Novelists in November

A WILD BLUE WONDER PRESS ANTHOLOGY

Published by Wild Blue Wonder Press LLC

ISBN: 978-1-962222-04-4

Cover Design by Hannah Linder Designs

Copyedit by Andrea Renee Cox

Formatting by Kellyn Roth

Wild Blue Wonder Press
P.O. Box 1156
White Salmon, WA, 98672
admin@wildbluewonderpress.com

Table of Contents

Introduction

WELCOME TO NOVELISTS IN NOVEMBER!

H ello, my friends! I'm Kellyn Roth, the organizer of this anthology and the founder of Wild Blue Wonder Press. Our goal is to create and publish Christian fiction that matters. When I was deciding on what my second published anthology with Wild Blue Wonder Press would be, I considered a number of options. Since I'd done one set in springtime, it made sense to do one set in autumn.

But what would the shared theme be?

As someone who has written a novel every November for the last ten years, it seemed rather obvious: a collection about Christian writers struggling along their own journeys as they create works of art for God's glory.

I'm so excited to share these eleven stories of writers seeking hope and inspiration through Christ with you! May they bless you as much as they have blessed me.

Sincerely,

Kellyn Roth

Melting-Pot Thanksgiving

ANDREA RENEE COX

Dedication

To the One Who called me into His family.
We're a mixed-heritage lot, aren't we?
Yet we're Your chosen family.
Thank You, Yahweh.
Thank You also for giving me the dream of writing.
What fun You and I have together in this gig!

"He fashions their hearts individually;
He considers all their works."
Psalm 33:15 (NKJV)

Pronunciation Guide

Eun-Ji = Un-Jee

halmae = hal-may

mandu = man-doo

Min = Meen

Wednesday, November 20

The End wasn't coming fast enough. Sarah Jones shoved up the sweater sleeve that had slipped to her wrist and typed as fast as she could to keep up with the characters in her head, but even that pace wasn't likely to beat her deadline and the upcoming holiday. Not to mention she needed to pick up her kids from school in—she checked the time in the corner of her laptop's screen—less than an hour. Once that happened, no more words would get written until her middle schoolers were tucked beneath their sheets, and then only if she had energy to spare for another thirty minutes or so.

Was that slice of time worth logging back on to her computer?

With only a week until the story was due, definitely.

"Lord," she whispered as her eyes closed, "please help me finish these last few chapters. You know I want time with my kiddos during Thanksgiving break, and who knows what Mama has planned this year. I'm sure she'll want to check out some hayride or pumpkin patch or carnival—like my kids are three." She looked up. "Would it be too much to ask for her to start understanding my life choices?" Sarah shut her eyes for as many seconds as it took to whisper, "Thank You; amen."

She took a sip of her now-cool cocoa and got busy again. The day would whiz by her if she didn't keep ticking things off her to-do list.

Reaching her page-count goal for the day was at the top.

Next to her laptop on the spacious dining room table, her cell phone rang. Why hadn't she silenced it? She usually did during writing sessions since her duplex neighbor and best friend, Kayla Prescott, was the backup number for the school. Unless Kayla was photographing wild animals, she always kept her phone on. She'd been eager to be placed on the emergency contact list when Sarah decided to become a foster mom.

Sarah saved her work so she wouldn't experience Lost Pages: Episode V.

Caller ID didn't make her feel any better about the workday interruption. She answered and hit Speaker so she could keep working. "Hi, Mama."

"Sweetie, I need a favor."

"I'm doing well, thanks. And you?"

"Sarah, are you listening to me?"

"Oh, that's nice. Is Daddy doing okay?" Then it hit her. Mama hadn't started with the usual congenialities. "I'm sorry. You caught me in the middle of writing a scene about a tower of trash cans and boxes in lieu of a ladder; the kids are rescuing a kitten this time."

A deflated sigh came across the line. "You and your stories. When are you going to grow up and get a real job?"

Sarah flipped her thick red braid over her shoulder. "You said something about a favor?"

"Well, yes." Mama took a loud breath, and Sarah braced herself. That was usually a very bad sign. "You see, I fell and sprained my wrist."

"Mama!"

"Hush now. I'm not done."

"Are you okay?"

"I'm *fine*. The doctor said I shouldn't lift anything more than a pound or two—"

"It was *one* pound, Felicity." Daddy's hollered comment sounded amused but insistent.

"—and you know my casserole dishes weigh at least eight without a stitch of food in them. I got the good stuff back when you were nothing but a cricket of a thing."

"What's the favor, Mama?" Sarah wistfully stared as the blinking cursor mocked her. If this call lasted more than a quarter hour, she could kiss her daily goal goodbye. Inwardly, she groaned; she wasn't looking forward to doubling up tomorrow—but she would silence her phone. Interruptions wouldn't be an option if she had any hope of hitting her deadline, already extended once due to an emergency in which Delonte Smith Jr.—or DJ, as he preferred—had beaten up a couple of school bullies and gotten his arm broken in the process. Sarah and her kids had sat in the ER for hours, with Eun-Ji wondering about dinner and missing *Halmae*—Grandmother—Min.

Sarah needed to call the hospital about Kim Min's broken hip. Eun-Ji would ask as soon as she got in the van this afternoon.

"I wondered if you'd do the Thanksgiving preparations for me."

Sarah zoned back in fast at that statement. "Thanksgiving dinner? That's next week. Are you kidding?"

"Sarah honey, please. It would mean the world to me if you'd help me out this one time." Mama's tone was syrupy sweet. "Daddy will bring over the turkey, thawed and ready for baking, the day before. And don't even think about doing that silly crumble thing on top of the sweet potatoes. You know your daddy likes the marshmallows better."

"I like the crumble!"

Sarah chuckled at her daddy's keeping her mom straight about who liked what. Although, no one would mistake that Mama knew exactly what she was doing spitting out things like that—getting her way.

"My book's due Wednesday ..."

"This is Thanksgiving! Can't your imaginary friends wait until afterward?"

Sarah took off her thin-framed, oversize glasses and rubbed at the tension between her eyes. "Not if my deadline's before."

"Why won't you help me? After all the sacrifices I've made for you—"

"Fine." Sarah set her glasses on the table. "But I decide on the menu, which means Daddy can keep the turkey."

"But—"

"No buts. You taught me the chef makes the menu. I'm holding you to that."

"But ... I don't like the crumble."

"If I rearrange my entire work schedule to do this favor, I'll create the menu. We'll do lunch at two, here at my place. My neighbor Kayla will be invited, too. If I have any questions or need a recipe, I'll call you."

They chatted a few more minutes, with Sarah finally getting out of Mama the full story of the accident. Sarah commiserated a little before making excuses to get off the phone. As soon as she hung up, she silenced the device, placed it screen down on the tabletop, and slid her glasses onto her nose. No matter how hard she tried to tap back into the flow of words, the only thing that ran through her head was, *I have to make Thanksgiving dinner—for the first time.*

"Lord, what have You gotten me into now?"

The car door snapped shut, and Eun-Ji ran crying up the curved sidewalk, her straight black hair flying out behind her and her light jacket slipping to expose a striped sleeve. Since the knob wouldn't turn, she kicked the door, though her attempt wouldn't have dented her favorite pillow.

Sarah let her have her muted fit because it was easier to reason with tweens after they'd had their cries and found their way back to normalcy on their own. Instead, she rounded her side of the car and raised the back hatch so she could grab a load of groceries on the way to their half of the single-story duplex.

Another door slammed, and DJ lugged Eun-Ji's and his backpacks as he passed Sarah on the way to the stoop. "It'll be okay, Eun-Ji. Maybe she won't be here for Thanksgiving, but there's always Christmas. Goodness, my mom won't get out of the clink 'til I'm grown and all, so one holiday hardly makes much difference." He dropped both packs between their feet and draped the arm not in a cast around her.

She shrugged him off, snatched up her bag, and looked at him with hot anger in her pitch-black gaze. "Halmae promised—she *promised*, DJ! She never breaks her word."

In the time it took Sarah—arms loaded with purse, sacks, and keys—to take two steps onto the sidewalk, Eun-Ji's head and shoulders slumped until she likely saw nothing more than her scuffed sneakers.

"She's breaking this one." The backpack slid down her arm, plopped back on the ground, and bumped against her leg.

Sarah unlocked the door and opened it.

DJ picked up Eun-Ji's bag and gently handed it to her. "Honestly, you get used to it after a while." He grabbed his own pack and trudged inside, all the steam of encouragement drained from his posture.

Eun-Ji hugged her bag and followed him. "What if I don't want to get used to it?"

"Eun-Ji"—Sarah trailed the girl inside and left the door open behind her to keep an eye on the open-trunked car—"Halmae is recovering from a bad fall, and hips take time to heal. There's a slim chance she'll be better next week, but it's more likely she'll be home by Christmas." She stepped into the kitchen, set the sacks on the counter, and returned to the hallway to welcome the hug she knew was coming.

The girl placed her backpack on a chair at the table, ran over, and wrapped her arms around Sarah. The girl trembled with sobs. After a minute, she looked up and said, "I want her to come home now, for Thanksgiving."

Sarah rubbed the child's back. "I wish she could."

At the table, DJ logged onto his school-assigned laptop, then spun it around to show Sarah. "Got my grades in. Wish Mom could see all these Bs. Never had such solid grades my whole life. Bro, wouldn't she be proud."

Sarah's brows jiggled upward.

"*Ma'am*, wouldn't she be proud."

"Better. She most certainly would. You've earned those marks, Deej. You worked hard all summer to close those gaps."

"Can I call the prison tonight, tell her about this report card?"

She hated to quash the hope glimmering in his chocolate eyes. "Remember, she already used her call this week."

He turned his computer back around and sank onto a chair. "Got homework." Using one hand and another pinky to type, he got busy on his assignments.

Sarah cupped Eun-Ji's face and smiled. "Want to help me bring in the rest of the groceries before you start on your own tasks?"

"No assignments today. Too close to Thanksgiving." The girl's voice wobbled on the holiday. She spun on her heel and slow-walked outside.

Sarah followed. Her grin widened. "You don't have to do that."

Behind the minivan, Kayla pivoted with hands loaded down with bags. "And leave this frowny-faced pixie with all the work?" She winked at Eun-Ji. "I wouldn't dare."

Eun-Ji hugged Kayla, grabbed a couple of sacks, and headed inside.

Kayla stepped closer to her friend. "Not good news from the hospital today?"

Sarah sagged against the taillight. "Recovery is slower than they expected. If there's another setback, it'll crush Eun-Ji."

"She already looked pretty down to me." Kayla's eyes sparkled. "I just took the best picture of a rare owl for this area that's going to knock her socks off. Full wingspan and everything."

Sarah glanced at the camera dangling from a strap around Kayla's neck. "Go on, then. I'll finish up here." As she gathered the remaining groceries and locked the vehicle, Sarah whispered a prayer for her kids to have their spirits lifted by the photographs Kayla brought to share. It was unfortunate that Eun-Ji and DJ faced disappointment this afternoon, and Sarah wished she could fix both situations to her youngsters' satisfaction. Only, she didn't have a clue where to begin.

Saturday, November 23

Fits and starts—that was Sarah's morning in a nutshell. The rain pattering on the roof and the lightning and thunder cracking the sky meant the kids were stuck inside. They'd already played numerous rounds of charades—without Sarah because these pages weren't going to write themselves. Being sequestered in her bedroom wasn't working. The kids nudged open the door at least a dozen times—to ask her to play a game, for a snack, for permission to get juice instead of water, and for help reaching something on the top shelf in DJ's closet.

Words were impossible today.

Something crashed in the living room, and Sarah immediately jumped off the comforter-covered bed and tossed aside her reading glasses. She found Eun-Ji crying and DJ crouching on the far cushion of the couch. Sarah squatted next to Eun-Ji, who clutched her elbow while curled up on the rug. "What happened?"

"It was an accident, Miss S, I promise." DJ edged over and stepped down gingerly as if he was afraid of shaking the floor and jostling his sister's injury.

Sarah threw him a glance. "What were you doing?"

Eun-Ji grabbed Sarah's arm. "He didn't do anything wrong."

Sarah softened her gaze as she looked down at the girl, who sniffled but affected bravery. "I'll be the one to judge that. Whatever happened, are you okay?"

Eun-Ji sat up, and Sarah prodded her elbow with soft fingers and moved her arm in a couple different ways, none of which extracted a bitten lip, gasp, or a blood-curdling scream. Once Sarah determined the girl had just whacked her funny bone, she reached toward DJ, but he didn't take her hand.

She couldn't blame him.

"I'm sorry I jumped to blaming you," Sarah said. "I never want to do that because I don't know what happened until I ask and listen. Forgive me?"

Though he nodded, he stayed quiet. The hurt in his eyes would need time to dissipate. He'd worked too hard over the summer to beat the stigma of his mom's being in prison, and in one accusatory glance and a few unkind words, Sarah had undone that effort and told him he couldn't rise above his past.

That wasn't at all what she'd intended.

She rose and gave him a hug, under which he stiffened. Stepping back, she forced her mouth into a bright smile. "Who wants to help me make desserts for Thanksgiving?"

Immediately, Eun-Ji popped up, raised her hand, and jiggled it through the air. "Me! Could we make strawberry cake? That's Halmae's favorite American food."

"We can even take her a slice this evening."

"Really?" The girl's voice squeaked, and she dashed down the hall to wash up.

"What do you say, Deej? Want to make a chocolate cake? Or we could do pies. Your choice."

He cocked his chin and blinked back pooled tears. "Do I get to lick the spoon?"

"Of course."

"And the bowl." He sauntered into the kitchen in the gangster-hitched lope he used when he wanted to appear tougher than he was and washed his hands in the sink before drying them on a nearby towel.

If letting him lick every drop of leftover goop—minus what little of it Eun-Ji consumed—would lift his spirits and let him know she regretted hurting his feelings, Sarah would hand him spoon after spoon after spoon.

By dinnertime, the house smelled like a mixture of strawberries, chocolate, pumpkin, cloves, pecans, and warmed apples, and the kids were happy and laughing again. Once they'd eaten, they donned light jackets and beanies, and each carried a plastic container encasing a slice of cake. Eun-Ji proudly carried two, one for her dear halmae and another for herself. The visit would be short, but they'd make the best of it.

This might be the closest thing to a Thanksgiving celebration the Kims would get this year, and Sarah intended for it to be as spectacular as a holiday could be in a hospital.

She ought to write a novel set in a hospital sometime because there were a lot of kids who dealt with terminal illnesses and extended stays in sterile, claustrophobic rooms. Maybe her next book would be inspired by the experiences of Eun-Ji and her grandmother. Sarah brainstormed a few plot points as she drove across town but locked away the ideas for later as the kids and she walked into Halmae Min's room—only to find a swarm of doctors and nurses dealing with a cacophony of beeps and bonks from the bevy of machines surrounding the head of the bed.

Eun-Ji dropped both containers of cake; one popped open, dumping the dessert in an icing-splattered, crumbly mess onto the floor. Weeping silently, she ran from the room.

Sarah thrust her own container toward DJ and dashed after her. After catching up just before the girl reached the bank of elevators, Sarah lowered to a knee and turned her around.

Eun-Ji surged forward and dampened Sarah's neck with tears. "What's wrong with Halmaaaeee?"

Sarah rubbed Eun-Ji's back. "I don't know, honey."

After a few minutes of offering comfort, Sarah rose. Eun-Ji snuggled against her side and sniffled. Together, they walked to the nurses' station. When Sarah asked for some paper towels to clean up her mess, the only nurse at the station offered to clean up the spilled cake. Sarah turned and beckoned to DJ, who held the plastic containers in the doorway to Halmae's room. The trio went to the nearest waiting room. They wouldn't be able to visit Min now, but Sarah knew Eun-Ji wouldn't want to go home immediately.

After claiming the seat next to Sarah, Eun-Ji looked her in the eye. "I'm not leaving until Halmae's okay." She laid her head against Sarah's shoulder and promptly fell asleep.

Sarah wished she could let her foster daughter stay here as long as it took to receive whatever news the doctors had about Halmae. But church was in the morning, and both kids needed to rest on their own beds.

After waiting nearly an hour with no word from any of the staff, Sarah glanced into the hall and then looked at her foster son. "DJ, come on."

"Where are we going? We're not leaving her here by herself." There was a stubborn jut to his jaw.

"Of course not. We'll stop at the nurses' station and ask for an update, but then we have to go home." Sarah rose and dug out her keys. Before she could wake Eun-Ji, DJ thrust his arm in front of his sister, blocking Sarah from nudging her.

"You heard her, Miss S."

Sarah gave DJ a small smile. "You know we don't always get what we want. Let's go."

DJ set down the containers on the seat next to him and crossed his arms, sinking into a deep slump.

"Now, Delonte."

A dragged-out sigh preceded his popping up to stand toe to toe with her. "She's an innocent, Miss S. She should get what she wants."

"Life doesn't work like that."

"It should."

"Grab the cake." Sarah woke Eun-Ji and wrapped an arm around her as they walked toward the doorway. She peeked back to make sure DJ was obeying her.

He snagged the containers and followed her as she got an update and headed to the car.

Her heart twisted as she drove home and got dinner for her kids. They might have laid up plenty of desserts, but there was one thing fewer to celebrate. Halmae Min had acquired an infection.

Monday, November 25

The kitten was out of the tree, but her owner hadn't yet been found. Only one or two chapters left until Sarah could write *The End* and send in the draft. She was excited to see what her kids thought of this one when it published next year.

If they were both with her then.

That was the thing with fostering. There was always the chance the kids would return home. For Delonte, that wasn't an option until his mom got out of prison and had a job and housing. For Eun-Ji, whenever her grandmother was released from the hospital, as long as she didn't need extended in-home care for her recovery, she would immediately regain guardianship of her granddaughter. That would be a wonderful thing, naturally, but it would certainly change things for Sarah—and DJ.

But she would make sure Eun Ji received a copy of this new middle grade novel.

When Sarah had gotten the two fictional kids and the kitten into a sad, soggy mess of leaves on the way home, her phone buzzed. She couldn't silence it today because Kayla had a zoo photography session. Was it the school calling? A quick check of the ID had her gathering courage for a different reason.

"Hello, Mama."

"Sarah hon, have you chosen the menu for Thanksgiving?"

"It's all decided."

"Are you sure? I mean ... Um."

"What is it?" Sarah saved her work and typed a couple more sentences.

"Are we having sweet potatoes?"

"You'll find out on Thursday. Just a few more days!" The perky tone likely wouldn't appease her mother, but Sarah tried it.

Mama harrumphed. "If you insist on choosing your own menu ..."

"Let's stick to your rule on that, Mama; it's a good one. I promise, it'll be a memorable Thanksgiving."

"Are you sure?" Mama's restrained emotion was pierced by a thin line of uncertainty, almost like she was afraid of losing her spot in the family if she didn't provide this celebratory meal.

"You know what? I think we'll have room for your spicy queso and a couple bags of chips. Would Daddy be able to help you whip up a batch?"

"Oh! He would be delighted to do that."

"What am I being volunteered for this time, Felicity?" Daddy sounded amused in the background.

"Not now, Caleb. You're sure it won't clash with the rest of the meal?" Mama's question couldn't dampen her excitement, and Sarah was relieved to have found a way to let her mother feel needed.

Plucking her glasses from her face and touching an earpiece against her lower lip, Sarah smiled at the thought of the meal to come later in the week. "Actually, it'll be a perfect addition."

For a few minutes, they chatted about several different topics, but Mama circled back to the meal. "What if I don't like the menu?"

"Mama ..."

"I'm serious, Sarah. I don't like not knowing what's going to be served. I know you like experimenting in the kitchen, but holiday meals aren't when that ought to be done." Mama sniffed, but it was all theatrics.

"If you don't like it, don't come."

"I never!"

"This holiday won't be spoiled for my children."

Mama gasped. "Why, they're not even yours!"

"In every way that counts right now, they're mine. They've both gone through a lot lately, and I want this holiday to be special for them." Sarah had never been gladder that her children still had school today. At least they didn't have to hear Sarah's half of this argument and figure out that Mama didn't consider them family.

"I don't like the sound of that."

"If anyone doesn't like the idea of a nontraditional, Sarah-picked-the-menu Thanksgiving ..." Sarah took a quick breath to steady the crickets hopping in her belly. "Don't come if it means upsetting the kids. Please."

Mama didn't respond.

"I have to get back to work. See you Thursday!" Sarah hung up and held her phone so tightly she thought she'd crack the glass screen. She stared blankly at the words on her laptop. Had she really just told off her mom? She was never going to hear the end of that, especially if the meal was a flop.

Lord, help me pull off this thing! It might have been a desperate prayer, but it was heartfelt, too. She set aside her phone and buckled down on the story before her. If she got it done by tomorrow night, she'd have all day Wednesday for prepping ingredients. She needed that time, if she could manage it, because this was her first Thanksgiving to create by herself.

Hopefully, Kayla wouldn't mind lending a hand.

Wednesday, November 27

The final scene came together so well that by midmorning, Sarah had gotten the kitten home to the kids' house—they'd adopted it when the owner said it was ready to be separated from its mother—and turned in the manuscript to her editor. She soaked in a deadline-free moment. Such relief to have this task marked off her mental to-do list!

As she tucked her laptop away and removed her glasses, she whispered a prayer of thanksgiving. It was a complete praise for God's helping her through this deadline with enough leftover time to get some dishes cooked and others prepared. She was grateful Kayla had agreed to watch the children today. There was no way Sarah would have gotten done and ready for tomorrow's meal with them underfoot.

A pounding on the door interrupted her prayer. She glanced up. "Thank You, Father. Help me with the next step: crafting an unforgettable Thanksgiving." Crossing the living room, she sent up another request. *Help Mama not spoil the holiday for my kids. They need this bit of happiness right now. Especially Eun-Ji.*

She opened the door and angled her head. "Brian? What are you doing here? Come in, sorry."

Her brother's jaw didn't loosen as he stepped inside.

"Everything okay?"

"Why aren't you answering your phone? Mama and Daddy have been trying to get ahold of you for hours. She's really upset about this Thanksgiving thing. She called me at work—called me *away* from work—to come check on you and be sure you're not destroying the meal she asked you to make." He strode into the kitchen and looked around. "Where is everything? Haven't you even begun yet?"

"Whoa, slow down there, slugger." When she caught up, she shut the fridge in his face before he could peek inside. She stared up a few inches into his gaze. "You don't get to come in here and get the scoop for her, no, sir. You get to be surprised like everyone else. Mama and I already talked about this; she knows the rule is the cook makes the menu. I'm sorry she's anxious, but I promise you: our celebration will be superb."

"You talked to her? When?" He deflated a bit, and his face lost its ruddiness.

"The day she asked me to take over and a couple days ago. We've covered the same material, and I'm tired of it. If she doesn't want to come, that's fine; I'll adjust; I'll even bring over some food and hand it off to Daddy." She sagged against the appliance. "I just want this to be a Thanksgiving we'll remember—all of us. Is that so much to ask?" Before she could stop it, a tear rolled down her cheek. She flicked it away, but he noticed.

"This means a lot to you, doesn't it, Sis?"

"The world."

He sent a swift text—probably letting an assistant coach know he wouldn't be back to finish the teacher-only workday—tugged off his dorky printed pullover, tossed it toward the living room, and quick-washed his hands, then dried them on a tea towel. "How can I help?"

Quirking her brow, she merely looked at him.

"If you're gonna wow Mama, you're gonna need help. Put me to work."

Her cheesiest grin came out, and she dug in the fridge. When she turned around, she held up two options. "Have you ever peeled and deveined shrimp? Or would you rather chop and parboil the cabbage?"

The remaining color leached from his skin, and he rocked back on his heels. "'Devein'? 'Parboil'? I didn't go to some fancy cooking school, Sarah."

She bit her lip to hold back the laugh wanting to burst forth. Her eyes would give her away any second, but her big brother was always a pretty good sport.

In fact, his eyes sparkled right back at her. "But I know how to chop. Hand me that cabbage."

With her hip, she nudged shut the refrigerator door. She tossed him the purple-hued vegetable, rounded the island, shoved up the sleeves of her coziest no-buttons sweater, and washed up before retrieving scissors and knives from a drawer. She handed one tool to her brother, set the other two aside, and fetched a pair of cutting boards. Finally, she gathered a few bowls of varying sizes.

They worked side by side, preparing not only the shrimp and cabbage but also peppers, sausages, and a wide variety of other delectables that would have her home smelling of baked pumpkins and nutmeg and all things autumn.

It was fun chortling and chatting with her brother again. Too long a stretch had gone by since they'd last relaxed in one another's company. He was busy with coaching and teaching, and she with writing and mothering. She ought to touch base with him more often. Besides, he didn't have a wife or children yet. Perhaps he would schedule some park time with her kids. They could use a strong influence like Brian's in their lives, particularly DJ, whose dad hadn't been in the picture since the day he was born.

Something buzzed beneath the surface of Sarah's thoughts while she worked. When they finally finished all the preparations they could do today, including storing a few cooked dishes and lots of ingredients for others in the refrigerator, she fetched bottles of water from the case on the floor and handed one to Brian as they settled on the sofa in the living room. "Bri ... have you ever considered what you'd do if you weren't a coach and history teacher?"

He nearly choked on water and coughed to clear his pipes. "Not coach and teach? I can't imagine. Never aimed for anything else."

"'Never'?" Clutching the bottle but not unscrewing the cap, she tried not to let her emotions surge. Would she always feel alone in this family?

"It was expected and an okay career for me. I understand teenagers well enough—if anyone above age twenty-five can—and teaching them to have discipline and determination but also to care about what makes our country great ... What responsibility could be more enjoyable?" Brian watched her carefully for a minute. "Why?"

"No reason."

"Aw, come on. You can't ask a loaded question like that but not tell why you wanted to know." He bumped her arm with his elbow. "Come on, Sarah-barah. Now's your chance to tell all."

She giggled at her childhood nickname. "Mama wanted me to be a librarian—like her."

"How could I forget when she won't let us?" His chuckle was dry. Was he also tired of hearing about Mama's dissatisfaction with Sarah?

"I never wanted to be a librarian. Still don't. But I love a good library. Mama's library, though she doesn't work there anymore."

"Retirement's been difficult for her. She volunteers, you know."

"At the library?"

He shrugged. "I told her she shouldn't, to let her successor find her own way for at least one school year before barging into her territory. You know Mama."

"Mm-hmm."

After a moment, Brian asked, "Are you happy, Sarah?"

"In most ways, yes."

"'Most ways'?"

She didn't answer. Her one aspect of discontent wasn't a concern he should bear. It was between Mama and her, and she held very little confidence that this holiday would do much to close the distance between one's hopes and the other's dreams.

Thursday, November 28

Thanksgiving dinner was ready.

Sarah fetched the hot pan of small soufflé cups of sweet potato casserole and set one of each type next to the place settings DJ and Eun-Ji were laying on the long dining room table.

DJ glanced over his shoulder and above Eun-Ji's head. "Miss S, do we really have to wear our Sunday best?"

"You may nix the tie, if you like."

"And the jacket? It won't fit right with this." He wiggled the cast-covered arm bracing a plate.

Sarah gave a soft smile. "Wear it through dinner. We'll pin the sleeve somehow. Afterward, you may change into everyday clothes."

"Deal." He set down the last plate, stepped around Eun-Ji, and held out his hand.

In all solemnity, Sarah gripped her foster son's hand. He'd hold her to this agreement, and she'd gladly follow through. They'd have a picture-perfect meal before they played or watched a game or any number of other things.

This would be a joyful holiday.

Eun-Ji finished with the silverware. Head downcast and shoulders drooping, she shuffled toward her bedroom.

Sarah finished with the casseroles and set the pan and pot holders on a corner of the table. Soon, she'd take it to the kitchen, but there was an attitude adjustment to be made first. "Eun-Ji?"

The girl paused but didn't turn.

Sarah went and squatted in front of her. "I know you're disappointed, but won't you put on a happy face through dinner?"

"I can't find a smile."

"Isn't there one thing you're thankful for today?"

The girl's straight black pigtails wiggled as she shook her head. "I'll be thankful when Halmae comes home." Tears gathered but didn't fall.

Sarah hugged her, then held her at bent-arm's length. "Will you try to be cheerful for DJ's sake? He's missing his mom just like you're missing Halmae."

"It's not the same thing."

"Maybe not, but hurt is hurt, yeah?"

Eun-Ji thought long and hard about that one. "I'll try. May I put on my dress now?" The girl's eyes glittered when she mentioned the outfit she'd been longing all week to wear.

"Now would be a fabulous time to put on your dress."

Once Eun-Ji scuttled into her room, DJ came out of his, struggling with a tie. He'd draped the cast-side part of the jacket over his shoulder.

Sarah barely held back a smirk. "Thought you were doing without the strangler."

"If this thing bites, I might bite back. Would you help me?" He tugged the lopsided thing until it was a little longer on the fat side than the skinny. "Besides, if Eun-Ji can be happy for me, I can wear a tie for your mama."

Sarah swallowed a grin and made quick work of the looping and tucking before adjusting the knot so it would be snug. "That's chivalrous of you, Deej."

He stuck a finger near her nose. "You better not tell. My rep would be ruined."

After pinning her lips together, she twisted a pretend key at the corner of them. Without moving her mouth, she mumbled, "My lips are sealed," but it came out as gobbledygook no one could understand.

DJ laughed heartily as the front door swung open.

"Ding-dong!" Kayla pranced in and shoved the door closed. She gave both DJ and Sarah quick hugs. "My kitchen is such a mess, but I've decided to deal with it after the party's over. No sense in messing up these"—she flashed her orange-and-brown nails—"any more than I already have. Who knew helping you with the fixin's would be so much work! Where's Eun-Ji?"

"Getting ready." A knock diverted Sarah's attention. "Would you check on her?"

"Remember to breathe. If they don't like it, at least we will."

Sarah mouthed *Thank you*. Kayla winked, grabbed the pan and pot holders from the table—who knew where she'd hide them, but at least they'd be out of sight—and skittered down the hall in heels that complemented her calf-length burgundy dress. Sarah smoothed her own emerald outfit, fluffed her burnished braid-crafted waves, and strode toward the entry but didn't take notice of where DJ landed himself.

She welcomed her parents and brother inside. All three were dressed to the nines—suits with ties for the men and a brown dress with low heels and pearls for her mom. Sarah took her mother's coat and ushered them toward the dining room, though her brother ducked into the kitchen to drop off a bowl of queso and two bags of chips.

Mama tried to get a peek at things, but Sarah kept her parents moving. Kayla whisked by and took the coat, disappeared momentarily, and returned with Eun-Ji, who wore a black-sequined dress with a smooth sash belt tied at the back and a red headband with a flat bow over her smoothly brushed hair, no longer in pigtails.

Sarah casually directed her parents and Eun-Ji to one side of the table while Kayla, DJ, and Brian took the opposite. Sarah paused at the head to round off things, and the empty chair on the far end was representative of Eun-Ji's halmae. Sarah's parents wouldn't likely be happy with this arrangement, but it was part of the ambiance of the evening.

Everyone stood behind their chairs, and Sarah took a quiet breath she hoped wouldn't betray her nervousness. "Welcome to our melting-pot Thanksgiving."

"Your what!" Mama pulled out her chair and plopped onto it in as undignified a manner as Sarah had ever seen, then adjusted the thin brace on her wrist.

"Felicity," Daddy rasped out of the corner of his mouth.

"This country has long been a melting pot of cultures and peoples, and this family now is as well. It is my hope that this Thanksgiving meal reflects each one of us." Sarah forced her smile to remain relaxed even though she wanted to cry over her mother's reaction to this different sort of celebration. "One of DJ's favorite dishes is seafood gumbo—shrimp and crabmeat, Cajun seasoning and diced bell peppers, among other ingredients. It has a spicy kick, but it's delicious, and there's cornbread to tame the taste, if you prefer."

DJ beamed a megawatt smile and cocked his chin just so to indicate how proud he was of this piece of his heritage. The gumbo was one of his grandmother's recipes passed down to his mama, and he'd helped her make it a few times before she'd landed herself in prison.

"Eun-Ji's halmae—that's 'grandmother' in Korean—favors mandu, a type of stuffed dumpling we usually call potstickers—"

"Oh! I love potstickers." Kayla licked her lips, anticipation dancing in her eyes.

Sarah would thank her later. "These are filled with ground turkey, parboiled purple cabbage, and seasonings. There's a trio of dipping sauces: ginger sesame, sour soy, and barbecue. All three are Kim family recipes, and Eun-Ji taught me how to make them—just as her halmae taught her."

Eun-Ji gave a bashful smile beneath dewy lashes. "Ginger sesame is my favorite, but Halmae likes sour soy best."

Brian winked at her. "I'm ready to give 'em all a try."

Mama gasped and pressed a hand to her chest while Daddy stared at the table in stony silence.

This wasn't going well.

Sarah tried to wrap up her explanation quickly. "Then, of course, we have baked turkey with dressing and"—she gestured to the table—"as you can see, sweet potato casserole two ways. Many other dishes, including one of my favorites: Mama's spicy queso"—she smiled at her mother—"and desserts await us, but first ..." She reached out to Eun-Ji and Brian. "Let us pray." She waited for everyone to hold hands.

Mama rose, sniffed, and reluctantly grasped Eun-Ji's hand while latching a death grip on her husband's.

Once everyone bowed their heads, Sarah shut her eyes. "Father, thank You for our melting-pot Thanksgiving and family. The people gathered in my home today, along with Halmae and DJ's mom, mean the most to me in the whole world. Please bless each one. And bless this unconventional meal to the health of our bodies. In the name of Jesus Christ, our Lord, amen."

Brian and Kayla choroused, "Amen," and Daddy mumbled along.

Mama didn't say a word.

Brian clapped once. "Let's eat!" He picked up his plate and motioned for the kids to lead the way into the kitchen.

As she passed by, Kayla squeezed Sarah's arm and smiled sweetly.

Sarah lifted her own plate and held it to her chest as Mama switched her crumble-topped potatoes for Daddy's marshmallow one. Sarah expected that, but it still stung that Mama wasn't willing to try the other type.

Sarah motioned for her parents to precede her to the line, and she was glad Brian chatted with DJ and Eun-Ji as they scooped up various foods. Yesterday's bonding with Brian had extended to the kids today, for which Sarah was eternally grateful. If only Mama and Daddy would get on board with the way Sarah's life was now. They had such beautiful foster grandchildren right in front of them, yet they both scowled over the foreign-to-them dishes and added only small portions to their plates.

At least Sarah hadn't nixed the turkey.

Mama barely touched her bowl of gumbo or the single mandu, but Daddy went back for seconds and thirds before the meal was through. He lightened up and carried on conversations with every member of the celebration, but Mama hardly managed a word when directly questioned. The corners of her eyes might have misted a time or two as well.

Sarah sent up more silent pleas through this one afternoon than she recalled having done in a lifetime of meals. Somehow, the family made it to the end of lunch and moved into the living room with desserts. Her brother found a game on TV, and Kayla tugged Eun-Ji upon her lap on an armchair so the guys, including DJ, could claim the sofa.

Before Sarah could step too far into the room, Mama touched her arm.

"Might I have a word with you?"

Sarah followed her mother into the kitchen, where Mama put her hands to scooping leftovers into an array of reusable containers. Sarah took small bites of banana pudding and chocolate cake, but she lost her appetite in the silence and set her plate aside so she could do the heavy lifting and shove things into the fridge.

It wasn't until the last of the entrées and sides were put away that Mama turned and squarely faced her. Sarah couldn't read her expression; this conversation could go either way.

Mama dusted off her palms. "Why must you always buck our family traditions?"

Sarah drooped against the island. Holding on to the peace in her soul was getting harder by the minute. Once again, she'd failed her mother.

"Honestly." Mama held out her hands, clearly exasperated. "I don't know where you get your notions sometimes."

Sarah took in a breath and sent yet another prayer for guidance and tact. What came out next wasn't anything like what she meant to say. "Have you even read my books, Mama?"

Her mother swayed back a step as if Sarah had shoved her. Mama's mouth gaped only briefly, as it would have been rude to continue much longer. "I don't see the relevance—"

"Writing is the first dream God gave me, and you're missing it." Sarah gripped the counter to anchor herself. She felt oddly confident in what she was saying, but it rocked her to the core to have to stand up for herself against her own mother. "Why? Why haven't you ever believed I could obtain my goals? Or observed that I actually *have* reached dream come true status—in more than one aspect of my life? Can't you see what God's done for me?"

Mama scrunched her nose. "Are you talking about the children?"

"What's wrong with being a foster mom? You know I've always wanted kids, yet when God finally blesses me with some—however temporarily—you keep yourself at a distance. I don't understand, Mama—help me understand." Sarah kept her expression open and willing to listen because she truly wanted to see things from her mother's perspective, to discover where she was coming from.

A rap came at the door.

Mama immediately took the excuse. "You should get that."

Sarah made no move to do so. Yet she didn't say anything either. She wasn't letting Mama off the hook so easily.

"I'll get it!" Eun-Ji called out before she pitter-pattered toward the door.

Sarah couldn't imagine who would be on her stoop. DJ's mom wasn't getting out for years, and Kim Min was in the hospital. Everyone else Sarah loved was already here.

Brian hustled past the doorway, which gave Sarah a mite of relief. Maybe he'd shoo Eun-Ji back into the living room and answer the door himself. Sure enough, Eun-Ji plodded by in the opposite direction.

Sarah refocused on her mother.

Mama shifted uneasily. "I never got what I dreamed of when I was a little girl."

When Mama didn't continue, Sarah asked, "What was that?"

"Your dad promised me adventure. I thought he meant we'd travel the world. But he took a job at the school, and in the summers, he took me camping at the lake."

"Not the grand escapade you hoped for."

Moisture glistened in Mama's left eye. "He promised he'd take me to see the Grand Canyon. It was the one place we both agreed would be amazing to see once in our lifetime. Only, I found out right before that I was pregnant with your brother."

"Daddy didn't want to go anymore?"

"Excuse me, Sis." Brian popped his head around the doorframe.

Reluctantly, Sarah looked away from her mother. "Yes?"

"I meant to ask before he got here, but could my buddy Nathan watch the game with us? He's in town for the weekend."

"The more the merrier."

"Thanks." He dashed in to kiss her on the cheek and hurried out again.

Moments later, Brian's college roommate waved on the way by.

She smiled and lifted a hand.

"He didn't want me to overexert myself." Mama snorted. "As if pregnant women haven't done more arduous things than sit in a car for a few dozen hours and walk around at a national park." The gathered liquid fell, and Mama swiped at it.

Sarah still didn't understand the connection between Mama's disappointment and her own dreams. "If you didn't get your aspirations, why have you tried so hard to discourage me from trying to obtain mine?"

"Because I didn't want you to experience such devastation!" Mama smacked the counter, and a fork next to a pie jumped at the impact. "I encouraged you to forget about writing and do something stable."

"Becoming a librarian like you ... which can be done in virtually any town in America."

"Whenever you got married"—Mama's chin inched upward—"you'd have a way of escaping your home for a while, even if it wasn't on a road trip."

"But ..." Sarah's memories flashed before her eyes and shifted in light of her mother's admission. Everything Sarah had known, every experience she'd had, had been an adventure to her. How had she missed the dimming of her mother's eyes in so much of their everyday living? "You held me back because Daddy did the same to you."

"He didn't mean to, of course. It wasn't my intention, honey—becoming demonstrative, manipulative, controlling ... none of it. Your brother pointed out those things the other evening, but that's beside the point. I only wanted your happiness. I couldn't stand the thought of you receiving nothing but anguish—like me."

"Don't you see?"

"See what?"

"I haven't been crushed; I've been blessed." Sarah came close, grasped her mother's hands, and squeezed lightly. "I always dreamed of being a writer ... and God provided a way for me to do so. I've dreamed of being a mom—but not necessarily a wife—and God led me to foster. The dreams He planted in me have come true. Can you see that?"

"Isn't it hard when the kids go back to their real homes?" Mama pulled out of her daughter's grip and wrapped her arms around herself.

"They long to be with their families more than me; that's natural, normal. I want the best for them, as every parent should."

"I do want the best for you!"

"That isn't what I meant, Mama."

"I wanted to roam the world. Even one excursion would have done the trick."

"Did you ever mention this to Daddy?"

"Once or twice, but those years were too tight to afford a trip, and *later* never seemed to show up." Mama sighed. "I don't even want the trips now, but letting go of them ... That was—is—the most difficult thing I've ever done—am doing."

"Hasn't our life together been amazing?" Sarah tilted her head as a million different emotions filtered over her mother's face. Was she running back through her memories to see where adventure tucked itself along the way? "Remember all those hayrides, Christmas lights, and birthday celebrations? The way you introduced me to the Sound Box Books—my first foray into the world of books. Did you know, when I was reading *My 'W' Sound Box*, I asked God what He wanted me to be when I grew up?"

"At age four?" Mama covered her open mouth.

"Mm-hmm. Ever since, He's instilled in me soul-deep loves of story and children." Sarah clasped her hands. "Remember how you told Brian and me stories about each animal at the zoo—you made every trip there an extraordinary trek for us. I could almost envision myself on a grand safari, meeting those lions and elephants and monkeys."

"You see odysseys everywhere you look, don't you?" Tears now coursed unchecked down Mama's cheeks.

"Every time my children tell me what happened at school. Every time they argue and make up. Each board game or new dish at dinner or trip to the grocery store ... Adventure is all around us, Mama. It's in the looking that we find it." She rubbed Mama's arm. "Through the books you introduced me to and the way you raised me ... You taught me that." Sarah's sigh was nostalgic. Was her mother understanding her a bit better now? Would she try to see things in a new light? Sarah couldn't stand that her mama saw their world as bleak and nothing to look forward to.

Mama grabbed a napkin and wiped the drips from her chin, then offered a tremulous smile. "The ... mandu, was it?"

"Yes." Sarah barely breathed for hoping.

"The mandu was unexpectedly delicious."

"Oh, Mama." Sarah enveloped her mother in an embrace that shared her heart.

"I'll try better, Sarah—to see you, to appreciate your work, to stop pushing you away from the things you long for." Mama pulled back but held on. "I honestly do want what's best for you."

Sarah's vision glossed, and a few drops ran free.

"How do you manage the grief when the kids ...? I'm ... afraid of growing attached only to have them leave."

"I muddle through and ask God to help me through any sadness that comes." Sarah shrugged. "All I know how to do is pour my love and prayers into the children. If I didn't … How miserable that would be for everyone involved! Besides, I would rather see them flourish and grow than hold them back because of my fears." She squeezed her mother's hand and wiped her own face. "The world is much better when love is present."

Mama crushed the napkin. "Will you show me your books sometime? I'd like to get to know this … *adventure* of yours." She winked. "Perhaps I'll discover my own in the reading."

Another knock interrupted whatever Sarah would have thought to say. "I better get it this time."

"I'll start on these dishes." Mama turned to the sink, moved a couple of desserts, and turned on the tap. Even though she shouldn't, she took off the brace and reached for a casserole dish but seemed to change her mind and picked up a plate instead. "I'll leave the heavy things for you."

At Mama's concession to her injury, Sarah grinned. She shooed Eun-Ji away and answered the door. Her mouth opened, but she hardly knew what to say. How—? But answers could come later. Holding a finger to her lips, Sarah closed the door most of the way. She scurried to the living room and put on as much of a straight face as she could manage.

The room went silent except for the game, which Daddy turned down some.

Eun-Ji leaned against Kayla's knees and blinked.

"Eun-Ji, there's someone here to see you." Sarah was surprised her voice came out evenly.

"Me?" The girl stepped forward.

"Mm-hmm." Sarah held out her hand.

Eun-Ji came and squeezed it tight. "Is it news about Halmae?"

"Why don't you come see?" Sarah walked with Eun-Ji but motioned behind her own back that her family should follow them.

When they passed the kitchen, Kayla rushed in to fetch Mama.

"What's going on?" DJ asked.

Someone, likely Brian, hushed him.

At the cracked-open door, Sarah nudged Eun-Ji ahead. "Go on. See who it is."

With great hesitation, Eun-Ji reached for the knob and slowly pulled back the door. "Halmae!" The squealed word was earsplitting. "Oh, Halmae!" The girl surged into the arms of the grandmother she'd worried would never return to her.

When Eun-Ji turned around, Sarah's heart melted at the sight of the matching smiles, one youthful and the other swathed in wrinkles.

Her father squeezed her shoulder, and her brother high-fived DJ and Nathan. Mama and Kayla stood near the back of the group but looked just as blissful as everyone else.

Eun-Ji led her grandmother through the family to the dining room, where she pulled out the chair at the head of the table, which was the highest honor the girl could likely think to give her beloved halmae. Eun-Ji tugged the next seat closer and perched on it. "Would you like mandu? We have your favorite: sour soy sauce. Should I warm some for you?"

Halmae Min patted the girl's hand. "Yes please, granddaughter."

Eun-Ji and Mama went into the kitchen, while the guys, who wore grins but would deny the emotion winking in each set of eyes, went back to the game.

The phone rang, and Kayla went to answer it.

Sarah sat on the other side of Min. "You've recovered?"

Min nodded once. "Enough to come home. Medication helped infection. A kind nurse bring me here. Doctor say I not take care of Eun-Ji." She tapped just below her temple. "He say my memory no good."

Alzheimer's.

Sarah grasped the woman's hand as Kayla called for DJ.

"What do you mean, Halmae?" Eun-Ji set a bowl of mandu and a smaller one of sauce in front of her grandmother, then leaned against her side, wrapping an arm around the woman's frail-looking frame.

Min looked at her granddaughter. "He say I forget things. Important things."

"Does this mean we can't stay together?"

Min opened her mouth, but Sarah got her words out first. "Of course it doesn't."

Both Kims turned quizzical and hope-filled faces toward her.

Sarah smiled at Eun-Ji. "Why, it couldn't be much harder to qualify as a guardian or caretaker for Halmae as it was for DJ and you, could it? I should have time for the training and paperwork before my next novel is due or the edits on the current one come back. I'm sure you wouldn't mind sharing your room with Halmae either, would you?"

"What about your deadlines?" Eun-Ji bit the inside of her lower lip as if all her dreams relied upon Sarah's answer.

"I'll have to shuffle things around a little, maybe request a few more months' time for each book, but they'll be doable."

"Oh, Miss Sarah, thank you!" Eun-Ji ran around and hugged Sarah with all the fierceness her petite body could manage. Afterward, she again perched on her chair.

Mama brought a set of chopsticks, a fork, and a small plate bearing a piece of strawberry cake and laid them on the table next to the bowls. Then she touched Halmae Min's shoulder and smiled at her. "Our granddaughter—if you don't mind ..."

Min lovingly covered Mama's hand with her own.

"She said this is your favorite American food. I thought you might like to enjoy it with the delicious mandu." Mama looked at Sarah. "Part of our melting-pot Thanksgiving is savoring different cultures at once."

"Thank you, dear one." Min tugged the plate closer and took the chopsticks Eun-Ji held out to her.

Sarah mouthed her gratitude to her mother, who winked and retraced her steps.

"Halmae Min," Sarah said, "would you tell your family stories to me while I record them? This way, we may preserve your family history for Eun-Ji to have always, sort of like a keepsake of culture. Would you like that?"

The elderly woman's eyes clouded, and she patted Sarah's cheek. "You kind lady, Miss Sarah."

"She's the best next to you, Halmae." Eun-Ji grinned.

Sarah's chest swelled, but her gut pinched. Eun-Ji would never have to leave Sarah's home, but they would eventually have to say goodbye to her sweet halmae. If Sarah could capture as many stories as the woman remembered and all the important family memorabilia from the Kims' home, Eun-Ji would have a collection of the heritage her grandmother cherished.

Sarah would do that for her.

Kayla came over and whispered in Sarah's ear. "You might want to check on DJ. His mom's on the phone."

"She was able to call?"

"Said she traded with someone with no kids."

Sarah skirted around her best friend and found Mama wiping countertops with a damp rag. Moments later, Mama abandoned the task, grabbed her wrist brace, and squeezed her daughter's elbow as she slipped from the room with a quick glance back at her foster grandson.

Leaning against a bank of cabinets, Sarah watched her son talk to his real mom while keeping his back to the room. He scrubbed his cheeks every few seconds. After he hung up, he sniffed hard before facing her.

"Mom said she was proud of me for keeping my grades so high."

"I'm glad for you, Deej."

He threw himself into her arms. "I wish she could've been here for your gumbo, Miss S."

Sarah pulled back and cupped his chin. "And to hug you?"

Her brave teenager nodded stoically despite the tears tracking down his face. "She was wrong in what she did, but she's still my mom."

"I know."

"Said she was glad I had you to take care of me."

"I'm glad, too."

"Is it okay if I stay here even if she gets out in a couple years?"

Sarah's heart lurched. "Why? Won't you want to go home to her?"

The devastation but truth in his eyes punched her in the abdomen. "I'll be in high school then. The one in my old neighborhood ain't good, Miss S. How do I know Mom won't mess up again and land right back in the clink?"

"If she wants custody, I have no choice, Delonte."

"I explained why I wanted to stay with you, and she said she'd rather me stay where I'm doing good. She ..." He took a deep breath. "She don't want me ending up in prison or shot to death in our old 'hood. She won't take me away from you and Eun-Ji, Miss S. She promised." He snorted and wiped his face. "Not that she sticks to much, but I think this is one promise she'll keep."

"Giving you a better life than she has is a huge expression of her love. You understand that, right?"

His chin notched upward. "Oh, Mom loves me, no doubt." A quaver made his lower lip twitch. "I'll miss her if she don't ever come visit."

"She's welcome here any time."

"I don't want you to adopt me. I'm okay sticking with the 'foster kid' status. Gotta maintain my rep, you know."

Sarah knuckled his shoulder. "Just so long as you know you can rise above it whenever you like."

"I think I want to be a coach like your brother. I'd get to blow the whistle and tell the other kids how to play ball. Might be fun." DJ smirked and hitch-stepped into the other room.

It wasn't long before Sarah heard him greeting Halmae. The game resumed its original volume, and laughter and boos and celebratory whoops created a delightful cacophony that punctuated this holiday.

Yet Sarah stayed in the kitchen awhile longer to soak in the blessings God had given her on this melting-pot Thanksgiving—the first of many. A new idea for a series of books fluttered into her mind. She smiled at the thought of writing a collection of stories based on her foster son and daughter and their family histories. She'd change names and details to some degree, but the books would pay homage to the cultures her kids used to know and bridge the gap between the ones they would build together in their mixed-heritage family.

Thank You, Lord. Your dreams for us come true indeed.

Sarah rejoined her family to delight in the remainder of the evening, finally glad that her mother had asked her to prepare the feast. Perhaps next year they could work together to create more memories for their clan.

A Note from Andrea Renee Cox

I owe a debt of gratitude to ...

Heavenly Father—thank You for guiding me to and through this story. I love my heritage of being Texan, American, Welsh, Irish, English, and American Indian (Black-foot), among others. You planted me in a melting-pot country and a melting-pot family, and I love both. But the best heritage I could have is one of faith, and You've blessed me beyond imagination on that front, for which I'm eternally grateful.

Family—Daddy, Mother, and Sis, thank you for your never-ending support not only of my writing journey but of my faith journey, too. Because you carve out space for me to grow within the safety and comfort of our home, I have felt loved and gained confidence in whom God has made me to be—and in whom He's training me to become.

Beta Readers—Bess, Grace A. Johnson, and Hannah Gridley, thank you for all the work you put into my little story. Bess, your cheerleading spirit is greatly appreciated. It's always great to be told I'm using my God-granted gifts well. Grace, you pointed out that Eun-Ji felt too young. If not for you, she'd still be a mix between an eight-year-old and the twelve she's supposed to be. Hannah, you ripped apart my story in *the best* way—and God used your work to help me see other unnecessary things and how to sharpen up certain aspects of the story. I'm glad you loved the mushy bits!

Wild Blue Wonder Press—Kellyn Roth, my fellow NiN authors, and the NiN street team, thank you for all the effort you expended to make this book a success. Kellyn, thank you for publishing *Melting-Pot Thanksgiving* in NiN. It's a joy to have my little story included in the collection. Fellow authors, thank you for the collaborative spirit with which you approached this project. Y'all made this journey fun. Street team members, thank you for the many ways in which you spread the word about this collection of short stories. I hope you know how much you're treasured.

Shira J. Rodriguez, my critique reader on MPT—Shira, your critique of my story was incredibly uplifting. I'm glad we could connect over our personal melting-pot backgrounds, among other things, while getting published together. Friends for life, girl!

Readers—thank you for choosing to read my story. It's a joy to have Sarah's journey be chosen by you for entertainment. I hope her journey in the midst of a deadline and family drama has inspired you in some way. If you'd like to check out my other books and some free short stories, follow my blog, or subscribe to my newsletter, please visit my website: AndreaReneeCox.com.

And As She Talked

BETHANY WILLCOCK

Dedication

To Bethany O'Brien,
My American counterpart, kindred spirit sister, and partner in crime;
the Anne to my Diana, Sherlock to my Watson, and Marianne to my Elinor;
who shares my love of all things unexplained, mysterious, and vintage.
Happy birthday! This story is for you.

He talked, and as he talked
Wallpaper came alive;
Suddenly ghosts walked,
And four doors were five;
~ "The Story-Teller," Mark Van Doren

And As She Talked

BETHANY WILLCOCK

There are no such things as ghosts.

*T*here are no such things as ghosts.

Autumn Greenwood pressed her palms against her eyes until she saw hot balls of light. *There are no such things as ghosts.* The Bible made that clear. Souls hanging between life and the afterlife just didn't exist. There were no such things as ghosts.

Right?

Carefully lowering her hands, she peeked up. No. It was still there. With a low groan, Autumn buried her face in her hands again. There was nothing she could do. She had lost her mind. What stood before her was impossible—utterly impossible. It defied all laws of reason and physics and everything the Bible taught. *There are no such things as ghosts.* But there was the catch.

This was a ghost of someone who'd never even existed.

And yet at the same time, it wasn't, because, well, there were no such things as ghosts. Autumn frantically shook her clouding head. This was ridiculous. She was a fully grown woman and well-respected novelist, and this was broad daylight on a November morning in 1947! And there were no such things as ghosts of real people, let alone imagined ones.

Then why, *why*, was she, Autumn Greenwood, currently staring in horrified helplessness at the ghost of the fictional character whose death scene she had penned only last evening?

A few days earlier

"Autumn! Here you are at last—we thought the train would never get in!"

Autumn hugged her older brother and unsuccessfully tried to disentangle her skirts from her two excited nieces. "So did I, Noah. I missed my train so took the next one. You're all looking well." She smiled down at the beaming girls. "And how you two have grown! Valerie, Lily, what are you now, six and seven?"

"Right you are!" Noah Greenwood grinned affectionately down at them. "Can't believe myself how fast they're growing up. And you are too! No way you're in your twenties already. Now then, Lily, let your Auntie Autumn have some space. She's travelled a long, long way and must be very tired. Here—" He turned back to his sister. "I have the Bentley ready and waiting. That all the luggage you have?"

"No, there's still the big trunk and carpetbag." Autumn led the way down the platform. "I hope there's enough room in your car. I'm afraid I always take up quite a bit of space when I travel."

Her brother winked at his daughters, who giggled. "Don't worry; we expected that, didn't we, girls? The Bentley has heaps of room. We know you're incapable of travelling light!"

Autumn joined in the laughter as the little party headed towards the car park. "But I *am* dragging my livelihood around with me. Not only do I need my typewriter, manuscripts, paper, pens, ink, etc., but also all my art supplies. You *know* I can't write a character properly unless I have their picture down on paper."

"We're only teasing you, of course." They had reached the Bentley and after loading Autumn's bags, Noah closed the trunk. "How's the new book coming along?"

"Splendidly so far." Autumn settled comfortably on the back seat between her nieces as Noah started the engine. "I'll show you the characters later, once I've painted them. It was such a long train journey, and there were so many interesting people on board, I was able to cast almost all the characters right off."

Several minutes later they rounded a corner, and Valerie tugged on Autumn's sleeve. "There's the inn, Auntie!"

Autumn adjusted her glasses and followed the direction Valerie was pointing. Her first impression of her brother's inn in the distance was most favourable. After his return from the war with a leg full of shrapnel wounds, Noah, having inherited his late wife's family house, renovated it, built a small cottage for the girls and himself right beside it, and flung open Mossfern Lodge to the public.

"It's honestly an artist's dream setting." Autumn smiled at her brother as they bounced up the stone lane. "And a writer's paradise. Tell me it has a library. I always write better in a library with a cup of hot tea and a ginger biscuit for company."

"Oh, you'll have all the library you could wish for; don't worry!" Noah laughed, switching off the engine. "The library is one of the inn's best features. It extends almost right up to the ceiling. We thought we'd put you in the east wing—it overlooks the grounds, and you can even see the pond from it. Good story inspiration, I should imagine."

"It certainly sounds like it!" Autumn gazed approvingly up at the high, ivy-covered stone walls. "This place is perfect. It looks like something out of a mystery book."

"Oooh, Auntie, you're writing a mystery this time?"

"Sadly not, Valerie. Mossfern would be the perfect setting for it—I can almost see my characters walking around these grounds as we speak—but I cannot write a good mystery to save my life!"

Her brother laughed. "Don't get carried away. You writers sometimes talk like you're living in one of your stories and the characters are real. Girls, you know that's the only reason your auntie has come to stay here, right? Not because she missed us, oh no; she just wanted a creepy story setting!"

"Noah—how could you!" Autumn swatted his head playfully, and her nieces giggled. "Girls, that's not true! Although, this place will certainly help my writing."

Lily and Valerie ran ahead to the arched doorway. Holding open the large wooden doors, they bowed low, waving their father and young aunt through the entrance with mock solemnity.

"Welcome to Mossfern Lodge, Miss Greenwood." Valerie bowed again. "It's such an honour having a famous author stay with us. Do allow us to show you to your room."

"Are there many other guests here at the moment?"

"No, don't worry. I know you need quiet while you're writing, and you must take all your meals with us in the cottage." Noah refilled her teacup and, handing Autumn a plate of ginger biscuits, sat down at the table under the library's French windows. "There's an old lady up in room ten, some journalists or some such on the first floor, a scientist chap in room three, and oh, a couple came in late last night. They took room seven near yours, but they shouldn't bother you. Only saw the wife; apparently, her husband's ill and needs quiet—doctor's orders. Shouldn't wonder if he'd been in the army, you know. A lot of soldiers came out of that nothing like how they'd gone in."

Autumn nodded sympathetically, noticing with a pang her brother's faraway look. "How's the leg these days?"

Noah sighed. "Not bad. Not better, but not bad. Struggle to climb the stairs sometimes, which is why I'm so thankful I thought to build the cottage. I can manage a small flight up to the bedrooms, but I couldn't have lived there with all those floors and wings." His face was sad. "The girls are doing better, too. At first, I thought none of us would recover from Evelyn's death; but with the Lord's help, it's finally getting easier for all of us, especially with the inn to keep us occupied."

Autumn gently patted his knee. "I'm so glad you decided to make it your full-time job. Especially as you decided not to send the girls to school but teach them here at home instead. They're doing splendidly, from what you say, and it's important for them to have you here right now."

"I know. I'm glad myself. I'm also glad I don't have to run the kitchen anymore, like when we first started up! At least now I can afford a cook and two maids."

"Oh yes, I was about to ask about that."

Just then, the library door burst open, and her nieces tumbled in.

Autumn smiled softy as she watched them. Evelyn Greenwood had been the gentlest, kindest, godliest woman alive, and she would have been so proud of her little family could she have seen them now. The recent war had a lot to answer for, not the least of which being the merciless London Blitz that had taken the life of Autumn's lovely sister-in-law. Autumn kept reminding herself that she would one day see her again in Heaven, but for now, they keenly felt her loss here on earth. She watched her nieces happily prattling to Noah, and suddenly, Autumn realised he was right. They *were* doing better. This inn and the complete change of scenery had been very good for them all. And, God willing, it would be good for her, too, and her writing.

Valerie bounded over and planted herself on the seat beside her. "How's the book, Auntie? Have anything to read us yet?"

"A little." Autumn reached for her black satchel. "I've started drawing some of the characters now, too. This library is giving me inspiration; it's a very nice place to paint and write in. Do you want to see one of the ladies? I finished her last night — here."

"Ohh, she's pretty!" Lily clambered up next to her sister, and they poured over the painting of a woman in a long light-blue dress. "What's her name?"

"Meredith, I think. I haven't made up my mind about her story yet."

"What time is she from?"

"Late last century. She's not the main character, but Meredith plays an important part later. I haven't got there yet, though, so I'm still not sure exactly what she does. She might die."

"Who did you draw to be her?" Lily wanted to know.

Autumn shook her head. "I don't remember. A woman I saw on the train, perhaps. That's the problem with me; I always remember a face when I see it but hardly ever remember *where* I've seen it before! Same thing with this dress. I know I saw an old Victorian-era outfit just like the one she has on in the picture somewhere recently, but I can't for the life of me remember where."

With thoughtful frowns, her nieces bent over the painting again while Noah reached over for his wellingtons and mac.

"Raining again," he remarked, nodding at the French windows leading into the garden. "I've got to get back to the cottage and check on our dinner, but you girls can stay here for now if you want, and I'm sure Auntie will read a bit to you if you ask her *very* nicely."

"I know!" Valerie suddenly exclaimed, jabbing her finger down on the dress. "There's a dress just like that up in the attic. Have you been up there?"

"Oh, yes I have, yesterday; now I remember. That's where I saw the outfit. It's old but really beautiful, just right for Meredith."

They nearly jumped out their chairs as Noah howled and flung a wellington across the floor, where it landed by a bookcase. Startled, Autumn and the girls gazed at it as a fluffy little brown-and-grey face with massive, surprised eyes peeked cautiously out before scrambling away in ruffled indignation and disappeared into a bookshelf.

"That cat again," Noah grumbled, retrieving the wellington. "I didn't mean to fling her, but she gave me such a fright! She seems fine, though."

"You have a cat!" Autumn leaped up and ran over to the shelf where the kitten was hiding. "Here, kitty, kitty!"

"You've done it now, girls." Noah winked as he opened the French windows. "Your aunt's crazy about cats."

"And proud of it!" Autumn called after his disappearing figure. Holding the purring kitten against her shoulder, she turned back to the girls. "I'm so glad you have a cat. I write so much better with a cat around to talk to. What's her name?"

"Boots, because she's always climbing into Daddy's wellingtons!" Lily grinned. "But she's so sweet nobody minds. Does Meredith have a cat?"

"Oh!" Autumn scratched her head and handed the kitten to Valerie. "I suppose she can have a cat; yes, why not! I'll add one in for her."

"Will she look like Boots?" Lily asked.

Autumn nodded, already starting to add brown and grey to her palette. "Exactly like Boots, though with a bit more white and orange, I think. I'll add her into this picture right here, sitting on the wooden fence by Meredith." She turned her easel so that the light was behind her. "I'll show you girls tonight when I've finished."

"What will her name be?" Valerie wanted to know.

Autumn glanced up as Boots disappeared with a squeak headfirst into the pot of marmalade on the tea table. She waited while the girls fished her out and washed the stickiness out of her fur with a hanky soaked in tea.

"Marmalade," she said. "She's definitely Marmalade!"

The next day, Autumn took a walk to the pond. Her head was full of her story, and in her mind's eye, she could almost see Meredith wandering the grounds, Marmalade in tow. Snatches of unwritten scenes played through her brain, and she unconsciously began testing lines of dialogue aloud, leaning over a little wooden fence that separated the grounds from the pond.

"Auntie?" Valerie's rather concerned voice startled her out of her musings.

"Oh my! You gave me a fright." Autumn laughed. "I was deep in thought."

"You were muttering to yourself. Was it the story?"

"Yes. It's always the story when I'm in the middle of writing one. Until I have it safely down on paper, I feel like I'm almost living in it. When you came up to me just now, for a moment I almost thought you were Meredith herself."

Her niece joined her laugh. "You're sounding like the story's real, Auntie!"

Autumn grinned. She pointed at the pond. "See that? Meredith would take a boat out onto the pond on a sunny day and watch the fish swimming lazily underneath."

"There *is* actually a boat." Climbing over the fence, Valerie led the way carefully down to the bank. "See that weeping willow? If you look underneath, there's a rowing boat half underwater, half on the shore. You should add it to your story."

"Oh!" Autumn stepped cautiously over to the tree and peered through its low-hanging branches. "My word. It does look rather creepy somehow, half-sunken like that. You're right; I'll just need to think how to fit it in."

"Have you done more drawings?"

"I've painted the house, and I'm working on this pond—lake in the story. Now I need to add the boat and willow. Oh, and I've been working on Philip's portrait—Meredith's husband? I read about him to you and Lily last night in the library. He'll be done soon, so I can show you girls later, if you want to read more."

"Of course we do! I like Philip and can't wait to see what he looks like."

"I'll have him finished by tonight," Autumn promised.

Back at the house, she stood puzzled in her room, her black satchel in her hand. *I'm sure I left Philip's painting with Meredith's. Yet only Meredith's picture is here now. Where on earth did I put Philip's?*

She jumped when the door creaked. For some inexplicable reason, Philip's face—or rather, how she pictured the character in her mind—flashed into her head; but then a fluffy face with two bright eyes peeked cautiously round the door, and Autumn drew a relieved breath.

"Here, kitty! Have you come to say hello? My, did you give me a start."

Boots padded over to her and, purring like a motor, rubbed her head affectionately against Autumn's outstretched hand. Autumn stroked her absently, her frown returning. *Where is that silly picture?*

"I must have left it on my easel in the library," she finally decided, addressing Boots, who was now rolling and stretching contentedly on her rug. "I've no idea why I'd have done that as I wanted to paint the grounds first, but it's the only place it can be. Still odd … I was certain I'd brought it up. Oh well. Kitty? You coming with me or waiting for me here?"

"You know she's a cat, right?" For the second time in two minutes, Autumn spun around, startled. Noah, leaning against the doorframe, smirked down at her and Boots.

Autumn blew out a long breath, trying to slow her racing pulse. "You can't keep doing that to me," she told her brother somewhat irritably. "My nerves can't stand it. Between you and Boots, I'll have a heart attack one of these days!"

"Right." Noah looked slightly confused, but he went on with his original point. "I was passing the door, and I heard you talking … to the *cat*. You do know that she doesn't understand a word you say?"

Autumn, huffing indignantly, picked up Boots and started past her brother towards the stairs. "So *you* say. She understands more than you give her credit for! Did you happen to notice if I left a portrait downstairs on my easel?"

"Er, no? Didn't notice it, sorry."

"That's fine. It must be there. I thought I'd taken it up to my room with Meredith's. It's her husband, you see, so I was keeping them together."

Her brother looked at her sideways as they reached the bottom of the stairs and turned towards the library. "You're talking about them as if they're real people! Next thing, you'll probably be talking *to* them! I don't know which is worse." Autumn glared at him, but he continued. "Talking to imaginary characters that *you* invented, or talking to the cat and asking it questions as though it's actually going to answer you. Why, next you know, you'll be ..." He stopped at her bewildered expression.

They had reached the library, and Autumn stood helplessly gazing at her easel ... her very *empty* easel.

"What is it?"

She shook her head and turned back to him with a small sigh. "Well, apparently, I didn't leave it down here after all. But question is, where in creation *is* it?"

"You sure it's not up in your room?" Noah glanced around the library as though he half expected the painting to be hidden in one of the bookshelves.

Autumn shook her head.

"Well, where else did you take it? Out onto the grounds? I saw you went for a walk earlier."

Autumn shrugged helplessly. "Anything's possible, I suppose, but surely I'd have noticed if I'd—no, actually, I couldn't have. I was talking to Valerie about Philip, and she would have noticed if I'd been holding his picture. Most odd."

"Well, you must have just absentmindedly put it down somewhere," said Noah comfortingly. "It's bound to turn up sometime. Meanwhile, weren't you also painting the house and grounds? Just finish those, and by then, the other picture will probably show up."

"You're most likely right. I'd just hoped to finish it today so I could show it to the girls tonight. But it doesn't matter. I do need to carry on with the garden. It's just annoying. I never used to be this bad."

"Don't fret; happens to everyone from time to time." Noah patted her shoulder before turning towards the door. "Dinner will be ready soon."

His sister nodded and smiled, but when the door closed behind him her puzzled frown returned. She was certain that she'd taken that picture up to her room. At least, she had been. Autumn pulled her glasses off, suddenly tired.

"Daddy! I know what happened to Auntie's painting!"

They were all sitting around the table in the cottage's cosy kitchen, enjoying the simple yet hearty dinner. Autumn and Noah looked at Lily in surprise.

"You do?" Noah glanced up, surprised.

"Yes! I think the Art Man took it! The papers said he likes to steal paintings, so he must have stolen yours."

Autumn looked over at her brother with her eyebrows raised. "Art Man?"

"Harold Newgate," Noah explained. "He's been all over the papers with his latest stunt. Apparently, he's a master art forger and thief, but during his last robbery at the Wilkes Museum last week, he ended up shooting a guard dead before fleeing the scene. The police are hunting high and low for him, but so far, no sign. The Wilkes Museum is only a few towns away from here."

Autumn's eyes widened, but she smiled at Lily. "Thank you, Lily, that's a very good thought, but I'm sure the Art Man wouldn't be interested in taking my picture. It wasn't even finished yet, and he's only wanting the big, expensive paintings by famous people that will get him lots of money when he sells them. Mine isn't worth anything. I'm sure I just put it somewhere by mistake."

"It will show up, you'll see." Noah took his sister's empty plate. "The minute you stop looking for something, it always shows up! It's a law or something. Now, you girls run off with Auntie Autumn and read the next part of the story while I clean up and get your baths ready. Off you go!"

"We'll have to go back to the inn. I left my typewriter and manuscript in the sitting room," Autumn told them as they buttoned up their coats. "I'll have these two back in time for baths and bed, Noah."

"I'm sorry we don't get to see Philip's picture," Lily said sadly as they hung up their coats in the inn's hallway.

"Me, too, Lily. Tell you what. I finished adding Marmalade into Meredith's picture. It's upstairs in my room. Why don't you go wait for me in the sitting room while I run up and get it, and you can tell me what you think."

"Ooh! Yes please!"

As Autumn slowly climbed the stairs, a strange uneasiness settled over her. She hurriedly tried to shake it. It was ridiculous. Just because she'd misplaced Philip didn't mean she wouldn't find Meredith now either. She *had* kept the two pictures together ... or so she'd thought. Autumn shuddered. Meredith's picture *would* be there, wouldn't it?

She reached her door and hesitated. At least the satchel was still where she'd left it. After opening it, she nervously rifled through the sketches.

Drawing out a paper, Autumn sat back on her heels and blew out a relieved breath. *There, you see? There was nothing to be worried about. It was right there just where you left ...*

Her internal monologue abruptly died away as she stared, horrified, at the picture she'd completed only the day before. Oh, it was there all right. There was Meredith, standing in all her old-fashioned finery beside the wooden fence, atop which Autumn had painted Marmalade, only ...

Autumn dropped the picture onto the floor and covered her eyes for a moment. Carefully, she opened them again and looked disbelievingly at the painting. *I'm losing it. I really am losing it.*

For where Marmalade should have been sitting by her mistress's side was nothing but an empty fence.

Marmalade was gone. Vanished. Straight out of her painting.

"Oh, Auntie! There you are! She's lovely, but I thought you put her on the fence by Meredith? She's very pretty, just like Boots."

Autumn's mouth went dry. "What are you talking about?"

Lily, surprised, gazed up at her. "Why, Marmalade, of course. But why didn't you put her in Meredith's painting? Or is she in both?"

Autumn somehow made it across the room to where the half-finished painting of the pond was perched on the easel. When she had left that picture earlier that evening, the boat had been empty. Now ...

If the girls hadn't been standing right there, Autumn would have pinched herself to make sure this whole thing wasn't some horrible nightmare.

In the boat sat Marmalade, exactly as Autumn had painted her ... in the other picture.

All through that endless reading session, Autumn's mind was spinning giddily. Had she really been so oblivious that she'd never noticed she was painting Marmalade into the wrong picture? Was that even possible? Somehow, somewhere, something wasn't right. If it had *just* been the cat in the wrong painting or *only* misplacing Philip, she could have put it down to carelessness or being too focused on her story. But both together?

Finally, Autumn reached the end of what she'd written that day and started gathering up her pages in relief. It was dark now—she must get the girls back to the cottage.

"Auntie, I can't remember what you made Meredith look like." Lily tugged at Autumn's woollen sweater. "Where's her picture?"

Sighing, her aunt unconsciously clutched her papers a little tighter. "I left it on my bed earlier."

Lily bounded out the door and up the stairs.

Valerie and Autumn stacked the pages neatly beside the typewriter, and Autumn shifted the easel closer to the window, nodding to a guest passing the door.

Lily burst breathless into the sitting room. "It's not there, Auntie. I looked everywhere—on your bed and in your black bag. Is it down here by mistake?"

"No, I had it in my room right before I came to read to you." Autumn swallowed the tremble in her voice. "Did you look under the bed?"

"Yes, but it's not there. Come see."

Autumn went to see straight away, her throat tightening with every step she took. Up in her room, they turned the place upside down and moved all the furniture. But after twenty minutes, Autumn sank back on her heels, helplessness washing over her like a cold wave.

Meredith's painting was gone.

"Maybe it's downstairs?" suggested Valerie.

Autumn shook her head. "No it's not, because I had it right after dinner. I didn't bring a picture with me when I came to read to you, did I?"

The girls shook their heads.

"That's what I thought. Oh well, never mind. Thank you for helping me look. You should be getting to bed. Daddy will be worried. It's very late."

"It *must* be the Art Man! He likes your paintings so he's stealing them to sell for lots of money!"

Autumn chuckled as she herded her nieces downstairs. "Thank you, Lily, but I promise you, my paintings wouldn't make any money. They're worthless to anyone except me because they help me remember what my characters look like. Come, get on your coats and boots, and I'll walk you back."

Only a thin glimmer of moonlight filtered down through the swaying branches high above as they hurried along the footpath to the cottage. The November chill was sharp and icy tonight, and Autumn didn't want to be out here in the freezing air any longer than she had to. They arrived breathless and flushed from the cold at the cottage's threshold.

Noah met them at the door and bundled them into the cosy glow of the warm kitchen. "I say, bit chilly, isn't it? I put on a pot of hot cocoa; should be ready any minute. Would you like some?"

Tempted, Autumn glanced at the stove but shook her head.

"No thanks, I'd best be getting back. It's late—I only wanted to see the girls safely home. Thanks anyway. They'll definitely need some, it's nippy out there."

"Daddy! Auntie's other picture's gone, too!" Lily burst out as soon as she was warm enough to speak. "I thought it was for sure the Art Man, but Auntie says it can't be. What is it, Daddy?"

"What? Another one?" Noah glanced up quickly. Autumn grimaced ruefully, shrugging.

"I must have just misplaced it, like Philip's. I thought I had it last in my room, but we searched, and it wasn't there. It'll show up."

Noah's brow furrowed, but he didn't press further. "If you're sure. Bit strange, though, misplacing two paintings in the same day. But you have seemed awfully moony since you arrived, so anything's possible. I mean, you were talking to the cat earlier—the *cat*, Autumn!"

She laughed with him, but a cold hand still gripped her stomach. Noah didn't even know about Marmalade's picture, nor was she going to tell him.

"Best be getting back." Autumn forced a smile.

"Night, Auntie!" her nieces chorused.

Autumn, lost in thought, trudged along the deeply shadowed footpath. There was something inexplicably strange going on here at Mossfern Lodge, and the worst was, it only seemed to be affecting her. The problem must lie with her, then. She knew she could get lost in her stories, and Noah was right that she had trouble sometimes discerning fiction from reality. That much was clear after her unbelievable mistake with Marmalade's picture. She really needed to wake up and pay more attention to what was going on around her. She really needed ...

A whisper of wind through the treetops sent a sudden chill down her back, and she stopped abruptly. She was about halfway between the inn and her brother's cottage, neither one visible through the dense wood, and far down below her, at the bottom of the grassy slope shone the glimmering pond.

Why had she stopped? Everything was silent except the breeze's whisper gently stirring the leaves. And yet something was there. Something. Somewhere. Watching her ...

With a start, Autumn realised she'd had this sensation of being followed, watched, for the last two days at least. Not always, but occasionally.

The pictures. Autumn sighed. Where *were* the pictures?

The sensation grew even stronger. She hastily glanced back in the direction of the safe, warm cottage. This was ridiculous. There was nothing out here to hurt her. Was there? Was that a sound she'd heard just now—something besides the wind? She swung back round to face the swaying shadows of the dark trees but didn't see anything. Or did she? Was that something flitting through the wood near the pond? Autumn strained her eyes. Nothing.

The wind rustled softly again, and this time, she almost could hear a voice in it ... a low, indistinct murmur. Then another gust whipped around her, and she was certain she could hear it, as if the wind was forming words and wafting them to her on the wings of a whisper. Words ... a voice in the wind, a woman's voice ... called out to her in a breathless whisper so low she wasn't sure if it really was a voice at all ...

"I'm at the laaaaaake! The laaaaaaaaake!"

Autumn's first instinct was to flee for the inn as fast as she could, but the nearly silent call arrested her feet, and before she realised what she was doing, she had stepped off the path and was stumbling down the slope towards the pond.

Only when she reached the water's edge did she pause, waiting, listening. After a few seconds, her logic caught up with her racing mind, and she shook herself.

"Autumn, old girl, you really are losing it. You honestly thought you heard a voice in the wind calling to you? Are you insane? Yes, you are insane. What are you even doing here? Get back up to the house straight away before you catch your death of cold!"

But even as she turned away from the pond, a gleam of white caught her attention, and she halted, peering through the dark. Something was moving slightly under the long willow branches where the rowing boat lay half submerged. She cautiously took a step nearer. Nothing had been there earlier when Valerie and she had been down here ... Autumn picked her way through the rocks and grassy tufts until she stood under the willow. She stooped and parted the branches ... and her breath caught in her throat, that now all too familiar fear washing through her.

In the boat, in the very spot where she'd accidently painted Marmalade, fluttered a sheet of white paper. She knew what it was before she even picked it up. Clutching it to her chest, Autumn turned and fled.

Back inside her room, in the safety of the warm light, she leaned against the bedroom door she'd locked and bolted behind her, trying to still her heavy breathing. Eventually, her heart slowed to a normal pace, and gingerly, she turned over the paper to confirm what she already knew.

It was one of her missing paintings.

Meredith's painting.

And what was more, Marmalade was back in it, exactly as Autumn had originally painted her.

Autumn's throat clenched as reality slowly dawned on her. She hadn't been mistaken. She *had* painted the cat into Meredith's painting, and yet ...

Did that mean ...?

After wrenching open her bedroom door, Autumn sprinted downstairs into the sitting room. Once she reached her easel, she drew a deep, shaky breath, steadied her hands, and spun it round.

Yes. It was as she'd feared.

Autumn sank to her knees. *Please Lord, am I actually insane? Please don't let me go mad! I must be going mad!*

The boat in the painting was empty.

Marmalade was gone.

"My word, you look pale as death! What's wrong?" Noah stared at Autumn in surprised concern the next morning.

She gulped. The girls looked worried ... She mustn't frighten them ...

Autumn hurriedly tried to regain her composure and laugh. "Oh, it's nothing, I just wanted to ask the girls something. Girls, last night, Marmalade *was* in the boat picture, right? You both saw her there?"

Her nieces blinked. "Of course, Auntie." Valerie answered. "We talked about it, remember?"

"I do remember, and that's what I'd thought, only ..." Autumn looked helplessly at her brother.

"What's wrong, Sis?" He was growing visibly concerned.

"I ... Well, it sounds so stupid. When I got back last night, Marmalade wasn't in that picture anymore. She was back in Meredith's."

"What?" Noah's startled exclamation joined his daughters'. "I thought you'd lost Meredith's."

"I had. I found her again in the boat on my way back last night, with Marmalade, like I'd originally had her. And gone from the boat picture."

"Wait, I don't quite follow." Noah held up his hand as the girls ran off towards the sitting room, presumably to check for themselves. "You found the lost picture at the pond? What on earth were you doing there in the middle of the night?"

"Oh, I—" However she tried to say, this would sound utterly insane. Autumn sighed resignedly. "She told me she was there. That is, I thought I could hear her calling to me. No, seriously," she said at his horrified expression. "It sounds mad, I know. But last night, I heard Meredith calling to me, saying she was at the lake. Down I went, and there's her missing painting. I know how this sounds, but you must believe me. I don't know what's happening to me, Noah. I think I'm losing my mind."

"All right, steady on." Noah blew out a long breath. "You have these characters on your mind so much, you're imagining hearing them talking to you. I suppose that can happen to authors. It's fine. I'm just confused how the painting got there in the first place. You must have put it there yourself."

"Must've, but don't see how unless I'm sleepwalking or something." Autumn shook her head helplessly.

"You're assuming it's your character you heard." Noah frowned. "But they didn't use a name, did they? Perhaps someone found your picture and really was calling to you about it for some reason."

Autumn thought hard. "I suppose it's possible. All I know is, I heard Meredith—I thought—calling that she was at the lake, and she was. Her picture anyway."

"Why do you keep calling it a lake?" Noah asked absently. "It's a pond, and not a very big one."

"Oh, well, you see ..." Again Autumn stopped, inexplicable fear clutching her. "In my story, I made it a lake," she whispered.

Noah stared at her. "Then, if it was a real person ..."

"Yes. They were very familiar with my very unfinished, unpublished story."

Noah squeezed her hand. "It's all right; don't you worry. We'll get to the bottom of this."

"Auntie, what do you mean? Marmalade is still in the boat picture, just like she was last night."

Autumn swung round and stared at Lily. "That's impossible," she murmured.

The girls led her back into the sitting room. But impossible or not, they were right. There was the painting, resting on her easel as she'd left it, and Marmalade sat contentedly in the boat. Autumn snatched up Meredith's picture ... no Marmalade.

She turned to Noah, her head spinning. "Noah, you must believe me!" She ran her hands through her auburn curls. "Nothing I see when I'm alone is real."

Sitting alone in the library, Autumn turned sharply at a slight scuffling behind her. She let out a breath of relief as a tail disappeared into Noah's wellington. She couldn't help chuckling. Somehow, seeing something so ordinary as a playful kitten soothed her nerves and steadied her pulse. *I really am a wreck right now if only a kitten can calm me down.*

Autumn gently picked up the wellington and tipped it over. "Here, Boots, you crazy kitten! What're you doing down there?" She grinned affectionately at the scrap of fur and claws scrabbling out the boot ... a grin that faded suddenly as she stared in horrified disbelief at the cat pattering away round the corner.

She'd only seen her for a moment, but it was enough. The kitten she'd just encountered was *not* Boots ... although it looked so very like Boots. In addition to grey and brown, this cat had patches of orange and white—in precisely the spots she'd painted them in her picture of Marmalade.

The wellington dropped from her hand, but Autumn stood frozen, gazing after the patchwork kitten. That cat was not Boots. That cat was ... was Marmalade! But Marmalade wasn't real! She'd invented Marmalade, she'd painted Marmalade, and she'd taken Marmalade's image out of her imagination and put her onto paper. Marmalade didn't exist!

This was too much. She wasn't losing her mind. She *had* lost her mind. She was seeing fictional cats as living, breathing creatures. She was hearing voices in her head, painting cats into wrong pictures, except she wasn't, and sometimes what she'd thought she'd done, she hadn't, and vice versa. She was becoming way too invested in her story, she needed to stop before it swallowed her completely, and she needed—

She needed Noah, that's what she needed. Autumn sprang to the door and sprinted madly out into the garden. She needed a voice of reason, someone steady and dependable who could tell her she wasn't mad, that God was still in control, and that she would be all right and just needed to rest. Or eat. Or take a holiday. Wait, this was a holiday. Well, something. Anything ...

There was Noah! Autumn almost sobbed with relief as she rushed towards him.

He straightened from his gardening and saw her. "I say! What's happened? You look dreadful."

Autumn slid to a halt and, trying to catch her breath, clutched the wall of the house. "Boots," she gasped out at last.

Noah looked even more concerned.

"Must—find Boots. Need Boots—hurry."

"I say." Noah dropped his spade and grasped her arm, steadying her. "Boots? Why? Your shoes look fine."

Autumn shook her head in frustration. "No, not boots, *Boots*! Kitten Boots! Must find her."

"Why?"

"She's—not Boots."

Noah stared at her.

She tried again. "She's Marmalade."

"Oh, she—got into the marmalade?"

"No! She *is* Marmalade!"

"Um ... all right?" Noah glanced around.

His sister groaned. She wasn't helping her case at all. "Never mind. I just need to find the cat. Have you seen her?"

"Erm, no. Not this morning. But we can look if you're that worried. She won't have run away. Try the tool shed."

They tried the tool shed—and the greenhouse and the cottage and most of the grounds. Eventually, Noah thought to try the kitchen, where the cook usually fed the cat and strays. Sure enough, there was a kitten, hungrily lapping up a bowl of milk.

Noah turned to his sister. "There she is, see? Safe and sound, nothing to worry about!"

Yes. There was Boots—normal grey-and-brown Boots. No orange, no white. No Marmalade. Just plain, ordinary Boots. The kitten looked innocently up at them and blinked contentedly.

Autumn turned and fled.

Across the deep water, the little boat sped recklessly. The dark-grey sky rumbled with angry thunder. But Meredith heard not the thunder nor saw the white streaks of lightning that split the threatening sky with fire above her. All she saw was the far-off bank and boathouse promising safety from the downpour that was slowly filling up the boat. But she had no time to stop to bail.

"We are almost there, Marmalade," she cried above the deafening rain, and the cat scrambled frantically up her skirt and tried to huddle on her lap. Instinctively, her mistress cuddled her, trying to shield her with her hand, and for a second, she let go of an oar. It fell with a dull splash into the lake just as a wave broke over the side of the boat, nearly tipping them both overboard.

"No!" Meredith shrieked, desperately clutching at the floating oar, but it slipped away and disappeared as another wave crashed over the boat, sweeping cat and woman into the stormy water in a moment ...

The clock chimed, and Autumn snapped her head up.

"My word. Dinner already." She glanced at the door and back at her typewriter and half-finished scene. Dinner. Yes.

Sighing, she stood and stacked the pages by the typewriter. She'd have to finish drowning Meredith later.

"Auntie, you *didn't*."

Autumn smiled tiredly at Lily's horrified expression. "I'm sorry, I'm afraid I had to. I did tell you Meredith might die."

"Yes, but did you have to drown Marmalade, too?" Valerie looked just as stricken as her sister. "She's a kitten, Auntie, a baby *kitten*!"

Noah glanced at his sister with a frown. Autumn knew he was concerned at her hasty decision, but it had seemed the only rational thing to do if this madness was ever to end.

She offered him a small smile. "I know what you're thinking, but if I'm getting so caught up in the story that I'm imagining I'm seeing Meredith and Marmalade, then surely those characters must go. They're the only ones that seem to be a problem right now. I thought, if I'm writing and painting them too much, stopping would end these ridiculous hallucinations."

"Whatever you think best." Her brother didn't sound convinced. "If you think it will make you feel better, give it a try."

Autumn sighed. "I didn't really want to, girls. I'm not sure. Maybe I'll take that scene out. I was just trying it to see if it worked." She rubbed her eyes and gazed blankly into her coffee cup. "Honestly, I'm too tired right now to think. I'll sleep on it and take another look tomorrow when I'm feeling better. Don't worry. They might not stay dead!"

"They better not!" Valerie was adamant.

"You should get back and turn in early," Noah said. "Try to forget the story for a bit."

Autumn nodded and drained the last of her coffee.

The November sun was barely peeking over the trees when Autumn awoke, and the dim dawn light beckoned invitingly from the glittering pond. All was calm and peaceful, and the confusion of the day before seemed to melt away with the retreating night. Autumn stood at her window, gazing at the grounds bathed in morning sunlight.

"I think I'll go read my Bible down there this morning, instead of here," she informed Boots, who yawned, stretched, and curled back into a sleepy ball at the foot of the bed. Autumn pulled on a comfortable jumper, woollen skirt, warm stockings, and boots, applied her makeup, and neatly did her hair before pinning on a beret. The morning was beautiful, but outside would be icy cold.

She spent a couple hours down at the pond, reading the Scriptures as the sun crept higher into the sky. The breakfast gong suddenly sounded faintly from the inn, and Autumn jumped up, startled. She hadn't realised the time, and she was starving!

As she turned onto the path, a soft sound caught her attention. She spun around. There was nothing there, and she couldn't quite make out what the sound was. A low humming, like a soft voice calling over the water to her. A woman's voice. Autumn took a step nearer the pond.

Yes, it was a voice. She could distinctly make out words now, and as she stepped along the bank towards the weeping willow hanging over the water, they became clearer.

Autumn froze in horror as the words began to sink in. They came drifting to her from the woman—was it a woman?—standing under the willow, every word turning Autumn's blood cold.

"Across the deep water, the little boat sped recklessly, while the dark-grey sky above rumbled with angry thunder that was creeping ever closer. But I heard not the thunder nor saw the white streaks of lightning that split the threatening sky with fire above my head ... "

The death scene. Meredith's death scene that Autumn had written only last night. She hadn't even read it to the girls yet. Nobody but herself had heard or read those words ...

Autumn yanked aside the hanging branches and stood paralysed face-to-face with the woman she had invented, created—and drowned the night before. In the half-submerged boat, Meredith stood in her long pale-blue dress clutching a ... no, no ...

Autumn gave a low groan and sank to the ground, burying her head in her hands. Meredith was clutching a patchwork kitten.

Marmalade.

There are no such things as ghosts. I invented her. She's not real. Please, Lord, help me stop seeing things that aren't really there.

Autumn peeked over her hands—no, Meredith was still there. This was hallucinating on a whole new level.

Meredith—or whatever she was—hadn't moved; now, however, she suddenly took a step forward and slowly stretched out the kitten towards Autumn, never breaking eye contact with her. *"We are almost there, Marmalade!"* she cried, in a low, lilting voice.

"Autumn?"

Noah's deep voice broke through the unnatural atmosphere, snapping Autumn back to reality. She blinked, then gazed in astonishment as Meredith dropped Marmalade into the boat, unceremoniously lifted her long skirt, and fled into the woods.

"What on earth?"

Autumn spun around to face her brother.

"Who was that?"

"You saw her, too?" Autumn nearly sobbed with relief. "Oh, thank you for seeing her, too! That means I'm not mad, even though she's all my own invention!"

"Autumn, what in creation? Who *was* that?"

"Meredith. My character. Yes"—she nodded at his startled expression—"now I'm seeing the people from my story, too, not just the cat!"

"That's impossible." Noah shook his head, his frown darkening. "Someone's having you on. *That* cat?"

Autumn followed his pointing finger to where Marmalade was climbing slowly out of the watery boat, her coat drenched and her tiny body shaking with cold. "Yes. That's Marmalade."

Noah strode over and picked up the dripping kitten. "No it's not. It's Boots, but there's some sort of powder on her." He held up his hand for Autumn to see the orange streaks on his palm.

Autumn sat down abruptly on the wet grass.

Noah was at her side in an instant. "I say." He helped her to her wobbly feet. "We'd better get you inside; you're all done in. Get some hot tea into you."

Autumn clung to his arm as they slowly climbed the steep bank. "Noah, don't you see? Boots! She's the solution to what's been happening. Someone's messing with my things and my head—or trying to. I'm not insane because you saw them, too, and it's really Boots! But why would someone do that to me?"

"I don't know, but we're going to find out as soon as you and the cat are warm and dry." Noah's face was grim. "We'll get to the bottom of this!"

"Here's your tea. Getting warmer?"

Autumn nodded mutely, shivering beside the fire. Boots snuggled down on her lap.

"It's some kind of chalk," she told Noah as he sat down. "On her coat. I've seen it before; some artists use it for pastel paintings. I don't use it myself, though."

"I was going to ask you about that, actually." Noah took a sip of tea. "If whoever used it didn't get it from your art supplies, then someone else here knows paints and art."

"You think it's one of the guests?"

"Must be, since they're always around, night and day, when these strange things are happening. Cook doesn't live on the premises, nor do the maids."

"So someone here at the inn is copying things from my story and trying to scare me with them. Why, nobody knows. But *how*? I'm still writing it—nobody's seen it."

"Where did you read to the girls, in your room?"

Autumn frowned. "No, the library usually, sometimes the sitting room. Why?"

"Well, those are public places. Couldn't someone have been listening? Behind a bookcase, perhaps, or in the next room?"

"Oh my, I see what you're getting at." She sighed and drained the last of her tea. "That must be it. I was going to say that the only part that wouldn't fit is Meredith's death scene. I haven't read it aloud yet, but now I remember, I left the whole manuscript in the library all night."

"So someone sneaked in, read the death scene, and decided to recreate it for you down at the pond this morning." Noah looked very stern. "Obviously a woman guest."

"But that still doesn't explain how things kept disappearing and reappearing in and out of my pictures!"

"No, it doesn't." Noah frowned at the teapot. "More tea?"

"Please. I suppose someone might have painted things in and out, but they'd have to be an awfully good artist to cover it up and copy my own art so perfectly that I couldn't tell the difference. Besides, seems like a heap of trouble for nothing."

"Wasn't nothing, though; that's plain." Noah handed her a new cup. "At first, I thought it was someone playing a prank on you, but with the amount of trouble they've gone to, it must be deeper than that."

Boots suddenly leaped off her lap, taking the teacup with her. It smashed at Autumn's feet, and golden tea spread slowly over the floor in a warm puddle.

"Oh!" Autumn cried.

"Oh, dear, don't worry. I'll get something to clean it up with." Her brother disappeared into the kitchen, and Autumn sank back with a sigh.

Who would do this, and why?

Noah returned with some sheets of newspaper. "This was all I could find." He spread them over the puddle. "Should soak it up if we leave them there for a bit. Now, who do you think would have been around to listen to you reading?"

"No idea," Autumn murmured absently. Her attention had been caught by an article on one of the newspaper sheets lying crookedly at her feet. She nudged it with her foot.

"What's up?" Noah followed her gaze. "Want to see that page?"

Autumn nodded, and he handed it to her. She peered at the picture and suddenly shrieked.

"What now?" Noah jumped to his feet.

She pointed excitedly at a man's photograph. "Him! That's Philip! My character—you know, the first painting to vanish? I must have seen this man somewhere and cast him as Philip."

"Autumn." Noah's voice was deathly grave. "That's Harold Newgate. Currently the most wanted chap in England. The Art Man."

Autumn turned pale. "Noah, what on earth?"

"I don't know. You must have seen him in the paper—his picture's been all over for weeks since the heist."

"No, that's impossible. I haven't looked at a paper since before I came here."

"But how else ...?"

Autumn shook her head. "You know I never remember where I've seen a face before. But I must have, somewhere."

"No, wait." Noah leaned forward and grasped her armrest. "Autumn, don't you see? That's it! If you haven't seen him in the papers, that only leaves one thing. You've seen him in person. Somewhere, sometime, you've run into Newgate. That right there is what all this is about!"

"Frighten me because I've seen Newgate?"

"Not quite." Noah leaned back. "You know this bloke has been on the run for several weeks. No one knows where he's hiding—except you. You've seen him, and he knows it and is doing everything he can to discredit you and make you look insane. The police would only laugh at you once they heard you've been seeing your characters and their cat vanishing in and out of paintings and coming to life. You wouldn't even believe yourself if you thought you were mad. Autumn, please try remember where you saw him. This is so important!"

"Oh my word." She put her head in her hands. "You're right. That's the only explanation. Someone as professional as Newgate could easily change my paintings."

"Wasn't Philip's the first to go missing? And the start of everything?"

"Yes, you're right. So he saw my painting of him—as Philip, obviously—got scared I would tell someone where he was, and decided to destroy my credibility and make me seem mad?"

"Seems like it. Can you really not remember where you saw him?"

"No, I'm trying. It might have been on the train coming here. Actually, no, no, wait ... It's coming back to me ... the second day I was here, I think."

"Yes?"

"I was coming out my room and bumped into someone. All my art supplies and pages went flying over the floor. It was one of my neighbours—I think the couple in room seven? You told me about them when I got here. Well, he was rather rude and didn't say anything, just sort of ducked past and back into his room, didn't even bother apologising or offer to help me pick everything up. I started Philip's drawing later that day, and I know his face was still fresh in my mind."

"It fits. We already established it must be a guest. And I never saw the fellow in room seven, only his wife."

"You think she dressed up as Meredith? The clothes I painted Meredith in are in your attic. And then they got hold of poor Boots and used coloured chalks to work powder into her fur to turn her into Marmalade!"

Noah set down his teacup and rose. "Well, joke's on them. You never remember where you see a face and seldom read the papers, so you had no idea your Philip character was really the most hunted fugitive of the decade!"

He opened the door and yelled up the stairs for the girls.

"Let them sleep in this morning, but I think I heard them playing up there with the dolls just now. Listen, Sis, this is very important. I don't want you here right now because you're clearly not safe, but I can't leave because someone needs to keep an eye on them until the police get here."

He handed his daughters their coats as they reached the bottom of the stairs. "Girls, something very important has turned up. Auntie will tell you all about it on the road. Listen very carefully to everything she says and be good for her."

He turned back to Autumn. "Take the girls in the Bentley and get down to the police station as fast as you can. Tell them we have him here and to send someone right away. Tell them I'm waiting for them and will make sure this fellow doesn't escape. After you've done that, the three of you wait in town. I'll call you at the hotel once the coast is clear.

You haven't eaten, have you? No? Nor have the girls. Go have breakfast at the hotel and then just wait." He herded them out the door. "Here are the keys. Let me start up the engine for you. You got all that?"

"Think so." Autumn climbed into the seat and gripped the wheel. "I just don't like leaving you here to deal with them alone. Why can't you ring the police?"

"Too risky; only telephone's in the inn, and who knows who could be lurking about. Can't afford to tip them off. Besides, I want you and the girls away in case things get unpleasant."

Autumn nodded. He was right. She needed to get the girls away from this place and get the police up here as fast as the Bentley could drive.

It was just past noon when the long-expected call from Noah came.

"He says we can go home now, if you've finished lunch." Autumn told the girls when she returned to the hotel table. "They caught the Art Man, and the police have taken him to prison."

"Was he the one doing all the mean things to your pictures?"

Autumn nodded. "Seems that way, Lily. You were right after all! It *was* the Art Man all along!"

"Mrs. Newgate is the most awful woman I've ever had the misfortune to encounter." Noah set the coffeepot on the table vehemently. "Her husband refused to talk even though he knew the game was up. She didn't so much confess to doing everything as outright brag about 'Dear Harold's' clever little scheme and all the things 'Dear Harold' managed to pull off and how brilliantly genius 'Dear Harold' was and how the world was just too stupid for him. It was her you saw down by the pond, and you also heard her calling quietly to you while walking back to the inn. She was sitting, taking notes, in the library behind a bookcase most nights you read to the girls. She was the one who fetched, carried, and stole various paintings for 'Dear Harold' to alter or hide. Notice they never returned Philip's picture, the reason for everything. They hoped you'd just forget about it with everything else going on."

"She sounds lovely." Autumn reached for the sugar tongs. "Charming lady. Perfect couple, by the sound of it. How long will he be put away?"

"Long enough, don't worry. The police couldn't arrest him fast enough. I still can't believe the amount of trouble they went to on your account. Mrs. Newgate openly told me that they wanted you to feel that your story was coming to life around you. They thought it might actually drive you mad if they kept it up long enough. Like you say, charming couple."

"Auntie, now that you know you aren't going crazy and you know what all the scary things happening really were, must Marmalade and Meredith still drown?"

Autumn laughed at Lily's anxious expression. "No, dear, they can live. I'll tear up that page as soon as we're done here!"

"Oh good, so you will carry on with the story, then! Valerie and I were afraid you wouldn't want to, after all this."

"Oh." Autumn shrugged. "Truth be told, I had thought I should take a bit of a break from it, just for a while. See, I had this idea for a mystery story."

"A mystery! Ooh, you think you can write a mystery at last?"

"Well, I could try my hand at it. Write about an author who suddenly starts seeing her characters and their pets appearing and talking to her until she's convinced she's bordering on the verge of insanity. And I'll call it *A Novelist in November*. How's that?"

Noah and the girls grinned, and Autumn winked.

"It would make a gripping story, don't you think? But sadly, I don't think anyone would believe it."

Acknowledgments

First of all, massive thanks to my sister, Lydia, without whom, quite literally, this story would never have been finished in time or even thought up! Thank you for sitting patiently through this five times, helping me edit it down into something legible, even at the expense of your own writing time, and for providing ideas, scenes, and names.

A huge thank you to my amazing writing buddy, Katja, for motivating and encouraging me each step of the way, all while listening to my writer's block rants and yet somehow managing to convince me not to ditch the whole thing! I'd be quite lost without you, and so would this story. I'm so glad we're in this anthology together.

Thank you to Faith Gilliosa for allowing me to borrow the real-life Boots and Marmalade and insert them into the story along with their names and all their adorable kitten cuteness.

Thank you to my fellow *Novelists* authors for all your support and help, particularly those who directly edited this story and gave me invaluable insight; Kellyn, Faith, and Andrea. I'm so honoured to be part of this anthology with you all!

And most of all, thank you to my dad, Shaun, who instilled a love of books in me at an age so young I can't remember a time before it; and to my mom, Stacey, who patiently taught me how to read and write in the first place!

This story would not be here but for you.

Reasons to Be Thankful

Hannah E. Gridley

J osie picked up her laptop and stared at the screen. Her mystery clues refused to fit themselves nicely into the story, and her deadline loomed. What was she going to do? She would go crazy if she didn't manage to have some outlet for her creativity, but her own mind was playing her false. As a homebound survivor of crimes, she had been sure this was her niche, her way of filling the empty hours while her husband worked.

She'd managed to write a story already, a cozy mystery with a cat that helped solve crimes. Her story had enjoyed modest success, and the publisher signed her to write another one, but now the words seemed stuck in her head. If she couldn't get them out, her safe career could be over before it really even started.

Reluctantly, she laid aside her laptop and limped to the sunroom, where her easel and paints were set out in the slanted autumnal light of an early-November midday in Virginia. She pulled on her cozy painter's smock—she was so messy after her injuries—and settled into her favorite hobby. Here was a watercolored little girl dancing through spring flowers; today, Josie could put on the final touches to make it perfect.

After a peaceful hour, the painting just needed to dry. Her heart relaxed as she viewed the happy little scene, which made her feel cozier than the falling temperatures that put a chill to her windowpanes. She went in and warmed a mug of cider as she thought about what she meant to paint next. She stared out the kitchen window, letting the heat of the drink soak into her soul. On the wooded slope behind her home, the last vestiges of fall color clung to the trees, browns and golds from the oaks and beeches against the scattered deep green of the pines and hemlocks. The lazy sunlight was giving way to a moody fall drizzle, and Josie loved the comfort of it.

The only thing to make it better would be the feel of her husband's arms around her or the sound of his voice nearby or the patter of a child's footsteps on the smooth hardwood floors. Having no child there when her husband was away at work left her achingly lonely and unable to ever feel like she had a chance to pour herself into another. To be a mom and to have no child in her arms was the worst sort of torture.

She went back to the sunroom after finishing her cider and doing some therapeutic stretches, ignoring the troublesome, fragmented first draft still in her laptop. She reached for her pencil to sketch out her next project when her phone rang. Her agent. Her stomach knotting, she answered the phone. "Hi, Tish."

"Jo! Do you have any progress to report?"

"I'm sorry, but I don't. My creativity with words appears to be completely dead."

"Jo, you don't have the luxury of that. I honestly don't care how messy that first draft is or how much we have to work with. But I can't do a thing with a blank page. How can I possibly get you to sit your rear on a chair and just get ink on a page?"

Josie sighed at Tish's strident voice. Josie had tried, so many ways. The very trying took out all the joy of the words she used to love crafting. There wasn't much she could say to excuse herself because that part of her brain simply wouldn't function. She seemed to forget the entirety of the English language when she sat down to force it. She hardly thought Tish was serious about wanting to receive the draft in Caveman. She was too much of an artist to be able to turn in something composed of nothing but "he sat, she stared, he sneezed, she coughed" type writing. Oh, why had she ever dreamed that she could do this?

"Jo? You there?" Tish pushed, her tone pitched a little louder. "Or did I lose you?"

"I'm here. I just don't know how to do it. How can I force it when I sound like I'm writing a chapter book?"

Tish blew out a breath. "Then write the stupid chapter book. But you promised me the manuscript last month, and I'm only able to give you to the end of November or your contract is considered broken. Listen, Jo. You signed a contract with us. I can't help you with no manuscript in hand. Publishing moves fast, and we don't have the luxury of waiting for artistry unless you're ahead in your projects. If you hand me a chapter book, we'll deal. Any words can be improved. No words are a fail. If you don't come through on this, your reputation is going to be shot in the publishing world, and you'll have a hard time ever getting your toe in the door again. Got it?"

Josie felt like crying. This was her outlet. Of course, Tish didn't know that. Didn't know that she was too afraid to leave home and go in public for anything. Didn't know about the violent attack that left her body shattered, her little son believing her dead, and her womb as yet unable to carry another baby. Witness protection wasn't a walk in the park for anyone, especially a woman who used to be the most outgoing and friendly face in her small town. "I got it. Are you serious that if I send it in, in that bad a shape, that you will read it?"

"Totally serious! I can't help you with nothing, but I can advise you with something. At the very least, we can go back and forth. But you must *start* something."

"Well, I guess I've started it, but I have no middle." Did Tish think saying the same thing ten times over would help anything?

"Start something different. It's possible to write a whole novel in a month. Or even a shorter story. Just give me something with all three essentials: beginning, middle, and end. Even if it's a dreadfully soggy middle. I still think you could manage to finish this one you're working on, but I will let you decide if you need to start something new. Got it? This is your last chance."

"I understand. I'll turn something in, even if it's short. It's very important to me to be able to write; I just can't seem to get past this brain freeze when I open my computer. Maybe if I try something a little different, I can make it work."

"If you can't do anything with a computer, that's fine. Take a notebook to the park and write away from home. Get a fancy pen and write with a moody shade of ink. Whatever it takes, *even* if you write the whole thing in calligraphy and then type it up. Many times, artists bloom best by a switch in the media they work with."

Tish didn't even know about the painting. That sentence stuck with Josie. An artist, switching up the media ... that was her language. She could understand that. Maybe Frank wouldn't mind if she did spend a bit of money on an experiment in writing supplies.

She went to her computer after hanging up with Tish and read over the pitiful thirty or so pages she'd managed to cobble together. It didn't even have a clear beginning, to be honest.

What if she did the crazy thing? Just jotting down whatever might come to mind? Then Tish would know she had made an effort. Josie couldn't honestly say it was "distracting" her from anything more important when her expected mystery was such a failure. Say she did write that little chapter book. Wouldn't it take her less than a week?

She leaned back and let her thoughts take her through some of the early readers she had just begun to check out for her little son, Paul, before she was ripped from his life by the accident that so nearly killed her. What was he reading now? He was a smart child and had already known his alphabet. But what if his grief at having his parents "die" could have set him back? She knew her aunt, her own foster mother, would be an excellent surrogate mom to him; she had zero worries on that front. But oh! How she longed to have him in her own arms. She would never get over that longing.

What if she could write something that he would read? He could never know it was from his lost mom, but maybe it would give her a tiny bit of influence over his life? She'd never considered writing for the youth market before, but it seemed like her only chance now. However, when she sat down before the computer screen, she once again had no available intelligence to string together more than three or four words at a time.

What was she to do?

Without the outlet of writing, how could she ever feel more than useless?

Frank left his car and carried his to-go lunch up to his office. He felt worn out, ready to drop. The week away from his wife on the case he'd just finished made him eager to get home and check on her. He had to admit, he was carrying so much weight at home that he had a hard time coping with the weight of the cases he dealt with on a daily basis as an FBI agent. He went to the break room and poured himself another big mug of stiff black coffee. He was just about to head to his desk when the outer door of his team's office suite creaked open again and the voice from his worst nightmares called out, "Agent Abraham? Have you a moment?"

Why was Moore showing up this side of the ocean, asking for Frank's boss? He froze. Would he be safe in the break room? Or was this the day his new identity died again? He wasn't wearing his sidearm right now, and he wished he was. He had no illusions that Moore wouldn't recognize him on the spot, and when he did, everything he knew as Agent Frank Jensen would be gone. Just as Josie and he had gotten a good new life set up again, too. Josie couldn't take another disappointment right now. How could he protect her? He'd failed entirely before.

He stood there, his back to the cabinets, as his coworker Agent Fraser made small talk with Agent Moore, now of Interpol. Moore's voice sent Frank back mentally to the worst days of his life, and the reason his little son had to be left behind with family. Frank had roomed with the man for three years while they completed an undercover mission and knew every inflection of Moore's voice. He used to call him one of his dearest friends until the day Moore shot him in the back and left him lying in a rural field to die. There was no evidence left, since the man was paranoid about leaving any sort of trace of himself behind. Just Frank's stunned body, shot with his own spare weapon, and only alive because Moore hadn't known he'd put on his bulletproof vest that day. And as Frank lay there, gasping for breath from cracked ribs and hoping to get home to his wife, some maniac in a borrowed pickup truck had deliberately run her down in the street as she was shopping downtown. She had very nearly died and would always be crippled, but the only clue to the crime was the borrowed truck being the same make and model as the one Moore had been driving when he shot Frank.

Agent Abraham had been their supervisor back then. By the time Frank got out of his own pickle and made it to his wife's side, Agent Moore had already reported Frank "killed in action on the last assignment" and headed off to his new job at Interpol. Agent Abraham, compassionate enough to climb in a car at midnight to go meet the panicked young man claiming to have been attacked and left for dead, had heard him out without telling others Frank was alive. It was Abraham who, although in the middle of transferring from the state office, believed Frank's story and helped him get a new identity, then hired him on at the Virginia office months later. However, try as they might, they couldn't come up with any evidence against Moore.

Agent Abraham would still cover for him, but how could Frank get out of the office without Moore seeing his face and realizing he lived through the attack? He really didn't want to go there yet, not until Moore was no longer in top favor with the State Department and the White House. Maybe someday more evidence could come to light, but until then, he wasn't poking sticks in the eyes of the government's favorite golden boy.

Just as he began to wonder if he could make any dash for safety, he heard Agent Abraham's door squeak open and Abe's voice say noisily, "Agent Moore? What brings you to the States? Welcome to my office. Come in and close the door so we can get some catching up done. You'll have to tell me about where you've been, what you've seen, and some of your most interesting cases."

The door closed, and Frank dared to peek out. Coast clear, he stopped only to grab the bag that contained his laptop, then scooted down the hall and straight down to his car.

No sooner did he gain his car than his cellular phone rang. A few minutes sooner, and it would have revealed his spot in the break room. *Josie.* He flipped it open and answered, trying to steady his voice and keep it from betraying his breathless hurry downstairs.

She didn't keep him more than a minute, conscientious as always about having him on the phone during work hours. It was just a quick request that he would try picking up a fountain pen or two and some ink for her to try, on his way home. Glad for the distraction, he agreed, then started his car and headed straight for a stationery shop he'd seen in town.

Frank had finished a too-large purchase at the stationery store and was halfway home when Abe called him.

"I'm out of the office," Abe said, getting right to the point. "I left early, too. I've scheduled you to leave town again in the morning, to catch up on the handwriting analysis conference this week, and the following week you'll be in a DNA developments conference. I'm sorry to send you away from home for so long, but Moore is stationed in town for the next couple of weeks and has assured me he's going to be dropping by often to catch up on old times, when I was his boss. I don't think he suspects anything, but I certainly don't want to test it. In exchange, I'm volunteering my niece to come stay with your wife. She's in between rentals and needs a place to stay, but she's also a black belt in three arts and a crack shot."

Frank's spirits sank at the news. Going right back out of town was the last thing he wanted to do, and neither of the conferences were things that particularly interested him. Worse was the idea of leaving Josie alone for two weeks after last week's absence, especially when they were trying to conceive before Christmas. The timing couldn't be more inconvenient with Josie's crippling deadline either. A militant niece of Abe's was hardly a consolation. "Thanks, Abe. I left as soon as I could slip out. I was in the break room pouring coffee when he came in."

"Thank God for your coffee addiction, then," Abe responded. "Funny if you owe your life to a pot of coffee. Go on home, and I'll email you the flight info tonight. No need to take time off for today's half day. However, I do have worse news."

Worse? Not good. "And?"

"It's officially not safe to bring your son home. Moore's made himself into a kind uncle, has been sending gifts, and apparently brought souvenirs to him from overseas the day he got back in the States. He brought me a Polaroid pic, which I'll set aside for you, but I will say unequivocally, if you try to move that boy out of Maryland, Moore will be on your tail faster than a chicken on a grub."

Frank's world crashed around him. It's exactly what he'd feared was the case because Moore had always viewed little Paul with a wide streak of ownership. Why would a single man with no family be so devoted to a small boy in rural Maryland? Was it guilt over killing Paul's parents or a suspicion they weren't really dead and might come back for him? Either could be true … but either one meant that it could cost Josie's life if she got her son back. Frank's one aim this year had been to get Paul home in time for Christmas, whether they did or didn't conceive their next baby before then, and now Frank's hopes came to a complete smash. Paul was safe where he was. Josie wouldn't be safe if he was with her. Besides, Josie didn't mind being a recluse, but could Frank and she require that of their little boy? Hardly.

"I'm sorry, Frank. I know what this means to you."

"I'm just glad I hadn't told Josie I was trying to bring him home to us."

"Right. It wouldn't be good to break her heart, too."

As he finished the last twenty minutes of his hour's drive home, Frank fought the blues that threatened to overtake him. He had to act normally for Josie, had to be cheerful to encourage her. He managed to stay on the road, but he couldn't say he really saw any of the vibrant fall color on his way home.

Josie hurried to the door as best she could when she heard Frank's car come down the gravel drive two hours earlier than normal. What a nice treat after his days away from home! His eager footsteps came in the house only minutes later, and then she was in his arms and getting well kissed. She let out a long breath of contentment. Somehow, when Frank held her close, she seemed to forget all the things she couldn't do and just remembered how much she loved this man of hers. Seven years together so far, and they hadn't grown the least bit tired of each other yet. It was God's mercy they hadn't, since their marriage was the only thing that had survived from their old life. In Frank's arms, Josie felt *normal*.

After releasing her, he held out the gift bag from the stationery store, which she hadn't even noticed he was holding when she threw herself into his arms. "Here are your new toys," he said. "You have several different nib sizes and ink colors in there."

"Oh, neat!" she set it on the nearby kitchen counter and emptied the bag piece by piece. "Oh, Frank, this is too much!"

"I had fun picking it all out. If you don't like any of the colors or styles, I can take them back, but if you like them, it's an early Thanksgiving gift. I have some not-so-fun news, so hopefully this helps you think of me the next couple weeks. I have been abruptly scheduled for two conferences and have to leave again in the morning."

"Oh no! I'm so sorry, Frank! But you'll be home for Thanksgiving, right?" She tried her best to keep her acute disappointment out of her tone and key it down to a more normal wifely longing, instead of betraying to him just how much of a clinging limpet she really was.

"You bet. I wouldn't miss it for anything. Then maybe I won't have to travel much for the rest of the year."

He sounded thoroughly tired out; Josie wished she could fix it for him. "Maybe you can take a long weekend or two in January," she added, since he'd already used up all but one vacation day this year, most of them on her doctor's appointments. Speaking of which, she had two of those next week that would have to be rescheduled. Oh well. Could she complain about anything? She couldn't even manage to write a book from the comfort of home, much less run around the country on a demanding job. But that's just one of the things that she admired about him. She'd indirectly managed to take so many things from him since her accident; could she say a single word against his job? She knew he'd worked toward his dream of being a field agent since middle school, and over her dead body would she make him feel guilty for hanging on to that dream. Besides, they needed the good insurance from it to keep their noses above the pile of health care debts.

"That sounds like a good plan," he said. "Now, I don't know about this next bit. Abe is assigning his niece to come be your companion while I'm gone, since you shouldn't be too long alone. Try her out, and if you can't stand her, send her away; but she will at least make sure you have groceries and get you to your doctor's appointments. Then we'll get back to normal by Thanksgiving."

A tumble of mixed feelings hit Josie. She hated meeting new people, with her scars and lameness, but she couldn't deny that it was hard to get through one week by herself, let alone two. Her fall risk left her afraid to shower except when the housekeeper was there. She couldn't deny she was running low on some groceries. "Can we afford that?" she asked.

"She's coming for room and board. She is in between apartments this month and is available overnight. I know it might be awkward, but we can trust her because Abe does. Maybe at least try her out?"

"Okay." She definitely wouldn't be finishing any book next week now. Oh well; at least she didn't have anything to prepare; the guest room was always clean, thanks to the housekeeper.

"Last thing; I'll need to work a little bit after supper tonight, to check my emails and print off my plane tickets. Other than that, I'm all yours."

Over the next few hours, she helped him plan what to pack for his trips and then spilled out the story of her writing woes. She showed him her watercolor last, and he loved it, as usual. If only she could make a living off her watercolors, too; but art was even fussier than literature.

Later, they sat in the sunroom with mugs of hot chocolate and cuddled away the autumn chill. The evening was perfect, and for a few hours, she let herself forget just how lonely she would be feeling the next night.

The next morning, Josie was up early to help fix Frank's breakfast and get him out the door in a timely manner. He needed to leave by 9:30 a.m., and Abe's niece, Tabitha, was expected at 9:00 a.m. It wasn't easy to leave her, especially without letting her know the real reason he was skipping town so fast. He didn't want to worry her, and there wasn't any reason to believe there was real danger to her if there was no easy link left to find her.

When the doorbell rang, Josie's heartbeat skipped despite her not being particularly excited about the companion coming to her. She saw the stares and unasked questions in the doctors' offices and wasn't keen on having them happen in her own home. It was just so very awkward to meet new people since her accident ...

Frank got the door and revealed a young woman on the taller side of medium height, straight light-brown hair hanging loose nearly to her elbows, her face framed by bottle-curl bangs. Her hazel eyes took in Frank first, then met Josie's gaze with a friendly smile. Josie held out her hand for a handshake, noting Tabitha's even white teeth and the freckles across the bridge of her nose. This looked like the sort of young woman she'd have wanted to be friends with back before the crash. The sort of open-eyed, frank-faced person she would have found easy to talk to. But now that she was so changed by everything, how could she hope to connect with that sort of bright, cheery personality?

Tabitha seemed to be pleased to meet them, and soon, her sunny personality was reminding Josie of herself before, as Tabitha looked through the house, saw the things Frank normally kept done, and quickly declared herself equal to all the tasks. That was a relief, since Frank hadn't had time to do more than a few tasks last night, and most of them would need doing sometime in the next two weeks. Frank helped carry Tabitha's bags into the guest room; then she took some time to settle in, letting Frank and Josie have a few minutes to themselves to say goodbye, which made Josie's heart warm toward her.

By the time Tabitha came out of her room, Josie had wiped her eyes and tried to put herself together again after her goodbye to Frank. Two weeks was going to be so long, and as soon as he drove away, she'd dissolved into a good sobbing session. Then she had gotten her new pens, seated herself at the kitchen table, and took time deciding which one she meant to try first. She had settled on using the Waterman with a medium nib, with a warm wine-colored ink that matched the barrel of the pen nicely. She wasn't sure what to try writing first, but then on glancing out the window, she thought of the cheerful watercolor she'd done this week. Who was the dancing little girl, and why? In a few moments, she had a freestyle poem skittering across the page. It felt so good to have the words flow again that she was lost to everything around her until she got to the ending lines.

She leaned back and stretched her stiff spine, realizing suddenly that she had a guest somewhere in the house. Was she still sitting in the guest room? Josie glanced around to see and found Tabitha ensconced on an armchair in the great room, crocheting happily. "Oh, there you are. Sorry; I had an idea to chase down."

Tabitha held up her crochet project and laughed. "No problem! You looked like something had you enthralled, so I grabbed this and settled in. I didn't know how long your muse tends to keep you captive."

"My muse has been hiding for months," Josie admitted. "I'm afraid my agent is very upset with me lately."

"That's too bad. Want me to try to jar it loose for you? I'm pretty handy to bounce ideas off of, if you want to."

"Maybe. That might be helpful." Josie wasn't sure, since she'd only really talked to Tish before about her writing; but she was desperate enough to try just about anything. It was already getting into the second week of November, and she didn't know if it was humanly possible to write a whole mystery in the space of just a few weeks.

"You have to know, I was so excited when Uncle Abe told me about you being an author. I used to help my mom with her stories a long time ago, but she mostly wrote for magazines."

"I don't feel very author-ish with a severe case of writer's block. It's been miserable."

"I bet it has. That sort of thing is so hard to deal with ... Mom hated it so badly." Tabitha pulled herself to her feet. "Shall we sit down and share a big pot of tea? I can listen as long as you need while we sip tea."

Josie hadn't had a good pot of tea in a while. "That sounds quite delicious. Let's do that."

She talked Tabitha through where to find each item needed, since the larger items like the teakettle and pot were still too heavy for her, and within minutes, the teakettle was bubbling merrily on the stovetop. Once the tea was ready, they sat down at the table, and Josie explained her problems to Tabitha with very little reserve. Nothing like desperation to break down barriers, it seemed.

Finally, after hours of chatting and note-taking, Tabitha made the suggestion that got everything to click into place: "Why, if you love kids so much, why not stick one in your mystery and see if that livens it up? If they're the right age, they could even be in on solving the crime."

That was it! She could write Paul into her story. Well, the imaginary version of him, at least. Have the lonely spinster sleuth get tasked with caring for a six-year-old boy who'd come to stay with her. Could that help salve the longing in Josie's heart? Or would it only make it worse? Either way, she had to take the chance. Had to dive right into the idea and let herself bleed across the page if she had to.

By evening, Josie had a decent outline scratched out. She still didn't want to be tied to the computer, and writing on paper did seem to help a little. Tabitha had quickly volunteered to help with whatever typing needed to be done once the story was started. They would take breaks for Josie to get up and stretch or walk around the room, but had stopped for very little else. Beyond the easy chatter of storybuilding, though, it began to sink in to

Josie that Tabitha didn't seem to see her as being any different from other women. She was cheerful and helpful but never stared at Josie's scars or spoke down to her as though her mind must be as slow as her gait. Josie felt her worries falling away as the day went on and Tabitha and she appeared to be starting a blessedly *normal* relationship. A friendship, maybe? She could only dream of having a good female friendship gifted to her again after so many years without and was still afraid it wouldn't last, but she meant to enjoy it while she could.

Operation Write the Novel was terrifically hard work over the next few days. Tabitha was a consistently beneficial sounding board and kept each of the scenes typed up as Josie wrote them down. Sometimes Tabitha even did the writing herself as Josie lay on the sofa with her feet up to ease her aching legs and back, dictating words from her resting place.

Tabitha helped her in other ways, too. "You need to be able to at least hold a teakettle enough to make yourself a cup of tea," she insisted, dragging out Josie's old physical therapy exercises and helping her dust them off, alongside nicely goading her into structural stretching exercises that helped ease some of the nerve pain Josie still dealt with. The amazing thing was, Josie didn't feel those suggestions to be some sort of "let me fix you so you can be more like me" push, but instead, a wish of wanting her to be more independent—especially once Tabitha heard about Josie's longing for another baby. "Oh, then of course we need to get your arms strengthened up a bit," Tabitha agreed. "I dare say, you can hold a newborn, but a squirming toddler would be quite another matter. You'll want to be able to cuddle that baby as long as possible." So Josie added in the exercises, the painful ones with the comfortable ones, thinking devotedly of the goal of holding her baby as long as she could.

Amazingly, sometime along the way, hope grew in her alongside watching her manuscript grow. She was only twenty-six in years despite how creaky she felt. She had time to work on having another baby. She began to let herself think in terms of *when* instead of *if*.

They pushed to complete at least one chapter a day, and on several days, they managed two. On the seventh day, they managed three; on the eighth, four; and Josie began to honestly believe the book might get done on time, maybe even early.

That Monday, though, Josie woke with a smashing headache. How could she get anything done? Tabitha tucked her up on the sofa and busied herself quietly with various household tasks. By lunchtime, Josie's headache eased and they got a chapter done in spite of her. The pattern repeated the next day, waking with a terrible headache that grew better by lunchtime. Same for the next day, which would already be a loss since Josie had her doctor's appointment; at least that was in the afternoon, so her head felt better.

Josie answered the nurse's questions by rote, grateful to be out of the crowded waiting room, where she had once again endured the sideways stares she hated so much. Tabitha had tried to keep her talking, but it didn't work. Nothing would ever change those stares. Would Tabitha herself see Josie in a new light after seeing how it was? After a few minutes, Josie was nothing but silent, trying to imagine herself far away from the area. It was a relief to be called back for her blood draw and ushered into an exam room all by herself.

Finally, the nurse was done, and the doctor didn't leave her waiting long. Dr. Leeper was a no-nonsense sort of doctor who always got right to the point. "Feeling okay, Mrs. Jensen?" she asked.

"Other than a bad headache every morning this week, yes. Just regular aches and pains."

"That's normal. No morning sickness yet?"

Josie's breath caught, and the room swirled around her. "Say what?"

"Good things in your blood work, Mrs. Jensen. Looks like you're finally pregnant."

"Am I really?!" Josie exclaimed, feeling the world shift.

"Yes indeed. Should be about five weeks along, by your chart. Early but real. Congratulations."

Josie burst into tears. Eight months or less, and she would have a baby in her arms.

Suddenly, everything was different.

Tabitha knew something was up but held in her questions until they were safely in the car. "Was it bad news?"

Josie laughed through another wash of tears. "Oh, no. I'm finally pregnant. Two years of trying."

"Eeeeee! That's wonderful!" Tabitha shrieked, hugging her impulsively across the console.

After that, everything seemed to slow down. They stuck to one chapter a day doggedly, but it wasn't easy. Josie kept getting the headaches every morning that week, though she didn't develop regular morning sickness yet.

She was waiting to tell Frank, determined to see his face when she told. It wasn't easy for her when Frank broke the news to her on Thursday that he'd been asked to stay over and wouldn't be home until Wednesday next, but that was when she decided she would wait one more day and tell him next Thursday, which was Thanksgiving. But the weekend ended up being more productive again, and the story was nearing its end.

On Tuesday, Tabitha was at her side when Josie made the triumphant phone call to Tish. "I have a story done. It's not optimal, and I know it will need some good edits, but we have words. But I need to add my good friend who helped me as my coauthor."

Tabitha gasped and tried to deny the request softly.

"You wouldn't have had a book without her," Josie insisted. "She was my typist, and she helped me plot the whole thing. It's only fair, and I won't send it to you without your agreement."

Tish blew out a breath. "Well, it's highly irregular to add an author like that, but if the story is good, I don't think we have much choice. But if you ever do it again without notifying me first, it will be considered breach of contract."

"Of course."

Josie emailed the file to Tish soon after, and Josie and Tabitha pulled out a jigsaw puzzle to relax with. Tabitha stoked up a roaring fire as added celebration.

The day before Thanksgiving wasn't pleasant on the roads, but Frank was home at last. He pulled in beside Tabitha's car and dragged out his luggage. Agent Moore had set up shop right there in their own FBI suite while working a local case and hadn't left until this Monday. Frank was emotionally drained after much too long a time away, but it was over now. He walked in the house without stopping to do anything else, going straight to hug his wife. Small consolation that now he was home, he didn't have to report back to work until Monday morning. He'd missed her so much, worried about her so much.

When he leaned down to kiss her, he could see the joy in her eyes. "You got the book accepted?" he asked, hoping he was guessing right.

"Oh yes! Tish emailed me this morning and loves it. Huge weight off my shoulders."

"Good job, honey. That's great news!"

"I think so!"

Within an hour, Tabitha headed down the road to stay at her uncle's for Thanksgiving but with plenty of promises to come back the next week to work on possible edits, and to outline the next book in the series—which would, of course, contain the little-boy character both women seemed to love dearly.

That evening, with Josie to himself, he finally explained the visit from Agent Moore and the danger Abe had helped him avoid. She shuddered at hearing the man had been in town again but didn't criticize Frank for waiting to tell her.

After supper they sat down on the sofa to talk and enjoy a crackling fire together. She seemed completely worn out from all her writing because she dropped off to sleep with her head against his shoulder, almost in the middle of her sentence.

Her dark lashes curled against her cheeks, and he took in the view with gratitude overflowing in his heart. Someday, she'd see in herself what he saw in her: not the long scar on the left side of her face, not the bump where her nose had broken, not the irregularity in her chin where she'd broken her jaw against the hood of the murderous truck—but as a fighter; a miracle in the flesh; a gift from God to him when the odds said there was no way she could live through the first weeks and months; when the doctors had assured him gravely she'd wake up as a vegetable, if at all. Frank saw a beautiful woman, not an ugly one. He didn't mind the limp because the doctors had all said she would never walk again. But even if she hadn't fought her way back to this level of wellness, he knew he'd have always loved her. He loved her even more because she came back to him across the pain and loss and tragedy that robbed him of everything else.

He'd lose everything all over again just to keep her safe in his arms.

Thanksgiving Day dawned dim and windy. Since Frank and Josie had nowhere to go for family and had declined Abe's generous invitation, they slept in late and then heated the meal Frank had picked up at a local restaurant the day before instead of eating a normal breakfast. Frank made a number of lighthearted comments about them making their own traditions now that they were on their own, but Josie's mind kept going back to the pregnancy results hiding in her pocket. She couldn't wait to see his face and hear his shout of joy at her news.

At last, all the dishes were on the table and they were ready to eat. Frank reached for her hand to hold to say grace, but before he began to speak, Josie stammered out, "I've got one more thing to be thankful for," and handed him the paper.

He stared for one good minute, then gasped and gave a whoop of joy. "You're pregnant?"

She laughed in pure delight at the elation in his face. "Yes indeed! The doctor told me last week. Isn't it delightful? I'm so happy."

"Wow. That's fabulous news, Josie. I can't believe you managed to keep the secret for so long."

"Two days? I needed to see your face when I told you, so I wasn't tempted earlier. Still, yes, it did seem rather hard to keep, but I was sure I wanted to give this to you on our national day of thanksgiving, since it's the best thing that's happened to us in years."

"Are you sure you're up to the task?"

"Very sure! The doctor says I have to plan for a cesarean but is otherwise hopeful I'll be able to carry nearly to term. We have an appointment next week to see if we can hear a heartbeat."

Frank pushed out his chair and clasped Josie tenderly. "That's truly the best news we've had this year." He slid a hand into his pocket and pulled out a photo. "Mine's not as fancy. It's a recent picture of Paul."

With a gasp of excitement, Josie pounced on it and held it close to her face, studying every possible detail. "Can you believe how big he's getting?"

"No, I can't."

"Do you have a copy?"

"There's just this one."

"I'll put it where we can both see it easily, then."

She reached out and took a lid off one of the dishes, then used it to lean Paul's picture against. "There. Now we can pretend he's here, too."

Frank clasped her hand. "Good idea."

As he said the grace then, they thanked God for Josie's continued healing and for keeping them safe during the surprise visit from Agent Moore, but more than anything, for the gift of the son they couldn't hold close and for the new soul on its way to them in the coming year.

Rural Maryland
One year later

Josie held the little wrapped package in her hand and put kisses on it. Inside were her three mystery books, the third hot-off-the-press with the little-boy sleuth returning as a main protagonist. Tabitha's pen name was right below hers on the cover; with their friendship a solid one now, it seemed likely to remain there for some time. The publisher had already sent a contract for the next three books in the series. Josie also had a separate contract with another agent and publisher to write and illustrate children's picture books, but with Paul being seven now, it seemed insulting to give him a small child's gift. Let this gift be generic enough that her aunt and son could both enjoy the story.

Though it was years since Josie and Frank had ventured back to the town she grew up in, she noticed most things looked the same. One full year without word of Moore emboldened them to drive up in a car Tabitha rented for them and to drop their gift on the doorstep. Frank had picked out a pocketknife to include for Paul; Josie had chuckled at the gift but figured her aunt would keep it until the right time to give it to him. Now, after handing the gift package to Frank, Josie sat on the back seat of the humble sedan. It might be years before it was advisable to risk driving by again, and she wanted to etch the place on her memory despite the dark.

As Frank took the gift to leave on the porch, Josie ran a finger down sleeping baby Travis's pudgy little arm. He'd arrived safely on July 15 and was growing like a weed. Thankfulness for him still flooded out the edges of her heart when she thought of how lonely she had been without him. She hadn't even minded being wheelchair bound again for the last trimester before he arrived.

Frank hurried back to the car, but no one was stirring to open the door anyway, despite his sprightly ring-and-run moves. Perhaps they weren't home at all but were out at some event with friends. He climbed back into the driver's seat with a sigh. "They're not opening up." He knew she'd hoped for the tiniest glimpse of either Aunt Minnie or Paul, and for a moment the disappointment squeezed tight around her chest. She had to make him feel better about her dashed hopes, she thought.

"It's okay. Really." And, quite suddenly, she knew she was. Despite everything she longed for, she still had joy, still had God, and still had Frank. God had gifted her a new son and a new friend. She would never quit hoping to have Paul back in her arms, but every day, she knew the *no* to her prayers of getting her firstborn home might just be a *not yet*. She held on to that with all her heart. "God gave us a beautiful new baby, Frank. I'm thankful for every minute. I shouldn't be here, by what medicine said. Maybe next year we can have Paul back. Until then … let's go celebrate our Thanksgiving together. At home. We'll prop the picture of Paul up on the table and pretend like we did last year. Sound good?"

"Sounds very good." Frank fastened his seat belt and sent another long glance toward the small house where Josie had lived when they met and married and where their older son now resided. Josie knew Frank had as many longings about glimpsing their boy as she did. Then he reached back to squeeze her hand gently for a moment before starting the engine and easing the car down the road, heading back home.

Home was a different place than where it used to be, but it was good nevertheless.

Act in the Living Present

Katja H. Labonté

Dedication

To the Burdens.
Thank you so much for those amazing two days this spring.
It meant—and still means—the world to me.

Glossary

Ah bi'n: Québécois pronunciation of *ah bien*, loosely equivalent to the English phrase, "well then!"

Belle province: Beautiful province (Québec)

Berçante: Québécois term for a rocking chair

Bi'n sûr, Maman Jeanne: Of course, Mama Jeanne (lit. "very sure")

Ma belle: My beautiful (girl)

Madame: Mrs., ma'am/madam

Mad'moiselle, Ma'm'selle: Québécois pronunciation of *mademoiselle*, miss

Ma mère: My mother

Merci: Thank you

Môman, Pôpa: Dialect pronunciation of *maman* and *papa*

Mon ange: My angel, common Québécois endearment for one's child

Monsieur: Mr., sir

N'est-c'pas: Québécois pronunciation of *n'est-ce pas*, French phrase meaning "is it not (so)?" equivalent to the English "right?"

Oncle: Uncle

'Scuse moi, là: *Là* is an interjection meaning *there/now*, here used as emphasis to strengthen Jeanne d'Arc's protest. "'Scuse me, *but* ...!"

T he library was unusually sombre that early-November day. Rain tapped at the
window like a thousand tiny hands seeking entrance. Outside, the wind wailed like
a lost, lonely thing, and a few stray leaves drifted in endless circles on its wings. The grey,
harsh light of afternoon filtered through the heavy drapes, throwing the dark wooden
shelves into deeper gloom by its concentrated glare and faint outlines.

The library was empty save for a very still form sitting cross-legged on the floor, leaning
against one of the bookcases. She was nothing more than a girl, about sixteen years of
age, rather slight and small, with fashionably waved blonde hair, a straight nose, and large
brown eyes fringed with very long, dark lashes. She was not strictly pretty, but her face
was delicate and striking, and she was very daintily and elegantly dressed in a simple white
gown. A large tome lay on her lap, but she was staring straight before her, eyes unseeing,
lips parted, wholly lost to the world.

A door without shut with a bang, rousing her effectively; she started and looked
around, then clambered to her feet, as though her legs had numbed from their cramped
position, and crossed over to the unlit fireplace. Drawing her book close, she curled down
on one of the large armchairs that sat stolidly on each side and began to read again, careless
of the uncertain light crossing her page.

The library doors opened softly, and a young man of about one-and-twenty thrust
his head and shoulders in, glancing swiftly about the room. The similarity in their faces
spoke of close kinship, but his eyes were thoughtful instead of dreamy, and his cleft chin,
mild instead of yielding; when studied, his gaze had a steadfast firmness that belied the
compliancy of his soft face, while a slight quirk at the corner of his lips spoke of a hidden
roguish lightheartedness.

He caught sight of the girl now and slipped into the room, closing the doors behind him with great caution. Step by step, sure and soundless, he crept upon her, while she read on, oblivious to the world. At last, he was behind her, and with brotherly affection, he seized her hair and gave a quick, gentle tug.

She raised her eyes from her book and frowned but put aside the book willingly as he perched on the arm of her chair. "Home so soon?"

"Yes, I caught an earlier train. The maid said you were here alone, but she didn't know where Father and *ma mère* went."

"Father's at a business meeting, and *ma mère* went calling. I was lonely alone, so I came here. Somehow, it isn't so lonely with all the books."

"Yes, I suppose if I'd read *Robinson Crusoe* thirty-two times, I, too, should count him a very good friend." His tone was dry, yet somehow conveyed all the fondness that his words did not.

She tossed her head but looked pleased. "I didn't read *Robinson Crusoe* more than six ... ten ... well, twelve times. And you must have read Ballantyne's books dozens of times!"

"But *I* didn't read a single book three times a year as you did."

"Yes, I don't have that time anymore." An emotion very like guilt seeped into her regretful words.

"And a good thing, too. You become more cat-like every day. I was right in calling you Kitten, you see," he teased.

Myriam rolled her eyes, but she smiled a little at the old nickname—a nickname born long before she could remember, when the nursemaid had first announced to him that he had a sister. *"Come and see the surprise I have for you,"* she'd said, and little Rupert, longing for a kitten, was promptly convinced this was what awaited him. Loud were his wails when he discovered only a rosy-faced, scrunched-nosed baby! He had gotten over his disappointment quickly enough, but from then on, he had referred to her as Kitten—except in their mother's hearing. Mrs. Carey did not approve of nicknames.

"Kittens don't like reading," Myriam answered now, stretching slightly.

"They would if they knew how. And they certainly like cuddling under blankets and curling up in chairs and staring out of rainy windows. What are you reading now?" Rupert asked, reaching for her book.

"It's a new novel; it's only just come out this summer."

"Ah yes, a romance, of course, with a handsome hero to rescue my lady every few chapters ..." But his sardonic expression disappeared as he scanned the last page she'd read.

"Do you really think you should be reading this, Myriam?"

There was no condemnation, only interest, in his tone, but she could not meet his eyes as she flushed.

"It's very, very good writing," she retorted.

He waited, and she fidgeted silently.

"Well—perhaps not," she admitted at last.

"I don't know whether it's a bad book or not, but from what I've heard the girls at college drop, I fancy you could be reading much better stuff, that's all. And I think you're rather young to be reading Gothic romance, Kitten. Perhaps when you are older and know more of the world, it might suit you more ..."

"It's only a *book*, Rupert!" she protested, trying to take the book back.

He let go, but a fine frown creased his brow. "Books affect you as much, if not more, than anything else, Myriam. I'm not saying you *must* stop; I'm only warning and suggesting. I wouldn't want you to go places where you'd be hurt, and I don't want you putting things in your mind and heart and soul that will hurt you either." The tenderness in his tone was unmistakable.

Myriam held her book for a long moment, then regretfully laid it aside.

"Do you know when our parents will return?" Rupert asked tactfully.

"No; only *ma mère* will be having tea with Lady Alexander, and Father won't be back for supper."

"Very well then; I propose a tramp."

"In the *rain*?"

"Why not? 'We're not made of chocolate,' as Jeanne d'Arc says. It'll do you good—straighten out the kinks in your spine and neck. You bend over books too much—and why didn't you get more light? You'll ruin your eyes, *child*."

And Rupert loped to the window, then threw the drapes wide open to flood the room with pale brightness.

"Besides, it's not raining very hard," he added critically when Myriam joined him, ducking under his arm to see.

"It's very muddy," she observed with distaste.

"You have rubbers."

"Yes, but ..."

"Oh come now, it'll be an adventure." Rupert dropped the curtain and wrapped an arm around her shoulders, dragging her along with him as he strode for the door. "Run up and change, Kit, and wipe that *makeup* off your face—" He dodged as she tried to elbow him.

"It's only lipstick!"

Rupert paused and peered at her face. "Also eye shadow, pencilled brows, mascara, and rouge. *And* nail varnish," he added, seizing her hands as she tried to hide them behind her. "My, aren't we fine!"

"Well, not as much as the lipstick, anyhow. And I'm only *experimenting*. I'm not sure I like it yet."

"Do Father and *ma mère* know?" The amusement was palpable in his voice.

Myriam looked seriously affronted as she pulled away from his grasp. "Of course she does; it's her makeup! She suggested it."

The frown returned, sobering Rupert's face as all mischief left his eyes. He slipped his hands into his pockets, watching grimly as Myriam retrieved her book and set it away on a high shelf.

"You don't think I'd go behind their backs, do you?" she asked softly.

Rupert roused, shaking himself a little. "No, of course not. And certainly, you can wear it if you like. But I was only thinking what Father thinks of his little Myrie growing up ..."

"He doesn't know." And Myriam glanced away, guessing, with sisterly sensitivity to her brother's every mood, Rupert's similar dislike of seeing his Kitten now a young woman. After all, he'd been at university for the last few years, and the realization had come on him suddenly, and unpleasantly, that she too was becoming older. It wasn't all that long ago that they'd been playmates in the garden ... They'd been very close until his departure for college.

"I'll go change," she said, squeezing his arm as he opened the library doors.

"Be quick, then. I'll wait in the entry."

With a nod, Myriam ran up the big, curving staircase towards her room, and he was left to pace the hallway alone, hands deep in his pockets. His eyes lingered over the various expensive decorations scattered about. It was a luxurious place, this Carey household. Mr. Carey was the youngest son of a distinguished and wealthy English family, and his wife, a French heiress. When the Great War had broken out a year after their wedding, Mr. Carey returned to his lieutenancy in the British army, while an expectant Mrs. Carey left for Canada to escape the severest effects of the war. At the end of the conflict, he joined her there, and since neither were interested in returning to war-ravaged Europe, they built their mansion in a lovely little corner of Canada's *belle province*. Thus, the building was done up with the elegance that taste, and not money, can give—great paintings in handsome frames hung on the walls; rich carpet lined the stairs and covered the floors; plants, glass, lights, and mirrors wove their spell, creating an atmosphere of spaciousness and calm; simple, sophisticated furniture and ornaments stood about, unobtrusive and non-obstructive. The light, white, classical ambiance was much more French than English, bowing to Mrs. Carey's fancy more than to her husband's.

Rupert lounged for a few minutes, whistling; then, as the minutes stretched on, he put on his long mackintosh, brushed back his hair with a careless hand, pulled on his hat, examined his face in a mirror, and finally strode to the bottom of the stairs. "*Myriam!*"

"I'm coming, I'm coming!"

"Not quickly enough!"

The next minute, his sister came running down the stairs in a simple skirt and shirt-waist, a scarf knotted over her hair. She slipped on her mackintosh and rain boots, then turned and grinned at him. "See? No makeup, new clothes, and only *ten minutes*—so there!"

"I guess that's about as fast as you could make it. Come on!"

"Where are we headed?" she demanded as they splashed down the drive, shoulders hunched against the rain.

"I want to see Jeanne d'Arc ... I haven't stopped by since I went back to Ottawa."

Myriam nodded. The sturdy Québécoise had been Rupert's nursemaid for five years, until Myriam was born and Mrs. Carey thought Jeanne d'Arc too old to continue tending children. Her daughter Marie had taken her place and soon became established as Mamie, thanks to the impediment that had Rupert calling himself Wupet in his early years. But dear as Mamie had become to his sister and him, Rupert never forgot his loving nurse of yore and visited her as often as he could 'til he'd gone to university. Myriam herself never really knew Jeanne d'Arc, but Myriam was perfectly willing to accompany Rupert there now, especially after their separation of a full month.

"By the way, how's writing coming along?" Rupert enquired, slipping his hands in his pockets again.

Myriam frowned. "Well enough, I suppose. I've hardly written for ages. I had an idea last month, but I've started my story over four times now, and it never goes far before we're fighting tooth and claw. I can't hardly remember when was the last time it *flowed*. I certainly miss it."

"Perhaps you simply haven't come across the right idea yet."

"Well, I wish I would. It's very discouraging to pour out and get nothing."

At the disconsolation in her tone, Rupert wrapped an arm around her shoulders and squeezed. "Well, I *am* sorry, Kit. What are you working on now?"

They had reached the end of the drive. The gardener's sons were playing about by the ornate iron gates, and the eldest ran to open them. Jean-Pierre's bare head was sopping wet, but the grin on his freckled face spoke of nothing but contentment as he slammed the gates shut behind the Careys. Rupert thanked him with a nod, Myriam with a smile, as they turned onto the long, wet road.

Rain splattered on everything and splashed up from the puddles; sodden leaves squished miserably underfoot, too dejected to crunch joyously as was their wont. It was the very ambiance she had attempted to fit into her tale, but the ridiculous thing only kicked and squirmed and refused to come. Perhaps a mystery was not within her powers. A romance, then? No, she'd no experience with that. But this story must be "something splendid," as Jo March said—something *clever*, eloquent—something that would make people say, "Ah yes, Miss Carey ... a good writer, that," and look out for her next work. Something Mr. Aford, Father's friend who was head of a prestigious publishing house, would be willing to print.

It had to be something that would change the world.

"Aren't you going to answer?" Rupert enquired at last, flinging a pinecone away with a practised kick.

"No. I haven't an answer. I've started the story, and it simply won't work, and I'm tired of struggling. I'd rather forget about it."

"All right. Anything else you care to talk about?"

"Something entertaining, please."

At her tone, Rupert glanced at her with one of his little frowns but obligingly launched into the lively tale of a prank by the college wag, Frédéric Arpin, whose especial target was the pompous, crotchety old dean. Rupert was a good storyteller, and Myriam's face cleared as she laughed heartily over the dean's ultimatums and Frédéric's nimble excuses. Encouraged, Rupert turned the conversation into light, caring gossip of home and town, and Myriam chattered away. Rupert listened attentively, occasionally throwing in a bit of dry humour. The rain had slackened, and only a very light pattering could be heard if one stood quite still and listened.

Within a quarter of an hour, they reached old Jeanne d'Arc's little stone house, a relic of two centuries past and the Gagnon home for many generations. Rupert had no need to knock on the solid oak door; Jeanne d'Arc herself opened it, her weathered face one bright smile.

"*Ah bi'n*, you've finally turned up!" she exclaimed blissfully as Rupert's strong, young arms wrapped tenderly about her.

"*Bi'n sûr, Maman* Jeanne," Rupert murmured, dropping easily into the beautiful language he'd spoken from infancy. Thanks to the constant exposure to both Canadian tongues, he had become fully bilingual without knowing it, while Myriam was fluent but much weaker than he, since Mamie spoke more English than Jeanne d'Arc.

"And you've come too, *ma belle*," the old woman greeted Myriam courteously. "Come in, come in, both of you. I hope you haven't been too wet. Give me your coats and hats."

"And if we did get wet? We're not made of chocolate," Rupert teased as he helped Myriam out of her coat and shrugged off his own.

Jeanne d'Arc shook her head, shuffling towards the kettle hanging over the fire. "You speak loudly, *mon ange*, but chills kill anyone. Come near the fire; I'll have a good tisane coming soon. Take the rocking chair, *ma belle*, and you, *mon ange*, there's a chair by the table for you."

Myriam hesitated, loathe to take the old woman's *berçante*, but Rupert gave her a nod as he settled onto his assigned seat, and Myriam subsided obediently.

Jeanne d'Arc bustled about, preparing her tisane. "So you've come back from the university, *mon ange*. How is it going there?"

"Very well," Rupert answered enthusiastically. "My professors are satisfied with my progress, and so am I."

She nodded, satisfied. "And how is your health? You're caring for it well, I hope?"

"Yes, of course. I'm perfectly fit. You mustn't worry over me any longer."

The look of affection that passed between them gave Myriam a pang of mingled jealousy and envy—jealousy that Rupert loved another as much as her, and envy that someone cared for *him* so. Marie loved Rupert and her both, but there was no special bond between Marie and Myriam like there was between Rupert and Jeanne d'Arc. And as for Mother and Father, they cared no more for Myriam than for Rupert. Both children were only a hindrance to their parents ... and with Rupert's ill health and Myriam's lack of social grace, even a disappointment, as had been made clear to them often.

"Well, you must *stay* healthy," Jeanne d'Arc ordered, pouring the boiling water onto the tea. "I will always remember the days and nights I spent tending you. Oh, you were a sickly child! And your *môman*—'scuse moi, *là*, but no mother should be gadding about while her child is so ill." Righteous anger filled Jeanne d'Arc's honest voice.

Myriam glanced at Rupert through her lashes, catching a fleeting glimpse of—was it pain? Grief?—cross his face. To be sure, Mrs. Carey had been no more present in Myriam's childhood than in Rupert's, but Myriam, at least, had been a splendidly vigorous child and never missed the care of motherly love in illness. In the last few years, he'd astonished everyone by growing hale and hearty, and after a trial period to ensure the miracle was there to remain, he fulfilled his childhood dream, pursuing a medical career. He was now approaching graduation, and Jeanne d'Arc worried greatly lest the strain of study break his newfound strength.

"It isn't her fault; she is only doing what was done to her and what she was raised to do," Rupert said after a few minutes, his smile tinged with wistfulness. "She meant well after all."

Jeanne d'Arc grunted, but with true Québécois kindness, honoured the tacit request to talk of something more pleasant, launching into a recital of her trials with her summer garden. Story after story did she tell about her life, past and present. She was as splendid a spinner of tales as most of her nationality, and Myriam listened with pleasure as she sipped her tisane, enchanted by the picture of the stalwart, easygoing woman accepting the struggles of life and laughing away the pain. Open-hearted and outspoken, loud and unreserved, gossiping freely and sharing everything, she was a sample of the best in that poorly understood, affectionate, independent people that is Québec. Anecdotes both humorous and affecting she related, touching on the tragedy and comedy and beauty that make up existence.

"And what are you up to, *ma belle*?" Jeanne d'Arc asked Myriam at last, as Rupert leaned back on his chair with an abstracted air. "You are finished with school, *n'est-c'pas*?"

"Yes, but I don't know if I am going to university yet. Father wishes me to get a B.A. in English, but *ma mère* doesn't believe in the higher education of females." *Mère* wished Myriam to follow in her steps as a society queen, catching a husband renowned not so much for character as for family name and possessions. There was no need for university education in that.

"And what do *you* wish?"

Keen eyes fastened on hers, and Myriam hesitated.

"I don't know—*yet*," she admitted.

"Well, there's no hurry. You are still young," Jeanne d'Arc said wisely. "It's as well to be quite sure before you gain anything. Sometimes we must make our own paths in life."

She knitted in silence for a moment, then added, "Is there a boy yet?"

Myriam laughed as Rupert sat up suddenly. "Oh dear me, no! I don't believe Rupert would ever agree to that. Sometimes I think he intends to keep me forever, he grows so fierce when any young men come around!"

"You don't need any of those college cubs," Rupert growled. "When the right man comes, I shall let him—but he'll have to prove himself first!"

Jeanne d'Arc chuckled comfortably as she took up her knitting. "My father didn't want to let me go either. On my wedding day, as I prepared to leave for the church, he asked, 'Are you very sure you want to marry this boy? I can arrange everything for you if you change your mind.' He was joking, but he meant it a little, too. He cried more than *Môman* did when the priest married Marc-André and me. He loved Marc-André, of course—but after all, it's a big thing, watching your children move on. And *Pôpa* was so very fond of his children."

Silence fell again—a cosy silence punctured only by the homey, comforting sounds of clicking needles, crackling fire, creaking beams, and clattering rain. Myriam thought of Jeanne d'Arc's Pôpa, who had loved his daughter enough to try one last half-serious attempt at keeping her, and of her own father, who hardly noticed when she dined with him. She thought of her mother, who insisted on the path she herself had followed thirty years ago, a path leading to social recognition at the cost of domestic dysfunction; and she compared that narrow, gilded existence to Jeanne's hard, happy life.

Rupert was asleep on his chair; there was no one to hear her but kind, old Jeanne d'Arc, who always listened intently and who knew enough of life to offer sound advice.

"I do know what I want," Myriam said.

Jeanne d'Arc raised her head and looked in silence at Myriam.

"I want a good life, *Maman* Jeanne," the girl continued in something very much like desperation. "I want to change the world. I want to make life better. I want to beautify it. I—I want to be loved by a good man. I want to raise fearless, healthy children. I want to *live*. I—" She stopped, wondering if she'd expressed herself well enough in the language that never did come as easily as her maternal tongue. English words crowded on the edge of her mind. *I want to write something grand. I want to be admired and respected and loved.*

Jeanne d'Arc still said nothing, her dark eyes fixed on Myriam's face with a neutral expression that made her seem almost severe.

"How do I do that?" Myriam asked, her tone softening into pleading. "I don't want to live like my parents. I don't want to be alienated from my own child. I don't want to live in my great, handsome house, unaware of the needs and desires of my fellow man. But I don't know how to achieve that. What do I do? Shall I go to college? Shall I marry? Shall I travel? *What should I do?* I don't know—and life is so very vast and frightening—and *empty.*"

She caught herself, wondering at her own boldness in sharing so much of her heart, in baring those deepest desires of her soul that had tumbled about unexpressed within her. Would Jeanne d'Arc understand? Would she laugh?

The old woman resumed her knitting, a small smile curving her lips. It was not a derogatory smile—it was kind, wise, and motherly. "You have a big heart, *ma belle.*"

Myriam waited for more, but Rupert dozed on and Jeanne d'Arc knitted away wordlessly. The girl began to feel a little foolish.

"So what are you going to do about it?"

Myriam blinked at the wise Québécoise. "'Do'?"

"To build the life you want."

"Why—that's what I'm asking you. What *can* I do?"

Jeanne d'Arc smiled again. She deliberately folded up her knitting and pierced Myriam with those shrewd, loving eyes of hers. "My child, nothing comes in this life to those who do nothing."

"But—"

"Think, *ma belle*. What actions can you take—*however small*—what actions can you take *now* to bring about what you desire? You cannot do *every*thing. But you can do *some*thing."

Myriam stared blankly.

"What you just told me—what is the key point of it all?"

"Ah—I—well—" Myriam floundered.

"Don't answer too fast," Jeanne d'Arc cautioned. "*Think.*"

She began to knit again, and Myriam watched, pondering.

What *was* the key point? She wanted to marry—she wanted children—she wanted, like Meg March, a pleasant house and a good life—but was that really all she asked of existence? Or rather, was it all she wished to *put into* life? What did she really, truly, most earnestly desire? If she died tomorrow, what would she most regret—most wish to do today?

She wanted to leave a legacy. She wanted to make a difference. She wanted to point to

Christ. She wanted to work for Him. She wanted to please Him.

But how?

Small actions, Jeanne d'Arc had said. How could Myriam pull apart her lofty goal into small, actionable steps?

Thou shalt love the Lord thy God with all thy heart, and with all thy soul, and with all thy mind. This is the first and great commandment. And the second is like unto it, Thou shalt love thy neighbour as thyself. On these two commandments hang all the law and the prophets.

Loving God with all her heart and soul and mind. *That*, already, was a great, awesome charge to be worked on every day in thousands of small actions. If she loved her Father, she would love her neighbour—and from that love, all other fruits of the Spirit would flow out, and every aspect of the Christian life would be touched upon.

And if she did this—if she were so intensely in tune with Him—it was likely enough He would lead her along, teach her what to do, show her the steps to take ... for had He not promised "the steps of a good man are ordered by the Lord" and "in all thy ways acknowledge Him, and He shall direct thy paths"?

Something burst out into radiance within her, like a great lamp flooding her soul and mind with heavenly light. She could not contain the grin that stretched across her face. It all was so simple, so divinely simple! Every little action of love built up, prepared her for something greater. Besides, sometimes it was those in the background who did the most, who helped the most, who changed the world the most.

And that desire to be admired and respected and loved—she was silly enough, often, to want it in a social sense. But deep within, she longed for the admiration and love of good, godly people who respected her for her devotion, not her cleverness. She would rather write what God led her to and bless His people than garner the admiration of people whose lives did not align with hers.

Oh, how good He was to make everything fit together so well!

A log snapped in the fireplace. Rupert started awake and looked around sheepishly. Jeanne d'Arc and Myriam both broke into laughter, and he smiled as he glanced at his watch.

"Well, I see I've slept the time away. It's rather late; suppose we head home, Kit?"

Myriam rose and slipped into the coat Rupert held for her. As she drew on her gloves, he threw on his own coat, took his hat in hand, and bent over the old woman for a kiss.

"May the good God keep you," Jeanne d'Arc said as tears stood out in her faithful brown eyes. "Take care of yourself over there among the English, *mon ange!*"

"I will. Take care of yourself too, *Maman* Jeanne ..."

It was still raining when they stepped outside. The autumn world was as bleak and gloomy, the discarded leaves as pitiful, the sky as sunless as before. But there was a warmth in Myriam's heart that made the day beautiful somehow, that helped her notice the brightness of a patch of moss, the colour of a bird's coat, the curious swirl of a cloud.

"Rupert," she said as they walked along, "is there any way I can help in the community—any charity I can assist or something of the sort?"

Her brother glanced at her, brow furrowed. "Perhaps, why?"

"Well, I thought, since I have no real work just now, I might invest and help out." She scrubbed her hands against her coat, suddenly feeling awkward. *Mère* and Father gave to charity in an offhand, impersonal, dutiful way; she did not want to copy that pattern.

Rupert shrugged. "I haven't really heard of any, but I suppose, if you asked the curé, he would be able to answer. Or the prioress at the convent. What made you think of it so suddenly, Kit?"

"Jeanne d'Arc." Myriam nodded reflectively. Tomorrow she could go—she could ask Monsieur le Curé. He was a kindly old man who always gave her peppermints when he saw her about in town. He would know what she could do. Myriam did not belong to his church; Rupert and she were members of the little Baptist chapel across the river, while their parents conventionally attended the Anglican church nearby. But Monsieur le Curé was an easygoing man, and she was sure he would have no scruples in assisting her charitable endeavours. The Québécois were hugely community-minded people. Surely there would be something ... some little way she could begin to help.

And who knew? Perhaps she would find writing inspiration and material by moving into this new pursuit. Perhaps the "something splendid" she searched for would be found in doing, not waiting. The thought put an extra skip into her step. *Thank You, Lord!*

"I always forget how much I loved home until I leave," Rupert said whimsically, avoiding a mud puddle. "English places just aren't the same. My mind and tongue might be English, but my heart and my words are Québécois. Professor Blythe says that will be a help to me as a doctor."

Myriam nodded. A bilingual physician would be a great gain to this place, and Rupert would get along excellently with both the French and the English. Generally, there was not much interaction between the wildly different cultures. Myriam preferred the

Québécois. She was used to this people, rough and friendly, shouting, debating, gossiping benevolently about anything and everything they had heard and experienced; English speakers seemed cool, rigid, almost untrustworthy to her. Truthfully, she was too mixed to fit with either group. She had been born and raised here, had been playmates with many of the young folk in her childhood, yet she was not a Québécoise. It would have made no difference had her people been poor. They were "English," and the Québécois might welcome them and love them, but it would take a generation or two for the culture to seep in.

How could she help when she did not really fit in? If only she'd worked harder to learn the language better and integrate more fully ...

She looked at him curiously as he tramped carefree, whistling, hands in his pockets. He loved Québec even more than she did, fit in better with the people, belonged here more. She was *Mad'moiselle*, sometimes *Ma'm'selle*, Miriam; but *he* was always Monsieur Robert—a variant of his English name, which was so unwieldy in French. Did he feel English or French? Canadian or Québécois? How much better he was suited at helping the people here. They loved and trusted him more because he loved this land, this culture, much more expressively than she did. It would be easier for *him* to try to help the community than for her.

"You realize I'm going to question you about why you want to see Monsieur le Curé, of course," Rupert remarked lightly as they reached home and Jean-Pierre opened the gates for them.

"How nosy you are, dear brother!"

"No more than you. Have you forgotten the time you wrote me a ten-page letter demanding an hour-by-hour recital of my first week at college?"

Myriam turned towards him menacingly, and he ducked, grinning.

"Or the time you asked poor Winslow about our daily routine ..."

"Rupert Ralph Carey!"

He raced away, and she rushed after him, laughing in spite of the embarrassing memory. They burst into the house together, Rupert dodging wildly and she, shouting threats. It was a moment of pure joy—one they had not experienced together for many months.

"Rupert. Margaret."

That voice—perfectly controlled, perfectly womanly, and "ever soft, gentle, and low," as Shakespeare said ... the voice that had never failed to bring them up short and remind them to conduct themselves as model children—still had the power to make them both instantly, silently sober up, brush down their clothes, remove their headgear to pat their hair into order, and let the housemaid take their coats.

"Good afternoon, Rupert. It is good to see you again." *Mère* glided over, holding up her face for Rupert's perfunctory kiss. She adjusted the lapels of his suit jacket and pulled his tie straight, her quiet face never morphing even slightly into the tenderness one would expect to show after his month of absence.

"*Merci, ma mère.*" He almost bowed, and an awkward frown marred his handsome face.

Myriam looked away and busied herself with her hair in a mirror. What was there to say to this woman—the woman they belonged to and loved but who had always been so remote? *Mère* had plenty to say *to* them—she made her forcible beliefs and intentions gracefully, firmly, unwaveringly known—but she never spoke *with* them. Everything tended to their social reputation, which, in itself, bound up her happiness. Had she ever done a useful thing in her life? *Anything* to change lives?

"Dinner will be served momentarily. Please make yourselves presentable as quickly as possible. Margaret, there will be a concert Friday evening, and you will attend with us; I have commissioned a new dress for you from Madame Lund already. My maid will help you dress that night when I am finished. Yours is hopeless; I have given her notice and hired you a new one."

Myriam nodded obediently as her mother glided away. Concerts weren't so bad, she thought as Rupert and she hurried upstairs. She'd have both an opportunity to watch people *and* quiet time to muse and let inspiration strike. The social aspect of it all was the rub; no one talked of anything remotely interesting, for they avoided any topic that might be the slightest bit controversial; and besides, few of them really had anything to say to *her*. Women her age hereabouts only ignored or mocked her. Tutored at home and rarely straying therefrom, she did not fit into their cliques and culture.

Another missed opportunity to influence and do good.

Well, if she could not do good among the wealthy community, she could perhaps share her wealth with the poorer people. There were certainly folks about here in need. The only difficulty was, that wealth did not *exactly* belong to her. To be sure, she had an allowance; but would Father allow her to give her money away? She was afraid to ask. If he said no, she'd be back where she started—helpless.

Hope and fear raged in Myriam all that evening. Dinner was more silent than usual. Rupert was in a thoughtful mood; *Mère* only spoke to announce her plans or coolly critique something; Father ate quickly and ignored them all. In such quiet, Myriam had nothing to distract her mind, and *Mère* had much more reason than usual to criticise her table manners.

"Really, Margaret, you are positively careless tonight," *Mère* said almost angrily. "You must not take walks anymore if they fatigue you to this extent. I'm sure I don't know why such terrible weather would appeal to you, anyhow. It is *not* ladylike to come home with your hem six inches deep with mud."

Myriam choked with laughter at this unconscious, unexpected imitation of Miss Caroline Bingley, but *Mère*'s attention was diverted from her by Rupert.

"Going somewhere tonight, Father?"

"Yes, business calls. Leaving as soon as I'm finished."

At this brief announcement, Myriam's heart descended to her boots. If she did not catch Father tonight, she would be forced to wait for whenever she saw him again to question him about her money. *Mère* would never allow money to be "wasted," *especially* on people she disliked. But *Mère* never contradicted Father ... at least not outright. She'd never wanted Myriam for a name, but Father had insisted on naming his daughter after a French peasant woman who'd saved his life in the war. *Mère* had yielded gracefully, but never in public or private did she call Myriam by aught other than her middle name—*Margaret*. Nor did Father ever seem to note that quiet defiance.

But if Father gave Myriam permission to spend her money as she liked, *Mère* would not trouble herself to argue as much as she would make her disapproval known otherwise.

On the other hand, if Father refused, Myriam's plans were shot. She squirmed at the thought. After the glow of this afternoon, she was not ready to let go of her intentions. But—

The steps of a good man are ordered by the Lord.

If this idea was the Lord's, He'd see it through. If not, He would lead to a different path. This was not about her at all—it was all about Him.

"Father, how much money do I have?"

It was a bombshell of a sentence. Rupert stared, *Mère* frowned, and Father raised his eyebrows, his eyes never leaving his plate.

"Isn't your allowance enough?" Father demanded.

Myriam leaned forward eagerly. "Can I do what I like with it?"

He looked up then, really noticing her for the first time in years. His gaze was shrewd. "What do you want to do with it?"

"I want to help some people."

Rupert's eyes widened in surprise, and *Mère*, tense and puzzled, put down her fork. But Father only sized Myriam up for a long moment, then returned to his soup. "Do what you like," he said briefly.

God had directed her path.

The kitchen was unusually dark this late-November day three weeks later. Rain drummed on the roof like a million dancing footsteps. Outside, the wind was voiceless, shaking the trees shorn of their leaves. The feeble white light of early morning straggled through the bare window, uncertainly illuminating the simple room and so hiding the imperfections of the old wooden furniture.

The kitchen was empty except for a girl sitting very straight and still in a rocking chair before the dead fire. Myriam's eyes and nose were red and swollen, with tear streaks along her cheeks. Her hair lay loose and lank about her shoulders; her severe dress was black, unrelieved by any ornament. On her lap lay a slim volume, but she was staring silently through the window, eyes wide, lips pressed tightly together, wholly lost in some uncomfortable reverie.

A young man appeared in the doorway, his sensitive face marked with horror and grief. His steps rang on the wooden floor, but the girl never moved. Slowly, sadly, he approached her. It was not until he laid a gentle hand on her head that she looked up.

"How is it, Rupert?"

He shook his head, and tears shimmered in her eyes again as he dropped onto a chair by the table.

"It's very bad." His voice was low, but he could not conceal the quiver it held. "It seems Father invested in the stock market, and there was a crash yesterday—not a very large one, but it took everything we had."

Myriam gasped, and her brother buried his head in his hands.

"It was the shock that killed him," Rupert continued dully. "And of course, the reaction is what ended *ma mère*. We're horribly in debt—it seems we haven't yet paid off the house and other extravagances—and of course, everything's being repossessed. We can only hope the sales will cover all the debts ... We won't have a penny, but at least we'll be free."

She could not repress a whimper at the last words, and he reached out to grasp her hand. He could not console, but he could comfort.

Myriam never forgot that horrible, wordless half hour. For a time, she did not think about the future or the present ... only of the past. It was true that she had never been close to her parents, but she loved them still. To picture life without Father was not so very hard; he was seldom home, nor did he notice her much; but the thought that he was no more, that she could never again watch him, speak to him, embrace him ... that they could never better their relationship, never enjoy her children sitting on his knee ... the finality, the *vanishment* of it all, was almost too great to grapple. And *Mère* ... so distant, so chilly, but still *ma mère*. Myriam did not have to be told her mother had died of a broken heart and wounded pride. Without her wealth and her husband—the only soul she truly loved—she had nothing to live for, no strength to fight. The tomb had claimed her scant days after it received her husband.

There were only Myriam and Rupert left in the whole wide world. Alone, friendless, without a way to support themselves.

Myriam caught back a sob, but Rupert heard it and raised his head. His face had hardened with determination; the latent strength of his character expressed itself in that firm gaze.

"Don't worry, Kitten," he said quietly. "We'll manage. God has not abandoned us, and He will provide a way. We're not destitute, and we can both work."

"But there's *no* work, Rupert!"

"There isn't *much*, but there is *some*, and our Lord promised to provide, Myriam. What Psalm is it that says, 'I have been young, and now am old; yet have I not seen the righteous forsaken, nor his seed begging bread'?"

Myriam sniffled, wiping her face with her sleeve. "I think it's thirty-five or something. And we're hardly the seed of the righteous."

"I thought it was thirty-seven, and you know what I mean. Use a handkerchief, child!"

His unnatural burst of anger startled her, and she could not repress a sob as she answered. "It doesn't really matter, does it? And I haven't any!"

"Well, here's mine, anyhow," said Rupert contritely, his voice softening.

She dried her eyes and blew her nose; Rupert refused to reclaim his property, at which they both laughed.

"What will we do now?" she asked softly, when the trembling smiles had died away and they both sat staring through the window.

"Well, I told you most of what Father's lawyer says. It seems *Oncle* Léon gambled away all the Saint Cyr fortune at Monte Carlo and is quite hopeless himself, so there's no help from *that* side of the family. And none of us know what other relatives we have in France; the war upset everything so much. As for the Careys, I understand there was some unpleasantness when Father married *ma mère*, but Barrow says they would certainly take us in for the sake of the name, if nothing else. He counsels us to return to England and hunt the Careys up—says he'll lend us the amount for second-class tickets and a few hundred pounds, to repay when we can. Very generous of him, too, for Father left him with a few unpaid bills."

Myriam said nothing. To leave her home was inconceivable. But what else could they do? In England, they were almost guaranteed support, while here, they would have to join the uncertain hunt for work ... which, at the worst, they could take up over there if the Careys proved unforgiving. Mr. Barrow's advice certainly seemed sound.

"Monsieur le Curé offered us his presbytery for as long as we care to stay," Rupert added after a minute.

"He's a darling," Myriam murmured. "He's been the one helping me these last few weeks, you know. I've purchased many things for different families, and he delivers them for me because I don't want them to know it was me. He's very understanding."

Rupert was silent, but his eyes told of his pride in his little sister, and Myriam blushed with pleasure. In the three weeks since her mission had been given to her, she'd done her best to fulfil the needs she could, making the rounds of the town and growing familiar and friendly with the people. It gave her a thrill and a purpose—a little something every day that made a difference in her life and in those about her.

Most people were kind and accepting, but the children were the quickest to adopt her. They artlessly admired her clothes and hair, prattled their admiration of her home, questioned her about the inside of the mansion ... Tears filled her eyes again at the thought of dear little Élisabeth and Johanne ... Paul, Denis, and Rolande ... Alexandre and Lisette. It hurt to think she could no longer distribute candies, books, and toys—would no longer see their eyes light up, their smiles flash out, their little worlds broaden. She'd been so happy helping.

"You're crying again," Rupert murmured, drawing her close.

Trying to hold back the sobs, Myriam snuggled against his tweed jacket. "It's very silly, I'm sure, but ... Rupert, I'll miss being able to help them!" There, her voice choked off, and she cried out everything she had held in for the last few days. Wordless, Rupert leaned his cheek against her head.

Myriam did not cry very long; she was too self-conscious when by herself in her room, let alone before her brother. Within minutes, she began to regulate her breath and calm herself. Rupert still remained quiet, and Myriam, rather embarrassed by her outburst, went to the sink and splashed cool water over her face.

"Reading Longfellow now?"

Rupert's voice carried a tinge of surprise, and she looked around to see him studying the book she'd left on her chair.

"I like poetry. I simply don't it read very often. I came across one of his poems in another of his collections some days ago and decided to read a volume of his work ... I haven't gotten very far yet."

Some days ago. When home had been safe, her parents still present. When she'd been able to do things. More sobs built up; she buried her face in a towel and tried to regain control again.

"Ever read 'A Psalm of Life'?"

"Yes, some years ago."

"I discovered it in college. Thought it was pretty great." Rupert flipped through the pages slowly. Then he stilled and began to read aloud. Myriam was not sure she wanted to hear him, but she could not ignore the words he recited with such feeling.

> *Tell me not, in mournful numbers,*
> *"Life is but an empty dream!"*
> *For the soul is dead that slumbers,*
> *And things are not what they seem.*
>
> *Life is real! Life is earnest!*
> *And the grave is not its goal;*
> *"Dust thou art, to dust returnest,"*
> *Was not spoken of the soul.*
>
> *Not enjoyment, and not sorrow,*
> *Is our destined end or way;*
> *But to act, that each to-morrow*
> *Find us farther than to-day.*
>
> *Art is long, and Time is fleeting,*
> *And our hearts, though stout and brave,*
> *Still, like muffled drums, are beating*

Funeral marches to the grave.

In the world's broad field of battle,
In the bivouac of Life,
Be not like dumb, driven cattle!
Be a hero in the strife!

Trust no Future, howe'er pleasant!
Let the dead Past bury its dead!
Act,—act in the living Present!
Heart within, and God o'erhead!

Lives of great men all remind us
We can make our lives sublime,
And, departing, leave behind us
Footprints on the sands of time;

Footprints, that perhaps another,
Sailing o'er life's solemn main,
A forlorn and shipwrecked brother,
Seeing, shall take heart again.

Let us, then, be up and doing,
With a heart for any fate;
Still achieving, still pursuing,
Learn to labor and to wait.

A long silence stretched when Rupert's voice died away. The rain had ceased, and on a sudden impulse, Myriam went to the window and opened it, seeking the cold, harsh, wet air.

"He wrote this after his first wife died," Rupert said thoughtfully. "While still a young man, I think. I've always found it rather inspiring, but it means much more now than ever before, doesn't it?"

"I don't see how." Chilled into changing her mind, Myriam slammed the window shut and dropped onto her chair, feeling ridiculously inclined to pout.

"Why ... because life is not purposeless. We simply can't afford to let it slip by. The whole point of life is to live it well—to better our lives constantly. Granted, it's rather discouraging that time is so rapid and we are so slow; but we can choose to *do* something about it. We *can* make a difference if we try. We can change people—change the world itself—if only we learn to be patient and work hard and *wait*. Words to live by now, aren't they?"

"But what can you do when you have nothing?" Myriam whispered, tears resurfacing. "I thought I could make a difference by giving away. Now I can hardly care for myself. How can I change lives when my own is so empty?"

"But it's *not* empty, Myriam. You have so much still. You have youth. You have a character that is naturally joyful and loving. You have many friends about you who care deeply. You don't only have *material* things to offer, Kit. You have *yourself*."

"Yes, a very great thing, I'm sure!"

"Lay off the sarcasm; I don't like it," Rupert retorted with a touch of elder-brother testiness at being crossed. "You know what I mean. One can make life beautiful, Myriam, and that is worth as much as making it easier. So you can't give things away. What about all those stories I hear you told the town children, that made them so happy?"

"But those stories aren't *worth* anything. I wanted to write something *splendid*. All I produce is foolish little tales about life. There's no depth, no real writing. Just ... scribbling."

Rupert raised a quizzical brow. "Apart from the fact that your penmanship really *is* atrocious, I disagree. Your 'foolish tales' are something pleasant the children look forward to. That's worth something in itself."

There was truth in what he said, little as she liked to admit it. Some indistinct memory stirred within Myriam ... one about a quote on princesses and the populace, from Burnett's *A Little Princess*. Sara Crewe had also gone from riches to rags, and she had discovered that though she could no longer "scatter largess to the populace" and feed her friends with her surplus wealth, she could still share her imagination and brighten their hard lives with her tales. Somehow, the silly reference was comforting.

Myriam had pursued her own ideal of changing lives so persistently that she had failed to consider the Lord's. Perhaps changing lives wasn't only achieved with splendid things but with constant small ones ... and maybe those small steps were still valuable because they were easier to follow than running strides. Perhaps all she really had to do in her life and her writing was to follow the greatest Man there ever was, without worrying about how "splendid" were the things He led her to—which would make the biggest difference of all, for then her footprints would lead always to Him ... and that was the most splendid thing anyone could ever have.

That would be a life well lived, a life worth living. And the love that came to His faithful followers was far more satisfying than any critical or lofty praise by her peers.

Rupert rested his chin in his hand and stared thoughtfully through the window. "I feel quite unprepared for everything that's just happened," he said, almost to himself. "I'm sure I haven't the skills or knowledge to do everything right and take care of things as I ought. It's rather daunting. But I've concluded to simply make do. 'Do what you can, with what you've got, where you are,' as Squire Bill Widener says."

They both laughed a little at the quote from Theodore Roosevelt's *Autobiography*, which had been Rupert's favourite childhood book, but the words struck Myriam. Perhaps that was what Jeanne d'Arc had meant. Something, however imperfect, was worth more than the elusive, empty perfection in a hoped-for future. One couldn't change the past, but one could start impacting life *now*. Regrets were worthless; small actions now built up into something greater later.

Hadn't the gardener once told her many of the spring flowers and vegetables were planted in autumn? There seemed a significance to that. If the summer work had been shirked, it was too late, come fall, to mourn over a lost year; but one could sow seeds and plant the bulbs for *next* year. Autumn might signal the end of a season, but it also meant preparation for a coming time of growth, please God.

It was true she had missed opportunities by her past choices. It was true that she no longer had the scope for influence she'd once had. But she need not give in because of her circumstances. Perhaps all that mattered was to waste no energy on looking backwards to bemoan the past or idly, hopefully, await a future, but to "act in the living present," however small that action might be. Doing whatever she could, with anything she had, wherever she was.

Rupert rose from the table and stretched. "Well, Kitten, life marches on, and there are many things to do before we leave home. Are you ready to 'be up and doing' with me?"

Tears threatened, but Myriam smiled. Perhaps someday she could be an author half as worth quoting as Longfellow.

She said, "Like 'a hero in the strife!'"

Acknowledgments

This story is my first venture into sharing about my people, the Québécois/Quebeckers, aka the people who live in that French-speaking province of Canada—Québec! There's a lot of historical context and tension that I won't go into here, but I'm just grateful to have the opportunity to explain a bit about our culture and who we are. I put bits about my ancestors in here, and I hope I was able to do them justice.

First thanks go to Chels & Court for making me watch *The Man Who Invented Christmas* (2017) and *I Heard the Bells* (2022). I never would have gotten this written if it wasn't for Longfellow and Dickens. Also, to Liss—thanks for getting me there; and to Mr. & Mrs. B. for their hospitality; and to literally everyone for the amazing, wonderful conversations that sparked so much of this story.

Second thanks go to my faithful partner in crime, Bethany. My dear Watson, whatever should I do without you? I can't imagine where this story would be without you endlessly supplying me with ideas, cheering me on, sending me inspiration, and fangirling over Rupert. I'm sorry he's fictional … ;)

To my lovely alpha readers, Serenity, Cat, Lydia, and Bethany, and my awesome beta readers, Akira, Naomi, Courtney, and May: thanks for reading the rough drafts of this story and making it so much better! Your compliments bolstered me up when I needed it. And Heather, you were the best critique partner! Thank you for every kind word and helpful note. Finally, many thanks to Kellyn, Kelsey, and the rest of the team at Wild Blue Wonder Press who made this story better and got it out. I'm so sorry if I've forgotten anyone—your input was valid regardless.

And to wrap up where it all started … thank You, Lord, for giving me the ideas I needed and guiding me along every page. This story comes from the most real and raw parts of my heart right now, and I pray that it serves to glorify You and help Your daughters.

My Heart Still Sings

Faith D. Cox

Dedication

To God Who has blessed me with these words; my family; all the people struggling with life changes; and those striving for a deeper relationship with our Lord, Jesus Christ.

"Be still, and know that I am God ..."
Psalm 46:10 (KJV)

Chapter One

Hearing "Kaylee McKenzie" over the loudspeaker, and the roar of the crowd, never got old. I was one who relished the announcement and seeing my name in the headlines, but I certainly didn't want to be the one to pen the story for the newspaper. On that blustery November afternoon in Texas, with my feet bare and my sandy-blonde hair amiss from wearing a swim cap, I slid my warm-up pants and lightweight jacket over my one-piece swimsuit, approached the indoor platform, and stood with the silver and bronze medalists. No matter how many times I stood on the podium and received the largest trophy, gold medal, or blue ribbon, my heart always sang.

I had worked my way to this point through relentless workouts and innumerable aching muscles. I knew how it felt to stand on either side with my reverie of reaching the top seeming so far away. If it weren't for the quirkiness of my mom toting her work bag and being willing to spend hours sitting on a bench or on a poolside corner chair, grading essays or working on her never-ending work-in-progress novel, I might not be standing on this platform today. Although I had spent the majority of my life in a pool being coached on correct swimming forms, it still seemed like a dream.

Most athletes were told to give 110 percent. My private swim instructor, Coach Bennett, never accepted less than 125 percent—or it was an extra hour's workout.

As I opened the refrigerator, Zach entered the room. "Hey, Kaylee, will you take the trash out tomorrow if I give you a dollar?"

"I've got my own chores to do."

As I reached toward the second shelf, Zach squirmed past me, stuck his head into the appliance, and gawked at the inner casing as Mom and Dad entered.

"Kaylee, how about you invite Shane and we go out for dinner tonight to celebrate your win?"

"Sure, Mom. Thanks!"

I tugged at my brother's shirt, but he jerked away.

Dad leaned against the counter. "I think you'll be needing another shelf in your bedroom."

I beamed with excitement. "I'll help you paint it."

Mom set her gaze on her younger child. "Zachary Aaron McKenzie, why do you have your head in the refrigerator?"

Zach poked his head out. "I've got to learn how this thing works if I'm going to be a repairman."

"Son, you're only thirteen."

I rooted my way in front of Zach and grabbed a peach. "You're such a dork."

Zach opened a nearby cabinet drawer, retrieved a screwdriver, and stuck his head back into the refrigerator.

"Close the door. You're wasting electricity." Mom's stern voice meant her patience was wearing thin.

Dad approached his son and grabbed the screwdriver. "Do you realize your sister just became the number one swimmer in Area?"

Zach slammed the appliance door and snarled. "I'm trying to learn how to keep people from getting zapped, and all she does is play in the water." He brushed against me on his way toward the doorway. "Life's not fair!"

Mom gazed at my little brother as he stomped out of the room.

I took a bite of the peach and followed Zach.

"Kaylee?"

I stopped and shook my head as I heard that familiar tone in her voice. *No, no, no, no, n o.* I gritted my teeth and turned around slowly.

"Have you thought about entering 'Novelists in November'?"

I moaned. "Are we really having this conversation again?"

"The deadline is in two weeks."

Does she really think she's informing me of something I don't already know? "It's your creation, Mom, not mine."

"I began this writing contest for all the high school students."

I bit my lower lip, took in a breath, and released it. "I don't mean to be disrespectful, but it's a total waste of my time."

Mom's jaw dropped. She was speechless, which only occurred on a rare occasion.

"It's only my opinion." I took a step away and then faced my mother again. "I'm sure there are some geeks who will be enthralled with your idea."

"It would be nice if my own daughter would give it a try."

I shook my head. "Besides my useless journalism class, the only writing I'll be doing is in my journal."

Mom clasped her hands together, pleading. "Oh, Kaylee, I do wish you would reconsider."

I waved as I walked away. "Not my thing, Mom. I'm not a nerd!" *Only two weeks, and the submissions period will be over—until next year.*

As I sat on my bed and gazed at my new award sitting beside me, I held the journal to my chest and thought back to the many coaches I had since the age of four. No doubt, Coach Bennett was the toughest, but without him, I wouldn't be where I am today. Now, five years later, I almost knew as much about him as he had learned about me. He was a widower with two grown daughters and one grandson, and I knew I had a second dad if I ever was in need of one.

Placing another trophy on my personal awards shelf, amidst a backdrop of swim champ posters, was always exhilarating; although, how I got my athletic genes from an electrical engineer and a teacher was still a family mystery. My dad was Mr. Fix-It, and my mom was delighted to grade English papers and create words on the back of a grocery list.

On a regular basis, my creative writing didn't venture far from the telling of my swimming successes. I glanced at my hand to be sure ink hadn't leaked. *Will I ever get past this paranoia? That ink explosion happened in fourth grade.* Without a doubt, I would not be winning any medal, gold or otherwise, for a writing competition. *Why would I want to compete in such a nerdy contest?* Even in elementary school, I often had to stay in from recess for not writing my name on my papers.

I checked one more time for an unwanted ink blob and retrieved my very first blue ribbon from my nightstand. It's the only one I kept by my bedside—I was only six years old when it was placed into my small hands. My parents obviously saw some talent in me or they wouldn't have hired personal coaches, but they really had no idea of the road we would travel together through the years.

I chuckled as I recalled stories of my scrawny, socially awkward dad as head of the chess club in high school, not the quarterback, and my shy mother with wire-framed glasses, not the all-American basketball player. My dad spent weekends experimenting with batteries and wires while my mother stayed hours at the library researching and writing poetry and short stories just for fun. Well, that's what she called it. I was so different than my parents. If it weren't for them attending the same church at the age of fifteen and serving senior adults a Valentine's Day dinner to earn funds for a mission trip, I might not even be here today.

I'm almost certain my mother had a voice in my becoming a writer for *The Mostly Truthful Tribune*. Just as I had a strong feeling there was more gossip than truth on the electronic pages of the small-town Elmont High School newspaper, I believed my mother had a powerful suggestion for the counselor concerning that vacant chair and her daughter's junior class schedule. However, there was a slight possibility I could be mistaken and was randomly picked without any hint of persuasion from my mother. At least in today's journalism society, we lived in a computerized era. I didn't have to carry around a notepad and pen unless the laptop went on a blitz, at which time, I was forced to risk the explosion of ink in my hand.

I tapped the pen and gazed across the room at my most recent trophy. I don't recall the last day I wasn't in a swimming pool, but I do know where my life was headed.

Chapter Two

I rolled over and punched the alarm clock as my head bobbed to the upbeat tune of "My Turn Now." I threw off my covers. Steven Curtis Chapman certainly knew how to put a pep in my step at 5:00 a.m.

I retrieved my wallet, gazed at my very first driver's license, and grinned. *Mom will no longer be my taxi driver.* I peered out the window and saw the Xterra in the driveway. It was the car my mother bought right before marrying my dad, and now it's mine. It might look ancient to other people, but I didn't care. I finally had wheels of my own.

I dropped my towel and dipped my toes into the water.

Coach Bennett blew his whistle. "Take five laps and work on your breaststroke."

I sneered. It was a bad habit of mine when I heard something distasteful. The muscles behaved automatically, and up went my upper lip. "How about butterfly or backstroke?"

"You know my rules, Kaylee. Work on your weakest stroke first."

I snarled and moaned as I swirled my foot in the water. "Let me start with the front crawl today, Coach."

"That's your best stroke."

I couldn't hold back the smile. "And the most fun! Two hundred or four hundred meters, it brings me home every race."

Keeping his gaze on me, Coach stepped closer to my side. "You have to be proficient in all four strokes to be an Olympic contender. If you don't master all quarters of the race, you won't be bringing home any medal."

I slapped a hand on my hip and raised my chin. "I'll be bringing home that Olympic gold. You just watch and see."

His stare cut through me.

I let out another involuntary moan and quickly covered my mouth.

Coach glanced at his watch. "I don't have time to waste. There are other athletes."

Without turning, I knew exactly where Coach's finger was pointing—between the ropes at that painted black, underwater line.

As I turned, I caught a glimpse of Coach's raised eyebrow, which meant he was getting more than a bit irritated. I tried to hold it back, but it was no use. One more groan escaped through my vocal cords as I went down the ladder.

"Give me five laps of breaststroke."

In my peripheral vision, I saw Coach with his eagle eyes upon me. *I can swim with the mermaids. Why can't I get the tempo right on my breaststroke?*

"Give me one hundred twenty-five percent, Kaylee!"

"Yes, sir, Coach." I took a deep breath and went under.

After our rooster, Henry, and my alarm clock sounded simultaneously, I delved into my early-morning devotional and prayer time. Next, I went to the pool for an hour-long workout and then I was back behind the wheel to head home to grab a quick shower and a couple of boiled eggs. Coach had strongly urged, or rather practically demanded, I lay off the donuts and pancakes. I licked my lips for weeks, but even pumpkin pie didn't sound good last Thanksgiving.

I couldn't get Coach's words from yesterday out of my head. I found a new resolve to do whatever it took to be a participant in the Summer Olympics, and I was determined to honor the Lord with the athletic ability I had been given and bring home the gold.

Hearing the crunching of the red, orange, and yellow leaves underneath my feet, I scurried up the steps, entered Elmont High School, and glanced at the black-rimmed, oversized clock on the wall. 7:45. *Only twenty minutes until the bell rings.*

Shane approached and grabbed at my books.

I quickly tucked them closer to my chest. "Sorry, I'm late on a deadline."

Shane mumbled, "Again?"

Why can't I escape this journalism class? It's insane having to come up with so many written words. I gazed at him with puppy-dog eyes. "Thanks for understanding."

"Go; you don't want to miss your deadline."

I squirmed in and out between people as I scurried down the hallway. *My life would be so much simpler without this time-wasting newspaper class. Why two semesters?*

Shane yelled down the hall. "Are you free for a movie Saturday?"

I glanced back. "Yeah, if I survive the jungle of journalism today." I smiled as I whisked around my main source of information: the gossiping trio.

I took one last glance at Shane Donaldson. *Wool or faux fur? Which sweater should I wear this weekend?* Being a bit of an extrovert, it only took me two days to discover common aquatic interests with the new guy and a mere three weeks for him to start carrying my books to class.

By the time third period rolled around Monday morning, my mohair garment was back in the closet, and I was ready to hit the pool. "Hi, Coach."

Coach Blakey glanced at her watch. She had been Elmont High School's girls' swimming coach for fifteen years. She stayed well-informed of any new rules and trained us to be competitive swimmers. She expected our best effort and didn't accept excuses. God had put two of the best coaches in my life. Without their expertise, my Olympian reverie would be unobtainable.

A few minutes later, Coach Blakey blew her whistle. Without hesitation and without turning her direction, I could mouth every word alongside her raspy voice, "Molly, you're late again. That's four extra laps."

Thanks, Mom. Maybe one day I'll admit my appreciation aloud and let you know how thankful I am for your training me to arrive early. I took a deep breath, dove under, and kicked my feet as I caught sight of the black line.

Fifth-period English was a double whammy. I detested stringing words together on paper, and my mother was the teacher. She wasn't a bad one. My fellow classmates assured me she was one of their favorite instructors, even though I'm pretty sure she bought red ink pens by the dozen every year and enjoyed using them. It was just since she was my teacher, I got a little more teaching, or nagging, at home about speaking grammatically correctly and the more than occasional reminder to enter her highly valued writing contest.

Mrs. McKenzie, as I had to refer to my own mother in class, eyed me. "Class, don't forget to sign up for 'Novelists in November.'"

I gazed downward and shrank forward. *Could there be anything more embarrassing, and boring, than spending hours making up stories about fake characters?*

Mrs. McKenzie held up a book. "Turn to page one hundred twenty-seven."

Does she really think she'll create the next Ernest Hemingway or Jane Austen?

With her sight off me, I pushed myself up and grabbed my book. *In just three more weeks, I can stop dashing out doors and avoiding Mom ... until next year's contest.* I opened the book and flipped pages to 127.

As soon as I entered the dreaded newspaper class, I felt my normal seventh-period headache brewing. The smiling and waving from the class geek didn't help. As I sheepishly returned the gesture, I still couldn't believe it was the only elective available with an empty chair.

Mrs. Arnold, with an ink pen protruding from her hair, approached, swinging a paper. "Kaylee, why are your articles always the shortest?"

I shrugged. "It's not intentional. It's just my style."

I grimaced and couldn't hide my gaze upon that writing instrument next to her face. *Why do geeks always carry a pen behind their ears?*

"Mrs. Arnold, I'll help Kaylee."

I glanced and saw those plastic, hexagonal-shaped, bronze-framed spectacles across the room, next to that empty chair. The class nerd smiled and pushed her glasses up on her nose. *Why is she torturing me? What have I ever done to her?* I seriously tried to control my sneering lip. *I've never even known her to exist until now.*

I whirled around. "Why should I write more if I can say it in fewer words?"

"Kaylee—"

"A few of my contributions are actually true." *Were Mrs. Arnold's cheeks turning a tint of red?*

Mrs. Arnold let out a loud sigh—or was it a growl?

I took a small stride toward the vacant chair. *I'll never understand writers.*

"Where do you get your information?"

I stopped in my tracks, grinned, and turned to face Mrs. Arnold. "I hear plenty of good ideas as I'm being shoved through the hallway. Oh, and the girls' locker room—there's always chatter as I'm changing into my gear."

The class chuckled, and Mrs. Arnold marched closer to me. I stretched my neck to peer around her. *Someone must have sneaked in after me and closed the door.*

Liliana raised her hand. "Mrs. Arnold, I can help Kaylee Friday afternoons."

Mrs. Arnold smiled. "That's a great idea. Thank you, Liliana."

After gathering control of my gaping mouth, the words spilled out. "I can't. I've got swim practice."

Mrs. Arnold removed the pen from behind her ear. "On Friday afternoons?"

"Yes, ma'am." I nodded. "Twice a day with my private coach."

Mrs. Arnold glanced at the paper in her hand. "I expect more than five sentences next time, or we will return to this discussion."

I slid onto my seat to the left of that wavy auburn hair and the unsightly eyewear of Liliana Royston, and I stared straight ahead. *Mom always says, "If you don't have anything nice to say, don't say anything at all."*

Chapter Three

As I sat with Shane during the worship service in our fifty-year-old, red-brick auditorium, I glanced around and leaned closer to him. "I've known most of these people my entire life."

"I've never lived in one place more than three years," Shane whispered.

I couldn't imagine what that would be like. *New house, new school, new friends.* Then the thought really soaked in. "How long do you plan to stay in Elmont?"

Shane grinned. "My dad promised we'll be here until I graduate." The warmth of Shane's hand grabbing mine gave me a sense of security as Pastor Richter approached the pulpit. He was filled with enlightening messages that would quite often, if not always, step on someone's toes—and mine were not exempt from the bruising. The sermons were uplifting and, at the same time, powerful truths to help us walk in faith and trust more in the Lord.

Pastor Richter opened his Bible. "Please turn to James 4:8." In the silence, you could hear the thin pages turning. "'Draw near to God and He will draw near to you ...'"

Upon returning home, I helped Mom in the kitchen to allow me a chance for some girl talk to catch up from the busyness of the week and to check in on upcoming schedules. Sundays seemed to be a time of truce. We never discussed the undesirable writing contest.

I diced a tomato and dropped it into the salad bowl. "Coach has increased afternoon practices to two hours."

Mom pulled the lasagna out of the oven. "I miss taking you."

"Really? I thought it would be a relief."

She smiled. "It was good work time for me, and even though I wasn't in the pool, it was still time we spent together."

"Thanks for all the years of chauffeuring me around."

"Oh, sweetheart, we'll need to find new ways to bond."

I nodded before I realized what was coming.

Mom stretched, retrieved a pen from a drawer, and laid it on the counter. "Maybe 'Novelists in November'?"

What happened to our unspoken Sunday agreement?

I tossed the pen and then the salad as I heard Dad and Zach having their father-and-son bonding moments a room away. Although my little brother could be a bit chatty and a little annoying at times, I cherished my family. I soaked in most of my parents' wisdom and instruction knowing one day, in the future, I would be wearing that same footwear as I trained my own children.

Nevertheless, on more than a rare occasion, my opinion wasn't in total agreement with my parents' advice. They listened to my side and then explained where they were coming from concerning our differences. I mostly agreed with my parents, and as I now knew, it had to do a great deal with God being the Leader of our home. Sometimes, as teenagers fall prey, I was too confident, on the verge of being a know-it-all in some areas, and had to be wrangled in—or be allowed to make my own mistakes.

Knowing I had the State swim meet coming up within a few weeks, I had all intentions of playing it safe. I knew to be cautious. It was the last meet of the year, and scouts would be there. I planned to be on a college swim team as I pursued a career as either a personal trainer or a sports nutritionist.

However, being the month of November, I was a bit antsy to get outdoors before the winter weather set in. I was competitive in swimming from the age of six, and sometimes that ambitious spirit ventured into other areas of my life. I wasn't about to stay indoors and bond over Mom's pet project.

Mom carried the hot dish to the table, and I followed with the salad.

"You always do a great job with lasagna, honey." Dad took a bite, and Mom grinned.

Was that a compliment, or did it mean Mom didn't cook anything else very well?

Zach set his glass on the table. "Yeah, remember last week when you had to throw out that burnt hamburger stuff?"

"Zach!" Dad's voice was a bit unusually gruff.

I looked at Mom and smiled. "Grilled cheese sandwiches are great anytime."

Zach scooped up a forkful of pasta. "Can we go horseback riding this afternoon?"

Dad swallowed a sip of iced tea. "It works for me."

Zach turned his gaze toward me. "Will you go, Kaylee? You haven't been all year, and the stables are only twenty minutes away."

I shrugged. "Sure, swim practice isn't until six o'clock on Sundays."

Zach almost jumped off his chair. "Yay!"

I didn't remember the last time I had seen my little brother's eyes beam so brightly. "I'll see if Shane wants to go, but we'll just be bystanders. Neither of us wants to chance a broken arm or leg and miss our final meet and the opportunity to get offered a letter of intent."

When we arrived at Schneider's Riding Stables, I slid on my favorite purple pullover sweater, knitted by my grandmother, to guard against the chill in the air. As we neared the well-maintained stables, the Criollo horses immediately captivated me. Their strength and beauty were breathtaking, and it had been quite a few years since I had ridden.

As Zach signed up to ride Rosy, their youngest mare, owner Bobby Schneider approached. "We've got a couple of geldings saddled and ready to ride. Are you two interested?"

I looked at Shane, and he shrugged. "Whatever you want."

I gazed momentarily at the handsome horses. *What harm could a trot be?*

Before I realized, Shane and I had signed our names on the list. As I sat atop the gray horse, Bobby handed me the reins. "His name is Pepper. Just chat with him, and you'll have a friend for life." I immediately felt a calmness and wondered if I had overthought the concerns of a Sunday afternoon ride and should have considered one more often with my little brother.

On the other hand, my parents had never been prone to sit atop horses. They preferred their feet on solid ground and were happy to relax with one another and chat about life while they enjoyed the peaceful moment of time and watched our horses frolic in the pasture. I guess that's how life was after twenty-five years of marriage.

I recalled once my parents went to get cards, stood side by side, picked out cards for each other, and never saw them until their anniversary three days later. Although a bit dorky, that continuous excitement and love was something I wanted to have someday in my own marriage. Shane and I had plans for those wedding bells in about seven years, though they weren't set in stone—I didn't have a ring on my finger yet.

For some unknown reason that particular Sunday afternoon, I felt the strong urge to join in on the ride. As we went from a trot to a gallop, the bounce on the saddle was a welcome change. Unlike the confines of four white, painted walls around the chlorinated pool and a tight cap on my head to reduce drag time to gain those extra seconds, I had the breeze through my hair and no boundaries of a painted line or lane ropes. There wasn't a ticking of a stopwatch or a high-pitched whistle. As much as I craved swimming competitions, I greatly needed this time of relaxation. Being in God's beautiful nature and riding one of His magnificent animals was exhilarating. The smile on my face could not be swiped away, until that moment—that life-changing moment.

Chapter Four

I didn't remember the unexpected movement of the horse rearing on his hind legs, the hard hit to the unforgiving ground, or sprawling in such an awkward position—unable to move and unconscious. I didn't personally see the panic in everyone's faces or the abundant tears streaming down my mother's cheeks. I didn't recall the stoic look upon my father's face, the silence from my usually inquisitive brother, or the path being worn by Shane as he paced back and forth on that green field. I didn't recollect the sirens, paramedics, or the ride to the hospital.

Those were all lost moments for me.

It was their memories wrapped around my life, verbalized to me—a segment of the air I breathed—that I would never capture. It was only the other people who remembered every minute of the horrifying ordeal—until my eyelids finally opened.

My first sight was familiar faces, but distraught like I had never seen before. Suddenly, a nurse dashed into the room calling for the doctor. It only took a minute or two to realize I was lying on a hospital bed, but I had no idea as to the reason. *Was it a swimming accident? Did I win?*

Zach burst his way to my side with tears streaming down his face. "I'm so sorry, Kaylee. I know you like horses. We never should have gone."

My brow scrunched. *So it must have something to do with horses.* I began to raise my hand to feel the soreness on the back of my head, but the needle, with the extended tube, taped to my arm disrupted the movement.

"It's all my fault," he mumbled in between sobs. He grabbed hold of my hand, which meant this was a serious matter. Most of the time, he thought I had cooties.

It must be more than just a broken leg. Are they both broken? I glanced toward my legs—no bulging cast underneath the covers. I lay speechless trying to recollect even one small detail.

As Mom stepped forward and kissed my cheek, I could tell she was trying to hold back tears, but she wasn't completely successful. "Do you remember anything, sweetheart?"

I shook my head.

"Do you recall riding a horse?"

"Pepper?" It was a bit hazy but was beginning to register in my brain.

Mom and Dad nodded.

"Where's Shane? Is he okay?"

Mom, Dad, and Zach stepped aside, and Shane approached from the corner at a turtle's pace. I had never seen him so solemn and distraught. His skin appeared a little pale, and his hand trembled as he touched mine.

"Did I miss the swim meet?"

Shane shook his head.

"Did I cause you to miss your competition?"

Shane cleared his throat and ruffled his hair as he did when he was upset, like when he didn't get the official time he wanted at a swim meet or when his parents were arguing again. He got so frustrated at things he couldn't fix.

Why the frustration now? I'll be out of here by the end of the day.

"It's in two weeks." He finally got the words out.

I grinned. "I still have time to practice my strokes. I'll be ready."

A tear descended from Shane's face.

"Shane?" I looked at Mom and Dad, and all I was greeted with were stoic expressions. I turned my gaze toward my little brother. I could always trust him to tell me the truth without any fluff. "Zach, what's going on?" Their faces weren't this gloomy at Aunt Beatrice's funeral last April.

I glimpsed at the blanket and saw my left toes, which had found their way outside the covers. I moved them up and down.

I attempted to do the same with my other foot. "Why can't I wiggle my right toes?" I faced my mother, who had been by my side through swim practices, every competition, and all my strained and cramped muscles. "Mom?"

I hit my right leg. Nothing. No pain. No sting.

My voice rose an octave with a sound of panic. "Mom? Dad?"

I beat my right leg and still felt nothing.

Mom sat on the chair beside me and grabbed my hand. She glanced at the Holy Bible on the tray. "Kaylee, you've been here seventy-two hours."

"I feel fine. Let's go home."

Mom glanced at the liquid flowing through the tube. "The morphine is helping with that."

"'Morphine'? You know I'll be disqualified."

Mom scooted to the edge of her chair. "You won't be making it to the swim meet, sweetheart."

My jaw dropped. "Of course I will. I have to be there."

Mom took a deep breath and released it slowly. "The doctor says it's just not possible."

"I'm not missing the State meet. I don't have to win gold, but maybe I'll still get silver or bronze after this unwanted three-day ordeal."

Tears fell down Mom's face as she stared downward at the hard, tile floor and then gazed into my eyes. "Kaylee, you're paralyzed."

"What? No! I can't be!" I moved my toes up and down. "I can wiggle my toes."

"Yes, on your left foot."

Dad, Shane, and Zach just stared in my direction. I felt like a meerkat in a zoo.

Mom gave a quick look to Dad and squeezed my hand harder. "It's monoplegia."

"'Mono' what?"

Mom glanced at my hand, seemed to realize she was squeezing a bit too tightly, and loosened her grip. "Monoplegia. The fall injured your spinal cord, and your right leg is paralyzed."

"For how long?"

In unison, everyone gasped for a breath.

I lifted my shoulders and looked sternly at Mom. "For how long?"

She wiped away tears and swallowed hard. "Permanently."

My head hit the pillow. I shook my head in silence for at least a full forty-five seconds as I stared at the ceiling. "I'll work the muscles. I'll rebuild."

Shane approached my side. "It won't work."

"You don't know what you're talking about."

Mom put her hand on the blanket and patted my right leg, although I didn't feel a thing. "Honey, the doctor explained it to us in detail."

I glanced at Zach for a hint of exaggeration or sarcasm, but his facial barometer held firm.

I swallowed hard and felt a tear slip down my cheek. Although my voice cracked, the words inched their way out. "Are my swimming days over?"

Mom, barely above a whisper, said, "I'm afraid they are."

I saw Shane lower his head right before the room began to spin and stars appeared. That's the last thing I remembered.

Chapter Five

"Kaylee. Kaylee! Can you hear me?" I faintly heard Mom's voice and slightly felt the nudge on my shoulder. As I was trying to speak, her voice became louder and the nudge stronger.

"Kaylee, we're all here. Dad, Zach, Shane, and me. Open your eyes, sweetheart. Please, come back to us." I had never heard Mom with such a desperate plea, not even when she begged me to join her boring writing contest.

My eyes blinked rapidly a few times and closed again.

"That's it. Try again, Kaylee." I could hear Mom's gentle voice, but I couldn't get my eyes to remain open.

"Kaylee, we need you to open your eyes." *Is that panic in Dad's voice?*

Slowly, I forced my eyes open and saw everyone gaze upon me. I turned my attention to my feet and saw my left toes moving, but not my right. Tears plunged down my face. "It wasn't a dream, was it?"

Mom shook her head.

I could feel the anger boil. "Why?"

Mom sniffled. "We don't always know the reason."

Dad attempted to take hold of my hand, but I pulled away. "God is still with you."

"Really? I'll never swim again, and I can't even walk!"

Dad pulled a chair closer to my bedside and sat. "You're still with us. We love you."

"Do you know what a burden I'm going to be to you?"

Tears descended along my mother's cheeks. "God will help us get through this together." After pulling a tissue from her pocket, Mom dabbed at her eyes, but she couldn't stop the waterfall.

"I can't even take a shower or get into a bathtub by myself."

Mom reached for more tissues. "The doctor has given me a list of therapists." She patted away more tears. "We'll get whatever help you need to regain some independence."

"Why didn't God just let me die?"

"Kaylee!"

I turned my head away from everyone and shut my eyes. I don't know if, in those two syllables, it was fear, pain, or disappointment in Mom's voice, but as soon as I said those seven words, I knew they pierced my mother's heart. Maybe she would just assume it was the medication talking, and maybe it was.

I had never seen my dad cry—until today. He didn't even shed a tear at his sister's graveside service. I'm not saying he never released a few waterworks before, but if he did, it must have been behind closed doors. Seeing Dad's emotions in this moment sucked the air right out of me. It was almost as wrenching as when Mom told me I could never swim again. Dad was always so strong and confident, but not in this instant, when his shoulders and head drooped and tears poured as he made his way out of my sterilized hospital room.

Zach stepped into Dad's place by my side. "I'll do your chores, Sis." My little brother just grew up a few years in a brief moment of time, right before my eyes. He was the one always begging and offering me a part of his allowance to take out the trash or sweep the floors when his turn rolled around, but today he was keeping his money in his pocket and volunteering to do extra work.

"Zach, we'll talk about chores later. Kaylee is going to gain her strength back and be able to perform some daily tasks."

Is Mom in denial? Does she really think my life will return to any type of normalcy?

Zach threw his arms around me and sobbed.

I attempted to comfort him with a pat on his back. "Hey, if I ever get my own refrigerator, you can come fix it anytime."

Zach stood straight, nodded, and sniffled as he scrubbed his sleeve across his wet cheeks.

I made eye contact with Shane for a brief moment and saw the cascade of tears. He shook his head and walked out of the room.

"Shane! Shane!" I stared at the doorway, expecting him to return.

Zach ran after Shane, and Mom picked up the Bible and began reading Psalm 118. "'Give thanks to the Lord, for He is good; For His lovingkindness is everlasting.'"

I felt like I was gasping for my final breaths—before drowning. I had always been confident in the water, and in my faith, until that moment.

Chapter Six

Lying in bed was now my preferred place to be. Crural monoplegia was the rarer form of monoplegia; it affected a lower extremity of the body instead of an arm.

I had nothing left. My life had ended.

I wasn't the extrovert that I once had been. I cried, prayed, and felt sorry for myself.

God, why did You take my swimming away?

I had bursts of anger and bouts of overwhelming sadness. It was easier to just stay in my room; however, Mom did not allow that. She knew the importance of my mental health along with the physical. I was grateful for my support team, but I still had moments of feeling rejected, useless, and unimportant.

As I entered the living room, I bumped into the wall and then the sofa. I moved the joystick, and the wheels went to the left. "Not that way!" I dropped my hand to the side and stared at the floor as I sat there in frustration.

Driving a motorized wheelchair was not the same as driving a car. I wondered if I could control the steering knob better if I had been one of those kids who played computer or video games all day—but that wasn't for me. I had enjoyed being an athlete. I even missed the grueling workouts. If I had the chance to work on my breaststroke, I would do it gladly without a whimper. Now, I'd never feel the senses of accomplishment and joy again as I had when I stood on those platforms and the judges placed awards into my hands or around my neck.

It was near impossible learning how to function with monoplegia. As if the physical rehabilitation wasn't enough, the mental was even more unfathomable at times. If I didn't have God to lean on, I would have already lost my courage, strength, and mind.

As I maneuvered my wheelchair and parked facing the sofa, Mom entered. I sure missed the days when I could step into a room without the aid of a joystick. It was very awkward for people to speak to my backside. Although clumsily at the moment, it was up to me to adjust my angles and move into the correct position to communicate face-to-face.

"Why does the therapist have to come four times a week?" I sat on the strange vinyl seat of a wheelchair as Mom approached the plush sofa.

"We have to keep those muscles moving, and you're not able to do it alone."

"Why don't you let Zach help me? He'd enjoy torturing and humiliating me."

"Cindy Johnson is well qualified and the best therapist in town. If anyone can help, she's the one."

I let out a loud groan, one that had been bottled up for quite some time.

Afterward, all I heard was silence. *Where's the reprimand? Does Mom wish she could do the same?*

A tear slipped down my cheek. "I used to swim for hours. I won gold medals."

Mom came over and sat on the chair next to me.

I wiped away the lone tear, only to open the floodgate.

I felt the warmth of Mom's skin as she settled her hand on top of mine. "We are family, and we're here for each other."

"This doesn't just affect me. It has changed all our lives." As much as I tried, I couldn't stop the weeping. "And, I lost Shane."

"That day changed his life, too."

Between sniffles, I was able to get out the words I held deeply in my heart, "I thought he loved me."

"Life isn't always so simple. You're both still young, and you've only known each other for a few months." Mom swiped at unsuppressed tears. "I'm sure he's scared, too, after something so traumatic."

I nodded, but no words came.

"He just needs time to figure out what's best for him and his future."

Mom grabbed a tissue and dabbed at my tears, but I was most certain one tissue wasn't going to make much difference.

Although I was Therapist Cindy's first patient with crural monoplegia, she didn't come any less prepared. She had done her research and brought her bags of exercise equipment, but every session had been a great humiliation and an annoying waste of time. As she moved my right leg up and down about eight inches, I couldn't feel a thing. I didn't know which was the worst: my aching heart, my limp leg, or the two-wheeled posture control walker in the corner. *It has a built-in seat. How embarrassing! Could I be any more mortified?*

As always, Coach Bennett was by my side on therapy days. I didn't know if he wanted to be supportive, learn the exercise techniques, or see if I would be able to swim again someday. I was quite certain the last one was of most importance to him; but in reality, he was probably here for all three reasons. Although the sessions didn't seem to make any difference with my condition, he never let his disappointment show. He knew a positive attitude was not only beneficial but also a requirement for a successful athlete.

Part of my routine included working out my good leg, arms, and core. The therapist explained it was important to strengthen my entire body to assist with the monoplegia so I could return to some independence. Coach always took a turn in the exercising of my lame leg, counted as I lifted weights with both hands, and, as usual, spoke words of wisdom. His presence was always a welcoming moment of my day. Even when Coach didn't say it verbally, I heard him in my head repeatedly, *"Give me one hundred twenty-five percent! Push hard! Harder, Kaylee!"*

While Therapist Cindy was raising my right leg, my mind roamed to Pastor Richter's sermon a couple of months ago, *"'Humble yourselves in the presence of the Lord, and He will exalt you.'"* Even with my extremely active schedule before my accident, I enjoyed chatting with people whenever I found a few minutes in my busy routine. I always considered myself a polite individual, and I held doors open for my elders as I entered buildings. I was irritated when I heard others snicker at Eddie Fisker as he hobbled down the hallways with his forearm crutches, but I never really considered what life was like having cerebral palsy. My priorities were to go from class to class and make sure I was on time for swim practices.

My goal in life was to stand in the center on the podiums at every swim meet. I had the best support group of family and friends to help accomplish my desires of an overflowing bookshelf of trophies and a path paved to become an Olympian. If someone was ill or hurt, I prayed for them. I read my Bible daily, and I went to church. I never thought myself to be prideful, but I also never thought much of the specific needs of others and how their difficulties affected their lives.

As Therapist Cindy was now massaging the muscles in my leg, my mind traveled back to that horrifying accident. If I were able to redo the past, I wouldn't have gone horseback riding. I would have been satisfied watching Zach, and I wouldn't be sitting here, weighed down with the regrets of one day. Under the keen supervision of my dedicated, stern coach, I would be practicing my strokes in the rectangular, city pool. I never would have chosen to be confined to this cold, unwelcoming wheelchair. Discovering humility hadn't really been a part of my life, not even when Tammy Sullivan beat me by three-tenths of a second in the 200-meter breaststroke. It was always my most difficult stroke.

Do I always make excuses when life doesn't turn out the way I planned it?

As I sat there, unable to move my bum leg, I silently prayed. *Dear Lord, please forgive me for my insensitivities to others. Please forgive me for being prideful. Show me Your plan for my life to share Your love with others. I come humbly before You, and I accept Your will. Thank You for Your mercy, and I want to draw nearer to You. Please guide me and teach me Your ways. Amen.*

As I looked up, Coach was finishing massaging my leg. *When did he take over?* I couldn't feel the difference between Therapist Cindy's and Coach Bennett's massages. I couldn't feel anything in that limb. As I gazed toward Coach, his eyes met mine. Not a word was spoken audibly, but in the silence, much was stated. One event was all it took to change our long, sought-after Olympic future. All the hours spent toiling together, and now neither would ever touch the gold. One life did affect another. I saw the pain and disappointment in his eyes. It was time for my coach, my friend, to move on with training other athletes. It was time to let go, but my heart would always hold a special place for Coach Bennett. As he was leaving that day, he glanced back, a tear escaped, and he walked out and closed the door.

Chapter Seven

I wasn't prepared for what happened three months later.

Being home alone, I answered the knock at the door and snarled as I glanced at the apparatuses before me and then lifted my gaze to his. "I didn't expect to see you again."

"I can't say I expected to be here."

Coach followed me into the room and offered the crutches. "Don't you think it's time you dive in a little deeper?"

I shook my head. "One slip, and the humiliation might just put me six feet under."

Has Coach been talking with Therapist Cindy? I made it perfectly clear that I have no intention of stepping away from the safety of my four-legged walker. With its build, no one can encroach upon my space.

"Don't you have someone else to coach?"

He leaned the crutches against the wall.

I gazed at Coach, hardly believing he was standing in our living room. "Doesn't someone else need you to get them to the Olympics?"

"It's not my calling."

"Or maybe you're not listening."

Coach chuckled. "Oh, I've heard the Lord very clearly."

Coach came every day for two months and continued to help me improve my core and upper body strength along with my balance. It's one thing to hop on one leg when you're a kid, but it's something totally different to walk with one leg and have the other hang like a noodle without any additional support.

Although I had previously been a fit athlete, I struggled to gain the different muscle strength needed for everyday independent living. I had taken my life for granted, but not anymore. I appreciated each miniscule accomplishment and gained an even greater respect, which I didn't think was possible, for Coach Bennett. He could have found another athlete and still obtained that gold, but he didn't. He stayed by my side and worked with me endlessly and tirelessly.

Mastering the crutches proved to be difficult. I don't know if it was a mental block, losing the security of the seat attached to the walker, or the soreness under my arms. I just couldn't seem to keep my balance with the dead weight of my lame leg and go a distance with them. It was extremely disappointing and frustrating. I could feel depression sneaking in.

Coach Bennett opened the door. I, dressed in shorts and a T-shirt, wheeled into the building. I gazed at the water. It seemed decades since I had swum in that chlorinated city pool.

"What are we doing here, Coach?"

Without saying a word, Coach approached the side of the swimming pool, and I followed.

"Coach?"

He engaged my brakes. "We're going for a swim."

"I can't."

"Sometimes we don't know what we're capable of doing until we give one hundred twenty-five percent."

I glanced at my leg. "It's going to take more than that."

Coach grinned and bound my legs together with a band. "This will keep your right leg from falling, but you'll have to use more upper body strength than before."

I glanced at my banded legs. "This must be how mermaids feel."

Coach Bennett grinned as he lifted me. "They sure know how to swim."

I chuckled.

Coach smiled. "I have missed that laughter."

I stared at the pool before I met his gaze. "Thanks for bringing me here, Coach."

He nodded. "You have a life to live." He carried me into the water. "We'll take it slow. I'll be with you every moment."

I nodded and swirled my hand in the water as Coach carried me, safely in his arms, deeper into the pool.

"Try moving your legs."

I stared at my motionless lower limbs.

"Do you recall how much my daughters struggled to get their high school and college diplomas after their mother passed away?"

"I remember."

In a familiar stern voice, Coach continued, "Give me one hundred seventy-five percent, Kaylee."

I gritted my teeth and stared at both legs as they moved in unison.

Coach gazed at the underwater stripes. "One day, you'll be swimming across this pool again."

"I won't be winning any medals."

"Success isn't always measured in gold, silver, or bronze."

I gazed at my legs as they went up and down.

Coach watched in silence before speaking. "I'm sorry I left. It was just too heartbreaking to watch you suffer."

"I don't blame you. I would have left, too, if I could."

Coach Bennett glanced at my legs as I mustered enough strength to continue moving them up and down a few more times before I stopped and panted as I attempted to catch my breath.

"I expect you to be in proper gear next week."

"Yes, sir, Coach." I grinned. I never expected to hear those words or to ever wear a swimsuit again.

"You're a fighter. You've never let me down."

I smirked. "Except that one day when I was thirteen. Remember that extra hour's workout?"

Coach hesitated. "It was the only basketball game of Lori's I ever missed."

"Coach?" I could feel my throat tightening.

"Rules were rules, but you learned your lesson."

I stared at him. "But at whose expense?" I wiped away a couple of tears I couldn't withhold.

"We can only move forward in life."

"I'm sorry, Coach."

"We all make mistakes. It's what we do with them that's important."

I nodded.

"You're an inspiration, Kaylee."

Did I splash water on Coach's face, or is that a tear trickling down his cheek?

"When you're ready, you have a story to share with the world."

Chapter Eight

A s I sat at my desk, in a new taupe sweater and with an ink pen in my hand, I thought back to that traumatizing horse accident last November and the fearful reality of awakening in a hospital. I glanced at my journal, rubbed at the smeared blotch of blue ink on my finger, glimpsed at the leaking pen in the trash can, and began to write.

A year has passed since the abrupt devastation of losing my beloved swim dream and the dire heartache of Shane's leaving, but I think it's time I consider Coach's advice and write a novel.

Will I have the right words to express such immense losses?

I never fully comprehended the reason for the accident, and no one ever discovered what spooked Pepper that afternoon. However, I came to understand, after heavily scribbling in a tower of journals, how difficult it was for Shane to be around me. He was hurting, too. In a short amount of time, we had built dreams together, but they suddenly vanished in that pasture. There wasn't any reason his dream to the Olympics should have to end just because mine did. In time, it made sense how it would be unsettling and a bit frightening to have a monoplegic wife. We were young and not prepared for what lay ahead under such circumstances.

The first six months home from the hospital were terrifying, grueling, and rehabilitating. Coach Bennett's encouragement and coaching skills kept me alive. God planted him in my life not only for swimming but also to help me see I still had a future, even if I wasn't chasing gold. He helped me realize my world hadn't ended; a new life had begun.

As a newborn, I didn't know the effort I expended to accomplish menial tasks. However, having a disability at the age of seventeen, I was quite aware and felt all the pangs required to achieve success. I had to adapt to a leg that didn't work and learn new ways to get dressed, fetch a cup of tea, and get from one place to another amidst a plethora of other duties in my daily routine. The simplest task was no longer taken for granted.

As I looked back, I knew God never left. Coach Blakey visited a few times, but she was never a woman with much self-expression other than guiding us with verbal commands and the blow of her whistle. Several of my teammates visited a couple of times, but then they strayed away with the rest of them. I probably would have done the same if places were switched. Their demanding athletic schedules and creating high school memories didn't allow a great deal of time to adjust to the tragedy of a classmate. Shane never returned to my side. I caught him, many times, glancing at me in the hallways, but he remained at a distance. I came to realize he had to have time to figure out where his life went from here.

Through Liliana and *The Mostly Truthful Tribune*, which I graciously stepped away from since I wasn't ready to hustle around gathering stories my senior year, I stayed enlightened of Shane's gold-medal wins and his scholarship offers to a variety of universities. It also appeared he was on track for the Summer Olympics after our high school graduation.

I continued swimming twice a week and accomplished the feat of swimming a few yards by myself. Coach Bennett said he was asked to train a young man for the Olympics but declined as he was already training a star athlete.

Was that young man Shane?

Dad and Mom considered transferring me to a school for severely disabled students, but I figured if Eddie could make it at Elmont High School, then I could, too. In fact, he and I enjoyed battling out chess matches on our lunch breaks.

God placed Liliana in my pathway the year before in that dreaded journalism class, but I hardly even noticed her—or at least I tried not to. When longtime teammates left, Liliana stepped up. She attended a different church in town with her grandmother, but we became inseparable on Sunday afternoons as we played board games, card games, and created fictional heroes, heroines, and villains. Even Zach joined in the games but seemed to vanish when Liliana and I got immersed with our literary characters. Old friends might have disappeared, but God brought new ones into my life.

I thought by going to church on Sundays and having my daily Bible study that Jesus Christ had been Center of my life. However, I learned my spiritual walk needed to grow deeper. I had been a swimmer for a reason, but it was time to share my story, and my faith, with others. I let the Lord lead my dreams, goals, and every moment of my life. God never promised us an easy life as Christians, but He promised He would never leave us.

Maybe one day, I'll write my autobiography; but for now, my entry into the "Novelists in November" contest for English IV revealed my story through a relatable, fictionalized character. As I typed the words, I put my heart out there for the world to see. My physical, mental, and emotional challenges were opened and on display. My disappointments, pains, heartaches, and vulnerabilities were exposed on the pages through an Olympian trampolinist named Katie—a nineteen-year-old who suffered tremendous losses and discovered the future didn't always arrive as planned. A spinal cord injury, from an eight-meter twist landing that went wrong, prevented her from performing in the final round of the Olympics, and she missed the opportunity to take home the gold, or any other, medal.

A part of living was not knowing. Although I had a thought-out future, I learned it wasn't guaranteed. I lost tremendously and suffered greatly. However, as I lived in the current moment, I trusted my Lord, Jesus Christ. He kept me alive for a purpose and put an ink pen in my hand. The Lord replaced my lost dreams and relationships with new visions and friends. Quite unexpectedly, He gave me a desire to write.

After closing my computer, I smiled. *I might not win, or even place, in this writing competition, but I am a novelist. I create and bring fictional characters to life. It's one way I can share God's love and bring inspiration and hope to the injured, heartbroken, and disappointed. I have suffered and walked in their downtrodden shoes. Stumble as I may, my heart still sings.*

As I heard, through the intercom system, the familiar two words, "Kaylee McKenzie," a warmth came across me. I stood and steadied myself with my crutches. Today was the first day I had the confidence to trade my walker for crutches out in public, but I didn't expect to be the center of attention. As I glanced at the stage, it appeared to be a long stretch from where I stood. As I felt all eyes upon me, I inhaled as deeply as I always had before diving into a pool, released the breath slowly, and began my path to the front of the room. I clopped with one left foot and two crutches as I dragged my right foot's toes. It wasn't with the fast pace I had in the past, but I felt the accomplishment of still being a part of this world—a feat for which I would never receive a medal, but a success I would carry with me for the rest of my life.

I was a few steps away from the winners' platform when I realized I still had an ink pen behind my ear after having stopped and written notes on my way inside the auditorium. *I'm such a nerd!* As I climbed the ramp, I chuckled with delight.

It wasn't a swimmer's medalist platform, but it was a stage. It wasn't a gold medal placed around my neck; it was bronze. *Does the college have a writing contest? Can I bypass the silver next year to reach the gold?* I felt my competitive spirit come alive, and I knew I might be in competition with Mom concerning the need for those red ink pens.

As I stood in front of the crowd admiring the first-place medalist, Liliana Royston, I could hear the autumn rain beat against the metal roof. My thoughts began pouring for my next novel. *Will my protagonist get drenched in a pool, or is she going to end up in a downpour of rain?*

As the crowd's applause brought me back to reality, I realized that the dreaded newspaper class had been a blessing in disguise. It not only provided me with a devoted friend but also taught me how to gain the skills of researching and writing fictional tales.

Is this how my mother felt during all those hours of waiting for me during swim practices? No wonder she never complained.

A Note from the Author

Foremost, I want to thank my Heavenly Father. This short story wasn't what I originally thought it was going to be. Through His grace, it is much more beautiful! He gave me words of inspiration and hope to share with those struggling with difficult times and those desiring to have a closer relationship with Him.

As I attempt to learn how to navigate the technological necessities of writing, I would like to thank my husband, Richter, and my daughter Andrea. I can't thank you enough for answering my questions with such kindness and precision.

I would also like to thank my husband, Richter, and my two daughters, Andrea and Kristy, for their continuous support. God has blessed me with a wonderful family!

Thank you to my beta readers: E.F. Buckles, Richter Cox, and Amy Reep. Your comments and suggestions were extremely helpful in the development of this work.

Thank you to Bethany Willcock, my fellow author and critique partner. I'm glad we were paired together, and I appreciate your swimming expertise, comments, and suggestions. Any remaining errors are my own.

This story would not be included in *Novelists in November* anthology without Kellyn Roth and the Wild Blue Wonder Press publishing team. Thank you for coaching me through the process and being such a blessing.

To my readers ... Through Kaylee's struggles and accomplishments, I hope you have found a bit of encouragement and enjoyment. May Kaylee be an inspiration to us all! If you would like to connect with me, read my blog, or keep updated with my writing career, please follow me at faithdcox.com. I welcome new friends and appreciate your support and comments!

Tollemache House

KELLYN ROTH

Dedication

For Aimee, who irritates me almost as much as Effie. I love you much more than I love her. Though I'm not really sure I would choose you over pig farming.

I t was a beautiful day for writing. Stormy clouds swirled over the London residence of the Duke of Ridgewell, flinging droplets of water against the wavy window panes. From her window seat in the Harriots' over-prioritized library, Lady Euphemia Adley stared down at the gray, windswept streets. A well-sprung carriage rolled by, but none of the *ton* dared stroll along the pavement as they usually did around this time of the late morning.

Effie leaned her head against the frame of the window and closed her eyes. Her head was throbbing, and today was an inconvenient day for a headache. For Effie, wife of Lord William Harriot and sister-in-law of the notorious Duke of Ridgewell, must write her fourth novel ...

... and it must be her second bestseller ...

... because she must support her family ...

... because of the idiot who was currently sitting upside-down on a chair across the room with a newspaper over his face, insinuating that he knew better than she did how a novel ought to be written.

To be fair, Philip Harriot, the Duke of Ridgewell, believed he was responsible for the success of her third novel, the first one published by Hadfield Books, her husband's publisher. But it wasn't true. Effie was a good writer.

She *was*.

Hence the reason why she knew better than to confide anything in her brother-in-law. And yet, unwilling to admit her lack of inspiration to her husband, Effie had told Philip.

And Charlotte, William's younger sister.

And Florie, Effie's younger sister.

She rather thought the headache might be due to their input more than any legitimate malady. Especially since all three of them had chosen to inhabit the library with her, offering suggestions and interrupting her every five minutes with inquiries about her well-being.

It was sweet.

It was also maddening.

"The problem," Philip mumbled from the chair he was slumped over, one leg somehow thrown over the back, "is that Effie refuses to take my excellent ideas. I gave her a plot for a novel last night. She refused to write it."

"The one with the haunted abbey?" Charlotte asked, glancing away from her morning tea and gossip rags to smirk at her brother.

Philip jerked upright, his stabilizing leg flailing as he struggled to maintain balance. The paper fluttered to the floor. "Yes! And the handsome duke who fights the ghosts for the gorgeous woman who adores him and sees past his mysterious exterior."

"You're not mysterious," Florie protested. "You're kind!"

"Thank you, Florie. You are my new favorite sister." He stuck his tongue out at Charlotte, who ignored him.

Effie rolled her eyes. She was never going to finish anything at this rate. "You are neither mysterious nor kind, and I am not writing a book about you, Philip." The last thing the London upper class needed was another novel about a rake like Philip presumably doing strange things.

Philip tumbled to his feet. "Perhaps I shall write it myself."

"When was the last time you wrote anything?" Charlotte asked, tossing her paper aside. "Other than scrawling your signature on any promissory note that is presented to you."

"If you must know, my favorite niece and I exchange letters every day. Granted, I write with big lettering so she can read it, but I am capable of writing small."

"Fabulous." Charlotte stood in a single fluid movement and straightened her skirts. As always, she was dressed to the height of fashion. "Come on, Phil. And Florie, for that matter. Let's give Effie the rest of the morning alone. We're getting in the way, and she needs to finish that novel or we'll all be living on the streets. I don't do well out of doors."

No pressure whatsoever. Effie cast a look over her shoulder. Charlotte was one of her dearest friends, but she could be a little ... much.

Philip laughed. "Oh, come on, Lot-A-Dot. It isn't as desperate as that. Perry will take care of all of us if we ask nicely." Perry Burton, Lord Dalbury, had married the elder daughter of the Ridgewell family. William and Charlotte adored Perry, who had supported the family through years of loss and poor leadership, and Effie found she liked the bookish earl, too.

"If Xannie lets him," Charlotte said. Alexandra Burton, formerly Lady Alexandra Harriot, could be a bit difficult to deal with. Effie wasn't sure she'd had more than five exchanges with the Countess of Dalbury thus far, and every one had made Effie feel very small.

But no one could be as hard on Effie as her own thoughts.

Once her family had disappeared, Effie turned her eyes to the breakfast tray she rested at an angle on her lap and the sheets of papers resting on it. The crisp, blank whiteness stared back at her, taunting her with its uselessness.

William loved Effie's writing. In his mind, she was the most talented author in the world—and that ought to be encouraging. He'd practically married her because of it, she thought, though he'd cited other qualities, of course.

Yes, it was delightful that her husband believed in her. His faith in her talent was like a warm, comforting blanket.

She just had a tendency to mistrust warm, comforting things. So often they proved untrue. Effie had spent her whole life proving herself to everyone—her distant father, her mildly evil cousin, her former publishers, the London upper class. It was a hard habit to break.

Unfortunately, the heavy weight of "proving herself" was not conducive to the creative process.

She set the tray aside and ran her hand over her eyes. The headache refused to ease. It was born of the strain, perhaps, of this fourth novel needing to be perfect.

Perfection was a hard mark to reach. Unachievable, some might say. But so much depended on the success of Hadfield Books.

However, to Effie, at least, the biggest benefits of another successful novel would be keeping William happy. Oh, maybe he would protest if she voiced that thought; her own recommendations were few, and she so wanted him to succeed in this area. Hadfield's was not tied to the dukedom, and William still struggled with feeling like his very soul was entangled in his brother's title, as if nothing really belonged to *William*—it was all Philip's.

With a sigh, Effie stood. She should lie down for a few minutes until her husband emerged from the office, where a few of his friends had gathered for their biweekly book club meeting.

She started back from the door as it abruptly opened, and a tall figure stepped in. Her brother-in-law, the Earl of Dalbury, smiled at her a bit bashfully and absently pushed his spectacles up his nose. If anything, the round frames only served to highlight his dark-blue eyes.

"Oh, sorry. Did I startle you?"

Effie shook her head. "Not at all, my lord."

"Perry," he reminded her. "If you're comfortable with that. I would understand if you were not. I consider us siblings, but I know we are newly acquainted. William sent me in to get a book he left me—he said it was on the side table ... Oh, there it is." His long legs took him swiftly across the room. He was as tall as William, but ganglier, if that was the right word. Still, he moved with a self-possession that William didn't have. "I really do hope I didn't interrupt anything. William says you are writing another book."

Effie shuddered. "Well ... yes."

Perry paused, his keen eyes taking her in as he turned the novel he'd collected over in his hands. "Not going well? I've heard that finding inspiration can be difficult for any artist."

Effie pressed her lips together. There was a burning behind her eyes—and she longed to tell someone. The earl had a softness to his expression, almost fatherly, that prompted her to confide in him. "Please don't let William know, but it's been a challenge. The idea I have ... it's not suitable." For whatever reason, the only idea that had come to her was that of a character—a married woman going through the ups and downs of her first year of marriage. However, that was hardly appropriate writing material for a romance author. She didn't want to write about an unhappily married couple, which was, in her mind, the only source of conflict she could introduce. If she wanted to write a romance, she must write about a single woman instead.

She just didn't want to at the moment.

"I'm sorry to hear that." He gestured toward a chair. "Would you like to talk about it?"

She took the seat, and he lowered himself onto the chaise opposite of her. "I feel like I'm dry of inspiration. Like I've used up all my good ideas, and now I have nothing left. It doesn't help that this year has been ..."

A slight smile ghosted across his lips. "Novel-worthy?"

"Yes!" Effie exclaimed. "But I already wrote *that* book. So now what?"

He nodded. "That's more than fair. Well, perhaps you need a rest from day-to-day life."

Effie laughed. There was nowhere to escape to, but there also wasn't much to escape *from*. Not now. Her husband adored her, she lived with her best friend and her sister, and though the duke could wear at her nerves, William did a good job making sure she felt comfortable nonetheless. "There's nothing terribly overwhelming about my life, honestly."

"A change could help. My wife, I believe, is similar, but she will never admit it. This last year has exhausted her, and she refused to rest after our last child arrived. Not that she ever does, but the birth was hard on her, I think." He paused, inclined his head, and then seemed to nod to himself. "What if you were to accompany Alexandra to our country estate, Tollemache House, in Surrey? You could write there; it's very peaceful, almost picturesque. This time of the year, it'll be cozy. And Alexandra won't bother you. She can prepare the household for Christmastime; we'll all be going down in December, and she likes to plan."

Effie pressed her lips together and shook her head. "I couldn't do that. I wouldn't presume—"

"Even though it's a short journey, I'd feel ill at ease to send Alexandra on alone, but she could use a rest, though don't tell her I said that." He grinned wryly. "She would never admit to exhaustion, but ... she was attached to the Harriot estates. Philip losing Northstrand, and in such a careless way, broke her. She grew up there, and I think it's taken a toll on her to know it's lost to the family, perhaps forever."

Solemnly, Effie nodded. She believed the same of William, though he was bearing up well. However, Alexandra seemed fiercely traditional, and traditional people did not always take well to change.

"I'll think about it," she said, not intending to think about it at all, "but I'm sure William won't want me to go." They'd only been married a month after all. What bridegroom would want his wife in another county while he remained in the city?

"We'll see about that. Just give it some thought." Perry rose and walked to the door. "I want you to be taken care of, Effie. In some ways, I blame myself for not interfering when it came to Philip—though he could scarcely be reasoned with, especially since he came into his majority, I might have spoken to him. And I feel that it is my job, therefore, to encourage the Harriots to rest at my estate if they need some time in the country."

"Oh, but I'm not—" Then she stopped herself, for she was a Harriot, and she would only disappoint Perry if she admitted she didn't see herself as one of the family.

With another little nod, Perry left Effie alone to think.

The carriage pulled up outside the Dalburys' London town house the next morning, and Effie, who had come over to Alexandra and Perry's for an early breakfast before her departure, stepped through the door, surrounded by her entire family, all determined to see her off. She smoothed her hands down the front of the skirt of her dark-blue traveling dress and watched the footman hop down to open the door.

They were traveling lightly, as a second carriage would follow carrying Alexandra's maid and her young son's nurse, along with their luggage.

Effie had no maid of her own, and the idea of possessing carriages—let alone taking both on a brief trip out to Surrey—was as foreign to her as the distant lives of royalty. But, it appeared, neither were unknown to her new family—the Ridgewell dukedom was, of course, heavily entangled in the monarchy, and the Earl and Countess of Dalbury were both very familiar with the prince regent, enough so that Alexandra referred to him as "Prinny" with a blasé flip of her delicate hand.

The earl himself stood to the left of Effie, his hand on the shoulder of his elder son, his daughter on his hip. The countess pressed a kiss to her husband's cheek, then her daughter's, then to the top of her son's head, before turning to the nurse who stood silently beside the carriage. She accepted the bundle of her youngest child, Baby William—named for Effie's husband—and stepped into the carriage.

So it was time to set off, then. Effie took a deep breath and pressed her hand briefly to her stomach. She was not exactly an unsociable person, but Alexandra unnerved her in a way few others could. She had a strong personality, whereas Effie was generally fairly quiet, at least in most situations. William brought out the protective side of her, the side that would do anything for the ones she loved. But when left to her own devices, she wasn't sure she existed at all, whereas Alexandra Burton, Countess of Dalbury, had *presence*.

Effie turned to William, at first facing the black buttons of his equally black waistcoat, but William tilted her chin up for another stolen kiss. William was private with other people, but with her ... She knew him well enough to understand that his regard for her was special. That *she* was special to *him*. It was a great gift.

"You'll write to me?" The words were repeated from multiple identical requests. William wanted to make sure their separation was minimal at best, despite the fact that he was the one who had pushed her to go.

"I can stay," she reiterated for the hundredth time in the last twelve hours. "Even now, darling. I can stay."

William's Harriot Hazel eyes softened, but he shook his head. "No, much as I'll miss you, it means so much to me to know you will be able to rest. It's been a busy year for you, and you deserve a respite. My family is ..." His eyes trailed to where Alexandra was giving strict orders about how things ought to be run in her absence. "They can be excessive," he settled on at last. "You deserve time to yourself, and Alexandra will be too busy at Tollemache House to bother you. Besides, it is only a month." He smiled. "We'll all come down in December and enjoy Christmastime together. By then, you may have finished your novel. What a treat that'll be!"

Effie faked her own smile. She wasn't sure she had the novel in her at all. But she must force one out—somehow. For William. For their family.

She had protested leaving William most of last night—and then capitulated and started packing.

After all, Effie owed William so much—and she must write.

Before she knew it, she was in the carriage with her sister-in-law and three-month-old nephew, at first jostling through the narrow cobbled streets of London and then eventually through buildings growing scarcer and scarcer until Effie and company were truly in the countryside. It was a gray first day of November, certainly, but no more than was normal, and though the air held a bite, it was comfortable within the confines of the carriage and beneath her cloak.

Alexandra said nothing. Her eyes were alternatively on her son, who slept in her arms, and out the window. Her face was lined unpleasantly, as if some great burden were being foisted upon her. Effie only hoped she herself was not that burden. She believed she wasn't. After all, Alexandra had intended to make this journey long before Effie had committed to joining her. That was what the earl had said.

Seeing that Alexandra truly had no interest in a conversation with her, Effie reached into her bag and pulled out a notebook and some pencils. William had sharpened them for her that morning before placing them in her bag; he was endlessly thoughtful like that. She could not work with a quill at present, but she could still make progress during the journey.

She began scratching away, forcing herself to write something. Unfortunately, the lack of inspiration continued, and though Effie wrote down her one, useless idea—the one involving the married woman and her boringly devoted husband—she mostly found herself scribbling unconnected thoughts.

She didn't feel like herself today, and that frustrated her. She did acknowledge that her monthly should be coming in a day or so, and usually that would affect her mood. She must soldier on nonetheless. For William.

With a sigh, she set the notebook aside and raised her eyes to his sister-in-law to find, unnervingly enough, that she was staring at Effie. No smile graced Alexandra's lips when she caught Effie's eyes with her own—so like William's, but somehow colder despite the warm hazel—but neither did she look away.

Effie swiftly dropped her eyes to young William, who had woken and was cooing on his mother's lap.

"He's a handsome boy," Effie observed. "William was so pleased for the namesake, and I cannot imagine a more darling one."

She looked up just in time to see a softening in Alexandra's face. Apparently, complimenting the baby was the right choice.

"He was my biggest baby, too," Alexandra offered in lieu of a peace talk. "You can see how big and fine he is. He looks like Perry, you know, except his eyes, which are, of course, Harriot Hazel."

The baby's eyes were milky blue, but Effie didn't contradict her.

"What were you writing down?" Alexandra asked.

Effie examined Alexandra's face—and grinned. She couldn't help it. She'd broken through. That was the first time Alexandra had asked her a question ... ever. "I'm supposed to be writing down ideas for my next novel. Unfortunately, these"—she gestured at the notebook—"won't do."

"Why not?" Alexandra's keen eyes flashed over her form. "Aren't they quality ideas?" Her tone indicated that it was probably a very simple matter to come up with "quality ideas" and the fact that Effie hadn't indicated a major flaw in her character.

Effie took a deep breath and let it out shortly, refusing to allow her sister-in-law (who she wasn't even sure she liked) to cause her immeasurable anxiety. Even though that was a very real possibility. "No, but my character idea is a married woman."

"And?"

"I write romances." Sensible romances, but romances nonetheless. "I don't want to write about infidelity or unhappiness—I'd rather write a husband and wife who get along well." The type with the marriage she aspired to have; the type with the marriage she hoped she *did* have.

Alexandra didn't frown—she was too much of a lady for that—but her eyes darkened.

"Personally, I have never enjoyed romances. Too silly. I'd rather read a book that gets right to the point of the matter and stays there."

"I write books that are sensible, but I'd rather not—"

"Romances cannot be 'sensible,'" Alexandra proclaimed airily. "Far better to write about a married woman. Someone staid, unaffected by the nonsense of young love. You should write that book."

"Lady Dalbury," Effie said, fighting to keep her voice calm, "it's honestly none of your business what I write. I doubt you could understand the feelings William and I have for each other—or the kind of books I write—and I don't need your input. In the time since we've known each other, you've never read one of my books; why would you feel qualified to tell me what I *have* written and what I *should* write in the future?"

Alexandra stared at her a moment, then nodded and turned her eyes deliberately to the window.

Effie mirrored her on the other side of the carriage.

The rest of the trip was performed in silence.

Tollemache House was a lovely estate, Effie suspected, but at this current moment, it was drenched in rain and surrounded by swirling mist. If it wasn't a uniformly built, red-brick Elizabethan manor rather than a massive stone castle with many towers, it would be a fitting setting for a Gothic romance.

Surely this was the perfect place for Effie to write her next novel—practical and charming but with a mystical element.

She was relieved to escape the tight confines of the carriage and be escorted to a daintily decorated room at the top of the stairs where she was able to settle. It had three windows which looked out onto the front of the house with its rain-muddied lawn surrounding a large marble statue of what looked to be a man being consumed by fire.

How comforting.

It was late in the evening, and Effie heard the baby fussing as she worked with a polite but efficient maid to unpack her few belongings. She suspected the countess's chambers were across the hall from hers. The baby had quieted by the time a tray with tea and biscuits was brought. She dismissed the maid and changed into her nightclothes after a slight struggle due to the fact that she'd become accustomed to William helping her undo buttons.

Exhausted, she fell asleep although it couldn't be any later than eight or so. The tossing and turning over the unfamiliar bed that failed to contain her very warm, very comforting husband was minimal.

She woke refreshed and had breakfast in bed at an early hour, as she preferred, despite never requesting it. The servants of Tollemache House were certainly efficient.

Probably terrified of their mistress.

But she shouldn't think such uncharitable thoughts.

Once Effie had finished a rousing breakfast of everything the kitchen had to offer, she went to the escritoire in front of one of the windows and set out a pen and inkwell and several sheets of paper.

And then she sat.

And drummed her fingers against the oak wood of the desk.

And sat.

And rubbed her forehead.

And sat.

This is getting me nowhere.

Outside, rain steadily dripped on the already sodden landscape, the puddles in the grassy courtyard becoming small lakes and then larger lakes. It was a good thing they had arrived yesterday, as the drive leading up to the house must be impassible now.

At last, she rose and rolled her shoulders. She started toward the door, then paused. Other than Alexandra—who was clearly attempting to influence Effie's writing, something she was determined not to let happen—there was no one here to speak with.

No one here to share ridiculous ideas with her—or tell her she could accomplish anything she set her mind to.

Perhaps even speaking to Alexandra would be better than being alone with her thoughts.

Especially since right now, her thoughts were saying things like "You're a failure" and "You can't write another novel to save your life—or your family's livelihood." All lovely, positive thoughts.

Maybe she ought to reach out to Alexandra after all. Surely William wouldn't want her causing a rift with his older sister, even if she was, by his admission, difficult to get to know.

With a sigh, Effie slipped out into the corridor and into a gallery lined with portraits of past Dalburys. It looked down on the black-and-white checkerboard of the tiled entryway. Skirting around it, she stepped through what looked to be a private drawing room—though it was lined with books, so she supposed it might be an odd, open library—and came to a door that she believed must provide an entrance to the earl's and countess's chambers.

After a long hesitation as she stood before the massive oak door, she raised her hand and lightly rapped her knuckles against the intricately carved paneling.

Almost immediately, the door was opened by a maid, who slid her eyes over Effie as if she were not a member of the household, but a tradesman at the door. "Yes?"

"I wondered if I might speak to Lady Dalbury," Effie murmured with as much dignity as she could manage.

Another dismissive glance, but the woman stepped back. "You may wait in her antechamber."

Effie stepped forward into a room about the size of her own chambers that held a few chairs and a chaise lounge. She could feel Lord Dalbury's touch here—it was, after all, his home—in the massive amount of books that lined the "antechamber." She was surprised they didn't just give up the pretense and call it the library, though she knew there was at least one other room in the house bearing that name.

The maid slipped through a door opposite, and Effie heard quiet voices speaking before the maid reappeared.

"Lady Dalbury is unable to receive you today, milady." She bobbed a curtsy. "Lady Dalbury suggested I show you the library, or I can alert the rest of the staff if you have any needs."

Effie dropped her eyes. She was being dismissed. "No. No, that's all right. I'll just ... I'll manage." *Alone. Unwanted.*

Not even capable of writing the next great English novel.

The whirling winds and driving rain didn't wake Effie that night—it was instead a rap on the door.

Effie barely had time to sit up before the door was thrown open and her sister-in-law charged in. She stood, a lantern in her hand casting eerie shadows about the dark room, wearing nothing but a quilted, buttoned-up blue robe over her nightgown.

"Effie," Alexandra said with no further ado, "I need your help."

Effie blinked. "What time is it?"

"When I left my bedroom, it was 1:15 in the morning," Alexandra said. "It is perhaps now 1:19, as I spoke with the housekeeper briefly before coming to you."

"Oh." Effie slid her legs over the edge of the bed and caught up her own robe. "What can I do for you?"

"The estate has flooded." Alexandra sounded more irritated than horrified by this announcement. "As is often true, the downstairs, particularly the ballroom, is affected, but also, unfortunately, the servants' chambers. Further, when the river rises this high, it is inevitable that some of the tenants are at least damp if not in danger. Men will be sent out to help with them, and some may come here and sleep in the empty servants' quarters upstairs—or something."

"I see." Affecting a calm she didn't feel in response to Alexandra's mostly unruffled demeanor, Effie tied her sash securely about her somewhat nonexistent waist. "What may I do to help?"

"It is a fairly common situation, so all is under control, but I am afraid the baby will awaken and find himself alone and frightened. Perhaps you might listen for him?" There was a genuine reluctance in Alexandra's tone, as if she had not wanted to bother Effie at all but had felt herself forced to.

Despite that, Alexandra *had* asked. Hope bloomed in Effie's chest at the realization in defiance of her continued drowsiness. "I see. I would be happy to help with William—he is asleep in your chambers?"

"Yes. And he should sleep through this. It is only if he awakens that I fear I would not hear him, as I will likely be in the back gardens, and I cannot trust a staff member to linger close to the stairwell at all times, or upstairs, when they must all do their part to help."

"I see. Perhaps I could help in other ways, though? If all is needed is someone who is listening for any sound of the babe, I can be at hand in the great hall—to help guide people as they come and go—and still hear him. It is not much of a distance," she added, thinking that she had easily heard young William through several closed doors the night before.

Alexandra blinked then, as if she had not anticipated Effie's offer of help. Slowly, she nodded. "Yes, that would be acceptable."

"I'll dress and be at the bottom of the stairwell for instructions as soon as I can."

Alexandra whirled and left the room, taking the lantern and all traces of light with her. Effie hastily lit a candle and dressed, leaving her hair in a loose plait down her back.

In five minutes, she was scurrying down the grand curved stairwell, the carvings on the railings fearsome in the wavering light rising from the hall below. At the bottom, she met the housekeeper, Mrs. Emmerson.

"Lady Dalbury mentioned you might come down and help," the kindly elderly woman said with a smile. "She's gone to survey the damage in the ballroom—it seems we have puddles, though, and little else. Nothing like it used to be before they built up the embankment several years ago. But there will be tenants who are affected. Perhaps you might help see them settled, milady? I think Lady Dalbury would like to have a lady of the household representing her to anyone we must take in tonight."

Touched by being referred to as "a lady of the household," Effie nodded. "Of course. Where will we be directing them?"

Mrs. Emmerson succinctly explained the layout and a few other details, but in general, Effie simply needed to hand them off to a maid. Still, she understood the importance of such small gestures—greeting people at the door, telling them who to ask for anything they needed, making sure they knew where they were supposed to go and with whom they would talk.

The next hour passed in a blur, with no less than four families arriving at the door, cold and wet and bedraggled. The empty servants' quarters were prepared for any damp refugees that needed them. The currently empty nursery was also made use of, as were the extra guest chambers. Effie helped in any way she could; with all the staff skittering to and fro, she easily slid into the role of servant, when required, fetching linens and escorting folks to the upper levels.

Effie began to realize exactly why Charlotte didn't want to stay in the country with her sister. It was chaotic. A good chaotic, surely—the kind of chaotic bred from a family who took good care of those who depended on them—but still, not Charlotte's style.

The rain had stopped when Effie found herself stationed at the bottom of the stairs, now without a task. After asking for something to do—and being rejected no less than three times—and persisting—she was finally allowed to help carry fresh rags over to mop up the now dripping, muddy entryway.

Alexandra appeared, still with straight shoulders and a high chin. "I think that resolves everything, Mrs. Emmerson." She took a cloth from Effie, without asking, and wiped her hands. "At least for the night. We might all attempt to get a few more hours of sleep before dawn. If you could dismiss the staff and perhaps bring tea to my chambers, that would be appreciated. My sister-in-law will join me."

Stunned, especially as Effie had not been sure Alexandra even knew she was there, Effie just stood there with her lips slightly parted.

The squeal of an infant broke the silence, and Alexandra cast her eyes upward before turning and heading up the stairs.

A few steps in, she paused. "Effie?"

"Yes?"

"Are you coming or aren't you?"

Effie scurried after her sister-in-law, being led to a hidden door at the top of the stairs—separate from either of the guest chambers—that passed through a sterile, un-decorated bedchamber. The room contained a ridiculous amount of books, to the point that getting to the bed tucked in the corner was rather a moot point. It was further piled with books.

"Perry's room," Alexandra said with a toss of her hand. "I fully intend to have shelves built—or perhaps simply sort through the books and remove the less expensive vol-umes—but I haven't had a chance. We moved Theo into his own room on the second floor last winter, which moved all these books here. So now Perry doesn't really have a proper bedroom, as he should."

Effie rather doubted the earl had ever slept in his own bedchamber, but she didn't protest.

Another panel in the wall led them through a dressing room and into the countess's private bedroom. A large bed stood on a dais opposite from where the boudoir's entrance sat. Unlike much of the rest of the house, the room had been updated to a modern style. A balustrade separated the bed area from the rest of the simple, elegantly decorated, pastel room, which was remarkably free of books. Only a few scattered tomes rested on a side table or two.

Unlike the rest of the house, this room truly breathed "Alexandra Burton, Countess of Dalbury."

Alexandra went straight to her son and said a few calming words as she bent over him. Her expression softened, and Effie felt a need to step back as if she were an intruder to this private scene between a loving mother and her child.

"Mrs. Emmerson said you did well," Alexandra said, lifting her child from his lacy cradle. "She was effusive in her praise; she always is. Perry says it is not right to sack someone because they are heartfelt in their speech, especially if they are like an aunt to him. I suppose I agree." Her tone spoke more of resignation than agreement as she shifted young William to her shoulder and patted his back.

"That was kind of her," Effie said. She decided that she would ignore the fact that her sister-in-law had considered firing a clearly faithful employee because she was kind. It was best to keep the peace.

Alexandra carried her son to a chair in the corner and sat. "I imagine you did well enough" was her own "effusive" comment. She shifted William into the cradle of her arms, then froze, as if considering something. After a long moment in which Alexandra and Effie stared at each other—Effie wondered what on earth her sister-in-law was thinking—Alexandra spoke again. "You must remember that I nurse my own child, Effie. I know it's not stylish, but he is never far from me, and it has become convenient—even when at home and not traveling, as we were a few days since. I realize you may find it shocking, but it cannot be helped."

She cares about what I think about her? She feels I might judge her for something so basic, so human? "I don't find it shocking at all," Effie said firmly. "If I had a child, I would do the same."

Alexandra nodded and draped a blanket over her shoulder so she could nurse young William in some privacy, as she had in the carriage—that time without explanation.

Night was like that, Effie supposed as she sat on the chair opposite. It brought out confessions that daylight failed to, that perhaps would never be thought of at all during waking hours.

"You see, being a married woman needn't be unexciting," Alexandra commented. "There's always something to do to keep the household running. *My* household tends to flood." There was more humor in Alexandra's voice than Effie would have anticipated.

Effie laughed softly. "You're referring to our ... earlier conversation? About my next novel?"

"Of course."

"It wasn't because married women are unexciting that I didn't want to write about one—it's just that romance readers won't expect it."

Alexandra frowned. "I hate to see anyone limiting themselves in such a way. Especially a relation. You don't seem the type of woman to avoid risks—and why shouldn't you publish something where a married woman is treated like an actual human being and not just a prop of her husband's? Someone should. Besides, surely there's *passion* in marriage. Isn't that what romance readers want?" She scoffed. "That's what I've heard, at least. '*Alget qui non ardet.*' It's one of the Dalbury mottos—'He grows cold who does not burn.' I find it overly dramatic, but it's true of love."

Effie shrugged ... but in truth, Alexandra had a point.

Why was Effie so unwilling to rock the boat when she claimed that was the whole reason she wrote novels in the first place? To bring forth truths of life, provided by her Creator, and to exercise creativity in a way that might hope to inspire others?

Soon, the baby was asleep and in his cradle, and Mrs. Emmerson appeared with a tea tray, which Alexandra and Effie took at a table in the antechamber so as to not disturb young William.

"You'll stay with us, Mrs. Emmerson?" Alexandra suggested as the housekeeper turned toward the door. "Please, take tea. You must be as wrung out as we are."

The housekeeper nodded gratefully. "That I am, milady."

They sat around the table in comfortable silence, holding steaming cups of tea.

"You know, Mrs. Emmerson," Alexandra said, setting her teacup aside, "my sister-in-law is an author."

"I had heard something to that point, Lady Dalbury," Mrs. Emmerson said smoothly.

Wonderful. She's going to try to get the housekeeper on her side. Not that Effie was as disinclined to pursue her idea as she had been before, but still—she didn't need to be influenced by Alexandra any more than she needed to be influenced by the rest of the *ton*. Effie took a sip of her steaming beverage and prayed for patience.

"I read her book *Calliope* yesterday," Alexandra said off-handedly.

Effie nearly spat her tea out. Had she heard her sister-in-law correctly?

"Indeed, milady?"

"Oh yes. I realized on the carriage ride down that I had been remiss in not reading it. It's an excellent book, I think, though perhaps not to my taste. You would enjoy it; I'll loan you my copy."

And then, while Effie stared at her with presumably wide eyes and open mouth, Alexandra rose, walked across the room, withdrew a copy of Effie's first novel and handed it to the housekeeper.

"Thank you, milady," Mrs. Emmerson said. "I always enjoy a good story."

Effie's mind spun. *Why did she read it?* She supposed Alexandra's dedication to duty was just that strong, but she hadn't had to compliment the book. Alexandra was not the type to be, as she put it, "effusive" about something that she had not truly enjoyed.

After ten minutes or so, Mrs. Emmerson rose and left, and Alexandra, too, stood and directed her hazel gaze piercingly at Effie.

"I shall see you in the morning. We must give you a tour of the grounds, though they are sure to be soggy, and the ballroom is a lake—don't laugh; it's not funny. But you must see the house and gardens nonetheless. I don't like this time of year because all my flowers are dead, but at least the trees still have some of their leaves. Perry said it's a good time to write a novel, so you must write yours. Perry says I need to rest—this year has been straining or some such nonsense—but I disagree; I need something to do. I suppose fixing up the grounds—again—will suffice. At least the embankment has been raised, but Perry really needs to ask the property owners to the north about a dam ... or something to relocate the water so our tenants aren't flushed out of their homes like rats every winter and spring that it decides to rain more than normal. Why are you looking at me like that?"

"Why are you being nice to me?" Effie asked. It was the plainest way she could think to phrase the question, the one that felt least confrontational and most unavoidable.

Alexandra blinked. "Have I not always been nice to you?"

"I thought you hated me," Effie confessed. "Or at least, I thought I wasn't good enough for your family."

Alexandra's brow furrowed. "You're an earl's daughter."

"A disgraced earl's daughter. An impoverished earl's daughter. And I write."

The look on her sister-in-law's face was nothing short of comedic. "More women ought to write. You have a brain; you should use it. That's why I want you to write about this married woman. You're just right for William—and for the Harriots—but he didn't marry you to sit about and do nothing ... nor would you, I don't think. But William told me you tend to insert yourself into your novels. I thought, if you wrote about it, you might become accustomed to being a part of our family sooner. Was I wrong?"

Effie cocked her head. She had never thought of that before. "I suppose not."

"Then do it. I am rarely wrong," Alexandra added airily. She turned and walked behind the balustrade. In a softer voice, she called over her shoulder, "I shall see you in the morning, Effie. I don't sleep in late, even after a night like this."

"I don't either." Effie never had been able to sleep in, even when she had her Season and was out dancing—well, standing at the edge of a ballroom watching other people dance—all night.

"Excellent. I knew we should get along, if we only got to know each other."

And they did.

∞

The book was finished.

Last night, minutes before the clock struck midnight, an exhausted Effie had written The End in big swirling letters, set the papers aside, and collapsed onto bed.

This morning, she had risen early, washed the ink from her fingers as best she could, and put on her prettiest dress.

For William was coming today.

Oh yes, and the rest of the Harriot family in addition to the Burtons, to spend Christmastime at Tollemache House. But William was the most important.

It was just beginning to snow as she stood by the fountain, watching the carriages roll up the driveway and grow bigger and bigger until, at last, they stopped, William stepped out, and she was in his arms.

Of course, she had to draw away from him to greet Florie and the rest of the family, but he kept his hand at her waist. She understood. Though the time alone in the country had been conducive to finishing her book, she was not eager to part from her husband again any time soon.

"I heard the house flooded," Perry was saying. "I did hope those embankments would solve that problem ..."

"That's not terribly surprising, dear." Alexandra's voice held a heavy dose of *I told you so*. "We really must come up with a solution."

"Of course, of course. But at least it wasn't as bad as it has been in the past."

William pulled Effie to his side with the hand he'd retained. "Tell me about your novel," he said. "I must hear everything at once."

"I'll tell you while you settle in," Effie said, tugging him away from his family and into the house.

In her bedroom, she kissed him and fussed over him a little and then she sat down to tell him about her novel. It was the tale of a happily married woman dealing with some conflict largely involving her siblings. Of course, her husband was loving and supportive and aided her in philanthropic pursuits that helped the main character restore her relationship with her siblings ... all the while facing the scorn of society.

"Hmm." William tossed his jacket over the end of the bed and turned to her. "It's different, Effie—I'll give you that."

"But will it sell?"

"It might. It should. I know there are some people who will buy it just because you're the Duke of Ridgewell's sister-in-law ... and I know you can write anything in a way that captures the mind." He came across the room and kissed her cheek. "Either way, congratulations on finishing it. I know it meant a lot to you, and that's what matters, more than the book sales or anything else. I'm proud of you."

"Thank you, darling."

"I'm not surprised you decided to write about a married woman, honestly." William grinned. "You tend to write yourself into your novels."

Why does everyone keep saying that? She did have original thoughts—occasionally. "The character is inspired as much by Alexandra as myself," she admitted.

William winced. "That both amuses and terrifies me."

"Besides, the character can't be inspired by me," Effie said, reaching up to straighten William's cravat. She took a deep breath. "The woman in my story wasn't able to have children for a long time because of dramatic plot reasons. But I am already with child, and we've only been married a few months."

William stilled, then put his hands on her arms and held her back. "You're with child?"

"Yes, I am."

"Are you sure?"

"As sure as I can be."

"*Effie,*" William said emphatically and pulled her into a tight embrace. "I'm so glad."

"I am, too." It had been torture to keep from writing to him when she'd begun to suspect in the last two weeks, but it was worth it to tell him in person, to see his face. "I'm afraid I have to tell you Alexandra guessed, so she knew before you, but I didn't tell her."

William withdrew and rolled his eyes. "You cannot keep anything from Xannie, if she wants to know it. I don't blame you."

"But she was good to me." Effie hesitated. "Kind, even. I hope we can be good friends. If nothing else, she gave me the push I need to write a book for myself and for the Lord, not for money or fame or the good opinions of others."

He looked at her in wonderment for a moment, then smiled. "I suppose Perry is right; you never know what you're going to get with Alexandra."

"No," Effie said with a little shake of her head. "You certainly do not."

A Note from the Author

Hello, dear reader! Thank you for taking the time to explore the pages of my short story—and all of *Novelists in November*, for that matter!

I'd like to thank Katja H. Labonté, Cate VanNostrand, Abby Elissa Johansen, Analise M., Elisabeth Aimee Brown, Serenity Helzerman, and Cari L. for being my fearless alpha readers, as well as my wonderful critique woman, Kelsey Bryant, and my editors, Michaela Bush and Andrea Renee Cox. All of you have provided a valuable contribution to not only this story but to the entire *Novelists in November* collection, and I am beyond thankful!

I'd also like to thank Brett Harris, Kara Swanson-Matsumoto, and all the lovely people of the Author Conservatory who have delighted in these characters (Philip and William especially). Someday, I'll be publishing more in this universe—and I have all of them to thank for it!

And finally, thank you to our entire *Novelists in November* team (from the authors to our social media manager to our editor) for pulling this off!

On a historical note, Tollemache House (pronounced *toll-mash*) is inspired by a real house in England: Ham House. You can find pictures and floor plans online, but I did tweak several things about the layout. I only adjusted the layout as far as different set of residents (the Dalbury family) might have adjusted them, should they have been the owners!

I do not believe Ham House has ever flooded, and I am not sure *any* part of Surrey floods as badly as my fictional estate, but what can I say? I am an Oregonian. I am used to watching people try to build on swamps. I hope you will forgive me this creative liberty, too.

If you would like to get to know me better, consider visiting me over at and joining my email list. You'll receive a free novella—and membership into my exclusive friendship club. (Was that cheesy? I like to think so.)

TTFN!

~ Kellyn Roth

Finding Beauty in the Suffering

KATIE ZELIGER

Dedication

To the girl who feels far from grace, the one living with broken dreams and shattered memories: may you know peace and find beauty in the midst of your suffering.

Chapter One

"What do you mean I got *in*?" Rowena screeched at a pacing Laney.

"... so we just have to pack our bags, don't forget your travel pillow, it's a long flight." Laney continued talking over her, gesturing excitedly, but Rowena wasn't listening. "... and the meals are already taken care of. You're going to love it there! My time last year was absolutely life-changing!" Laney came to a stop in front of Rowena where she sat staring blankly out the frost-paned window.

Winter was coming early this year, frost coated the newly carved jack-o'-lanterns on their front stoop. Rowena fixed her eyes on hers, the too-big smile and crooked, down-turned eyes that caved in slightly giving the pumpkin an eerie face.

"Winnie, are you even listening to me?" Laney snapped a couple of times in front of Rowena's eyes.

"I didn't sign up for this; I'm not going." Rowena pushed up from the gold velvet armchair and strode across the living room to the large bookcase. She took her time selecting a book, fingertips brushing against the ragged cloth bindings. She skipped over her father's threadbare Bible as bile rose in her throat. Rowena grew up going with her mom and dad and two brothers to a little white church on a backcountry road, but she stopped the day her father died.

"I know, I know, I know." Laney covered the distance between them with a giddy gallop. "But you're, like, made for this program. The National Novel Writing Month retreat is in Germany this year and they already accepted you and"—she turned away, brushing her hair behind her ears—"I knew you wouldn't sign up yourself after what happened."

At that, Rowena blinked back the tears and wrenched a tattered, cloth-bound copy of *Frankenstein* from the shelf before stalking back to the armchair by the window. She read *Frankenstein* every year before Halloween. It was a tradition her father started when she was young. The old chair moved feebly under her forceful plop. Laney squatted next to her, but Rowena scooted the chair to face the window—away from Laney.

"I know it's only been a year since ..." Laney trailed off kindly. "But you're a great writer, Winnie. You can't stop doing what you love. Your dad wouldn't want you to give it up just because he isn't here anymore." Laney spoke softly from just behind Rowena's shoulder.

Rowena flinched at the mention of her dad. *Dad* had become a curse word in their home. When either her brothers or she spoke it aloud, whatever activity was going on would still and all gazes would drop to avoid making eye contact, as if saying his name would usher him back from the dead to yell at them for upsetting their mother. So *Dad* became something whispered under their breath to avoid an emotional reaction.

If they mentioned him at all anymore.

Rowena worried they were slowly forgetting him by sealing him in memory boxes and family picture albums. Her chest burned with the agony of tears unspilled, and she cleared her throat, turning the page to chapter one.

"Winnie, please. Come with me. You know what your dad would say, 'Don't let us hold you back, kiddo.'" Laney came around, pestering at Rowena's stonewall fortitude. "Please, please, please?"

Rowena blinked back the tears, looked up from the pages, and snorted when she took in Laney's puppy dog look. She begged, hands clasped together, big bottom lip out-turned for a full pout. "Quit that; you look pathetic."

"That's what I will be if my best friend ditches me last minute for the trip of a lifetime." Laney froze in her crouched position.

"What about work? I'm just supposed to call off for two weeks?" Rowena snapped the book closed and crossed her arms over her chest.

"I already talked to Mr. Yannecky for you, and your brother offered to pick all your shifts."

Mr. Yannecky owned the video store and arcade in town. It wasn't exactly the future Rowena imagined for herself after high school, but it turned out funerals were expensive and three kids on a single parent's income didn't exactly leave much room for a college education.

"You did *what*?" Rowena spat, causing Laney to wince from the bite her words left.

"I thought you would be happy ... I took care of everything for you. But I guess if you really don't want to go, I can cancel everything and see if maybe I can get a full refund. But I don't know ..." The line in Laney's forehead dipped as her gaze dropped to the floor.

Rowena felt the stirring of fresh emotion she desperately needed to avoid.

"All right, fine." Rowena rolled her eyes. "You don't have to be so dramatic. When do we leave?"

"Oh thank you, thank you, Winnie! I love you, you know that?!" Laney leaped up and hugged Rowena around the neck. "We leave November first, of course!"

Chapter Two

Two planes, a taxi, and twelve hours later, the girls stood with their luggage in tow in front of Château Chambéry. The squat beige taxi crunched down the circular gravel drive back toward the small town an hour outside the airport. Its taillights were the only glow in the dusky night. A brisk November wind howled through the trees and kicked up leaves in the taxi's wake, leaving scattered crimson foliage at Rowena's and Laney's feet.

Rowena couldn't admit her excitement or her nerves during the flight; instead, she drowned it out with loud music and scary movies, much to Laney's dismay. Laney, however, doodled and journaled the whole flight, growing bubblier and bubblier as they got closer.

But now, as Rowena peered up at the looming castle, she felt a sudden prick of panic run cold in her blood. What was she doing here? The whitewashed stone staircase before them led up to an expansive double-door entrance. Paned glass filled the doors, and on either side, ensconced lanterns held real candles burning in the evening dusk. The flames flickered with each new gust of wind.

"We're finally here; can you believe it?" Beside her, Laney let out a squeal, dropping her suitcase handle in exchange for Rowena's arm. She jumped and jostled Rowena in her excitement, but Rowena just glowered back.

One of the ornate glass-and-wooden doors gave a low groan as it opened, and a woman in a large black bird mask curtsied before them. She held out her brown peasant dress so it barely grazed the stone as she lowered herself. She rose and approached them silently to take their bags.

Laney shot Rowena a quizzical look, but she deadpanned, "All right, I'm out. I don't know where you brought me, but I ain't doing this." She pointed after the fowl-faced servant. Rowena dug her cell phone from her pants pocket and held it higher, looking for service.

"Come on, I'm sure it's nothing; let's just go in and find out what's going on." Laney beamed a hundred-kilowatt smile at her sour friend and tugged her by the arm up the grand steps.

When they hit the landing, the door opened again. This time, a woman with stark white hair coiffed in a regal style met them.

"I am the Atelier. I am your host for the workshop." She looked them up and down, taking in their yoga-pants-and-hoodie ensembles with a curling lip. "Welcome. I will show you to your room." She lightly touched a crystalline brooch that clasped a cape over her black fitted dress. She turned without holding the door open for them, and Laney lunged to grasp the handle before it closed.

The Atelier clicked down the hall on black pointed stilettos. The girls scurried to catch up, passing through the chestnut foyer, following her flowing black cape down the dimly lit hall.

"This will be your room," She stopped in front of an open door and gestured abruptly.

They paused to peer inside. Laney nudged around Rowena to step inside and twirled slowly, taking in the room. Vaulted ceilings boasted intricate paintings of cherubs and angels. Thick, woven curtains hung over floor-to-ceiling windows. Laney whispered her awe and flicked her saucer-shaped eyes to Rowena. Rowena tried not to bring her down at the moment but was genuinely concerned whether or not they had fallen down a rabbit hole just now.

The luggage sat neatly in the corner beside a crackling fireplace. As Laney approached her suitcase, a figure stepped into the center of the room. It was the bird-masked girl. Her dress blended into the curtain as seamlessly as camouflage. Laney sputtered with a start and leaped back from her luggage.

"If you need anything, my office is on the third floor," said the Atelier. "Do not disturb the artists in residence; they are in the midst of an immersive installment. Your unstructured writing session begins now, and lessons will commence tomorrow. The common areas have a strict quiet time curfew, and dinner will be in an hour in the ballroom." The Atelier looked Rowena over, then squinted at Laney. "Be respectful, and we won't have a problem."

With a curt nod to the lady in the mask, the Atelier preceded her from the room in choreographed silence.

"What about—" Laney began to ask after the Atelier, but she had already clicked down the hall and up the stairs. "Well, she doesn't seem very friendly."

Rowena had never heard Laney grumble before and stifled a chuckle. Laney laid her luggage down and pulled out her laptop case, a Bible, and a journal. Rowena squinted at her and decided it was just the jet lag talking. Laptop case under one arm, Laney paced around the room slowly, touching all the surfaces with her free hand. She stopped in front of a solid oak writing desk, lightly feeling the back of the leather chair.

"Do you mind if I write for a bit?" she asked Rowena, who nodded. "I think I need to do a little devotional and prayer time before I get started, you know." Laney gestured vaguely after the Atelier.

"Okay, I'm gonna go look around." When Laney got her Bible out, Rowena knew that was her cue to leave. If Laney noticed the tension that shifted in Rowena, she was at least kind enough not to point it out.

As Rowena crossed the room to the doorway, she thought about a time when she used to be as faithful as Laney was at doing devotions. Rowena hadn't done them in over a year. She couldn't bring herself to even look at a Bible anymore, let alone open one, despite having grown up in children's church, earning gold stars week after week for her Scripture memorization. The memory turned her stomach sour. *If God was so good, why did he take my dad away?*

"I'll be back before dinner ..." Rowena said from the doorway, shoving the thought down deep. "I mean, unless they plan on feeding us to the birds." She paused to turn and wink at a shocked Laney.

Laney laughed, and the tension Rowena felt between them melted away.

Rowena paced the herringbone hardwood floor down the white and gold–accented hallway back to the foyer. At the opposite end of the foyer was a ruby-red-carpeted staircase that split, circling up and up. She climbed carefully, noticing the traction had worn off her favorite Converse.

The second-floor balcony opened over the foyer with a majestic dangling chandelier above. Under the large glass windows behind her were wide panes where two marble busts sat flanked by golden candelabras.

She traced her finger along the engravings of each bust.

"Dr. Guillaume Moreau and his wife, Martine, still haunt the place," came an American accent from above. The first American accent she heard since arriving in Germany, actually—not counting Laney. She turned to see a man leaning on his arms at the railing a floor above. "Although, you hear more stories of his untimely demise, perhaps murder, they say."

"Who were they?" Rowena asked, looking upon the busts. Dr. Moreau had a shiny, bald head, lifeless eyes, and a bushy mustache. While he was carved looking straight on, Martine's bust had her chin inclined as though baring her neck or looking away. She had a short fringe carved above her brows, and the rest of her hair was pulled atop her head in delicate curls and twists.

"Dr. Moreau was a philanthropist, made his money being a part of the Mittelstand, but when he died, the money disappeared." He wiggled his dark eyebrows at her in a suggestive way. "Makes for great storytelling."

Rowena looked at the busts with new eyes, trying to see their history unfold. How did he die? Where did the money go? The thought of death lanced through her. She had heard her mother sobbing on the phone to her aunt late one night. *"I don't know how we're going to make ends meet on one salary ..."*

"Seems a little desperate to exploit someone's pain for the sake of a story," Rowena snapped, turning back to the railing, but the man was gone. She rolled her eyes in disdain. She ran a hand through her black hair, which she flung over her shoulders.

She continued down the hallway, touching the bone-and-gold-inlaid wainscoting as she went. Dotting the ceiling, chandeliers dripped with crystals, the light refracted from them painting the shadows in slashes of rainbows.

At the end of the hall, stately double doors were thrown open, and she caught a glimpse of a colorful tapestry and billowing sheer curtains letting the night air in. She peered in to find several masked people posing in a variation of frozen mannequin positions. She halted and swallowed a gulp of shock.

Less than a foot to her right was another peasant-dressed bird girl, this one wore a tight corset over fluffed linen skirts. Up close, Rowena could see the beak was papier-mâché; faint newspaper headlines stood out under the whitewashing. The beak jutted out of the center of the mask several inches before sloping down at a crooked angle. There were only slight cutouts for eyes under peaked brows. The mask was attached to a brilliant white-feather headdress that bobbed slightly by the wind from the fan overhead.

In front of each posed masked person was an easel and a sketching artist perched on a stool. Despite Rowena's interruption, they all sketched quietly. She tiptoed noiselessly behind each artist to garner a glimpse of their creations.

She loved visiting art museums. As a kid, her dad and she would be the last ones left in the gallery pondering brushstrokes, while her Mom and brothers sat outside the gift shop licking ice cream cones from a nearby cart. In this hushed reverence, she felt her heart ache for her dad. He would never savor a Monet again. She would never hear him compare Rembrandt to Vermeer and argue with her when she laughed. He loved Vermeer's painting *Girl with a Pearl Earring*.

"My Pearl," he would call her, and she would dismiss it because she didn't have the blonde hair like the girl in the painting. *"My Black Pearl,"* he would rephrase, curling a finger through her silky, raven hair. Tears tugged at the corners of her eyes at the memory as she reached up to twirl a strand of hair.

"Don't move." A sharp ripping sound filled the otherwise stagnant air, followed by a crumple and light tsk-tsk of paper skidding across the hardwood. She was so caught in the moment, she didn't hear where the voice came from. Afraid the Atelier caught her disturbing the artists, she ducked her head and swiveled.

"No, no, not like that." She caught the gaze of an older artist with a cream apron tied across his waist. He looked at her above his easel, thin-rimmed glasses perched precariously at the tip of his nose. "Do not move," he emphasized carefully with a thick French accent. "Your pain is visceral; I must capture it." His eyes darted between her and the canvas as he wildly moved his charcoal-laced hand across it, capturing her figure.

She had never been drawn before. She became very aware of her hands, empty and frozen in mid-air. Where was she to put them? She slid them slowly to her sides and tried to relax her fingertips by feeling the starch in her denim. Her face pinched tight with emotion, and she panicked, realizing it was on display for a room of creatives to see. She wiped at her eyes and straightened her shoulders.

"No! No! No!" The artist tore another sheet from his canvas. He leaped to his feet. His eyes were a wildfire threatening to consume her if she moved again.

Her pain was not for entertainment.

Rowena shoved her hand out with a growl, *stop*, and muttered, "I didn't sign up for this," before bolting toward the hall. She narrowly missed colliding with the Atelier, who couldn't open her mouth fast enough to scold Rowena before she was turning another corner and climbing higher, to the third floor.

She huffed as her shoes slid a bit on the carpeted stairs. The third-floor landing was a stark contrast to the second-floor's wide-open, light-filled space. A long, dark hallway intersected the landing. Grand bay windows jutted from the space, flanked by built-in bookshelves. The wooden frame had ornate carvings that she longed to touch. In front of the large windows were plush Victorian armchairs; they touched back-to-back, facing the bookshelves nearest them and it felt like a place she could find solace. She sighed.

She ran her fingers along the edge of the old tomes but didn't recognize any of the names. Most were in German, some Italian and French, but only a few in English. She flopped down on the chair and let out a guttural groan. She didn't want to be here. She should be at home with her mom and brothers. It was too soon for her to be away from home. She shoved her hands under her armpits and leaned her forehead down to her knees.

"Pull yourself together, Winnie," she whispered to herself between jagged breaths. "Why can't I seem to escape death?"

A throat cleared and made her jump.

She pinched the tears from her eyes and turned on the armchair to look over the side, and came face-to-face with the American man from earlier, who now sat on the chair behind her.

He leaned on one arm, book folded open on his lap. His gaze raked over her in a calculating manner. "Shouldn't you be writing?"

She took in his face, dark hair swept back to reveal his broad brow and ink-drop eyes. He didn't look much older than her. Maybe mid- to late-twenties. The candle on the windowsill flickered, and she caught sight of the reflection in his eyes. She grimaced, he was *too* good-looking. That meant he was either a jerk who knew it or a wounded bad boy who needed the approval of others—neither of which Rowena had the capacity for.

Her eyes trailed down to the book that teetered on his lazily crossed knee. The cover was folded back around, and there were words written in the margins with various arrows and underlines to indicate the reference.

She cringed. "Shouldn't you take better care of books? Ever heard of spine training?" She turned back on her chair. She cursed herself and her display of emotions today. She had made it all year without anyone so much as hearing her cry, and now today alone, twice she had been caught in the throes of grief. The embarrassment and self-loathing flashed heat across her fair skin.

She tucked the pain deep down in the locked part of her heart and swore to stop feeling, to stop being so weak and pathetic. She exhaled, although it sounded more like a dragon's breath, and she imagined her anger was fire flowing from her nostrils.

"My, my. 'Pull yourself together, Winnie,'" the man said patronizingly before lifting the book from his knee and picking up where he left off.

Red-hot shame flared through her, and she pushed off the chair with great force. "What would you know about grief anyways?" Mustering all the courage she had left, she lifted her head high and padded back to the room with Laney.

"Successful expedition?" Laney asked without looking up from her journal.

"Far from it. This place is weird, and the people are awful." Rowena threw herself face-first on the double bed.

"Maybe you just need to sleep on it, although ..." Laney looked over at her, proceeding carefully, "I bet some time with God would help a lot."

Rowena groaned her disapproval into the covers.

"I'm not going to nag, but I'm just saying ... I haven't seen you spend time with God lately, and I think it would help. I had a great prayer time while you were gone, and I really feel like God opened this door for us for a reason, like we're supposed to be here. You know?"

The question fell on the room like a blanket. Rowena hadn't talked to God since her dad died. The family missed the first two Sundays after his death, and while her mom and brothers eventually went back, she stopped going altogether. It just wasn't for her.

"You know I don't believe in that stuff anymore," Rowena murmured. She didn't want to fight, but she didn't want Laney to make this whole trip some revival reunion either.

"Okay, I'll drop it—for now. Let's go get dinner." Laney closed her journal and strode to where Rowena lay like a rag doll. She hauled her up and looped an arm around hers to pull her out the door.

Chapter Three

B AM.

BAM. BAM.

"What is that?" Laney cried from where she was curled up on the other double bed.

Rowena rolled up on one elbow to turn the bedside table lamp on. "What time is it?" She looked at her phone.

2:14 a.m.

BAM. BAM. BAM.

It sounded like a battering ram crashing into the front doors.

"I don't know, I'll go look," Rowena mumbled, sliding from under the covers and stuffing her feet in her shoes. She grabbed the black hoodie she wore on the plane from the top of her bag and pulled it over her head, then fluffed her long hair out from under it.

"Take a flashlight!" Laney whispered.

"I don't have one; do you?"

"Oh ... no." She shrank back, pulling the covers into fists under her chin. "Don't die!"

"Gee thanks," Rowena said, swiping her cell phone from the charger and turning on the flashlight.

Rowena pulled the door open ever so slightly to peer down the hall. After dinner in the ballroom, they had met a few of the other writers here for the NaNoWriMo Retreat. A few of them popped their heads out of the bedroom doorways that lined the hall.

The banging continued, echoing through the lofty château. It was coming from outside. Following the hollow thudding noise, she stepped through the foyer and out the main entrance, then across the grand stairs. She peered over the wrought iron railing and could see a faint fire flickering around the side of the château.

She was about to go back inside to bed, having figured a guest was rudely keeping them awake, when a warmth filled the night air around her. She looked over her shoulder to find the too-beautiful man. He had silently closed the distance between the château's threshold and her.

"Shall we investigate?" He threaded his fingers through his hair to sweep it back before slipping down the steps.

Rowena groaned and glared after him, debating if she could return to her slumber having never known the culprit of the sound. Knowing her active imagination, she decided she *definitely could not* and trekked haltingly down the stairs. The nip in the air tightened her joints, and she rocked slowly down the steps, giving her bones time to wake.

Mr. Beautiful was a few strides ahead of her and snaked around the château's grounds, clinging to the shadows. The thuds continued rhythmically, once, twice, thrice, and again. When he reached the corner, he turned back holding a finger to his lips, and she drew close to peer over his shoulder. There, under the starlit sky were the artists in their masks sitting on couches and armchairs with floor lamps lit around a blistering fire.

Rowena scoffed at the ridiculous setup, a living room outdoors. It must have been moved after everyone went to sleep; the chairs she spied by the fire were the same ones she had seen scattered throughout the château in her earlier exploration.

The masked men and women spoke lowly from their cushy seats. If she hadn't known any better, she would have mistaken a subtle laugh for the fire crackling and a scorned remark for an owl's calling to the night. But here, she was close enough to make out the syllables and consonants from the blur of hushed tones. It wasn't all English, but it was its own lullaby of sorts, animated and hypnotizing. It was the first time she heard the masked people speak. They had all been stoic throughout the day, aside from the one artist who yelled at her. She wondered what their immersive installment had been about.

The man in front of her looked over his shoulder with a bewildered grin. He was apparently wondering the same thing.

She ignored his gaze and scanned the grassy hillside to find the source of the perpetual noise pollution. On the hilltop were two figures silhouetted in the moonlight, one with a gun blasting up at an angle.

BAM.

BAM. BAM.

"What the heck are they doing?"

He followed her line of sight to the hill and laughed. He stood up straight and trailed back toward the entrance.

"Excuse me, where are you going?" She followed him, reaching for his shoulder.

He turned and cleared his throat. "Let me see if I can get this straight." He wiggled his Adam's apple with his right hand and feigned a girlish pitch. "Ever heard of skeet shooting?"

He was mocking her.

She licked her lips with one eyebrow cocked high. "All right, I'll give you that; that was pretty good." She laughed and peeked over her shoulder to look back at the hill. "So skeet shooting, huh? I thought that was, like, a British-daylight thing, not a German-middle-of-the-night thing."

When she glanced back, he was already gone. Only a faint "Mm-hm" on the wind came as his response. She peered ahead and caught the entrance doors slowly shutter to a close. A pit of aggravation opened in her gut, and she cursed the well of feelings bubbling up inside of her.

Rowena turned back to watch the artists. Some danced by the fire, while others blew out smoke and looked up at the stars. They had a freedom about them; they expressed themselves so openly, it seemed. A twinge of jealousy hit her as she watched. *What must that be like, to feel without worrying that something bad would happen?*

Chapter Four

The ballroom was alive with fresh morning chatter as Rowena followed Laney through the breakfast buffet line. She pushed up her sleeves and reached for yogurt and muesli. Rowena had donned her usual attire, black skinny jeans, a chunky cable knit sweater, and Dr. Martens. Her long braid dangled over her shoulder as she stooped to reach for the clear glass milk jug.

"Winnie, look at all these people! Do you think they're all writers?" Laney held her tray of toast and jam close to her ribs as her eyes glistened like baubles taking in the room.

Rowena managed a half-hearted "Mm-hm" in reply.

"I don't see any masks today, though, do you? Ooh, look, it's the Atelier!"

Rowena followed her pointing finger across the room to see the château's host in her signature black cape flitting about the room.

"Do you think that's her real name? What is 'Atelier,' even? Is that French? Why is everything here inspired by the French if we're in Germany? I haven't even seen a beer or bratwurst yet." If Laney kept going at this speed, Rowena would sign up to be the clay pigeon in the next round of night skeet.

They found two open spots next to an aged woman with bright-pink hair and bangs that stuck straight out from her forehead. She had some faded tattoos along her hairline and a smattering of face piercings that drew Rowena's attention.

Across from the woman was a tall, thin Latin man. He wrinkled his nose frequently to balance the thick white frames on his face.

Neither seemed interested in morning chatter, although that didn't tamper Laney's extroverted morning steam.

As the breakfast clamor dwindled, the Atelier stood at the head of the room and clinked a glass with a tiny fork. The tinny clang reverberated through the room, catching everyone's eye. "May I have your attention, please? It is with sincere delight that I welcome this year's National Novel Writing Month writers to our third annual retreat!"

A light applause filled the room.

"Today, you embark on a journey with a feverish bunch of miscreants. As Oscar Wilde said, 'A writer is someone who has taught his mind to misbehave.' You will have two weeks here in Château Chambéry to find the strength to unleash that which you hold so tightly, pack so neatly, and trifle with so tenderly. It will be torture. It will be agony. And it will evoke such freedom, you'll never want to do anything else." The Atelier paused to survey the room.

The audience hinged on bated breath.

Rowena cringed inwardly at the idea of upending her proverbial mixed bag of emotions.

"Our resident artists will roam the halls and the château's grounds freely for a few days more; thank you for allowing them the respect and space their immersive installment demanded of them." She set the glass and fork down to clasp her hands, signaling she was almost done. "A couple of housekeeping rules: don't bother the ghosts, and they won't bother you."

At that, Laney's elbow shot right into Rowena's ribs.

Rowena didn't hear the rest of the Atelier's closing statements, she replayed what Mr. Beautiful had said upstairs about the ghosts. Chairs scraped back from the table around her as she nursed her bruised ribs. She gave Laney the side-eye and followed the crowd toward the garbage.

Laney was at her side already. "Did you hear what she said about ghosts? Huh-uh! I don't do ghosts. You know I can't do that. We have to go back to the room and pray right now." She started tugging at Rowena. "Winnie, come on, please."

"Laney, chill. They're not gonna hurt us, and besides, they're probably not real, just another tourist trap or lore to stimulate writing prompts." After dumping her barely touched breakfast, she turned back to Laney. "Did you hear what she said about our lessons? I thought there was some sort of structure for the retreat."

"Yeah," Laney said with a dismissal wave, her mind clearly still on floating ethereal entities.

"Well?" Rowena crossed her arms over her sweater and waited.

"I guess we have a class on the third floor after breakfast?"

Rowena spun her friend around and marched her back to the bedroom. While Rowena gathered her books and pens, Laney quickly prayed around the room, anointing the windows and doors to ward against evil ghouls.

"I don't think they care that you're here. I'm sure they've got bigger fish to fry. You know, like 'unfinished business' or whatever." Rowena offered, trying to de-escalate her friend's building fear, but Laney didn't slow and continued praying quickly and quietly to herself.

Twenty minutes later, they hiked up to the third floor, following the flow of others to the first door on the left. Rowena hadn't made it farther than the landing of the third floor yesterday, but this unique and stunning room was just around the corner. The room was wrapped with polished chestnut wainscoting and painted crimson between exquisite leather and gold–flecked wallpaper. A small sign near the entrance warned guests not to touch the rare wall decorations or their oily hands would ruin it. Rowena smirked at the printer paper poster and wondered if it really worked to dissuade guests.

Laney skipped into the room and trotted ahead to sit with the writers they met over breakfast. She had managed to coax a name out of the pink-haired woman, Sonnet Walker, and now Laney waved Rowena over, but she shrugged and shook her head. *Not this time.* If Rowena was going to participate—be forced to feel—she was going to do it on her terms. She continued walking the room's perimeter slowly, taking it in from every vantage point.

A low-slung velvet couch sat beneath an oil painting that took up the entire eastern wall. It was a scene of hunters chasing galloping hound dogs through an autumnal won-derland. In front of the couch was a cowhide coffee table littered with ceramic coasters and forgotten teas. The room was staged with various seating areas placed in prearranged groups. Rowena took a seat near a smattering of brightly cushioned, velvet-backed chairs and dropped her bag at the corner of a low table beside it. She pulled out her notebook and pen case, then positioned them haphazardly on the table before her.

"You are here for a reason," a voice full of authority boomed, and Rowena shifted on her seat to see where it was coming from. The door to the classroom slammed shut, rattling the paintings on the wall.

"And while I don't care what that reason is—it's between you and whatever muse you choose …"

She turned again, and over her shoulder, Rowena saw Mr. Beautiful cross the room in strides. He briskly deposited his laptop bag on the writing desk in the corner before doing an about-turn, commanding the attention of the room with his swift movements and piercing gaze.

His drawn-out pause quieted the room as he searched the students' faces. He slowly rolled up the sleeves of his pressed button-down shirt, revealing cords of muscles. Rowena's eyes flickered away to the windows in annoyance. *This showboat is the writing instructor? Great.*

He continued once both sleeves were rolled tightly just below his elbows and he patted at his buttoned vest. "I do care what you do with the imponderable gift of creativity that lies within you. You will not squander talent, at least not on my watch." He cocked his wrist, facing his watch toward him now, to take in the time. "Speaking of which, it's time to begin. Everyone take your seat."

The sound of shuffling feet and bags thudding to the ground reminded Rowena of her recent attempt at collegiate scholastics. Before her dad died, he was a professor at the school she attended. She made it six weeks into the new semester before being there without him became too much. She didn't so much "drop out" as "drop off." When she stopped going to class or showing up to exams, they marked her out.

The memory soured in her mouth and distracted Rowena long enough not to notice Mr. I-Know-I'm-Gorgeous standing in front of her, waving a pile of printed papers.

"Already communing with your muse, I see." He snapped his fingers, drawing her gaze back to him. "That's great, but there will be time for that later. Pass these out to everyone."

Rowena didn't move, just slid her gaze up to meet his. His eyes swirled with mischief, and his dark hair dangled into them. Daring him to challenge her, she regarded him a moment longer. But he didn't bite; instead, he smirked and set the papers down on the table in front of her and resumed his spotlight.

Rolling her eyes, she rose from the chair and passed out the papers. It allowed her to look over the paper. It looked like any regular syllabus: paragraphs of insights and objectives dotted the page with motivationally colored language, followed by bullet point assignments and bold-print deadlines.

Her eyes flicked between the pages and the classmates she handed them to when she saw what she'd been looking for, his name. "...Mr. Edward Clancy Broussard, a two-time *New York Times* bestseller and award-winning novelist, with one novel optioned to become a major motion picture..." His bio read like a dating app, and if she hadn't had other interactions with him, she might have mooned over him like the rest of the class was doing.

She finished passing out the papers and returned to her seat.

"Your first assignment"—Mr. Broussard cleared his throat as he leaned back on the desk—"is to write about your life through important textures. Pick three moments from your life and hone in on the texture in the memory. This is about feeling, not the sentiments but tangible things, visceral reactions. No word limit. You have ten minutes and then we'll share. Go."

Rowena stared at the blank page of her notebook before her. Texture. She could do this. At least it wasn't a writing assignment about *feelings*. No, this was the opposite of feelings. Perfect. Her pen hovered over the page. She waited for the spark of creativity in her brain to set off the chain reaction that led to writing. Texture. Blue. Blue jeans. Denim jacket. She started writing, and an image came to mind. Her favorite photo of her dad was of him holding her as a baby, and he was in a denim—

No, no. Try again.

She took a deep breath and scratched out what she wrote. A beautiful tapestry came to mind, intricate woven designs in red, fuchsia, and sunset orange. She could see herself reaching out to touch the fabric at the museum, and over her shoulder, she smiled at her—

Rowena's eyes shot open. *No, no. No.*

Think about the least Dad-esque thing ever, she challenged herself.

"Time's up," Mr. Broussard crowed from the back of the room, where he was walking circles around the various groupings of writers. "Let's have a couple people read theirs out. Be sure to listen for the visceral connection of feeling." His gaze swept around the room before landing on Rowena.

As though in a daze, one more image flitted into her mind as she stared abjectly. Brown, rugged, handmade paper, cut in small slips, rolled, and filled. Cold metal pressed into her palm, a heavy flick of the lid, and fire lit the dark. She inhaled, it was the first time she'd ever run away from home, the first time she figured out how to numb her emotions. It was the night he di—

"No." She hadn't realized she'd said it aloud or pushed the table away from her until all the eyes in the room landed on her. She panicked and shoved her notebook into her bag.

"Winnie ..." the soft voice of Laney found her in the disquieted room.

Embarrassment rouged her cheeks, and she fled from the room, unwilling to hear whatever snarky thing Mr. Broussard may have to say.

Outside, she looked for the safest place to hide. Down the hall, past the landing, was another set of double doors. She stopped to peer through to an empty balcony. She pushed through the doors just as it began raining. *Great.* She thought about returning to her room but thought better of it. There was a small roofed alcove she could tuck into. Besides, no one would try to enjoy the balcony in the cold November rain.

She stuffed herself in the stone alcove and slid her back down the wall until she sat with knees crunched to her face. Squeezing her eyes, she tried to shut out the images, but they wouldn't relent. Her dad's denim jacket, the museum tapestry her dad and she loved, the joint she rolled to forget him. The tears started coming now. The looming cloud of loneliness and grief found her at last.

What kind of daughter was she? How could she be so heartless? She had balled up every memory of her dad and treated it like garbage, shoving it in a dark place to be forgotten. The cries turned to sobs and she burrowed deep under her arms. Thunder rolled and cracked above the château, and she was glad to know the sky was crying with her.

A barrage of photos flashed to mind, a mix of images of her mom and dad, and ones with her brothers and dad. It hit her then; she had been so engulfed in her own grief that she couldn't see theirs. She forgot he was *their* dad, too, her mom's husband. She allowed her pain to eclipse any sense of logic or love. She had holed up in her mind, thinking she was keeping everyone safe this way, but really, she was keeping everyone out.

She thought of the strange artists dancing and laughing by the firelight last night. She'd never seen anyone move with such freedom, and she wished she had what they had: the ability to feel.

Rowena let all the tears fall. Every thought she had of anger, sadness, hurt, or anxiety came tumbling out in soft waves of sobs. She cried until her gut hurt and she could no longer hold herself up. She lay down in a fetal position, allowing her cheek to flatten against the grooved balcony flooring. She waited out the rain, crying harder while the thunder obscured her tears.

When the rain stopped, she didn't know how much time had passed. Maybe minutes, maybe an hour? She pushed up to sitting and wiped her face before looking around. The afternoon sky was gray, and it was freezing. She had lost all feeling in her fingers and toes. Her core vibrated gently in chills.

How had it taken me flying to Germany to get all this out?

Her gaze dropped down to the bag she kept her notebook in. A small gold cross keychain was stuck on the outside; a baptism gift her dad got her when she was twelve.

Even though she couldn't talk to God after Dad died, she couldn't bring herself to remove it. She was afraid her dad would see or that God would and then punish her dad for it. Silly, she knew.

The balcony door creaked open then, and Rowena caught her breath and held it.

"Winnie?" came a familiar whisper.

She exhaled and peeked around the corner. It was Laney with a worried look on her face. As soon as she saw Rowena, she ran to her and embraced her. "Mr. Broussard sent me to look for you, we're on a break, but—" Laney got a good look at Rowena then and saw the tears and shivering. "What are you doing out here? You're gonna catch a cold! We have to get you inside."

Rowena tried to emote, but her face was either too swollen from crying or too frozen from the cold to laugh. "Not yet. Just wait a moment with me, will you?"

Laney opened her mouth to say something but closed it, looking closely at Rowena.

"I've not been a good friend," Rowena started.

"No, Winnie, I—"

"Let me finish. I have to get this off my chest." A solitary tear trickled down her cheek. "I have been awful to you. I've been angry ever since my dad died. I hate that he's gone, and I hate that God took him away. But it's not fair for me to push everyone away. It's not right for me to act this way, especially how I've been treating you. I'm so sorry. And I know I don't deserve it, but I need a favor." At that, Rowena paused to look up at Laney.

Laney had tears in her eyes, too, and she sank to her knees to be at eye level. "Anything."

"Will you pray with me? I don't know what to say, but I know I need to talk to God. I just need help doing it. Can you say the words for me?"

Tears rolled down Laney's cheeks as quickly as they slipped down Rowena's. "Of course." Laney scooted close to her best friend and took her hand.

"Dear Jesus, help me pray for my friend." She took a deep breath before continuing, "Jesus we repent for pushing You away in our darkest hour of need; we repent for not allowing Your light in when we needed it the most. We are so sorry for the way we've been acting out in grief and anger, and we ask for Your forgiveness. I pray for Winnie and ask that You help her heart to heal. Help her feel *all the feels* and know that it's okay not to be okay. Thank You, Jesus, that You are a Man much acquainted with grief and sorrow. Thank You for not shaming us for having messy feelings. Please help us walk through this pain together with You. I pray You would give her a sign that You are with her, that she could sense Your presence around her. Please shield us from evil that would try to take advantage of us when we are vulnerable. Protect Winnie's heart and mind and give her Your peace. In Jesus's name, I pray, amen."

Rowena took a deep breath and opened her eyes. It was like whatever was dimming or clouding her vision before had rolled off and everything was brighter now. The anxiety that sat on her chest all day every day lifted, and she took her first unencumbered breath.

"How do you feel?" Laney asked, carefully eyeing her friend.

"Better." And when Rowena smiled, it was genuine.

Laney threw her arms around her and pulled her in close.

A throat cleared behind them. "Hate to break up this very meaningful and emotionally charged moment, but class resumed and we're waiting for you." Mr. Broussard pushed off the wall he was leaning on, leaving Rowena to wonder how much he heard. He stood there a moment while Laney helped Rowena up.

"I'd like a word with you, Rowena." Mr. Broussard crossed his arms, sending a shiver down Rowena's spine.

In trouble already? She dusted herself off as she got to her feet.

Laney shot her a furtive glance before disappearing through the double doors.

"I remember what it was like being a teenager," he began, scrutinizing Rowena. "It's hard, especially being in a different place—"

"That's what you think this is about?" Rowena scoffed, but it was less potent than before, dampened by her emotional exhaustion. She stepped around him to head inside.

"What is it, then?" He grabbed her arm, his fingertips a feather-light pressure.

"Why should I tell you? I don't owe you an explanation." She shook off his arm and sulked back to class.

Chapter Five

Inside the classroom, Mr. Vain-and-Arrogant continued with lessons two and three, conflict and conflict resolution in stories. They made Rowena wary not just because Laney pinched her leg, pointing out Rowena was the class act for them, but because of the palpable tension in the room. It seemed that Rowena wasn't the only one carrying a burden.

After a short bathroom break, the writers returned for the last session before dinner. The room swelled with emotion like a balloon about to pop.

"Today's final lesson is on healing." Mr. Broussard pulled a chair to the front of the room and sat on it, then leaned forward, forearms on his knees.

Rowena whipped her gaze to Laney, who shared with her a nervous smile to soften the blow.

"Every so often, a writer finds themselves in the conundrum of wanting to write about what they're going through but not wanting to bleed on the reader." He leaned back on the seat, interlocking his fingers across his vest. "Perhaps you've read an author's story and came away scarred or read an eyewitness account and walked away carrying the victim's wounded worldview. We've all come across it at one time or another. And here's the thing. As writers, it is our job to tell the story. But it is not our job to wound the reader."

A raised hand got the instructor's attention, and he gestured openly to the person.

"How do we do that, then? If writing is most accurate as close to the event as possible, how can we both wait to heal and write accurately?"

"Editing. Revisions. The process of writing is as much putting pen to page as it is erasing and rewriting." Mr. Broussard leaned forward again, scanning the room. "You have to heal. You can't write unhealed words, or you will bleed on your reader and wound them. You will break their trust." His eyes landed on Rowena for a beat before continuing around the room.

"New assignment." He stood and stretched out his legs. "Write an allegory for grief: one thousand words, fictional, due tomorrow. Class dismissed."

"How on earth am I supposed to heal *and* write an allegory on grief by tomorrow?" Rowena groaned into her pillow. She was sprawled over the top of the quilted bed in Laney's and her room that evening after dinner.

"You heard what he said about editing. I don't think he expects anyone to heal overnight. Maybe he just wants us to be aware of it?" Laney twisted from the desk, where she was already diligently typing away, to face Rowena.

"Yeah, maybe." Rowena lifted her head up to look at Laney. "What are you writing about?"

"My mother always used to say, 'No use crying over spilled milk,' and I think there might be something to that." Laney twisted back around to type a few lines before glancing over her shoulder. "Winnie? Love you, mean it, but if you're just gonna sulk, can you do it somewhere else? Pretty please?" She stuck out her bottom lip and trained those doe eyes on Rowena.

"Yeah sure. I'll be back before bed." Rowena grabbed her notebook and pen from the desk, and Laney snaked out a hand to catch her before she left.

She pulled her into a hug. "You can do this, Winnie. You made a huge leap toward healing today; don't stop now."

Rowena smiled as they broke apart. Her friend was right. And Rowena knew just where she wanted to go to write her story.

The second-floor artists' room was cleared out since their immersive installment was complete. She wandered around the room, reimagining where the artists' easels were placed. She shook off the embarrassment she felt the last time she was here as an idea for a story came to mind. Rowena shrank down on the floor, having found the perfect vantage point, and began to write.

"Welcome class." Mr. Broussard clapped, getting everyone's attention. "Today will be our final day together. The Atelier will teach tomorrow, and next week will be one-on-one mentorship, publishing panels, agent pitching, and unstructured writing sessions."

He came around the desk and leaned on it. Rowena took in his mulberry-colored tailored suit and cursed herself for noticing how sublime it made his skin and hair look.

"Yesterday's assignment was to write a short story that was an allegory for grief. Let's chat about your themes and metaphors before we pick a few to read. Who wants to share? How about Malcolm?" He pointed to the Latin guy with thick glasses that Rowena met on the first day.

She tuned out his story about Frogger and looked over her own. Her fingers trembled coldly as she reviewed what she wrote last night. She was up late writing and didn't have time to edit it. She prayed Mr. Broussard wouldn't call on her to read.

Next up, Laney shared her story inspiration about spilled milk, and everyone chuckled.

She scanned the story again. A small tug in her heart made her proud of her work. She had discovered something meaningful about her grief and she almost wanted to share it.

"Winnie?" Mr. Broussard's usually smug face was soft with the question of her name. She wanted to chuckle. Had she scared him that good?

Letting out a shaky breath, she stood and cleared her throat. "I was inspired by the artists who were residents with us." She quickly looked around the room to gauge a reaction. No one was laughing at her; they were just patiently waiting to hear what she had to say like they had with the others. "The world's most renowned artist suffers a tragic loss. His studio is burnt to the ground along with everything he's ever worked to create. The loss is so painful that he throws all that's left of his art supplies into the sea.

"He leads a miserable existence, refusing to create ever again. Until one day the king demands he paint the royal portrait. The artist's refusal lands him in jail. While in prison, he is tortured by his creativity, which constantly concocts wonderful images desperate to be painted. After ten years, the king offers a reprieve, and the artist concedes. He is frail and certain he has lost all talent by this time and that by creating a benign portrait of the queen will suffer no loss greater than what he's put himself through these many years.

"After the king has him showered and dressed like a proper man at court ought to be, the artist is given a room with every instrument and supply he could possibly require. He gives himself over to the process and in doing so, loosens something magnificent within himself. Every stored emotion, every repressed image he bore during the decade spent in prison, spilled out of him. His painting technique now was more skilled and nuanced than before, the underpainting richer with deeper tones than he ever felt drawn. The painting became a living, moving, beautiful work of art before the court's very eyes. In the end, the artist weeps, 'If I had known sooner how to use my grief for good, I would have.' And the queen comforts him, 'You didn't need to suffer alone; there is beauty to be found in shared suffering.'" Rowena closed her notebook. "And that's it. I mean, it needs editing, but ..." She looked down to avoid making eye contact with anyone.

The room was silent.

Then a slow clap began.

Her eyes shot up and around until they landed on Mr. Broussard. His eyes glistened with a disarming amount of pride. She quickly looked across the room to Laney, whose jaw was still hanging open. *Girlllllll*, she mouthed.

"I thought you had it in you." Mr. Broussard winked at her, holding her gaze for a moment.

Rowena felt the embarrassment of a compliment undeserved after she treated Mr. Broussard like crap. *Sorry*, she mouthed through a wince.

Mr. Broussard nodded cordially before moving on to the next student. Rowena sat down and collected herself. A small heat crept up Rowena's neck, filling her with a giddy sense of accomplishment. She did it.

"If I had known sooner how to use my grief for good, I would have." When she wrote that line last night, she was so enthralled in the story that it only made sense for the artist to speak them. But vocalizing it here and now in front of others, she realized the words had a compounded interest. They resonated deep within her. Grief didn't have to be an isolated experience. There was beauty to be found in it, comfort to experience when it was shared.

Maybe Laney was right. Maybe God did bring them to this writing retreat for a reason. Maybe it was time for Rowena to lay down the weapon she made her grief so she could start to heal.

Laney wiggled her fingers at her from across the room and pointed heavenward with a wink.

Message received.

Acknowledgments

This story wouldn't have been possible without God, my Comforter in the midst of my own periods of grief. I am grateful that God presented this opportunity to share Rowena's story with you and also for the many moments before now that have led to this. He is such a faithful Companion in the dark night of the soul, and it is my hope that you will find peace in Christ's embrace in your own dark moments.

I owe a great many thanks to my husband, Keith, without whom I would not have taken the time to write this story. He is my biggest cheerleader and speaker of truth when I need it most. I am so grateful to have someone who listens to my ideas and champions my dreams. Thank you.

The Lost History of Lavender Lockbourne

SHIRA J. RODRIGUEZ

Dedication

To Papi,
who believed in me when no one else did.
To Mami,
who taught me as no one else could.
To Nevi,
who loved this story when no one else had.
To Alizah,
who heard me the way no one else has.
And to my Jesus,
Who penned my story into the fabric of space and time
as only the greatest of writers could.

Chapter One

November 20, 1984

I 've always had irrational fears. Heights, big dogs, and any six-legged creature with an exoskeleton longer than an inch. Even ice cream gave me anxiety. (Does it never give you anxiety to see that drop of ice cream lazily crawling down the cone and hold you tense as you wait for it to inevitably spill onto your waiting finger below?)

So you can imagine how surprised I was when the cancer specialist, a man with slick blond hair and a tiny sprig popping up from the back, came to my pallor-stricken, thumb-rubbing, trembling self and said, "I don't know how to break this to you gently, Miss Leoni, but I'm afraid your test came back positive," and amazingly, I felt nothing.

For the first time in ages, something happened and I felt nothing.

You can imagine how many times I've run through that strip of memory, more times than the old-time movie editors scanned each frame to see where they ought to cut the film and paste the next shot, taking inventory of every piece and detail. I've even determined the exact color of the room—pea green—and the exact sound of the parchment paper crinkling and shuffling under my red corduroy pants as I sat on the examination table. I remember the long mirror on the back of the door and the reflection of my face staring back at me. It was so pale beneath all the makeup I wished I hadn't slathered on so generously. I remember the smeared mascara under my right eye that I hadn't completely wiped off after I cried in the car with my cousin Rita on the way here and the somewhat swollen look of the corner of my mouth where my finger had unsuccessfully wiped at the bit of lipstick that managed to land just south of my lips. My hands had trembled so, I couldn't even get that on without smudging it, too.

Yet, when I left the office and walked out to the car where Rita sat with her feet on the dashboard, waiting for me, eating popcorn and reading Peanuts comics (she always ate popcorn and read Snoopy's antics when she was anxious), my heart had resumed its normal pace and I felt the blessed blood flow back into my face as I turned the ignition.

The tennis shoes flew off the dashboard, and the comic scuttled to the glove compartment. "What did they say?" Rita asked, popcorn still clutched like a life vest in a storm.

"Three to six months."

When I glanced at Rita's face as I drove down the highway, she just stared at me with half-parted lips. I didn't dare peek at her before. I thought it might do something to my nerves and send me crashing into another car, thus speeding my imminent death before leukemia got me. Not a bad idea, actually.

Wait ... was I really going there?

"What?" Rita said. "That's impossible."

"The doctor said there was no mistake about it."

"That's impossible," she repeated, shaking her head. "You're only twenty-six!"

"Twenty-five, to be precise. I've two weeks 'til my birthday."

"Even worse!" Rita's hands flew in my peripheral view. "You're practically making my case for me."

Rita was a paralegal, which meant she basically did everything a lawyer did but got half their paycheck and none of the credit. She was working on passing the bar exam, which she had optimistically taken and optimistically failed three times already. But that didn't quench her thirst for justice and love of debates, even when it was a lost cause. She was a patron saint of lost causes, actually. *"Even Rockefeller hit rock bottom before he shot up,"* she always insisted, a piquant smile playing at the corners of her mouth.

I, on the other hand, was the shy, romantic, cloistered novelist with thick glasses, a perennially lopsided messy bun, and baggy crocheted sweaters. I was a turtle person — the person who always scuttled home to her little shell as soon as possible. It was the highlight of my day, actually.

To be completely fair, I'm not all mousy. I'm reasonably studious, surprisingly observant, decidedly creative, and, I would even dare say, remarkably intelligent. But I've been described by more than one person as a breathing monument to all things oxymoron.

I was the novelist who'd sold millions of copies but couldn't bear to hear the words *author event* without turning pale as printer paper.

To put it another way, Rita was Gatsby and I was Nick. She always drove the storyline, like the kick drum in a song, while I followed.

So why the flashy red corduroy pants today, you may ask.

That was all Rita. She had dressed me this morning, pontificating on the importance of "confidence" and "girl power" and why I needed it today. Well, not even Rita's girl power benedictions could save me. I'd cried in the car anyway.

"It doesn't seem fair!" Rita said.

Her words swept me back to the present and left me feeling a little disoriented. "What doesn't seem fair?"

"I don't know; the results, the prognosis, maybe? Life?" She slapped her edition of Peanuts against the window, nearly upsetting the half-full popcorn holder on her lap. "And you're all cool and everything, and I'm the one who's all worked up. I don't understand it, Vannie." Rita still used the pet name that had stuck somehow when we were little. She never called me by my full name, and that was perfectly fine with me. Lavender was the name only lovers should use, not cousins.

"I don't understand it either." I bit my lip as I swung the wheel and turned into my apartment's parking lot. Even I was confused. Why wasn't I trembling from head to foot in full-fledged terror? My mind had always been too ready to imagine my *Titanic* dreams sinking and my fears floating while my heart sank down into the cold waters of life. Maybe I was calm because I wasn't waiting anymore.

Everything's worse in the heart-pounding, soul-blistering, pulse-grating reality of waiting for something to happen.

And then it does.

And then, it turns out, it's not so bad. Because it's a relief from your terrified waiting.

I'd known I hadn't been doing so well, health-wise. Everybody knew that. The sheets soaked in sweat every morning ought to have been a tell-tale sign, along with the cheek-bones that now made valleys of my once rosy face. The constant three-hour nosebleeds that had made me go through three tissue boxes just this week. The countless takeout boxes I handed to the worn, open hands of homeless people dawdling on the street because my stomach turned at the thought of anything more than a little lukewarm coffee all day. But, I don't know; I guess I just thought something wouldn't happen. I was young. I could take a lot, right?

Apparently, there's only so much your body can take before it gives out.

Even at twenty-five.

"So my birthday is coming up," I began, hoping to distract Rita from her troubled musings. "And I think I want to do something different."

"Okay." Rita squinted at me and stopped midway through unbuckling her seat belt. "Did that doctor give you the wrong medicine or something?"

"Why?" I shrugged. "It's not like I'm a hermit."

"I hardly know you, you're acting so weird right now! Normally, you are totally a hermit crab. You don't do 'different.'" She slapped the rolled up edition of Peanuts against my arm before she rose out of the car and stretched her legs.

"Well, now I do," I insisted, scrambling off the seat and leaning my arms on my car's top. I didn't sound convincing, not even to me, though. "I've wanted to do so many things, but I was always ... you know." I gesticulated wildly in the air. "Me." I finally landed on the word, inept as it was.

"Yeah." She chewed the end of the pencil she'd been doodling mustaches onto Charlie Brown with, her other things squeezed into the crook her left arm. She was probably thinking about whether she should add spectacles on Snoopy once she got to my apartment. "I know what you mean." She paused again, and I heard her tap her toe against the pavement. "So where do you want to go?"

I'd given this some thought. I knew the answer to the question, *where would you go if you could only go to one place in the entire world?*

I was practically living that question.

"Yorkshire," I stated without blinking.

Rita did. Blink, that was. "Umm, not Rome, not Athens, not Paris? Yorkshire." She grimaced. "You sure you don't want to think again? From what I've heard, it's just hills—miles and miles of hills. And sheep."

"Nope." I shook my head and walked to the entryway of my complex, an enormous red-brick brownstone.

"Why do you want to go to Yorkshire?" Her breath turned into a little cloud in the chilly New York air.

I bit my lip. "I don't know. It sounds ... different."

"Okay, now you're lying." Rita put her rolled up comic hand to her hip and leaned her shoulder against the white door as I fumbled with my keys. It was a welcome distraction that kept me from thinking about how my cheeks were probably turning as red as my scarf.

"I never lie," I fibbed.

"Yes you do, all the time. Come on and tell me everything; just spill it."

The door clicked and I wrestled the key out of the hole, tumbling Rita — popcorn, comic and all — inside as it swung open. Her pencil clattered to the floor and once she regained her balance, she went searching for it under the furniture, too occupied to read the lie still written all over my scarlet face. Should I really tell her? Would she understand or think I was completely out of my mind?

But she'd grown up with me. Surely if anyone could ever understand, it would be her. Besides, she was probably coming with me anyway. If anything happened, I couldn't afford to be alone. Not anymore.

She was staring at me now, eyebrows lifted, the runaway pencil now behind her ear. "Well?"

I cleared my throat. "Because that's where Mom and Dad found me," I whispered.

Her eyes widened. "Oh."

She looked about the room, covered in white bookshelves as high as the ceiling and the occasional antique trinket or porcelain figurine in some nook or cranny. She had cast the comic onto a nearby vintage couch and now sat down by it. "You know they might not be alive, right?" she said, her strong voice lulled to an almost shy hush.

"I know," I said.

"It might be really hard to trace them."

"I know."

"And ... you might be disappointed."

"I know." I nodded.

She took up the comic again and rolled it up, looking at me. "Then why do you want to go? It's not like you don't have a family, Vannie. You have us."

I rushed over and took one of her warm hands in both of my cold ones. "I didn't mean it like that." I paused. "You're my real family. You all—my parents, Nonna, Nonno, you, the cousins—made space for me in your hearts, even though I don't really belong. I'm not even Italian! And yet you all were so kind, and welcoming, and—" I struggled with the idea that seemed too big to fit onto my tongue. "So like family, you know? I'll never forget that."

"You *are* family, and we love you." Rita hugged me. "That's all there is to it."

"But, you see, I've never stopped wondering. Wondering what really happened. For all we know, there was a cardboard box and there was me. Planted right on Mom and Dad's doorstep as if I'd grown there overnight. "

"And the locket."

"Yeah, and the locket. But, Rita, I want to know where I come from. Who they were. What they liked. How they spent their time and—" My voice faltered. "And other things."

"Okay," Rita said.

"Okay ... what?"

"Okay, let's go. To Yorkshire."

"Just like that?"

"Yeah. I mean, it's not like you have that much time, you know?" Rita laughed, getting up from the vintage rosebud couch and rubbing her hands on her washed-out jeans. "I'll stop by a travel agency and get tickets for London or Edinburgh or something and then start packing my bags. Tomorrow sound good?"

Now everything was moving too fast. I gulped. "Umm, sure?"

"Great! I'll call you first thing to let you know." And Rita left with a sweeping kiss and slammed the door, leaving me staring at it for a full five minutes.

Chapter Two

November 21, 1984

Rita didn't call me the next morning. She called me that night. The travel agency had found us two roundtrip tickets bound for Leeds Bradford Airport, departing the next day.

"I already called my boss," Rita effused. "Told him I was going to be out sick for the next four days. Doctor's orders. I tried to get a week and a half, but the best I could get was two days and then the weekend, of course."

"Rita, that's not right; you're not sick."

"But you are," she insisted over the phone, pots and pans clattering in the background. She was probably fixing herself some dinner. I glanced at the time on my vintage white clock on the battered bedside table. The hour and the minute hands both rested on the squatty ten.

"You should probably get to bed early, then," I said, rubbing my face. "I can't have you all cranky for tomorrow."

"I'm never cranky." A pot came down, presumably on the stove. "But I get it. You need to rest. See you tomorrow!"

The line went dead.

For a couple minutes, I just sat there, cross-legged on the quilted bedcover, the receiver on my lap, ruminating as the monotone hum of the phone echoed in the stillness. It had all been so fast. In twenty-four hours, my life had changed drastically. For better or worse, in less than a week from today, I would know everything about my past. Or at least, as long as everything went according to plan.

Life rarely went according to plan, though.

I spent all night spilling the contents of my drawers onto my bed and finally decided to simply stuff everything I could find lying around into the suitcase. I finally tumbled onto the bed next to the mound of leftover clothes at around 3:00 a.m.

The next morning, I bundled up in a long hazelnut coat with a brown mitten on one hand and a brown glove on the other and dropped by Rita's apartment, stamping my cold feet on her doorstep. I rang the bell like a cat playing with a swinging mouse toy before she came down, without makeup and with dark circles under her eyes, her hair a little worse for wear.

"Good grief, what's with the crazy bell ringing?" she demanded.

She still looked a bit groggy, and her face had wandering little lines where the creases of her pillow had formed beneath her cheek. But she trundled or stumbled her way to the cab I'd hailed and stuffed both of our capacious suitcases into the trunk.

"What'd you put in here, lady?" the cab driver asked when the trunk wouldn't close on mine.

"All my worldly possessions," I said.

"All her what?" He squinted at Rita, then shook his head. "You know what, I don't care about New Age. We're going to have to put the suitcase in the back with you."

So I sat in the back with my tattered old suitcase, whose handle had nearly fallen off along with one wheel, as we soon found out when we arrived at the airport. It kept hiccuping against the glossy floor until we decided it was easier to carry it between the two of us. Rita seemed to perk up in the plane and ordered a hearty breakfast of pancakes and bacon. But I couldn't eat. I clutched my 1957 copy of *Wuthering Heights* against my heaving chest until, to make matters worse, my nose started bleeding and stained the pages.

It was nearly five by the time we arrived, and my nose was still bleeding. Rita collected our luggage while I bought a jumbo tissue box at one of the stores near our gate's exit and clasped it in my arms for dear life. We boarded a bus that then took us to a train, where the passengers stared at the bloody wad of tissues pressed against my nose.

It took an eternity, but at last, we arrived at the center of Kirkby Lonsdale. It was an adorable little town, paved with cobblestones and flanked by quaint pastry shops, tea shops, and pubs. We found an old inn somewhere nearby.

"I think we can rest for now," I said as I finally flopped onto the pillows, the bleeding stopped for now, but my nose still red as raspberries from pinching. "I'll read something here, and we can go out and about on the dales tomorrow."

"You've been worn ragged. You should sleep, Vannie," Rita chided. "You haven't even had anything to eat! I saw a nice pastry shop with some English whatchamacallit, that sweet stuff that's in triangles?"

"Scones?"

"Yeah, scones. I saw them in the window. Blueberry ones, I think. You want me to get you some? And some coffee? Actually, no, that would keep you awake. How about some tea?"

I smiled. "That sounds amazing."

"Then it's settled. I'll hop off and get some and ask about the little cottages that your parents stayed in when they came. Toodles!" she sang out, blew a kiss, and scampered down the stairs.

"They only say that on TV!" I shouted after her, even though I knew she couldn't hear.

Her footsteps pattered up the stairs some twenty minutes later. She entered clasping the promised paper lunch bag and two disposable cups of pungent black tea. The warm smells of cinnamon, sugar, and melted butter, barely kissed with a tart, sizzling hint of baked blueberries, filled the empty room like a bird's song.

"I have good and bad news," Rita announced, holding out the bag. "Which one do you want to hear first?"

I stopped mid-sip. "Neither."

"Okay, I'll tell you the good news first." Rita flopped onto the other end of my bed and nibbled on her own scone. "Good news: the cottages aren't far. They're actually within walking distance."

"That's perfect," I said flatly and chewed a fingernail. "What about the bad news?" That horrible fear had swept into me again, as though someone had broomed all my fears back into my soul.

"It's not that bad," Rita said. "I asked the lady at the shop, and she said it was best to get to wherever we wanted to get to today. It was raining all last week, which made the roads impossible to get through. It's finally manageable today, but they think it might change. See?" She pointed out the window to the gathering gray chariots of clouds advancing on the horizon.

I stared at them for a good while. I saw them move, steadily casting a growing shadow over the slate-hued rooftops of the town. I could almost feel the scent of the rain through the barely open window.

"So what do you want to do?" Rita asked.

I sighed. "I guess we'll just have to change our plans. We'll go to the people who rented out the cottage Mom and Dad stayed in, or at least find out who owned them then, and ask them if they knew of any incidents around that time. The landlords lived in a big house, my dad said, so it should be on the map."

"Okay." Rita grabbed my coat and held it out to me. "I guess we're going up the dales."

Chapter Three

The dales were out of this world.

Have you ever gone to the beach? Well, imagine that the waves are bigger and made of ebbs and flows of grass instead of water, and that is the closest thing to describing the hills and dales on the English countryside. Even the smell of the air on those hills was wonderful. I think I felt alive for the first time. Happy. The sort of happiness that your lungs can touch and swell with as the scent of wildflowers and earth and rain and cloud permeates everything like a holy incense.

I almost forgot about my headache while wandering out there. Who could blame Cathy and Heathcliff for running around in this richness? Maybe they weren't as crazy as everyone thought. Maybe it was everyone else who was crazy, and they were the only sane people.

We strolled up and down the dales for a little more than a quarter of an hour, basking in it all until the rain poured. And I mean that it literally poured, as though some sneaky angels had doused a whole bucketload of rainwater onto us for their special pleasure. I hope they got what they wanted, because we were soaking wet, which also got our map wet. It was now practically illegible, ink blurred and lines mottled.

When we somehow got to the place we were headed for, we realized the house was much bigger than we'd thought. In fact, you might even call it a mansion. It was squarish and made of whitewashed brick. The pair of iron gates before it, narrow and a little rusted, clanged open as we entered, and our tennis shoes squeaked and splashed against the muddy ground. We rapped on the door with the brass lion's face knocker and waited.

"I don't think anybody lives here," I said.

"I don't know," Rita replied, eyeing the steps leading up to the door. "I've heard of places where people actually live in these old houses."

"You think? This house looks more like a museum than an actual residence. I wonder if they've got a heating system in there. I'm freezing."

Rita thought a minute and cocked her head. "We could just try the door," she suggested. She blew on her fingers and tried the knob. The door squealed open and swung a little in tune with the breeze.

The scent of toasting wood met my nose even before I saw the tangerine glow that licked the walls within. It seemed so inviting and warm, like a blanket pulled over your shoulder after coming out shivering from a swim in a cold lake. I didn't think; I just stumbled in and searched for a chair. I found a bare little stool in the corner, very rustic and full of splinters, and plopped onto it and rubbed my arms and legs.

My goodness, that fire was amazing! It warmed me up like one of my mom's steaming cups of coffee. It was only after I'd sat down that I noticed Rita's tense face and twitching lips. She was trying to tell me something, that much I could tell, but what?

And then, from the fireplace, I heard the echoing groan of a large chair against the floor and saw a figure rise from the dark shadow of a high-backed chair poised before the fire.

Chapter Four

The figure was tall and angular, and the thing that struck me most was her bearing. It was rigid, erect, stiff as a cold marble statue; as though she had been etched onto paper in hard charcoal lines. She was only a silhouette against the glowing fire that cast more shadows than light in the chamber. I couldn't see her face, but I could almost swear she had turned to me. I felt her stare for a while.

"And who are you?" asked a flat and poised yet deep female voice.

I supposed it was the figure who said it, but I wasn't sure, so I only stared, dumbfounded. Words seemed to vie for my attention, but I couldn't get any out even if I tried.

"I told you people live in these places!" Rita hissed.

"I'm sorry," I began, thinking I ought to get up but trembling too hard to do so. I wasn't sure whether I meant to address the silhouette or Rita.

"How did you come here?" the silhouette said.

There was a clip of feet from the opposite direction, the entrance of a hall, maybe, and another silhouette entered. "I heard the door. Were we expecting someone?" It was taller than the first silhouette and decidedly masculine in a vest and long black pants. "It's pouring outside. I can't imagine who'd come in this kind of weather."

"No one is supposed to come into the house without an appointment. I strictly forbade Meredith from letting people in. We're not some museum or petting zoo," the lady said. "Look how they're dripping mud all over my clean floor."

I looked down. It was true. My muddy tennis shoes had already created wet, pooling, brown stains upon the polished wood floor. I stared at them until I felt too embarrassed and wrenched my eyes away from the sight of them, only to behold ten — I counted them

— ten outrageously large deer heads poised on the wall, gaping at me with their empty, black, glassy gazes. It was unnerving, to say the least. Only the sound of the shower of rain outside kept me from running out screaming.

"You're not going to send them out, are you?" the man persisted.

"They came into it; it's their foolishness, not ours. My deepest regrets." She turned to us, her tone completely desaturated of any regret. "But I can't have you stay; the house is not open to the public."

"Oh, we didn't come to see the house, ma'am," Rita said.

"Well then, I can't understand how that implicates me."

"We came to see you."

"Me?" The woman drew back.

"You see, we're historical researchers," Rita said too brightly, as if she were telling the guy at the hot dog stand how she could get him free tickets for Coney Island. "We just wanted to ask you some questions about one of the people who was renting a cottage from you some time ago, and we just so happened to get stuck in the rain. We're just not used to it, you know, the whole 'nice weather for ducks' thing!" Her forced laugh echoed against the walls. "Anyway, if you'd be so kind as to just let us stay here until the rain stops, that would be great. It should stop in, what, ten minutes, right?" She turned to me as if I were the weather man.

"Yeah," I offered vaguely and gave a weak chuckle, digging my hands deep into my skirt pockets. I didn't care about the rain anymore; these people squelched my earthworm-sized dignity like galoshes in the rain.

"They only came to ask questions," the man said. His voice sounded younger than the woman's did. Almost timid. "They'll be gone before you even have time to notice them."

"You are too soft, Edward," the woman scolded.

"If I could say something …" I raised my hand as if I were in school, but I quickly put it down once the woman turned to me.

She was staring at me now; I could feel her gaze in the darkness.

"Well," I began, "I'm sick, and it would be nice not to get sicker by staying out in the rain. I know we probably seem really rude, and I'm really sorry, but …" My throat grew thick. Why on earth was my voice failing me now—now, of all times? "We're just … really desperate." The words sounded wobbly, they walked a tightrope and were teetering off. Suddenly, a lump swelled somewhere between my tongue and my vocal chords. I blinked hard as if that would make it go away, rolling a fat tear down my cheek. I wiped it away fast. I wasn't going to make a scene. I just wanted to get warm. But why on earth was I crying?

The woman was silent for a long time. "You may stay, but I won't have any questions. I don't want to be bothered."

We stared at each other until I at last turned my eyes from her and sat down. This was better than nothing.

"Ten minutes," she repeated. "No more."

We spent what felt like an eternal verbal vacuum fidgeting and swinging our legs under us like children (I could see Rita was aching to whistle, and once she even puckered her mouth, only to have the woman stare at her). In the middle of it, the lady's eyes flickered to us. They were gray—I could see them now as the light from the fire danced on her face—and her hair was gray, too, fearfully and wonderfully coiffed in a Margaret Thatcher style, voluminous and short.

"I hope it's not contagious, this sickness of yours?" she said.

"No." I shuffled on my seat. "It's cancer."

Edward's head tilted to face me. I could now see his moused hair, all combed back except for the little wave over his forehead. "I'm sorry," he said. "My mother died of cancer."

"She's not your mother?" Rita pointed at the woman.

"No," the woman said, glancing at the timid gentleman. "His name is Edward Snow. My sister's godson."

"How did you come here, then?" I asked, leaning forward a little.

"My godmother was killed in a riot in Vietnam. She was a missionary," Edward said, his voice fingering the words the way a boy might graze the frets of a guitar for the first time. "And my parents died when I was young. I've lived here since ..." He glanced at the woman, but her grim frown dissuaded him from continuing, and he sent us a wan, apologetic smile.

We sat in a painful, monastic silence after that, all the more miserable for everyone's disinterest in breaking it until the woman again drew her stony eyes in our direction.

"You'll want tea?" she asked in the same tone you might use to demand an explanation from a misbehaving child.

"No, no thanks," I said.

"Well, I want tea. You'll not object to my having some?"

Even Rita froze for a second and blinked. "Uh, yeah, sure."

So the woman called for Meredith, but as the girl didn't come in the next five seconds, the woman nudged Edward and told him to tell the maid to make her tea.

Rita took up the opportunity to ask for a restroom. "You can practically smell the stress here; just look at those constipated faces they have!" she stage-whispered. She had never been good at being quiet. "Will you be okay alone? I don't want to leave you, but I thought it might give me a chance to take a peek out the window and see whether the storm will let up soon. We've already been here for more than half an hour. Might as well go somewhere else if they won't answer us. I'm sure somebody else has got to know something."

I nodded and squeezed her hand. "Yeah, that's okay."

Now the older woman and I were alone. We stayed silent for a long while, watching each other. At last, her bullet-gray eyes fastened onto me.

"Where did you get that?" she asked me suddenly.

I stared down at where she looked, where my fingers stroked the embossed lines on my locket, rising and falling on my breast to the time of my breath.

Then I glanced up into her face, and even in the orange glow, I saw it had gone pale, and the muscles on her forehead made stiff ridges upon her skin. Out of nowhere, her hands clutched my locket and snatched it off me, and then stowed it in her pocket. She sat back down. "That will teach you to steal from me. You'll depart from this place as soon as the rain stops."

I was so shocked, the air wouldn't squeeze into my lungs. I rose to rip it from her hands, but the room seemed to sway about me. I gripped a chair. "You don't understand, ma'am," I began, my face flashing with ice and fire under my skin, but the woman ignored me.

The floor felt like it was balancing on a ball, tipping drunkenly to one side and then the other. But the pictures weren't falling, they were fastened on the wall, and the fire, too, seemed to know which way was up, and the two highbacked chairs before the hearth... they stayed level with the ground.

But I couldn't balance.

The world was splitting into twos, twos of everything, even my hand turned into two, the floor seemed to be coming at me.

And then I crashed onto it.

And everything went dark.

Chapter Five

I remember the softness first and then the headache. And then I heard a groan.

"Shhhh, you're all right now." Rita's voice, more clement than usual, came from above me.

I turned a little, then stiffened and squeezed my eyes shut again, feeling the world spin around me.

"Hey, relax," A shadow urged — Rita's from the sound of it — stroking my arm.

"She's woken up?" another voice—deeper and mellower—said. I now saw a second shadow upon the white, fabric surface. They were sheets, bedsheets, and below my head was a pillow. I was on a bed in a strange, half-lit room. Above me stretched a canopy held up by the arms of great mahogany bedposts. I drank in the warm, liquid scent of a fire on the grate and the crackling sound that accompanied it.

I turned to the source of the two shadows. I knew the first was Rita—I'd know that form anywhere—but the other? I couldn't tell who it was.

"Hey." I stretched out my hand to Rita and felt her racing pulse as she squeezed it.

"Hey, drama queen," she said, balancing a warble in her voice. "You nearly had me there. All that blood—gosh, you were a sight!" She laughed, but it didn't tumble from her throat like a waterfall, the way it always did. It just tripped three steps and stopped. "Do you like your room? Edward was kind enough to bring you up here after you fell. I can't even leave you for five minutes, can I?" She stroked my hair. "I'm glad you're okay."

"Me, too." I squeezed her hand back. I turned to the other shadow, the one I supposed to be Edward. "And thanks for taking me up. You really didn't have to."

"It was no trouble," he said. I couldn't see his face, but I could hear the smile in the waves of his voice. "Mrs. Lockbourne was only too willing to let you stay when you fell. She said you fainted clean away all of a sudden, hit your head on the floor. We ought to call a doctor to see that you haven't got a concussion."

"No, I should be okay. There's no need to bother about getting any doctors. I'll be fine. Mrs. Lockbourne ... is that ..." I bit my lip. "Was that the woman next to you?"

"Yes."

"Oh," I said, looking down at the sheets. I wanted to tell Rita all about how the woman took the locket and thought I'd stolen it from her (which, seriously, who in their right mind did that to a complete stranger?) but the mere thought made me feel so exhausted and heavy. I'd explain it another time.

Edward continued, "You can stay here as long as you like. The storm still hasn't let up, but you're in no state to go out anyway." He had the sort of voice that made you feel comfortable immediately. There was an unassuming quality to it. It wasn't particularly beautiful or deep, but it had a kind timbre to it. It let the simple and gentle words be exactly what they were.

"Thank you." I tried to muster as much gratitude in my eyes as I could.

I felt his gaze rest on me for a long while. "There's something I can't quite place about you. Have we met? Before this, I mean."

I squinted. "Maybe we met in the subway or something?"

"No, I'm afraid I've never been to America."

"I've never been outside of America." I shook my head.

"Maybe you've read one of her books," Rita suggested. "She's a *New York Times* bestselling romance author."

Edward scratched his neck. "I haven't read much new fiction, though I would like to read *A Wrinkle in Time*. I've heard it's excellent. I didn't know you were a writer."

I smiled. "I don't usually tell people."

"Ah, well, I'm glad you told me." I felt his smile this time, like the warmth of steaming Earl Grey cupped in your hands. "Well, I'd best let you rest a little more so you can be off tomorrow."

He bowed and left the room, the scent of aftershave and cedarwood lingering behind, like Hansel and Gretel's crumbs. And then I remembered the headache, like a nightmare washes over you in a wave of memory. I'd almost forgotten it while he was here.

Funny, wasn't it, how you could forget a headache?

Rita patted my hand. "Let's get you changed out of those clothes. The maid just brought some up for us to borrow. Aren't these PJs cute?" She held up a white nightgown with a pink ribbon woven through the fabric and a baby bow just where the collarbone dips. "I mean, it's kind of giving me 'cherubic Victorian child' vibes, but you were always into that anyway, right?" She laughed, landed opposite me on the bed, and leaned her head against my arm, our breathing slowing until we matched breaths and just lay there together. I could feel the faint pulse in her forehead against my skin.

"I'm gonna miss you so much, Vannie girl," she whispered, her fingers searching for my palm. Our fingers interlaced, and she squeezed mine as if she was holding me from falling off a cliff. She didn't let go.

I was afraid she had almost fallen asleep when I said, "Me, too."

I felt her head turn and tilt up. "You'll be having such a good time, you won't even think about us. It's us that'll have to wait to see you again. You'll hurt for a little, but we'll hurt for a lifetime."

My throat grew tight, and some invisible boa constrictor slithered about my chest. I almost couldn't hear the breath escape my own lips. "I'm scared."

"I know. But you're gonna be okay." Rita patted my arm, her other palm still clutching my hand. "You know I wasn't that much into kids' books when I was little. But I never, ever forgot that part from that book about the bear."

"Paddington?"

"No! The one with the friend who was a boy? And the pig? Oh, and that rabbit guy who always reminded me of our family! You know, all his friends and cousins?"

"Oh, *Winnie-the-Pooh* by A. A. Milne?"

"'That the one,' as the venerable Whipsnatch used to say. We always watched those ridiculous cartoons on Saturdays over cereal. You remember that?" Rita rolled over, tossed her head back, and laughed. She had a rippling laugh; you could feel it in the air around you, like the ripples in a pond in Central Park in autumn. "Yeah well, I've always remembered it. The book about the bear, I mean. I don't know why. Maybe because it reminded me of you."

"Really?"

"Yeah."

"Well, which part was it?"

"You want me to say it?"

"Sure." I shrugged.

"Let me see if I remember it." She shifted and drew in a breath. "I think it's at the end of the book, some part with the mushy farewell ... Gosh, I can't remember it."

"Winnie-the-Pooh is *not* mushy." I laughed.

"Oh, when you've been around the court system as long as I have, believe me, Winnie-the-Pooh sounds decidedly mushy." She smirked. "But you know what, Vannie? Mushy or not, deep down it really is like that part where they're saying goodbye. You might be miles away, years in the past. But to me, it'll be like I've never said goodbye. I'll find you every time I see ink, smell you when the flower cart rolls down the street with lavender, and hold you when I hug your old coat with the missing buttons and your old-fashioned sweaters. And I can't help but think I'm really, really lucky. It's not everybody who has someone that makes saying goodbye impossible."

Neither of us could say anything after that.

So we stayed in silence on the bed, just drinking in each other's company as the night waned into the morning and another day passed into the annals of history, never to be lived again.

Chapter Six

With Rita's help, I walked down the august wooden staircase to breakfast the next morning, feeling like a tiny elf on a stair made for giants. Everything was just so massive about it. And to think, Edward had carried me up those stairs! My cheeks grew warm just envisioning it.

We at last entered the ample dining room, where a table set with an awe-inspiring breakfast spread awaited us. A generous platter of blushing strawberries and purple blueberries and rosy raspberries was at its center; bacon, crisped to perfection and a glorious mound of toast and butter the color of the sun were on either side of it, chaperoned by an elegant silver teapot with delicious steam whispering up its spout.

But all the sweetness soured with one look at the mistress at the head of the table. Either I had forgotten how pucker-faced she was, or she had grown grimmer overnight.

Edward also sat at the table but rose as we entered, yet somehow even his warm "good morning" sounded chilled in the presence of the North Wind.

We sat down.

Mrs. Lockbourne said grace and then, to my astonishment, she addressed me. "Miss Leoni, I'm afraid I've mistaken your locket for one of my own. I here return that which is rightfully yours. I hope you'll accept my apology." She passed a little gray pendant to a servant, who then passed it to me.

I knew something was wrong the moment I clutched it. It was lighter than I remembered, and this one had a heart faintly engraved on its center. It was also unrusted and newer than mine.

She was trying to trick me.

"Ma'am, I'm afraid you're mistaken. This isn't my locket." I passed it back to her.

"Oh, but it is." Her hand did not stretch out to take it. She eyed me, measuring me; we both knew that this was no confusion.

"I demand that you give me back my locket." A hot flush threatened to flood my face as my hands pushed me up and away from the table too quickly. I clutched Rita's blouse as my vision swam, and she sat me down. I couldn't see her face nor Edward's; they were confounded, I could imagine, but I never stopped for an instant staring into that woman's frozen gray eyes. I thought for a moment Mrs. Lockbourne's stony, winterous heart almost cracked under a tug of compassion. And then I watched her soul recoil from that warm spring wind.

"No, my dear, you are mistaken. This is your locket." And like last night, she left me alone with those words as she rose from the table and left the room.

That was all it took for me to sob my heart out into my pristine white napkin and stain it with my shameful tears.

Edward looked on in baffled confusion. "I sincerely apologize, ladies."

"What the heck happened? I don't get any of this." Rita grasped my shoulder. "Did you lose something last night? Please, Vannie, stop it. I can't stand to see you like that!"

"It doesn't matter. None of it matters anymore." I sniffed.

"Clearly, something has disturbed you." Edward walked over and laid a hand on mine. "I know she can, at times, be difficult, and I am sorry if she distressed you. Has this got to do with what happened last night?" He passed me a little handkerchief, this, too, scented of rich cedarwood, but my fingers only played with the stitched initials *E. S.*

"It's nothing," I said, wiping away a tear. What an utter fool I'd made of myself! I'd broken down in the middle of breakfast with total strangers who literally lent me pajamas to sleep in on *their* bed after I broke into *their* house because of my reckless idea to go waltzing off on the Yorkshire Dales in the rain. Oh, this was just getting better and better.

"You know what," I said, "I think the best thing right now is just to go home, you know? Back to my cozy apartment, where it doesn't rain cats and dogs. Forget the drama; it's better in the books after all. I don't need it. I don't need to know."

"Know what?" Edward asked.

"You're going to think I'm absolutely insane," I said, but he gazed back at me and shook his head with that quiet kindness that just seemed to flow like a river from his irises. It filled you, surrounded you, healed any little nicks or bruises with that infinite patience.

"Well," I began, "I had a locket around my neck yesterday. It's the one my parents found in a cardboard box at their rented cottage nearly twenty-six years ago. They don't know who my biological parents were. There was only me, the box, and that locket. My dad is a doctor, and he and my mom came here to vacation for a week. They'd been through a rough year and so they thought some time away from the city might be nice. The first night they come up here, a man showed up at their door, dripping wet. He said his wife was in labor. So my dad rushed over and helped with the delivery. It was a girl. They were very kind, but it was obvious they were also very poor, so he refused payment. He never saw them again."

Edward thought for a moment. There was a fire by one end of the wall, and he stared into it, his back facing us. "This locket, was it etched with three sprigs of lavender, by any chance?"

I started, and Rita clasped my arm as we both said, "Yes."

He turned and rubbed his eyes with a hand. "It was in front of me all the time. I knew something about you was familiar. Those eyes don't lie." He met my gaze. "You're Helen's daughter."

Chapter Seven

Edward began pacing the length of the dining room, a flush washing over his face. "I'm afraid you'll either be very pleased or horribly disappointed when I finish. So speak now or forever hold your peace. But you don't look well at all—forgive me; we'll leave it for another time."

"Is this about my parents?" I asked, sitting down at Rita's urging. "I would give anything to know."

"Yes, but it's not an easy story to tell. Or hear. You might not like it."

"Tell me."

He watched my face, my eyes, and there was such tenderness in his glance as though he already knew me. Or saw someone he used to know. His shoulders rose and fell with his sigh.

And then he left the room.

I stared at Rita and immediately saw a mirror of my own emotions upon her wide eyes and open mouth.

"What did I say wrong?" I whispered.

"I don't know," she said slowly, glancing out the door Edward had just left barely open.

And then it swung wide, and Edward himself walked back into the room with a book clasped like a bird's nest in his hands.

"I thought of telling you, but I believe you deserve to know the whole truth. You see, it was so long ago, I don't remember all the details. I didn't want to at the time. So I scribbled them all down and then ... forgot them, I suppose." He turned to the window and looked out, ruffling his hair as if searching for some thread to pick up, some hint of where to start, still clutching the book in the other hand. "But I suppose I ought to start somewhere."

"I usually like to start at the beginning." I said.

"Yes." He looked back at me and smiled, like the sun parting the clouds to take a peek at the world. "That's a very good place to start. Let's see, what was the beginning? Well, I suppose it's when I came to this house from Vietnam as a gangly, skinny, awkward boy of ten. A horrible flight; we nearly crashed into the Indian Ocean. The house was very different then. Mr. and Mrs. Lockbourne lived in this enormous estate with their son, Ralph Lockbourne. Now, you should know, Mr. Lockbourne was the wealthiest man around and had connections with the royal family. No one could rival him in those days. He was broad-shouldered and six feet tall, with a weathered face and satin hair that Mrs. Lockbourne would stroke before crowds at her parties. She said it was the color of his hair that had made her fall in love with him and claimed no woman would ever keep a lock in her grave as beautiful as that of her husband's."

Edward had been standing before the window by the fireplace, staring out the dew-kissed window pane during this first part, but he now shifted to eye the chair at the head of the dining table, where the lady of the house had sat not fifteen minutes ago. "Mrs. Lockbourne was a social but proud woman. She loved hosting great balls where she could show off her home, her husband, and above all, her son.

"I remember I used to always tag along behind him when we lived together. He was eight years older than I, and I idolized him like a god. Everyone admired him and I overheard not a few of the servant girls gossiping and glorying over his thick dark blond hair and blue eyes. I can't remember how many magazines came to take his picture. He was athletic, charismatic. He taught me to hold the bat in cricket and how to parry in fencing. He'd even take me with him to his father's library, where we would spend hours reenacting scenes from *Treasure Island* and *Huckleberry Finn* and even the *Odyssey*. He could have done anything he chose, absolutely anything.

"But he chose to marry my governess. I suppose he couldn't help it. She was pretty, very young, with hair as black as a raven's feathers and eyes like yours, that changed with her mood; sometimes they were brown as earth; at other times, gray like our streams; and at other times, the strangest color, something between emerald and blue. She had a knack for a good story; hers were often better than Ralph's. I loved her. You know, I wouldn't sleep until she had kissed me three times and sung a strange incantation that we had invented for fun. It was a spell for good dreams, she'd say. One time, she didn't come—I think her mother had bronchitis or something—and I sobbed into my pillow all night and was miserable all day until she returned.

"And then one day," Edward said, turning to me. "One little incident brought this house of cards into such ruin, it has never been the same. I've thought it over and traced it all back to that one day. I wrote it down while I attended my last year at boarding school, thinking someday I'd be famous enough to have it turned into a book. I haven't looked at it for years. But you may read it, if you'd like." He passed the little brown, tattered notebook to me.

I cracked it open. It smelled of pencil shavings and rubber bands and old paper and erasers. My eyes scanned the first lines, written in clear, impatient blue ink, words scratched out here and there and funny childish misspellings punctuating every other paragraph.

One day when I was about eleven—no, twelve—Ralph and I planned on spending our afternoon in the library. In we walk, and there, by Mr. Lockbourne's stock of philosophical works, sits my governess, her face hidden in Plato's Republic. *She shut the book when she heard the door. I'll never forget her face; it was pale and angry and terrified. I thought for a moment she would run away. But she didn't, only sat there and stared up at us staring down at her.*

"I'm so sorry, Mr. Lockbourne," she murmured, handing the book back to Ralph. "I thought the study was empty."

And Ralph just stares at her, amazed. "No," says he. "Helen, you have every right to be here. Please, stay here, read all you like. We'll be quiet as mice, won't we, Ed?"

If Ralph was fine with this new arrangement, then it sat even better with me. I nodded and plopped myself on the rug in the center of the library to read while Ralph crept into a corner and stole glances at Helen. At length, I don't remember how, we all started talking about the books we'd been reading, and it was so enjoyable, we agreed to do it twice a week. We called ourselves the Treasure Seekers. It had been my idea, and I felt very proud of it at the time, but I suppose Ralph couldn't have minded any name at all, so long as Helen joined us. And that is how we became a trio.

When Mrs. Lockbourne was not near, Ralph would take Helen and me racing through the dales on his motorbike. I had always thought it grand and wondered if it was the feeling eagles had when they rushed off a cliff and flapped their wings. Helen would always scream, "Careful, Ralph!" and squeeze me between them as if she was afraid I'd fall off, and Ralph's deep, rippling laughter would echo into the wind as he told her to hold on to him tighter. We escaped Mrs. Lockbourne's notice for about a year, until I came down with pneumonia. It was a horrid two weeks, and while Helen saw me rather less than I would have liked, her outings with Ralph continued, and I always watched them from the window. Confined on my bed, I waved as the motorbike sped past my window. When I turned, I saw Mrs. Lockbourne standing behind me with a bottle of medicine, her gray eyes hard and grim as a graveyard.

"Who's that young lady with Ralph?" she asked.

I groaned that my head ached and that I didn't know what she was talking about.

But Mrs. Lockbourne grasped me by the collar. "Don't lie to me. I haven't seen that girl for the last hour, and she's supposed to give you your medicine. Why didn't she come when I called?"

I stammered a series of meaningless syllables and phrases.

Then she slapped me.

I was so angry and ashamed, but I swore I wouldn't tell. At last, she gave up and sent a servant for ice and a towel for my swelling cheek.

I never again saw Helen in the house. When I recovered, another governess, a shrimpy, nearsighted woman with an obsession for Latin maxims, replaced her. I couldn't stand the sight of her, and Ralph shut himself up in his study for three weeks after that, leaving me alone.

Mr. Lockbourne seemed impatient to send me to boarding school after I complained about my new governess, and the Lockbournes sent me to a prep school in Edinburgh before the end of the month. Ralph still refused to speak to me—or anyone, for that matter. I spent six months at St. John's, sending letter after letter in apology to Ralph and going to bed in a miserable state every night. He was gone when I returned to the estate for the summer holidays, leaving Mrs. Lockbourne in an eternal resentment. One night, Mrs. Lockbourne and her husband, with glares that made me feel as though I was at some trial, sat me at their great dining table and asked me if I had received anything from Ralph. I shook my head and told of all the unanswered letters.

"Then I suppose you tell the truth," she said in exactly the same tone and manner she would have used if I had lied, and sent me back to my room.

That night, I heard a knock on my door, and afraid the being on the other side was one of the ghouls from Helen's old folk tales, I buried my head deeper into the sheets until I heard Ralph's voice—undeniably Ralph's!—from the other side of the door.

I opened it, and there stood Ralph and Helen, droplets of dew on their hair and flushed faces. She wrapped her arms around me and hugged me as if she never wished to let go. When she pulled away, tears glistened in her deep eyes.

"We're eloping, Eddy dear; Ralph's got all our things outside. We wanted to say goodbye." And she took me up again in her arms and kissed both my cheeks with the salt of her tears still fresh on her lips. Then Ralph stepped forward and gave a manly slap on the back. He smiled, but I saw the corners of his mouth tremble.

"You're not angry with me, then?" I asked.

He seemed startled at the idea and grasped my shoulders, now some six inches higher than they used to be, and looked me straight in the eye. "Never, old chap."

I couldn't stand to see them leave, so I closed the door and heard their soft tread fade into my imagination.

Chapter Eight

I closed the notebook and handed it back to Edward.

"We heard nothing of them after that." He played with its pages. "I later made some private investigations and found they lived some thirty miles north of here. I don't know what he did for a living; I suppose he was something of a jack-of-all-trades. Anyway, we knew nothing tangible of him for at least three years. And then one spring morning, some twenty years ago, we found a note on the doorstep signed by no other than Ralph Lockbourne. But when we read its contents, we thought he'd gone insane. It was the only explanation."

"What do you mean, insane?" I asked.

"Well, he wrote of where he'd been living and how Helen had died a short while after delivering a child, a daughter, and we could see the blotted ink where his tears had stained the note. He wanted Mrs. Lockbourne to provide for the child and raise her because he was no longer able to do so. But we all supposed he'd become schizophrenic because the note accompanied nothing of which it spoke—not Mrs. Lockbourne's locket, the old dog blanket, the cardboard box, or even the child—nothing."

As Edward finished that sentence, I sensed Rita's gaze rest on me, and she rose abruptly. "Edward, I think she's about to pass out."

"I'm okay," I said. I did feel lightheaded and slightly dizzy, but I was far too close to the truth to give up now. This was what I came here for. So I steadied myself against Rita's arm and spoke in a forced, even voice. "I have all those things you say your note lacked."

His hands trembled as he poured a stream of tea into his cup and smoothed away the bead of sweat upon his hair.

"But why leave the box and the child and the locket at Dr. Leoni's rented cottage that autumn?" I asked. "They received no note with the box."

"I wish I knew. Maybe he was afraid his mother wouldn't take the child; thought a childless foreign doctor and his wife might and the letter fell out when he changed his mind—I don't know. The only proof would be one of the items from the basket, Lavender."

He met my gaze, and some strange understanding passed between us. Without a word, he offered me his arm and walked me down the halls of endless paintings, past a hundred doors, and into a private sitting room at the other end of the house, where Mrs. Lockbourne stared out the window as if still seeing her son speeding down the dales on his motorbike. The sun now peeked through the clouds, turning the soft drizzle quivering on the pane into luscious diamonds of water. It was like the beauty of a smile through tears. Her back was toward us, and there was something almost wistful in the tilt of her head, the gentle stoop of her shoulders that hadn't been there before.

"He used to ride past here sometimes, didn't he, Edward?" she murmured. "Hallooing to us to come and watch him. Oh, my boy could have been the best of men."

"Hello, grandmother," I whispered, clutching Edward's arm.

She turned to me in a sort of sharp alarm and then looked away. Her lip trembled in the bleak, imperfect light. "I thought you'd stolen it or bought it. And then I saw your face ... and I knew."

There was no need to say anything. We shared blood through that locket, and I loved her despite every jealous mistake she'd made. The way she'd hurt my father and my mother, Edward and me. I didn't care that her soul spat out it could not love me back; life was too short for that. And I didn't know if I had a tomorrow or when we might ever be together again.

The one thing that is ever allowed us, even at the threshold of death's door, is our decision to give love or withhold it. There is everything to gain if we face our fears and love recklessly, radically, outrageously, despite it all.

And we have everything to lose if we don't.

We might find that, in waiting for people to deserve our love, we lose the joy of loving them in spite of it. Love, like every action in life, is a choice. You must face the fear of getting hurt and thrust yourself into it, cannonball into it like kids jumping into a pool on a sunburnt summer's day.

The only sure way to lose is if you never try at all.

But if you love them even when you're apart, they'll always be with you.

In love, no one can be lost.

I stepped away from Edward and took my grandmother's locket—the locket she had given my father and my father had left with me—from her palms. She made no resistance. Not a movement or a single breath. I saw she had replaced the photograph of my father within the trinket. My fingers kissed his cheeks and stroked his ironed shirt and passed over the lips I had never touched. And then I passed the locket to my grandmother and left the room in silence—without help, without pain.

I am packing up now to leave Rochester Hall. It's a blustery day on the dales, but the wind can't beat the spirit out of me. I plan to visit the old cottage and sit there for a while.

And then I plan to go home, Grandmother. I don't know how long I have, but I thought you might want to know me a little. So I'm enclosing this, my very last story, for you. It's in your sitting room, on the blue armchair Edward told me used to be my father's favorite. When your heart can find a little room for it, I hope you read it, and so our souls will get to know each other long after my body relinquishes its haunt on earth.

Always your own,

Lavender Lockbourne

A Note from the Author

Stories are journeys for the author, too.

(Did you know that?)

So many times as writers, we think that the journey is about our characters, about having them overcome challenges to reach that distant, unattainable—or perhaps just barely out-of-reach—goal. Dorothy finding her way back to Kansas. Huck tasting freedom for the first time. Caspian reaching the eastern edge of the world.

But often, the quest is only one part of the story, and the hero comes back with a good deal more. Dorothy finds she always had the power to go home. Huck discovers that freedom is a choice. And Caspian understands that it is the people that make the journey so full.

And like the heroes in these stories, every author goes out on a quest to tell a good story only to find that they've also become one in the process. Spinning stories, I think, is the one art that anyone can pursue without a coin in his purse. It is the essence, the atomic level, of reality. I think every real thing was once a story—a dream—in someone's mind, as this one was in mine.

But the person who started this story and the one who finished it are two very different people. The one was an anxious, starry-eyed girl with a penchant for philosophy and the arts and old-fashioned things. The other was a slightly reckless, humbled woman with the heart of a child who tightroped between what the world is and what it could be. I suppose, in a way, I'm both Rita and Lavender.

If my younger self would have seen the long trek it would take—the eyestrain, the sleepless nights, the grief, the aching loneliness—perhaps she would have preferred not to take that route. Had the hero say, "The journey's too hard."

But, you see, there is no story without the journey. And a writer cannot write what doesn't come from her heart.

What a writer doesn't pay in money, they pay in life lessons.

(Sorry to rain on your parade!)

But, oh, how grateful I am that God writes my stories and is wise enough to place a cast of characters who both sharpen and shape the stories into something beautiful.

My family—Papi, Mami, Nevi, Alizah, Abuela Lulu, Abuela Lita, Abuelo Alfredo, and Abuelo Carlos—are the primary players upon the stage, the people who have known my every entrance and exit from a scene. I will be forever grateful for the patience with which my stunning and incredible sisters Nevi and Alizah heard my story ideas, even when they sounded like garbled telegraphs. For Papi's immense support when everyone else thought I was absolutely nuts to forgo college. For Mami's warm embraces and de-stressing massages. For Nevi's and Papi's reading endless manuscripts and telling me, kindly but honestly, when something definitely didn't work. You are troupers. You are the biggest blessings in my life. And I don't think anyone in the world is half as lucky as me to have such an amazing family like you. Thank you for the sacrifices. Thank you for the prayers. Thank you for all the things I don't know about and perhaps will never know you did for the love of me.

And how can I forget the love so generously poured out by my precious fellow scene partners—my beta readers and writing comrades and friends?

My precious Morgan, Daejah, Gabriela, and Danicar, thank you for your prayers over my deadlines. You will never know how much the words *let us know if you need anything* can soothe a stressed-out soul! You are gems, and I love you all dearly. May God requite you abundantly, my loves.

My own beautiful Moriyah—are there words to fully capture what a sublime blessing your friendship has been to me? Few people can say that they found, as I have, a kindred spirit, and, my dear, I have without a doubt found one in you.

My lovely Lewis Club ladies—Grace, Ella, Savannah and Moriyah—what a precious gift you are! I feel so immensely blessed and proud to know such brilliant, kind souls as you. Thank you for hearing my heart and being some of the best friends in the world. Grace, my darling girl, I can always find a safe haven in you and how very grateful I am that we met—so like Anneish characters!—by apparent happenstance (though we both know that ain't true!). Ella, chatting with you is always a breath of fresh air, and your piquant thoughts on books always meander with mine in the most delightful of ways! Savannah, your sweet encouragements and beautiful heart have been such a blessing, and I'm so proud to know such a beautiful soul and girl like you!

My own precious beta readers and critique partner—Hannah Beth, Laurel Luhman, Moriyah C., Stephanie Crachiolo, Caitlin Miller, and Katja Labonté—thank you for loving this story with all your hearts and souls and for the time and effort you've put into this story and the boundless enthusiasm you've all expressed. This story is what it is because of you. I wrote this for girls like you. I never thought I'd be so blessed as to find such beautiful, bookish souls, and yet I have. You are treasures, my loves, always know that.

Hannah Beth, my dear, you loved this story from the very beginning and when I didn't even know if it would be published. Thank you for every beautiful, kind word and tender comment. I'm so grateful to know such a talented, Anneish soul like you, dear.

Laurel, your love for the *Wuthering Heights* allusions in my story and precious appreciation for my story's poetry warmed my heart so much! How beautiful to know someone understood and loved my story for its attempts at poetry as much as I did!

Moriyah, my own darling, you have always understood my stories like few people have, and your sweet comments are the sweetest balm to my soul. Thank you for loving my writing, no matter what it looks like or what form it takes.

Stephanie, your lively, delightful comments always made my day!! I had such a delightful time laughing and smiling at your funny comments and your kind, beautiful excitement for my story and for being so kind as to ask me what I wanted you to focus on. You are gold, my dear, and thank you ever so much for your wonderful, beautiful support.

My dearest Caitlin, I'll forever be grateful you took the time out of your busy days to read my little story and love it. You are a true friend, and I'll be eternally grateful God put you in my path. You are such a lovely soul, and thank you for the love and gentleness with which you pointed out where things could be altered and when they weren't quite working! God bless your wonderful editor's eye and storyteller's heart, love!

And to my own Katja ... thank you. Thank you, thank you, thank you for your *beautiful* comments that always made me smile. You loved this story as few others have, and I feel honored that you found so much delight in reading this and in the title! I absolutely loved working with you and hope we may again in the future!

Wild Blue Wonder Press—Kellyn Roth, my fellow NiN authors, and the NiN street team — and my own lovely Lockbournes!! Thank you, from the bottom of my heart, for all the work you ladies have put into this beautiful anthology. It's been one of the greatest joys of my life to work with each one of you and with Wild Blue Wonder Press, and I feel that everyone ought to be absolutely, divinely blessed with such a talented, supportive team! Kellyn, your work and dedication to these anthologies is truly inspiring. You are amazing, and I hope you know that. And, Andrea, thank you for your beautiful friendship and for trusting me with your own story. You've been such a beautiful gift, and I hope and pray we'll be friends for a very, very long time, dear! Heather and Bethany, thank you for your beautiful support on Instagram and my lovely ladies who helped me with Goodreads!—I owe you my utmost and sincerest gratitude. Without you ladies, I would probably still be wrestling with that funny and odd little monster, lol!

And to God—my Savior, my King, my Shepherd—the One Who Sees me. You are so worthy. Thank You for taking a little Latina girl and giving her a voice. Thank You for the sleepless nights where Your presence was my only comfort. For the days You saw me weep in my office at 5:00 a.m., crying out for guidance, asking why my life wasn't what it was supposed to be. Your plans are indeed not my plans, and Your thoughts, higher than mine. And I've learned it is far better that way. Father, would You glorify Your name through this story, that as Christ said, people would know this story by its love. Holy Spirit, would You write with me more and more every day and wake me with the kiss of Your presence in the morning.

And last, but certainly not least, my own readers. If you've gotten this far, you must either love me devotedly or be just as nosy and nerdy as me, lol! But in all earnestness, thank you. Thank you for loving this story and receiving it and its characters with open hearts and open hands. You are the lifeblood of why I do what I do. Never forget that, my loves.

If this story has given you even a ray of enjoyment and you want to share your thoughts, please know my door is always open on Instagram (@shirajrodriguez) and my online home away from home (bio.site/shirajrodriguez).

To Him be the glory forever and ever.

All my love,
Shira

Pages of Grace

HEATHER FLYNN

Dedication

To everyone who has ever wondered what their purpose in life is. May each of you find the wonders that God has in store for you!

"What can I get for you?" A man's voice cut through the fog that clouded Emilee Claymont's mind.

Without looking up and still a bit stuck in her own world, she murmured, "A slice of strawberry rhubarb pie would be nice if you have it, please."

"Would you like to try a new creation, miss? A freshly baked pie with strawberries, rhubarb, a little pumpkin spice, and all things nice? I'm thinking of calling it the Emilee Special." The man's odd comment and his barely suppressed laughter actually made Emilee come back from her orbit.

She looked up to see her longtime friend, Drake Bennett, standing there with a menu in his hand and a kitchen towel slung over his shoulder. Emilee rolled her eyes, laughing. "Nice try, Drake." She let out a sigh, then readjusted her thoughts. "So how's the diner doing today?"

Drake sat down on the chair across from Emilee at her little table tucked away in the corner where she always sat. She smiled to herself; there had been a lot of memories that had happened here over the years. In fact, this was the exact same table where they had met as teenagers. At the time, Drake was working as a waiter in the diner his family had owned for generations. On that fateful day, Emilee was supposed to meet a "secret admirer" for a date at the diner, only to find out some of her classmates had pulled a mean prank on her. So there she had sat crying in the corner while trying her best to drink a chocolate milkshake, which wasn't exactly an easy task. Drake had noticed her crying, and in an effort to help her to stop and smile, he had grabbed some glassware from a nearby table and attempted to juggle it. That may have ended badly with broken glass on the floor, but it had started their friendship, and she was extremely grateful for that. Sometimes it was hard to imagine that the awkward teenage waiter had become the man who now had inherited the Bennett Family Diner, owning and running it himself. Drake seemed happy and content in his work.

Emilee only wished she could feel the same way about her own job.

Drake brought her out of her reminiscing by asking, "So what's got you so far away today?"

Emilee tapped her fingers on the table, her mind on all of the uncertainties at the publishing company where she worked. While she loved getting to work with writers, it wasn't the same as getting to be a writer herself. "It's work. You know, when I first started out there, I thought it could be my ticket to getting into the writing world. Now I just dread the very thought of going in."

Drake's brow furrowed. "What's been going on lately?"

Emilee sighed. "Well, things started going downhill with the layoffs. That really tightened things up. We don't have the same amount of people anymore, so there's been an increased workload for those of us that are left." Emilee felt restless and full of questions. "I guess I'm just putting off going in as long as feasibly possible."

"I'm sorry to hear that. I didn't know things had gotten that bad. Is there anything I can do to help?" Drake checked his watch. "Oh. I guess it's pretty close to your work time now, isn't it?

Emilee nodded after glancing at her phone. "Yep, I'm running close on time. I guess I should be heading out." She stood and started toward the diner's door.

Drake walked along beside her. "Do you need a ride to work this morning? I can get away, if I need to."

"That's okay. I'd rather enjoy the beautiful day outside."

"All right, well, I'll pick you up this afternoon." Drake smirked. "So ... I'll save that new recipe for later, then?"

Emilee laughed. "No, I think I'll pass on that one. See you later, Drake."

"Take care, Emilee." Drake waved as he headed back toward the kitchen, and Emilee headed out the door and into the cool late-October air. If she had to pick a season for her car to break down, making her transportation either walking or getting rides, she was glad it was fall and not in the hot southern summer.

Emilee started down the street; she admired the quaint small town she had called home her whole life. Its cozy shops all had their windows decorated with the palette of autumn. The air was cooler today, and she smiled at the just-emerging colors on the leaves of the trees nestled along the street. Normally, she would take her time to enjoy this beautiful fall day—it was her favorite season after all—but she was already running too late for that. Within a few minutes, she had reached her destination, but she hesitated outside the door of the old, weathered brick building. She took a deep breath, trying to mentally prepare herself, since she had no idea what would be awaiting her on the other side.

When Emilee had started at Harding Publishing House several years ago, it had been like a dream come true. She had loved crafting stories since she was able to talk and was always having all sorts of adventures in her imagination. It seemed natural for her to pursue a career in writing since it was her passion. When she had seen the job listing for an opening at Harding Publishing House's Oakville branch, it had felt like this could be her big break into writing.

She had started out helping whoever on staff needed anything, and they had seen potential in her. As she continued to prove her determination and dedication, they started giving her on-the-job training for editing work. Although she'd have preferred to be writing her own books, she was thankful for the opportunity to dip her toes into the world of how books were made. When she had been offered the additional position of ghostwriter a few years later, she thought that would be the perfect way to get her foot into the proverbial door and allow people to at least catch a glimpse of her *own* writing abilities. Sadly, that moment never came, and she was still stuck in the shadows of someone else's name while feeling like she was hiding who she was and what she felt.

Enough putting things off. She opened the door and went to her desk. There were no new notes on her incoming requests bulletin board, so she powered on her computer. She sorted through new emails, sending the junk to the trash; however, one particular message caught her eye.

Before she got a chance to read the entire message, she was taken by surprise at the abrupt sound of an office door slamming shut. With tears streaking down her face, Laney Wilson, a graphic designer and as of late, social media manager, headed for Emilee's desk.

Emilee jumped to her feet, worry gripping her. "Laney? What's wrong?"

"I can't take it anymore, Em." Laney rubbed her eyes with her fists.

Unsure what to do, Emilee wrung her hands. "I'm sure it'll be okay. Why don't you sit down and take a breath? I'll get you some water, and you can tell me what happened. We can work it out if we work together."

Laney accepted the bottle of water Emilee offered from the mini fridge under her desk, but Laney stayed standing. "It's too late for that. I already quit. Without two weeks' notice. I'm leaving today, and I'll never come back here again."

"Laney, what happened to bring this about?" Emilee didn't know what to say. This certainly hadn't been what she expected when she came into work this morning.

Laney ran her hand through her thick, curly hair in frustration. "You know how they just had the layoffs the month before last?"

Emilee's chest tightened as she continued to listen to Laney.

"We all knew there would be more work to go around, and I didn't even mind taking over the social media accounts for the company. Mr. and Mrs. Weston called me into the meeting room this morning to tell me I needed to double the number of social media output. Not only that, but the other graphic designer had given her two weeks' notice only yesterday, and I would be expected to take on *all* of the graphic design projects. I don't mind the hard work, but this is beyond what I can possibly do in the hours we are allowed. There was no negotiating with either of them when I tried to work out a solution. Their *solution* was that I had a couple days to figure out a plan to do the work of two or three people. No raise, no extra hours paid. I can't do this anymore. So I'm packing my stuff and then I'm out of here."

Emilee numbly helped Laney pack her things into some boxes and then watched her leave. Emilee didn't know how much more loss this branch could stand. At this rate, she was nearly the last person standing, aside from the husband and wife who were the head honchos (or more professionally titled as the co-branch managers of this location) and a small handful of others. On top of the job-related stress Laney also had to deal with a stressful home life. Emilee made a mental note to do some special prayer time for Laney when she got home tonight.

Emilee let out a long sigh of relief as she stepped out of work at the end of the day. Thankfully, there in his old pickup sat Drake, waiting to give her a ride home. She put her backpack on the floorboard of the truck and swung herself onto the passenger seat.

"Did you have a good day at school?" Drake joked as he picked up the backpack, but then he groaned. "What have you got in there, a ton of bricks?"

"Homework?" Emilee gave a cutesy grin, hoping that would distract him. "Thanks for giving me a ride home. I hope I can get my car fixed sometime soon."

Apparently, jokes and gratitude were not enough to distract Drake. "Emmie? Don't tell me you are taking work home. Not when it's your birthday tomorrow."

Emilee fidgeted with her hands, refusing to look at him. "Okay ... I won't tell you, then."

Drake gave her a stern look, and she caved.

"Okay, fine. Laney quit today, so my workload *might* have picked up some more. It's okay. I promise I can take care of it. I just might have to do some of it at home. It's no big deal."

Drake put the truck in gear, then started down the road toward Emilee's home, but he wasn't done with this particular conversation topic yet. "I don't want you burning yourself out. You already do a lot for the company. It's not that I don't believe in what you can do, because you know I do. It's just that I can't stand to see you stressed out." Drake shifted the topic, but just a little. "At least you can get a little more money that way."

Emilee didn't know how to respond, so the rest of the ride to her quaint English-inspired cottage was silent. Should she tell him she was *not* actually getting paid for taking her work home with her? In truth, putting in some 'bonus hours' was not ideal, but it helped take a little off her plate so she could feel more productive during working hours. When he pulled into her driveway, Emilee started to get out without even glancing in Drake's direction. "Thanks again for the ride."

"Emmie, please wait," Drake pleaded.

Emilee turned to him and could not force herself to look away from his gaze, no matter how hard she tried.

"Please know that I meant no harm by what I said earlier. I care about you, and I want you to take care of yourself. Okay?"

Emilee felt a slow smile ease across her face. "I know. Thank you."

"Also, don't think you are off the hook about your birthday!" Drake tapped the steering wheel with a happy little drumbeat. "You had some birthday fun with your parents last weekend, right?"

Emilee nodded. "Yeah, we did it last weekend. There was an important meeting at church that they had to be there for as the pastor and his wife. I'm fine spending my birthday reading and stuff."

"Not a chance, Claymont. You'll probably just try to work." Drake grinned. "I'll be by tomorrow morning to pick you up."

Emilee looked at Drake skeptically. "What are you cooking up, Bennett?"

Drake winked at her. "Wouldn't you like to know?"

"You know I don't like surprises!" Emilee groaned.

"Tough luck," Drake said as Emilee got out of the truck, took her bag, and headed toward the house. "Be ready at eight!" he called out as he drove away.

Emilee shook her head, laughing. He was such a goofball, but sometimes she wished he was *her* goofball. She'd grown to like Drake as more than a friend over the years, and she just wished he would feel the same way about her. Why did she have such a hard time believing that could ever happen?

Night had fallen, and Emilee still found herself sitting on the back porch of the sweet little house she had inherited when her grandparents passed away. The manuscript in her hand was marked here and there with red ink, and she fought back a yawn. She should probably be headed for bed, but she was determined to get a few more pages, maybe even the rest of this chapter, edited on this work project tonight. She picked up her cup of tea and sipped it, savoring the mingling taste of the herbs all dancing in her mouth.

When she finally finished the chapter, she set the papers on the table next to her tea and looked out at the now-fading-away flowers of her garden. This "death" of the flowers was only for a season. A person just needed a little patience to see things come to life once more. She closed her eyes, enjoying the peaceful stillness that surrounded her and the calm it brought with it.

Growing up, this home had been a haven for her. Anytime she got to visit Nana and Pop, she had felt herself dreaming up all sorts of stories. Nana had been born in England, but circumstances had brought her to America, where she had ended up meeting Pop. The rest, as they said, was history. This cottage had been Nana's dream home, and Pop and his brothers had built it exactly as she described, including the lovely garden out back.

Emilee stood up, pulling her sweater a little tighter, then crossed over to the big tree that stood center stage in the garden. Her grandparents had planted this tree on their first wedding anniversary, with prayers and promises for the future whispered. She traced the initials carved into the wood. While her grandparents had planted the tree with love and hope, these carved letters were a sign of love from her parents.

Thoughtfully, Emilee meandered back toward the porch, where she gathered her things. Her sleep that night was fitful and full of dreams that leaned more toward being nightmares. None of them were vivid enough for her to remember the next morning, but overall, they stuck to her mind like gum to a shoe. They left her feeling held back in a way she couldn't explain. By the time seven o'clock rolled around, she was dressed, after much deliberation, in some nice blue jeans, a flower-print shirt, and a jean jacket. Now she was ready to go for whatever Drake had planned for her that day.

At exactly eight o'clock, the doorbell rang, and Emilee grabbed her purse. When she swung the door open, she was surprised to see Drake standing there in a nice brown, checked, button-up shirt with a beautiful bouquet of red and white chrysanthemums in a fist and a sweet smile on his face. "You look nice, Emmie." He handed her the flowers, and she breathed in the scent of them.

Emilee felt her face grow hot, so she quickly turned on her heel, waving Drake inside. She grabbed a vase in the kitchen, filled it with water, put the flowers in, and placed the arrangement in the center of her dining room table. She smiled; she liked the light and happy feel it gave the room. "Thank you. You don't look too bad yourself, Drake." She grinned at him, then asked a question she'd been wondering since yesterday. "So ... what's the big secret? What are we doing today?"

"Fixing your car?" Drake leaned against the doorframe that led into the entryway, his face didn't give any indication if what he said was meant to sound like a question or not.

Emilee gave him a quizzical look, unsure if he was joking or not. She almost thought she detected a mischievous glint in his eyes, but she couldn't be sure. "That's your idea of birthday fun? Besides, if you're serious, that's too expensive!"

Drake laughed. "Relax, Emmie. I thought we would take your birthday on the road." They walked out of the house, only stopping long enough for Emilee to lock the door; by that time, Drake stood at the truck's door, holding it open and waiting for her. "M'lady, your carriage awaits." He bowed deeply, laughing at his attempt to imitate a British accent.

Emilee climbed into the truck, then Drake climbed onto the driver's seat after having shut her door for her. Emilee turned towards Drake. "You aren't going to tell me what we're doing, are you?"

"You'll see soon enough." Drake smiled at her and then they were off and rolling down the road to whatever mystery destination he had in mind.

"Oh, Drake, it's beautiful!" Emilee whispered in awe, as they arrived at a beautiful park. The trees were at one of the most breathtaking points in their autumn transformation.

She admired the many colors—the beautiful yellows, reds, and oranges—that burst forth before her eyes. "I really enjoyed our drive."

"The drive? You didn't think the drive was all we were doing for your birthday, did you?" Drake shot her a teasing look, one eyebrow lifted. "No, no, my dear friend. There is so much more that awaits you!" With that, Drake hopped out of the truck and practically ran to open her door. Unexpectedly, he leaned close to her, taking her hand to help her from the truck. "Are you ready for this?"

Emilee felt her breath catch, and she shoved away the thought that these things could mean more than just two friends on a birthday outing. She forced a laugh. "Let's go see what you've cooked up."

Drake led the way through the park at a slow pace as they enjoyed the sights and sounds that met them along the way. He pulled out a Frisbee that he had tucked underneath his arm, then gave Emilee a challenging, yet playful grin. They tossed the disc back and forth as they enjoyed the spectacular weather today. Drake went ahead, saying that he needed to check and make sure everything for the next part of the surprise was in order. Emilee didn't mind; this time alone gave her a chance to just take joy in being in the great outdoors. There was such a wonderful sense of calm that she couldn't help but smile and lose herself in the moment. As a cool breeze brought a small league of leaves past her, Emilee stopped walking, closed her eyes, and spun around in a circle, feeling, for a moment, completely carefree. *This is shaping up to be a really good day.*

At that exact moment, she felt something hit her upper arm. Opening her eyes, she didn't see anything on her arm, but when she looked down at the ground, she was confused to find what looked to be a foam dart.

"Open fire!" Drake's voice came from somewhere nearby.

Emilee yelped, laughing while she tried to dodge more of the foam darts. "I'm un-armed!"

Drake stepped from behind a nearby tree, bent over with laughter. When he finally caught his breath, he said, "I'm out of ammunition anyhow. I'll reload, and you can get acquainted with yours." Emilee noticed he had not only one foam shooter in his hand but another tied by a string to his belt loop. He untied the string and handed the weapon to her.

What followed was a crazy foam dart battle that left them both panting and laughing.

"Okay, I give up! I was going to let you win anyway, since it's your birthday." Drake blew out a breath, hands raised into the air in a sign of surrender.

"Right." Emilee laughed, then stooped to pick up the darts that were scattered around on the ground. "Thank you; that was a lot of fun."

Drake motioned for her to follow him, and they walked farther along the path through the park.

"Drake? Do you still have more surprises up your sleeve?"

"I mean … I did wear long sleeves after all," Drake joked. "Hey, I helped you get in a workout, free of charge. You can't beat that kind of a deal. Besides, how can you come to the park without having a picnic?" In that instant, they crested a hill, and there in a nice grassy area near some trees was a blanket spread out on the ground. She could hardly believe her eyes at the feast before them. "I had it all made at the diner this morning and had someone deliver it for me so you wouldn't smell the food on the ride here. Are you hungry?"

"Absolutely!" Emilee pointed at a covered pie pan. "What kind of pie are we having?"

Drake laughed. "It's the Emilee Special, of course. It's only strawberry and rhubarb, no pumpkin spice, but it's still real nice."

They settled onto the blanket and ate their meal. Not only was it delicious but it was satisfying to just eat in the quiet with no pressure to talk. They often sat together in comfortable silence, and when they chatted, the subjects could end up going anywhere under the sun. Now was no different. Emilee was thoroughly enjoying this birthday celebration with one of her closest friends. "You know you didn't have to do all this, right?" She looked at Drake, who was finishing off his second slice of pie.

"I know I didn't have to, but I wanted to." He smiled softly. "You needed a break, and you deserved it." There was a pause as he fidgeted with his fingers. "Could I ask you something?"

"Okay?" Emilee had no idea what to expect. While, yes, he was a goofball and great at making her laugh, their friendship was no stranger to deeper conversations as well. They shared their secret wishes and dreams (at least … most of them), prayed together, and consoled each other when things didn't go as they might have planned.

"First off, I want you to know I'm not trying to pressure you about anything whatsoever, but when was the last time you wrote?"

Drake's question left her stunned for a second before she responded. "I write all the time."

His voice was soft as he continued. "Maybe for someone else. When was the last time you wrote for *you*? When did you last put pen to paper on the things God has poured into *your* heart? I know that's all you used to talk about. You'd be dreaming of someday getting your words out there for others to read, to let others see what God wanted to say through you."

Emilee felt her eyes welling up with tears as Drake spoke. Everything he said was true. Writing had always been something that made her feel so free. With a pen in her hand or a laptop at her fingertips, she felt a power that brought her unspeakable joy as she watched the story flow forth from her mind into something tangible. Something that felt like it was her *purpose* to be doing. That was something, if she were truly honest with herself, that she had not felt in a very long time. She felt so stuck. She wasn't sure when her fire had been doused and she had stopped believing in herself.

"Emmie, I'm sorry. I didn't mean to make you cry." Drake reached out and touched her hand briefly.

"No, Drake ... Don't be sorry. Everything you said is true." She accepted the handkerchief he offered and wiped her tears. "I feel like I've lost touch with my words, with what I want to be saying in writing. It's like there's some wall blocking my path that I can't see any way to get around."

"You know I am here for you in whatever way you need. If there's any way I can help you with getting back to that place, just say the word, and I will do whatever I can."

"That means more than I can put into words." Emilee let out a jagged sigh, one last tear falling down her cheek. "I really think I needed to hear that."

"Well, it'll be November in just a couple of days, and I know you used to always talk about taking part in that writing challenge. Why not join the Nanobot Wrimoth?"

"The *what* now?" Emilee laughed, then realized what he meant. "Oh, Drake! NaNoWriMo; it's short for National Novel Writing Month." She thought about it for a moment. He made a good point. It *was* something she'd always thought about doing but had just never taken the time to try. "You know what ... yeah, why not? It couldn't hurt."

Drake smiled. "Atta, girl." Then he stood and walked over behind the nearby tree. He returned with his guitar case in one hand and a canvas bag in the other. She almost thought there was the lightest touch of a blush on his cheeks as he pulled his guitar from its case. "I thought a great way to end our da ... day here would be with some worship time. I mean, that is, if you don't mind."

A huge grin broke out on Emilee's face. "I would love that so much."

Drake started strumming, and together they sang songs of worship. Some of the songs were classic hymns and others were more contemporary, but with each new song, they both were praising God more and more. Drake would sometimes sing a song while Emilee just sat and soaked it in. She felt peace listening to the strings of the guitar and his voice and the meaning behind the words being sung. All these things swirled straight to her core, and she felt so lighthearted. As they sang the last few words of "Amazing Grace" without music, she didn't think it could get much better than this. Drake put his guitar away, then pulled their Bibles from the canvas bag.

He handed Emilee her Bible. "I grabbed it while you were distracted with the flowers and the vase."

"How sweet and clever of you." Emilee smiled, flipping open her Bible. "Where should we start?"

Together, they studied their Bibles, sharing what thoughts came to mind when they read. When they had finished, Drake asked if they could pray together. Drake offered to take the lead.

"Father God, thank You for Emilee. Thank You for putting her into my life and for letting her be born and becoming the wonderful human being she is. We thank You for the day we have shared today and for many more to come. Please let us always chase after Your will and show the light of Your love in all we do. Let us always remember when the weight of the world feels too heavy and we feel like giving up that You never left us and are for us! Help us each and every day, Lord. In Jesus's name, we humbly pray, amen."

They gathered all their things and started leaving the park. It was slow going, but neither of them minded it. The ride home was mostly quiet but peaceful. When they pulled into the driveway, Drake turned to Emilee. "I have one final surprise for you."

"Really? What else could there possibly be?"

"So I really did get your car fixed while we were gone today. You're all good to go. You don't have to walk everywhere, and you can feel like you have a little more freedom."

Emilee was stunned speechless. This was far too generous a gift, one she didn't know she could ever repay.

"It's a free gift, Emilee ... I wanted to give this to you."

"Thank you, Drake. Today truly has been wonderful." They said their goodbyes as she was climbing out of the truck, and then Emilee waved as he headed off down the road toward his own home. Emilee basked in the memories and emotions of today. It had been a blessed day. As she let her mind replay through the events of the day, she couldn't help but think how closely it resembled a date. Could Drake actually have feelings for her?

By the time the first of November rolled around, Emilee had been thinking a lot about what Drake had said. She'd felt a little spark in her heart of her love for writing once more. So she decided to dig into some old files that had story ideas and started works-in-progress. There was one in particular that caught her attention. She couldn't quite put her finger on what it was about this story idea, but it resonated with her, and she thought she could do something with it. She didn't know if she could succeed in writing a novel of her own, but she wouldn't ever know if she didn't give it a try. There was still the occasional voice of doubt that tried to creep into her thoughts and make her question if she was really called to write or telling her she should forget writing on her own and stick with what she'd been doing. When those thoughts tried to attack her, she would get away to a quiet place, to pray and listen to worship music while working on *her* writing project. It wasn't always easy, but it felt right.

The fact that she had extra time in the morning at home since her car was now fixed was helping her tremendously. All that she needed to do to get started was to find a quiet place to sit and start typing. She found herself choosing to spend more of her free time building her *own* story, rather than using it to get in extra (unpaid) work hours. A part of her felt guilty for not devoting as much time to her day job as she once had, but she was learning to readjust her mindset as far as that was concerned. She believed that it was because of this that she found herself smiling more often as she went to work. She still dreaded it, but the days were a bit easier because she had something else to fix her focus on when things were hard.

Around the middle of the month, Emilee was shocked at how far she had come on what she was writing. What she was doing might *actually* be a book someday; she could almost feel it. This was her opportunity to be more than just a machine cranking out someone else's ideas. She had an extra hop in her step as she went into work and started her day.

"Miss Claymont, may we see you in the meeting room?" Emilee was surprised to see Mrs. Weston, one of the co-branch managers, beside her desk. She was standing there as still as stone and ramrod straight, her expression unreadable.

"Yes, ma'am." Emilee nervously followed behind her. *What could this be about?* She wondered to herself if she was to be next on the chopping block. For a moment, doubt crept in, and she thought that writing her own words might have stolen focus and time on cranking out better results for work. She did her best to shove that thought away. She didn't owe this company her time outside of working hours. It was nothing to be ashamed of if she chose to write in her free time because it was her own to do with what she saw fit.

When they entered the meeting room, Emilee was shocked to see not only Mr. Weston sitting at the head of the table but several other individuals she didn't recognize along its sides.

"Please have a seat, Miss Claymont." Mr. Weston motioned to a chair at the far end of the table, the only open seat now that Mrs. Weston had sat down.

Emilee sat slowly, afraid she would miss her chair otherwise, given the nerves that were threatening to rattle her apart.

"Do you know why we have called you into this meeting, Miss Claymont?" Mrs. Weston asked in a tone nearly empty of emotion.

"I ... No, I can't say that I know why," Emilee finally managed to say.

Mr. Weston spoke now. "The individuals you see here with us today are some members of the board from headquarters ..." He studied her, and she wasn't sure if he was pausing for emphasis or to make her crazy with anxiety.

"We've lost a lot of employees as of late, for some reason," Mrs. Weston said in a mournful tone that didn't sound very believable. Did she expect anyone to think she truly didn't know why there had been so many of their employees leaving the company? Emilee couldn't believe the gall of this woman. Sure, Laney had quit, but most of the others that had been 'lost' had been laid off. Mrs. Weston added, "It's unfortunate, but it happens, I suppose."

Mr. Weston piped in again. "The Oakville branch of Harding Publishing House is going to be closing our doors. Of course, Mrs. Weston and I have been offered positions at headquarters. All current employees will be notified of termination immediately."

Emilee blinked, momentarily at a loss for words, she was in such shock. "'Termination'? 'Immediately'?" It seemed she could only parrot what they had last said. She was jobless. All of her coworkers, those who were left at this point, were unemployed. Just like that, a normal day coming into work, only to find out they were all being tossed out into the street like trash. Her mind threatened to race away with her, but she did her best to rein it in. What could she do for work?

Mrs. Weston smiled; however, it didn't seem to reach her eyes, making it feel hollow. "You, Miss Claymont, are being offered a position at headquarters as well. If you do choose to accept the offer, you will need to make plans to move as quickly as possible so you can start ASAP. I'm sure you can find some adequate housing that would be suitable for you."

If Emilee had been shocked before, she could have been knocked over by a feather now. "I'm being offered a position at headquarters?"

One of the others in the room, a short man even while seated, interjected, "I'm Andrew Harding II, Miss Claymont, the owner of this company. Are you questioning our judgment in offering you a position?" He looked at her with an icy glare. "We can retract our offer if that would be preferable for you. We were under the impression that you were an employee of exemplary quality and a master of multitasking skills. Were we wrong for thinking this?"

"No, sir. I mean no offense to any of you, Mr. Harding, sir." Emilee struggled to know how to react or what to say. "I ... I only ask that you allow me some time to think it over."

Mr. Harding answered her, a smug look on his face, "We will allow that. Please begin cleaning out any personal belongings from your desk area; when you've finished with that, you may go home." He slid a business card with his name and the address of the headquarters to her. "I'll have my people send over an email with a contract and what we will be expecting from you in this new role. We look forward to hearing your answer, Miss Claymont."

"Yes, sir."

Emilee functioned on autopilot as she left the meeting room, heading straight for her desk to clean everything out. When she had everything securely sitting in a little box, she double-checked the area. It was all clear. She heard Mrs. Weston call the name of one of her remaining coworkers, and she dreaded for them what they were about to hear. It baffled her that she had been selected as the sole regular employee to be offered a position at headquarters. One minute, she had been thinking she was fired; the next, she was being faced with a new opportunity. The question was, should she even consider it?

Emilee walked into Bennett Family Diner and found her way through the crowd to her normal seat. She noticed that nearly every table was full. She didn't mind waiting; she couldn't say she was all that hungry right now anyway. This just felt like a safe place for her to escape to. To fill the time, she pulled out her phone, checking to see if there were any Help Wanted ads for local businesses. She hadn't decided whether or not to accept the new job offer yet, but she wanted to keep her options open.

"Emmie! I didn't expect to see you today." Drake was practically huffing and puffing as he approached her table. "What ... what would you like?"

"To start, for you to catch your breath." Emilee shot her friend a worried glance. "Do you have a minute to sit?"

"I wish I could, but we are short-staffed today. We just had one of our cooks quit because his family is moving, and one of the waitresses had to go on maternity leave." Drake's attention was drawn to a nearby table, where someone was asking for a refill, then he looked at Emilee. "I'll catch you later?"

Emilee nodded and watched Drake rush away. A few minutes later, a waitress brought her a slice of her pie of choice. Emilee had noticed on the menu that Drake had followed through with his threat. He *actually* had listed the strawberry rhubarb as the Emilee Special. She quietly ate the pie, thinking about the decision she had before her to make. After paying, she silently slipped out of the diner and got in her car, then got lost in her thoughts as she drove home. She was grateful for the weekend; she wanted to talk to her parents about this to get their thoughts on the matter, too.

Saturday had come and gone. She had spent a while yesterday talking and praying with her parents about this new job offer and if it was what God wanted for her. She continued to wait for the promised email with details about the position, hoping it would bring more clarity to the situation.

Now it was Sunday, and church service had just ended. Emilee stood up from her seat on the pew, feeling some much-needed peace after listening to a message she desperately needed to hear. She watched with a smile on her face as her dad mingled with his congregation. It made her heart happy to see him fulfilling his purpose and touching people's lives. Her mom had fallen into the role of a pastor's wife perfectly as well. No stereotypes or tropes, just real people who were serving God. Emilee felt tears start pooling up in her eyes, and she did her best to blink them away. She wished she felt clearer about what her *own* purpose was because she felt so uncertain at times.

She decided to wait for people to slowly mingle their way out of the church. After all, she didn't mind being one of the last to leave. Her eyes met those of her sweet friend of many years, Winnie Holt. Winnie raised an eyebrow, mouthing the words *"Are you okay?"* When Emilee just shrugged in response, Winnie leaned over and whispered something to her husband, who nodded and started the process of leaving with their kids. Winnie wove her way through the crowd until she reached Emilee. "Okay, sis, we need some time to hang out." They hugged, and Emilee couldn't think of a reason to object.

Emilee sighed. She didn't really feel like going out, so she offered, "I can fix us lunch at my house, if you want."

Winnie gave two thumbs up. "Perfect."

Emilee and Winnie were some of the last ones out of the church. Emilee hugged her parents, and the four of them chatted for a few minutes. Winnie and Emilee walked over to Emilee's car, then on the way to Emilee's cottage, the pair made small talk. Once at home, Emilee made them each a sandwich from stuff she had in her fridge, then placed them on the table. When they had both settled onto their seats, Emilee let Winnie say grace over the food.

When the prayer was finished, Emilee looked over at her friend. "Anything exciting and new going on with you, Winnie?"

Winnie shook her head. "We can talk about me later. What's going on?" She reached out and touched Emilee's hand. "I'm here for you." That was all it took for the floodgates to open, and Emilee released her pent-up tears like a raging river. Winnie stood up and came over to Emilee to wrap her in a bear hug. "Spill your tea."

Emilee shared with Winnie how she had been feeling so drained from her work. She told her about how she had started writing for herself again and how she had been feeling a freedom that she had not experienced in some time. Then there had been this offer about a new position she still didn't know any details about. She continued to share thoughts she hadn't even realized had been weighing her down. She even told Winnie about the complicated emotions of her situation with Drake and whether he could like her as more than a friend.

Winnie listened patiently, taking everything in. She clasped her hands in front of her as she locked eyes with Emilee. "For starters, about Drake, didn't he ask you out when we were in high school?"

Emilee was caught off guard by that question. "I … I don't think so?"

"He asked you to that movie … And you told him you didn't want to go."

"That wasn't a date, Winnie." Emilee protested. "He was just asking as a friend." She thought about different instances with Drake over the years. Suddenly, she wasn't so sure anymore. "Wasn't it?"

"That man has been head over heels for you for over a decade now, Emilee. You have feelings for each other. I think everyone but you two can see that." Winnie tapped the table with her painted fingernails. "Also, the birthday surprise you described that he took you on was screaming *date*."

Emilee felt dumbfounded. "So ... you think ... there could be more between Drake and me than just friends?" When Winnie shot her a look that said *duh*, Emilee continued, "How did I not pick up on that?" Her heart danced with a thrill of hope at the possibility that there might be more for Drake and her.

Winnie reached across the table and grasped Emilee's hand. "You tend to not believe in yourself and what you can do. You believe in everyone but yourself. It's time to shift that thinking." Winnie continued, her voice calm and determined, "As far as this work situation is concerned, I recommend you *take five*. By that I mean, even in circumstances where time might be hard to come by, just take five minutes and give it to God. No distractions, just you, God, and His Holy Word. Sometimes all He needs is just five minutes to turn your day around and change things in a way you never could have imagined."

Emilee and Winnie continued talking for a little while longer until Winnie's husband showed up to take her out to dinner. Emilee thanked her friend for everything and waved at the happy couple as they drove away.

Emilee thought about what Winnie had said, so she grabbed her Bible and headed for the old tree in the center of the garden. She sat down, then leaned her back against the rough bark. She didn't care that the ground was damp and cool; this was where she wanted to be right now. This was the place of so many memories of her family. So many dreams and prayers had been poured out in this spot. Emilee closed her eyes, not trying to stop the tears streaming down her face. "Oh, God ... what do I do now? What is the right choice with this job situation?"

On the one hand, if she moved to the city where the company's headquarters was located, she wouldn't necessarily have to take everything she owned with her. Harding Publishing was a good two hours away. Maybe she could even come home on the weekends. It might give her more opportunities for her writing to be noticed. She wasn't the biggest fan of being in the city, so she had to ask herself if she would enjoy being there for most of her waking hours. A long commute didn't seem like the answer either, because it wouldn't allow much time for sleeping between work and travel time.

On the other hand, if she didn't take the job, what would she do for a living? She knew God would provide, but the uncertainty of it made her nervous. While she was a hard worker, the likelihood that anyone in this small town would be looking for someone whose résumé primarily showed a writing-related background wasn't very probable. She thought of Drake and what Winnie had told her and wondered if there really could be more for them than friendship. She felt sick to her stomach with a toxic mix of frustration and worry as her thoughts nearly made her dizzy from going around in so many circles.

Emilee felt the weight of the Bible sitting on her lap, and she released a sigh. *God, please help guide me in this decision. I don't know best, but You do. Help me to see Your will in all of this. I don't want to do any of this without You.* On the inside cover of her Bible, she noticed a note from her Granny—not the one who she had inherited the home from, but instead her last living grandparent. "To Emilee, my sweet first grandchild. Don't let worry bring you down. I know that's easier said than done. Always remember your worth is found in God and who He says you are, not in the world and it's ever changing opinions. Love, Granny."

She continued to flip through her Bible and ended up in the book of Habakkuk. The second part of the fifth verse in chapter one resounded within her. *"For I will work a work in your days which you would not believe ... "* Emilee felt God's presence wrap around her. She continued to read her Bible, finding verses saying in Proverbs to *"trust in the Lord with all your heart"* and in Romans that *"all things work together for good to those who love God, to those who are the called according to His purpose."*

Each of these verses found a place to rest in her heart like a dove in its nest. She didn't miss out on the word *purpose*, something she'd been feeling like she had been missing out on, something that God had known all along for her; He was just waiting for her to see it. That night she slept with dreams of possibilities and the hope she had found within the pages filled with God's grace and mercy.

The next morning, Emilee awoke early and listened to worship music on the radio while she was fixing herself breakfast. She smiled at several of the songs being about God's grace. She checked her email on her phone as she was eating and saw the very email she'd been waiting for. As she read its contents that described the position and then scanned the contract, she was surprised.

Suddenly, it was all starting to make sense why they had told her she would have to move to headquarters rather than having a choice to work remotely on editing and such. They wanted her to be a glorified secretary. Of course, they didn't come out and admit it in so many words. However, it was plain to see on top of her already existing roles, she would be expected to answer phone calls, run errands, and do other on-site desk work. The contract also suggested, in cleverly disguised language, that she would be getting a decrease in pay. Emilee had already felt what decision should be made last night in her time with God, she felt this new information confirmed all of it.

She picked up the business card; it was time to call Harding Publishing House and let them know she had made her decision. After being put on hold multiple times, Emilee found herself on the phone with none other than Mrs. Weston, who didn't sound nearly as confident as she once had.

"Mrs. Weston? This is Emilee Claymont. Please notify Mr. Harding I'm not interested in his offer. I appreciate the time I spent with the company and the lessons I have learned. However, I see no future for me there."

The other end of the line was silent, and for a moment, Emilee thought that the call might have dropped. Mrs. Weston spoke, but something in her voice was different, humbler. "Good for you, Emilee. I wish you the best."

Emilee smiled, astounded at this turn of events but grateful for seeing God putting more changes in the works. Mrs. Weston and she said their goodbyes but not before Emilee added that she would be praying for the Westons. When the call was finished, Emilee let out a sigh so deep it felt like it came all the way from her toes.

She was pulled from her thoughts by the sound of the doorbell ringing. She opened the door to see Drake standing there in front of her.

"Emilee." His eyes had an almost desperate look in them. "I need to talk to you."

"Of course, come in." Emilee led the way to the kitchen, offering to make him something to eat or even a cup of coffee or tea, but he declined. They sat down at the dining table, looking at each other for a few silent moments before Emilee broke the silence. "Is everything okay, Drake?"

"Winnie told me about your job offer ... I know it may seem selfish of me, but I can't let you make a decision without making something clear between us." He locked eyes with Emilee, and her heartbeat picked up in speed. "I've cared about you for a long time,

Emilee Claymont. As more than just a friend. I know you didn't want to go to the movies when we were kids—"

"It wasn't you; it was the movie. Plus, I just don't care about going to the movie theater." Emilee smiled. "Sorry for butting in; I just wanted to let you know that."

"Oh ..." Drake seemed to gather his thoughts. "Well, Emilee, I just want you to know I can't help but pursue you and the beautiful woman of God I have watched you blossom into over the years. You are such a beacon of His grace and love that I'm left astounded. That's why I took you on such an extravagant day for your birthday. I wanted you to feel how special you are. I even almost slipped and called it a date that day. I don't know what decision you are going to make about the job, but please know whatever you end up doing, I'll always be praying for you and supporting you."

Emilee watched, started to respond, but stopped because she was unsure what to say.

Drake's Adam's apple bobbed up and down, and he blinked. When he spoke, his voice was raspy with emotion. "I love you, Emilee Claymont."

Emilee wiped at tears that had pooled in the corner of her eyes. "I never thought I would hear you say those words. I couldn't make myself believe they could possibly be true. I love you, too, Drake Bennett."

Drake visibly relaxed. "That's a relief." He smiled. "Like I said, whatever decision you come to, I'll do what I can to help you through it."

"I turned down the position."

"You did?" Drake's eyes brightened.

Emilee smiled. "That wasn't what God had planned for me. I have no idea what exactly He does have in store for me, but I know being there was not it. Just like the 'two roads diverged in a yellow wood,' I'm taking 'the one less traveled by.' God knows more than I do, and He sees what I can't possibly see. I know He has a fantastic tapestry that He is weaving together for my future that is beyond what I could ever imagine."

Drake looked like a shy schoolboy as he looked down at the table, then back up at her. "Is it weird to ask you to be my girlfriend *after* I've already told you 'I love you'?"

Emilee laughed and felt like her heart was dancing with pure joy. "Of course I'll be your girlfriend, you goofball." She smiled. She didn't know what was in store for them, but she trusted God with it, and she would do her best to enjoy each moment He gave them.

Thanksgiving had come and gone, and Emilee had to admit she was relieved. It was nice to spend this first Thanksgiving as a couple with Drake—they had taken the time to visit with both his family and hers—but she was ready for things to slow back down to normal once more.

She was also beginning to adjust to the life she was now finding herself in and truly enjoying it. Drake had offered her a position at the diner and let her adjust her hours there around her schedule as needed. She had really enjoyed getting to interact with the customers, and of course, she didn't mind being around Drake a little more.

Emilee's writing project she started working on for National Novel Writing Month was nearly completed. She was astounded at how many words had flowed out of her mind and into existence. When she had last sat down and started reading what she had written so far in her novel, she was amazed to see God's grace sprinkled throughout the pages. The sense of accomplishment was a nice boost of confidence, and she realized writing was something she was called to do. It was a part of who she was, and if she wasn't writing, actually writing the words that were waiting in her heart to come into existence, then she was betraying herself. From now on, she'd keep writing, even as the other things in life around her were changing. She would write what God was calling her to. Why? Because *this* was her purpose.

Acknowledgments

First things first, I thank God for His many blessings. He put a dream and a story in my heart from a young age. He is the One Who gave me a purpose in my life, and I want to do everything I can to fulfill that. I'm so thankful He gave me this opportunity.

I also want to thank everyone in my life who has impacted my own story and for believing in me when I might not have been able to believe in myself. To each of you, my sweet family and friends, thank you; I'm so blessed to have you in my life. A special thanks to Daddy, Momma, and Granny for always believing in me and my writing. Of course, I can't leave out my sweet husband who has been by my side through this whole process, encouraging me and helping me in whatever way I needed.

I want to add an additional thanks to my Writer's Club who encouraged me to take the plunge and try to write a short story for this anthology.

I can't forget this wonderful team of ladies I've been blessed to get the opportunity to work with on this project. They have become a community that has encouraged me and helped me grow so much.

Of course, before I go, I must thank you, dear reader. I'm grateful that you saw fit to use some precious time out of your day to spend with me and my story.

The Sound of Healing

AVRIE SWAN

Dedication

For Grandpa. Thank you for always sharing your stories with me ... even the hard ones.

Chapter One

St. Ignace, Michigan
November 1958

The sound of barking spiked fear, cold and raw, into Rebeka Wagner's heart. She ran, the frosty air making her throat burn and her lungs ache as she darted through the forest. Each breath was like a dagger, and every step sent pain shooting through her spine.

The heavy snow clung to her skirts and tried to weigh her down, tried to slow her footsteps, but Beka continued on, her small arms swinging. Branches slashed at her face and snagged her clothes as she ran, twigs scraping against her bare cheeks. Though she wanted nothing more than to stop and catch her breath, the warm hand that held her own tugged her forward.

"Almost there," a young voice urged from beside her, a voice that she trusted beyond all else. "We're almost there, Beka. We just have to run a little bit farther. We can't stop now."

"Beka, are you awake yet?"

Rebeka shifted on the bed and groaned, the nightmare fading into a haze at the back of her mind. It wasn't the first time she had experienced the dream, nor did she suspect it would be the last. At least she no longer jolted awake in the middle of the night with a pounding heart and sweat trailing down her spine.

"Beka! Did you hear me?"

The high-pitched voice cast the last vestiges of sleep from Rebeka's mind. "I'm sorry, Eleanor. What did you say?" she asked.

Eleanor's impatient voice returned, this time slightly louder. "I was asking if you were awake. I need to leave for school, and the walk hasn't been shoveled. Father already left for work, so he can't do it."

"You're more than capable of doing it yourself," Rebeka mumbled, rolling over.

"If I shovel, I'll get snow on my new shoes! And my skirt will probably get wet, too. Do you have any idea how embarrassing it would be to show up to school like that? And don't tell me to change. The bus arrives in five minutes."

Rebeka waved a hand in the air without looking up. "It can't be more than an inch or two. You'll survive."

Her sister huffed in annoyance. "Fine, but don't expect me to do you any favors in the future." Retreating footsteps sounded as the fourteen-year-old walked down the hallway, and the front door slammed shut shortly after.

Rebeka sighed and pushed herself upright, gazing around the bedroom. Word-covered pages littered the wooden floor and the writing desk in the back corner. They were words that formed Rebeka's entire world, the story she had spent months developing.

After stepping from bed, Rebeka carefully plucked each paper from the floor and arranged them so the title page faced outward. *The Treacherous Journey*. She smiled, the horrible dream fading from memory as she thought of her story. What she wouldn't give to be like her heroine, Adelaide. Adelaide certainly wasn't afraid of night terrors. She was brave, beautiful, and outspoken, a girl who took trouble in hand and solved it with a charming grin. In short, she was everything that Rebeka was not.

Rebeka set the papers on her writing desk and twirled a strand of hickory-colored hair around her finger. There was only one critical flaw with Adelaide's story, a flaw that Rebeka hadn't been able to solve during the night—it was without an ending. It was a problem that required immediate attention, which meant eating breakfast and getting straight to work.

The bell above the door released a loud chime as Rebeka entered the diner, sighing in relief as warm air surrounded her. Music filtered softly through the radio that sat behind the counter and settled in the air like a warm blanket. The diner itself had only a few tables, each surrounded by a cluster of old, wooden chairs, and a countertop with metal stools. Though it was humble in appearance, the building was the central hub of activity for everything in town—a place to huddle over mugs of coffee while whispering gossip, a place to celebrate good news, and a place to sit at the window while pondering the future.

The smell of fresh pancakes and sausage led Rebeka to wander farther into the room, where she took a seat at the counter and withdrew her notepad. Opening to a blank page, she stared down at the empty sheet of paper and willed her mind to come up with something inspired.

"Rebeka! What are you doing out this early? Did you miss breakfast again?" The voice was punctuated by a soft pop and the smacking of lips.

Rebeka looked up, the corners of her mouth lifting when she caught sight of her friend. "Hello, Nelka. I did come here for some breakfast. However, I also came here to see if you could help me finish my story."

Nelka leaned one elbow against the counter, her jaw working the gum that she always seemed to have in her mouth. She appeared to have wrangled her blonde locks into what Rebeka assumed was the latest fashion, a strange combination of curls mounded atop her head and stuck through with a pencil. "What makes you think that I have the answers you need? You're the author. I flip pancakes for a living." She laughed, the sound booming through the small room and making several of the customers look up from their meals.

Rebeka crossed one leg over the other, tugging absentmindedly at a strand of hair that had fallen over her cheek. "I don't know. Maybe I just wanted to get away from the house."

Nelka raised one brow. "Did you have a hard time sleeping again?" Rebeka's face must have been telling, for she shook her head and sighed. "Oh, Beks. You stay here, and I'll get you some fresh pancakes. They're on the house today." Before Rebeka could reject the offer, Nelka turned and sauntered into the kitchen, her apron strings bouncing as she went.

Rebeka exhaled slowly, a smile creeping onto her face. It was good to have friends who cared.

A few minutes later, Nelka returned with a plate of steaming pancakes. "There you are. Eat up, now. You could use a helping or two." She set the plate on the table, along with a cup of coffee. "I put some cream in the coffee, how you always like it." She ended her sentence by blowing and popping a gum bubble.

"Thanks, Nelka," Rebeka murmured, slicing her knife into the buttery pancakes. "I've never tasted anything as good as your pancakes."

Nelka fisted a hand on her hip. "I know you haven't. If only I could get you to try my biscuits. I'm telling you, you'd never want to eat anything else ever again. If they hosted a contest for best biscuits in the world, I'm dead certain I'd be the winner."

Rebeka swallowed, feeling bile rising in the back of her throat at the mere mention of the food. *"Come on, Beka! You have to eat."* Rebeka glanced down at the proffered food. *Bugs, small and black, writhed on brick-hard biscuits.* The memory made her shudder, and she set the fork down with a loud clatter. "No thanks, Nelka. I'm sorry, but I just can't stomach biscuits. It's nothing you've done."

Nelka shrugged. "If you say so. Now, what do you need to finish your story?"

"I'm not sure. Adelaide crosses thousands of miles to find her hero, braving raging storms and terrible monsters to reach his side. But now that she's found him, I don't know what to do."

"What more is there to do? She found him. That's it. The end." Nelka waved a hand in the air. "There doesn't have to be anything else."

"But I feel like there should be. It ought to be romantic somehow." Rebeka closed her eyes, letting her mind drift. "The hero could sweep Adelaide off her feet and say something like ... 'I've been waiting for you to find me.' Then ... they both sail off aboard the ship that he rescued from an army of pirates."

"Pirates? You never mentioned pirates," Nelka said, her blue eyes widening in surprise. "Did he really defeat an entire army of them?"

"He did, and with one hand, too." Rebeka made a stabbing motion with one hand and scribbled down words on her pad of paper with the other.

"Some man he must be," Nelka mused. "I wonder where I could find one of them. I would love to marry a handsome, pirate-slaying fella."

Rebeka giggled as she finished her notes and glanced up at her friend. "Nelka, I do believe you just helped me create the end for my story. Thank you for your help."

Nelka released another booming laugh, dimples creating deep divots in her cheeks. "Oh, Beks, I didn't do a thing. You did all the work. What are you going to do once the story is finished?"

Rebeka pointed to the radio. "I'm going to send it to that radio station I like for their writing contest. They pick a different winner every month and broadcast the story a chapter at a time for everyone to hear." She couldn't help the proud smile that bloomed across her face. "I plan to be the person they pick for the next reading."

"Oh, Beks, that's swell! You had better tell me if it gets picked. I'll put it on in the diner so everyone can hear."

"I will. I'll see you later, Nelka."

"See you later, Beks." Nelka waved goodbye and turned back to the kitchen, vanishing around the corner a second later.

Rebeka stood, clutching her notepad to her chest. Hope rose like a balloon within her as she grasped the pad, thinking of all the dreams she had captured in graphite on the paper. The radio had to take the story, had to broadcast it for others to hear. Rebeka cared too much to let her tale fade away.

Chapter Two

"Beka! Dinner is ready!" Eleanor called, her voice muffled behind the bedroom door.

Rebeka glanced up from the writing desk, her pencil lifting from the words she had written at the bottom of the page. *The End*. They were words she had wanted to write for a long time, words that encompassed hours of work and thought. Her tale was finished, the villain defeated, and the hero victorious. Now it was just a matter of submitting it for the world to hear. Rebeka released a quiet sigh, imagining the sound of her characters being brought to life over the radio. She would listen to every reading and cherish every word, knowing that the story was hers to share.

"Beka!"

"Sorry, Eleanor! I'm coming!" Rebeka set the pencil down and plucked the manuscript from the writing desk. After placing it on her bed, she fetched a closed envelope from her dresser drawer and set it atop the stack of papers. Using a piece of twine, she tied them together and then stood back to survey the finished product. She would have to run the package to the post office the second it opened tomorrow morning. She just couldn't wait any longer.

Rebeka left the bedroom with her notepad in hand and moved to the kitchen, inhaling the mouth-watering smell of roasted potatoes and chicken. She slid onto one of the chairs at the table, setting the pad of paper on the empty seat beside her. She didn't have to worry about anyone sitting on it. They only ever used three of the four chairs.

On the opposite side of the table sat her father, with his cane propped up against the wall behind him. His gray hair peeked over the top of the daily newspaper, and gnarled hands turned each page as he read. Rebeka knew there would be no speaking to him until after he was finished with it.

"Dinner!" Eleanor announced, setting a plate with a steaming chicken on the table. "I seasoned it before cooking, just like my cookbook said to do."

Father set down his paper, his blue eyes widening at the sight of the chicken. "My, Eleanor. This may be your finest dish yet. We're going to eat like royalty today."

Eleanor grinned and folded her arms across her chest. "I plan to be the best chef on this side of Michigan. You two are lucky that you get to sample my practice."

"We are very lucky," Father agreed with a low chuckle. His eyes seemed more tired than normal, the lines that fanned around them deeper and darker. It was as if he had aged years in the past few days, making Rebeka wonder if she was not the only one who was haunted.

Once Eleanor was seated, they bowed their heads. Rebeka sat quietly as her father said grace, though her mind was already drifting back to the story that sat next to her. By the time he said, "Amen," she realized with a twinge of guilt that she hadn't heard a word of the prayer. She sent up a few words of her own to make up for her absentmindedness. *Lord, please let the radio accept my book. Let them broadcast it so that others can enjoy it and so that my family can be proud of me. And please, help me to forget.*

Opening her eyes, Rebeka turned to the radio, which sat on a small stool behind the kitchen table. She turned the knobs, carefully adjusting the frequency until she reached the channel that she always listened to during dinner. It was the channel she loved the most and the one she hoped her story would be on. As she turned back to cut herself a piece of chicken, the radio's static retreated, replaced instead by a voice.

"Good evening, ladies and gentlemen. This is A.M. on the P.M. with your nightly reading. Today we are reading chapter twenty-nine of the book ..."

Rebeka forked a piece of food into her mouth, listening as the radio announcer continued on. He had a pleasing voice, deep and smooth, that was filled to the brim with expression. Every emotion was perfectly captured in his tone, and every pause left her holding her breath in anticipation. In short, Mr. A.M. had the perfect voice for narrating stories, which was why she was eager for him to read hers. Rebeka knew he would read it the right way, not in the sing-song tone that some of the other radio announcers used. He would pay attention to every emotion and small nuance.

"'The butler pushed open the hotel door, stepped inside, and froze.'" The radio announcer sucked in a breath as though he himself were the butler. "'Before him lay Mrs.

Hopps, her face pale and lifeless.'"

Eleanor gasped, her bite of chicken halfway to her mouth. "Not Mrs. Hopps! I was really starting to like her. I'll bet it was that creepy old Mr. Bluetwitch that did it."

Rebeka shook her head and waved her fork in the air. "I don't think so. He's far too obvious to be the villain." She flipped open her notepad to the page where she had been keeping track of the book's characters. "I think the real culprit is Miss Apple, the young schoolteacher. She's too nice. Only two chapters ago she mentioned how Mrs. Hopps refused to lend her a mixer for her bread."

"Speaking of books and stories, how has your writing been going, Rebeka? Is that book of yours almost finished?" Rebeka's father inquired, peering at her from across the table. "I haven't heard you talk about it for a few days now."

"I finished it before dinner," Rebeka admitted. "I'm going to take it to the post office tomorrow morning."

Rebeka's father hummed, returning his attention to his potatoes. "That's nice. Perhaps we'll be hearing your story on the radio once this one is finished."

Rebeka released a long breath. "I hope so. I really do."

One Week Later

Rebeka's breath hitched as she spotted the fence through the trees, a great wall that rose far beyond her reach. How would they possibly get past it? The hole that had once been there was long gone.

"Come on. We just have to get through this fence. We're so close," the voice at her side implored. "We'll be free, Beka. Free at last."

Then they were at the fence, staring up at the barbed wire that blocked them from climbing over. Rebeka knelt down and dug her numb hands into the snow at the bottom of the fence. She scooped the snow and frozen dirt from around the metal like a dog digging a hole, the dirt collecting beneath her nails as she frantically scrabbled and clawed. Thin hands joined her own, helping her to remove the dirt from the growing hole beneath the fence. Shouts rang out in the distance, prompting Beka to dig even faster, her heart pounding.

"Go, Beka! I'll follow right behind you," the voice urged. His small hands pushed her toward the hole that they had created.

Rebeka ducked beneath the fence, wriggling for all she was worth. He again pushed her from behind, helping her to move an inch at a time. After a minute of struggle, Rebeka emerged on the other side of the fence. She twisted around and waited for her best friend to join her.

"I'm stuck," he said fearfully. "Leave me here. Go, just go!"

"No! I won't leave you." Rebeka had left him once, and she never would again. She grasped his arms and tugged hard. There was a tearing noise, and then they were both on the outside of the fence. Rebeka sat back, ready to lie in the snow and rest, but his cold hands urged her up.

"Not yet, Beka. We can't rest here," his weak voice warned. "Not yet."

"Beka, an envelope came for you!"

Rebeka inhaled, trying and failing to open her eyelids. It felt as though they weighed a pound each, and she was powerless to fight their pull. She slumped over, wincing when a twinge ran up her spine. Why was she sitting up to begin with?

"Rebeka! You were meant to be cleaning out the bookshelf! What are you doing on the floor?"

Rebeka groaned and rubbed at her eyes, finally managing to get them open. Realization set in as she glanced around, feeling the hard side of the coffee table behind her back. She had grown so tired while sorting through the bottom of the bookshelf that she had quite literally fallen asleep while sitting up.

Looking up, Rebeka found her sister glaring down at her with an envelope in hand. "I'm sorry, Eleanor. I guess I was just sneaking in a little nap." She smiled apologetically. "Apparently, the floor is as good a place to sleep as any."

Eleanor rolled her eyes and blew a strand of chestnut hair from her face. "You really need to find a better sleep schedule. My biology teacher says staying up all night and sleeping during the day isn't good for your health."

Rebeka bit her tongue to keep from retorting. Her sister spoke the truth, but it was a truth she was loath to face. She would much rather stay awake all night with a book in hand than fall asleep and face the things that flickered like a broken record at the back of her memory. "I know. What is that you have?"

"The letter? The postman gave me this. It's addressed to you." Eleanor held the envelope out for Rebeka to see.

Rebeka's heart skipped a beat as she took the envelope, studying the address on the front. "It's from the radio. They must have gotten my manuscript."

"Well? Are you going to open it?" Eleanor asked, setting her hands on her hips.

Rebeka studied the envelope for a moment before lowering it to her lap. "No. I want to open it at the diner so I can read the letter with Nelka. She asked me to tell her as soon as I got it."

"Suit yourself." Eleanor whirled around on her heel and walked away.

Rebeka pushed herself to her feet and searched around the room for her coat. She had to get to the diner as quickly as possible, for the letter in her hand couldn't wait.

Chapter Three

A harsh wind blew frigid air at Rebeka as she rushed down the sidewalk, heading straight for the diner at the end of the street. Judging by the dark clouds that were making a slow but steady approach from the northwest, a storm was brewing over Lake Huron. They were a harsh warning to all that were out and about that they should not stay away from home for long.

After reaching the diner's door, Rebeka rushed inside, not sparing a moment to glance around her. "Nelka!" She darted to the counter. "Nelka, are you there?"

"Just a moment, please!" her friend's voice answered from the kitchen. A minute later, Nelka bustled to the counter, her brows drawn in concern and her jaw chewing furiously. "Beks! What is it? Is something wrong with your daddy?"

Rebeka shook her head. "No, it's nothing bad. I got a letter from the radio station and wanted to open it with you." She waved the letter in the air to prove her point.

Nelka placed a hand with chipped red nail polish over her chest. "Oh, thank goodness." She peered closely at the envelope, a smile growing on her face. "Now, that *is* good news. What are you waiting for? Open it!"

Rebeka nodded and sank onto one of the metal stools. "All right. I will." She slid one shaking finger beneath the flap of the envelope and carefully peeled it back, exposing the folded sheet of paper hidden within. With trembling fingers, she pried the paper loose and held it in front of her, not daring to unfold it.

"Well? Come on, Beks. You won't get any less nervous by sitting here and staring at it." Nelka leaned both elbows on the counter in anticipation.

Rebeka forced herself to take a deep breath and unfolded the paper, her eyes flying to the top. "'Dear Miss Willowsby,'" she read aloud.

"'Miss Willowsby'? Who's that?"

"My pen name." Rebeka focused her attention back on the letter. "'Our team has reviewed your story and found that it is not well suited for our program.'" Her throat ran dry and her heart sank to the very bottom of her toes as she continued on. "'While the writing is admirable, the story will not connect well with our listeners. Our program is intended for stories that are rich in depth and heart—not stories that are meant merely to amuse.'" Rebeka swallowed, feeling tears burning at the back of her eyes. "'Most sincerely, Channel 98.1.'"

There was a moment of silence as they both let the words sink in. Then Nelka hurried around the counter and wrapped Rebeka into a warm hug, causing the smell of bubble gum to envelop them both. "Oh, Beks," she murmured. "I'm so sorry."

"They said my story had no heart. How could it have no heart? I spent months working on it," Rebeka whispered dejectedly. Sadness, deep and hollow, settled in her chest. "That story was my everything. I spent every waking hour crafting it until it was perfect."

"Those radio people have no clue what they're talking about. Why, I'll write them a letter and tell them so." Nelka stepped away and plopped her hands on her hips. "I'll tell them just what I think of their treatment toward my friend."

Rebeka attempted to smile and failed. "There's no need for that, Nelka. The decision has been made. I have to respect it."

"Bah. I still think you should write them back." Nelka blew and popped a gum bubble, her stormy eyes softening. "Why don't I get you a warm cup of coffee and a donut? I know it won't solve anything, but a little bit of sugar never hurt anyone."

Rebeka nodded, still staring at the words typed out on the paper. "All right. Thanks, Nelka."

"Just hang in there. Things will get better. You'll see," Nelka said with a sympathetic smile.

As she turned to head back to the kitchen, the bell over the diner door jingled. The sound of deep voices entered the room, accompanied by a smell that Rebeka dreaded above all else. *Cigarettes.* She choked, memories flooding through her body and freezing her in place.

The dim glow of the cigarettes were the only thing she could see as she crept through the fields, the small piece of bread held tightly in one hand. On any other day, she might have thought of them as fireflies, tiny lights that flickered and danced in the blackness.

But they were not. Fireflies did not carry rifles, nor did they speak with harsh voices in languages that she could not understand.

The smell of cigarette smoke grew closer as she neared the fence. She had only a few feet more to travel, and she would be safe. Her heart raced like a frightened rabbit as a stick cracked beneath her foot. Rebeka paused as voices sounded close by. Would they find her?

A rock hit the ground a few feet to her right, shattering the silence. The men moved off in the direction of the thump, giving Rebeka the freedom she needed to squeeze her small body under the fence. Small hands found her as soon as she reached the other side, grasping her own reassuringly.

"Are you all right?" he whispered.

"I'm fine." Rebeka's shaking hands told a different story. "Thank you for saving me."

"I'll always save you, Beka. Always."

The smell of cigarettes grew stronger as the men drew closer. Chairs scraped as they sat down, clearly not planning on leaving any time soon.

Rebeka gasped for breath. She had to leave. *Run, Beka, run!* She jumped up from the stool with the letter still clutched in her hand and raced to the door. Nelka's confused call faded into the distance as Rebeka fled from the building and into the cold, the wind whipping her dark hair around her as she ran down the sidewalk, far from the diner and far from the memories that hounded her every moment. "Why can't I just forget? Lord, why can't You just let me forget?" she cried, her voice breaking into a harsh sob. She dashed headlong into the empty park before collapsing beneath one of the oak trees that stood like a barren sentinel among the empty fields. Drawing in shuddering breaths, Rebeka buried her head into her knees and crumpled the letter in her closed fist. Memories flashed in front of her eyes, each one like a knife in her skull. It was as if the storm brewing outside was also raging within her, drowning out all rational thought and surrounding her with dark clouds of fear. There was no way to escape it, no way to run from it.

"Rebeka?" The voice, deep and worn, with the same German accent that she had rid herself of years ago, pierced the storm in her head.

Rebeka glanced up, blinking tears from her eyes. Standing in front of her, his hand clutching his wooden cane, was none other than her father. At that moment, Rebeka felt five years old again, staring up at her father after skinning her knee. Though he had been a proud man, he had never hesitated to stoop down, pick her up in his strong arms, and carry her inside to put on a bandage.

"Father." Rebeka swiped at her face with one woolen sleeve. "Why are you here?"

Father blinked, his forehead creasing as he stared down at her. "You didn't come home for dinner. I looked for you at the diner, but Nelka said you had run away. She told me what happened with the letter."

Rebeka winced, turning away. "I didn't get chosen. My story wasn't good enough. I guess I was overambitious to think that it would be."

Father grunted as he lowered himself to the ground next to her and laid his cane between them. He set one of his hands gently over hers, the rough calluses brushing against her knuckles as he looked into her eyes. "Is that all that troubles you? Or is there something else that brought you here?"

"Sometimes I feel as though ... no matter how hard I run, I can't get away." Rebeka stared at the leaves that carpeted the ground in a patchwork of color beneath her skirt. "I try and try to forget everything that has happened, but it always comes back to haunt me. If not in my dreams, then in the biscuits Nelka offers me or the cigarettes that the men smoke in the diner. I'm so tired of being afraid. I'm so tired of remembering." She glanced at him. "Do you ever feel the same way?"

Father fell silent, letting the wind swirl softly around them. Then he released a heavy sigh, one that seemed as old as time itself. "Fear is a thing that none of us can escape from. I would like to say that I am strong enough to resist, but in the end, I am no stronger than anyone else." He paused, his lips moving wordlessly. "We ... we are all human, and humans will always be prone to fear. I was afraid then, and I am still afraid now. I was afraid for myself, but more than that, I was afraid for you. I was afraid for Eleanor." His voice dropped to a whisper. "I was afraid for your mother."

Rebeka glanced up at Father, watching the tears gather in his eyes.

"I thought I was a strong man. I thought I could protect you all. I was wrong. That fact still haunts me to this day. I wish I could have done more to protect you from the things that hurt you. I wish I could have been there to shield your eyes and keep you safe within my arms. But I could not."

"That's not your fault," Rebeka argued. "You were no safer than the rest of us. You were just in a different place, a place that you didn't choose to be in."

"True, and yet, it didn't stop me from worrying." Father straightened, fixing his gaze on a point in the distance. "However, in these past few years, I've come to realize something. All this time spent running, all this time spent hiding, I lived in fear of something that could no longer hurt me. I was living in fear of memories, memories that I could not change. And I thought to myself, why let the memories win? Why let them rule over me? I know it is not so easy to overcome them, but I have stopped trying to run. Instead, I am letting them come. I am allowing myself to feel each and every one of them, knowing that may be the only way to make peace with them." He frowned. "Does that make sense?"

"I suppose so," Rebeka murmured. "I'm just afraid of getting hurt, Father. I'm afraid of what I'll find hidden in the darkest corners of my memory."

Father hummed, looping an arm around Rebeka. She relaxed and leaned into his warm embrace. It had been a long time since she had been hugged by him.

"Rebeka, you can only shine light into the darkness if you turn around and face it. You have been running for too long. Stop trying to hide from the thing that is chasing you. Turn around and face it with courage. Do you remember Joshua 1:7?"

Rebeka nodded. "'Only be thou strong and very courageous, that thou mayest observe to do according to all the law, which Moses my servant commanded thee: turn not from it to the right hand or to the left, that thou mayest prosper withersoever thou goest.' You helped me memorize it when I was a child."

"Have courage, daughter. Do not let yourself become a victim of fear. We can face it together, you and I. Will you do that with me?"

Rebeka chewed on the inside of her cheek for a moment before replying. "I'll try. I don't know how, but I'll try."

"Good." Father raised one bushy brow. "Now, what are you going to do about that letter?"

"I don't know. The people at the radio station said my story was shallow. They said it lacked heart." Rebeka shook her head and moved from Father's arms so she could better look at him. "But how do I write with heart? I thought I was, but apparently, it wasn't good enough. They said they wanted a story that people could connect with."

"Rebeka, if you think about it, I believe you will find that there always was a story hidden within your heart." Father tilted his head to the side, his eyes knowing. "I think you were just afraid to tell it."

Rebeka tugged at a loose strand in her sweater, considering her father's words. Was there a story hidden somewhere within her? She thought back, realization growing within her. "You're right. There was a story I wanted to write. But I was afraid."

"The best stories are often the hardest to tell." Father smiled. "But I know you, and you can put any story into words. You're talented that way."

Rebeka felt a tiny seed of hope blooming in her chest, a tiny spark of light that began to block out the dark storm clouds that had swirled for so long inside of her. "Thank you, Father." She gave Father a squeeze. "Thank you."

"Do not despair, Rebeka. I have a feeling the best is yet to come." Father rose and offered her a hand. Together, the two walked home.

That night, as the town of St. Ignace went to sleep and the snow began to fall in the glowing lamplights, Rebeka set her pencil to a blank piece of paper and began to write.

Chapter Four

A thick blanket of snow covered the earth, draping over every tree and icing every fence post. The air was nearly silent, undisturbed by cars or voices in the early morning. The only noise came from the seagulls that released distant cries as they flew far overhead, their wings flashing white in the rising sun.

Rebeka plodded down the sidewalk, marveling at the tiny sparrow footprints that dotted the powdery white. It was a wonder the birds still remained with the weather growing colder and the snow growing higher. Still, she couldn't help but admire their tenacity for daring to stay. They were brave little creatures, those birds. Rebeka had a feeling she could learn a thing or two from them.

The diner door squeaked behind Rebeka as she closed it and moved slowly to the front of the counter. She could hear humming echoing from the kitchen, a tune that sounded similar to the Del Vikings' "Come Along With Me". Rebeka slid onto one of the stools at the countertop and waited for Nelka to emerge.

It took only a minute for her friend to appear with a coffeepot in hand, and she jumped at the sight of Rebeka. "For goodness' sake, Rebeka! You scared me half to death! When did you come in?"

Rebeka couldn't help but laugh. "Oh, Nelka, I'm sorry. I didn't mean to scare you. I had good news and wanted to celebrate with you."

Nelka shook her head, plunking the coffeepot down on the counter. "It had better be good for you to risk my heart like that. Let's hear it, then."

"You know how the radio station decided to air my new story after they finished *The*

Mystery of Green Manor? Well, they finished the book yesterday evening. That means Mr. A.M. will be reading my story over the radio tonight."

"Oh, Beks! That's wonderful!" Nelka bobbed up and down, her face lighting up. "I was starting to get impatient with all of this waiting." She took Rebeka's hands. "I'm going to tell everyone in town to tune in to channel 98.1 tonight. I'll put it on in the diner, as well. You deserve it for all of your hard work. I still can't believe you wrote that whole thing in three days!"

"Well, it's much smaller than my other story," Rebeka admitted with a shy smile. "Still, it did take hours of writing to perfect. I just hope that everyone will like it."

"They will, Beks. I just know they will. You have a talent most of us could only dream of." Nelka grinned. "I'm lucky to have you as my friend. It gives me the right to brag about how amazing you are."

"Oh, I don't know about that."

Nelka raised one brow. "Well, I do. And I know that this is a story nobody will want to miss."

Eleanor's excited chatter filled the kitchen as Rebeka entered and took a seat. "I told everyone at school today that my sister was going to be on the radio," Eleanor babbled, setting a plate of sliced meatloaf on the table. "Nobody believed me, so I told them to tune in and see. I wish I could see their faces when they realize that I was telling the truth. They're going to be eating their words tomorrow."

"Eleanor, that isn't nice," Father warned, flicking his newspaper. Though his voice was stern, it held a hint of pride, too. It warmed something inside of Rebeka, knowing her father was pleased with what she had done.

"Well, it's true." Eleanor slid into her chair and folded her arms across her chest.

Father lowered his newspaper. "Enough of that. Let's say grace so that Rebeka can tune in to the station."

As their father blessed the food, Rebeka sent up her own prayer. *Thank You, Lord, for giving me the courage to write this story. I couldn't have done it without Your guidance. Please continue to give me the courage I need to face my past. In Your name I pray, amen.*

"Amen," Father said from across the table. "Now, let's get that radio on. Eleanor, would you do us the honor of dishing out your meatloaf while Rebeka finds the station?"

Rebeka turned around and fiddled with the knobs, the nerves building in her chest. Glancing at her father and sister, she noted their eager faces as they stared at the radio in anticipation. She knew that Nelka would be doing the same at the diner, and so would many other people throughout town. It was wonderful to know that so many people wanted to hear her story, but in a way, it was terrifying as well. What if they didn't like what she had to say?

Joshua 1:7 ran through Rebeka's head. *"Be thou strong and very courageous."* Rebeka pursed her lips. *I will be courageous.* It had taken hours of hard work to reach this point, far too much for her to grow fearful at the last minute. She would listen to her story with her head held high, knowing that she was the one who had crafted the words.

The static of the radio retreated as Rebeka found the correct frequency, replaced by the voice she knew so well. "Good evening, ladies and gentlemen. This is A.M. on the P.M. with your nightly reading."

Rebeka released a shuddering breath and picked up her fork, shoving a piece of meat-loaf into her mouth as a distraction.

"Today we will be reading a short story entitled 'Beyond the Fence,' written by Miss Regina Willowsby. My team was very eager for me to read this story, as they think it will be an interesting change from many of the books we have read on this program. And so, without further ado, let us begin." With that, the radio announcer cleared his throat and began reading the story that Rebeka had dreaded telling for so long. It was a story that had been hiding within her for years, one that came directly and unabashedly from her heart.

"'It was a dark night in 1947, the kind of darkness that seemed to my ten-year-old self like it hid monsters within its black folds. I crept through the farm fields, my feet scraping against the frozen ground as I made my way closer to the place where the fields ended at a great wooden wall. The cold air made my scalp prickle, the hair shaved away long ago by the cruel men who had taken me prisoner and ripped me from my mother. The same men who had forced me to live like a dog. The same men who now stood guard with guns in their hands and cigarettes in their mouths.'" The announcer's voice seemed to waver as he went on. "'Beside me crept the boy who had become my best friend, Andy. The whites of his eyes flashed in the faint glow of the town's lights as he glanced back and forth, searching constantly for any potential danger. Though his body was frail and his face was sunken in, I could see that his eyes shone with determination. In his thin hands he held two potatoes and a stale, weevil-filled biscuit, the only food we had managed to get while begging that day.

"'A crunching sound echoed from somewhere close by, and Andy held out a hand, preventing me from moving forward. "Stay still," he whispered, every muscle tense.

"'We both froze in place, hardly daring to breathe as we waited for the guard to continue moving. For a moment, there was silence, and then the crunching of footsteps sounded as the guard continued on his patrol route. I let out a soft sigh of relief, and Andy motioned me forward.

""'We'll eat well tonight," he murmured as we came closer to the fence. "If you want, you can give one of the potatoes to Mrs. Bauer. I'm sure she'll share it with Eleanor."

""'That would be nice." I was lucky that Mrs. Bauer had agreed to watch over my little sister. It was only fair that I shared some of my meal with her in return. My sister was the only reason Andy and I hadn't run for the hills the minute we went under the fence. While I couldn't care for her, I would never leave her behind.

"'The unmistakable sound of a gun cocking brought us both to an immediate halt. Then the thick, suffocating smell of cigarette smoke surrounded us, and I couldn't help the cough that escaped my lips.

""'Who is there? Show yourself!" the guard demanded, the Serbian accent heavy in his voice. He was a few feet from us, close enough that there would be no avoiding him but far enough that he had not yet caught sight of us.

""'Go. Go, now!" Andy hissed, shoving the food into my hands. "We don't both have to get caught!"

"'I hesitated, torn between helping my friend and running for all I was worth. But then, I heard a sound that we both dreaded. A sound that meant danger for any prisoner that dared move outside the town. *Barking.*

""'They let the dogs loose!" Andy gave me another push, his eyes desperate. "Get out of here, Beka. Get to safety!"

"'The barking grew louder, and still I hesitated. "I don't want to leave you."

""'I can take it, Beka," Andy said. "Now, go!"

"'His words sent me over the edge. I turned and dashed through the field, my heart racing as I leaped over rocks and swerved around barren stalks of corn. I ran for the fence, not stopping until I had crawled underneath, back into the very place that held me captive. Once I was certain that I was not being chased, I knelt and peered through the hole, searching the darkness for any sign of my friend. "Andy?" I whispered, my shaking voice betraying my fear. In the distance came snarling, followed by what sounded like a cry. I sat back, tears running down my cheeks. I knew that Andy had been caught, an offense that could very likely lead to his death. Worst of all, I had left him to face the guards alone, running away like the coward that I was.

"'Later that night, I sobbed on my small pallet, the food lying untouched on the floor beside me. I couldn't fathom living without my friend, the boy who had shared his food with me and encouraged me when I was ready to give up. I would rather starve to death than try and continue surviving alone.

"'Days passed by with no sign of Andy's return. I spent the time in a daze, moving aimlessly around the camp, unable to forget what had happened. At night, I was haunted by the empty pallet next to my own, a stark reminder that my best friend was gone.'" The announcer paused, and it was a long time before he next spoke. When he did, his voice was strained, as though the words pained him to say. "'The following evening, my misery was interrupted by a knock on the door, so faint that at first, I thought I was hallucinating. But then it came again, this time a fraction louder. After creeping from bed, I stepped up to the door and carefully cracked it open. There in front of me, his face covered in bruises and his arms hugging his red-stained side, stood Andy.

"'"Can I come in?' he asked, his voice a mere croak.

"'I nodded and stood aside, scarcely able to believe that he was alive. As I watched, Andy stepped a few feet into the room before collapsing on the floor. I sank to the ground beside him, tears running down my cheeks as I pulled his head onto my lap. "I'm sorry," I sobbed. "I'm so sorry."

"'Andy shook his head, a tiny nudge from side to side that seemed to cost him a great deal of effort. "Don't be sorry, Beks," he whispered. "It wasn't your fault."

"'"But it was. You got hurt because of me."

"'"No. It was my idea to leave town." Andy let out a rattling sigh and coughed, the movement making his entire body seize up. "Will you do something for me, Beks?"

"Anything," I whispered.

"'"Tell me one of your stories. A nice one, where the hero defeats the villain and rises up in a cloak of glory. I like those ones best of all," Andy said. "They make me believe that someday we might actually make it out of this place."

"'"Do you really think so?" I murmured, leaning my back against the wall of the tiny house. "Do you really think we might someday be free?"

"'Andy nodded. "I know so, Beks. We just have to believe it."

"'We would, in time, escape from that awful place, along with Mrs. Bauer, Eleanor, and many others. Though we would lose sight of each other after rejoining our families, I never stopped wondering what happened to the boy who saved my life that day. I would forever go forward, hoping that he was safe, wherever he was.'" The radio announcer fell silent. Just when Rebeka thought he was finished, he spoke again. "'And though she did not know it, the boy wondered the same thing about her. He would forever wonder what became of the girl who told him stories that kept him alive throughout those hard times. For while Beka thought he had saved her, the boy knew that, in a way, she had also saved him.'"

Rebeka glanced up, fixing her gaze on the radio. "Something's wrong. I didn't write that."

Silence settled over the room as they waited in quiet anticipation for the radio announcer to resume speaking. From the radio came a sharp noise, as though someone was taking a quick breath. Rebeka jumped on her seat when the radio announcer's voice came back over the speakers.

"This has been 'Behind the Fence,' written by Rebeka Wagner. Thank you all for listening. Good evening." The clicking of the radio signaled that the microphone had been turned off.

For a moment, they stared across the table at each other. Then, Eleanor shrugged. "Well, that was an odd way to end. He didn't even announce what he'll be reading next."

Rebeka let out a shuddering breath, realization building in her as the announcer's words played over and over in her mind. *It couldn't be. Is it possible?*

"Rebeka? Are you all right?" Eleanor asked. "You look a little pale."

Rebeka glanced up, her heart thundering. "I never told the radio announcer my real name."

Chapter Five

Two Days Later

The sharp whistle of the train cut through the air, disrupting the silence and pulling Rebeka from her slumber. She lifted her head from Andy's shoulder, gazing with growing hope at the approaching locomotive.

"Do you think our parents will be on that train?" she asked. "Do you think they've come to take us home?"

"I don't know. I don't even know where home is." Andy fixed his eyes on the train. "But we'll find out soon enough."

Rebeka sighed, placing her mittened hands on her lap. It was nice to have warm clothes, even though they were two sizes too big. "What will happen if our parents do come, Andy? What if I never see you again?"

Andy shook his head, a smile on his face. In his eyes burned determination and a promise, one that Rebeka knew he would never break. "We'll find each other, Beka. It may take days or even years, but I know that we'll meet again. You're too wonderful to stay hidden from the world, Rebeka Wagner. Someday your stories will be read around the world—and when they are, I'll know who wrote them."

The harsh cries of the gulls rose in volume as Rebeka left the wooden boardwalk, stepping onto frozen sand. It was not what she would normally consider a good day for traversing the beach, but she had much to think about, and a walk was the perfect way to sort through her thoughts. She ambled slowly along, her footsteps crunching as she moved closer to the place where the sand met the water. The winter air sent chills running down her spine, and Rebeka tucked her hands into her pockets to keep them from turning blue. Once she reached the edge of the lake, she paused, staring down into the blue depths. Though the wind was bitterly cold and snow caked the ground, the lake had not frozen. It was like a living creature, tossing and turning in a sapphire tempest. Oftentimes, Rebeka had imagined glittering mermaid tails and ancient leviathans hiding in the deep, waiting for an unlucky fisherman to pass by overhead. The thought made her smile as she watched the waves crash forward and retreat.

Footsteps interrupted her musing. They were heavy and measured, as if the person they belonged to was uncertain. Rebeka waited for the person to continue down the beach, but instead, they stopped. She remained facing the water, waiting for the person to speak. To her surprise, no voice interrupted the silence.

Slowly, Rebeka turned to face the stranger. Her breath hitched as she caught sight of the person standing before her, the words fleeing from her mind.

His hair was darker than it had been eleven years ago, a rich golden instead of sun-bleached blond. His face, too, was different, the skin healthy and shadowed by stubble. Despite his changed appearance, one thing remained the same—his brown eyes, filled with determination and that stubborn spark.

"Andy," Rebeka breathed, taking a step forward.

The man nodded, his eyes never leaving her own. "Rebeka."

Rebeka opened her mouth to speak, but for once in her life, no words came to mind. There was too much to say, too many stories to tell in one conversation.

Andy waited, his gaze understanding. He knew as well as she that there was no putting into words the emotions that they felt.

"I missed you every day," Rebeka finally whispered. "There were so many things I wanted to share with you, so many stories I wished I could tell you."

Andy stepped closer. "Then tell them to me, Rebeka. I want to hear them all."

"You do?" Rebeka's voice began to shake. How could he have been so close all that time? How had she not known?

Andy nodded, his eyes earnest. "Tell me a story, Rebeka. A nice one, where the hero defeats the villain and rises up in a cloak of glory. One where the hero reunites with his lost heroine at the end." He smiled. "I like those ones best of all."

Rebeka felt her own lips twitching as she looked up into his gaze. Taking a deep breath, she began to tell a story. *Her* story. The story that came from her heart.

Acknowledgments

When I first sat down to put words on a page, I had no idea who Rebeka Wagner was nor what her journey would be. It's not often that I start a story without really and truly knowing who the main character is. However, in Rebeka's case, I had the joy of discovering her as the story progressed. I came to appreciate her quiet life, which made it all the sadder when I wrote the last sentence and had to bid Andy and her farewell. I hope that you, dear reader, enjoyed meeting her as much as I did.

Rebeka's past was inspired by the displacement of the Donauschwaben people. At the end of the Second World War, the Donauschwaben were captured from their small farming communities in Hungary, Romania, and Yugoslavia and placed into internment camps by Yugoslav partisans. Because most of the men had been drafted into the German army several years prior, the majority of the people taken by the partisans were women, children, and elderly people. They were then forced to work long hours in labor camps, where a large number died due to the harsh conditions and poor treatment. Those who did manage to escape were left without a home to return to. Some, like Rebeka, were able to rejoin their lost family members and immigrate to America for a chance at starting anew. Others chose to remain in the region and wait for a chance to reclaim their homes and belongings. Most were never able to.

If you would like to follow along with my writing journey, you can do so by checking out my website (avrieswan.com) or following my Instagram account (@avrieswanwrites). I hope to see you there!

Between Moor and Mountain

KELSEY BRYANT

Dedication

For all the writers who long to write but can't ... I am praying for you!

L eslie Fraser wasn't about to cry. Yes, she had just fulfilled a lifelong dream. Yes, she stood on Scottish pavement. But the descent through solid gray clouds, the barest glimpse of fields and trees in the dusk before the plane landed on the runway, the small barren airport—none of it seemed like a dream come true. Surrounded by fog, dead tired after a three-hour flight delay, praying her phone would work as she tapped Tamsin McCray's number, Leslie was numb. Well, that quiver in her stomach might be nerves. Regardless, she was beyond caring.

"Hello, Leslie?" came a soft, warm brogue.

Thank God. "Yes, this is Leslie. Are you Tamsin McCray?"

"The one and only."

Beneath her numbness, the tiniest of thrills stirred within Leslie. Her hostess had a perfectly lyrical accent.

"I'm outside the airport now," Leslie said.

"Oh, lovely. I'll be just a minute more. I'm on the last roundabout before the entrance."

Leslie double-checked that Tamsin knew exactly where to find her, then they bade goodbye for the moment. Leslie's quiver grew a little stronger. Was that excitement?

She hadn't had much to be excited about in recent years, so the feeling was almost alien.

In about three minutes, a tiny, white, snub-nosed car pulled up to the curb in front of her, coming from the opposite direction than one would in America. The "wrong side of the road" driving would be one of many things that she'd get accustomed to again during the next three weeks. Almost every quirk of UK culture was endearing to her. She'd visited England nine years ago, at age twenty-one, and never forgotten any of it.

A short blonde woman popped out of the driver's seat. Grinning, she extended her palm for a handshake. "Leslie Fraser? Ye look so much like yer mam."

Leslie shook hands, then fingered her shoulder-length brown hair, plastered down by a beanie. Maybe it was her body's build that matched Mom's—broad shoulders, average height, average weight. Leslie always thought she took more after Dad; Mom's hair was red, and her features were more delicate.

"Hi, Tamsin. It's nice to meet you at last. Thank you so much for coming to get me." Leslie roused the biggest smile she could, but her eyes probably still looked tired.

The other woman pulled her gray coat more tightly around her. "And it's so nice to meet ye! It's me pleasure to have ye. I couldnae do anything less for me best American friend than take in her daughter. Now, let's get ye in the car out of this damp. I wish the weather would have greeted ye more warmly."

"Well, it is late October," Leslie said.

As Tamsin extricated the vehicle from the confines of the airport, she said, "I imagine ye want to rest a day or two before havin' any adventures."

Leslie nodded against the headrest. Now that she sat in near darkness, weariness blanketed her. "Yes," she managed to say. She wished she could be more polite, more vivacious, more interested, but that tiny spark of excitement had deserted her and she wanted only to sleep.

Tamsin chuckled. "There'll be time to discuss everything when ye feel up to it."

"Mm-hmm." Leslie didn't want to miss her first survey of Scotland beneath the clouds, but it was so dark she couldn't see much anyway. Her eyes drifted shut.

The car ride felt like a dream of flying through darkness pierced by spots of gliding light. Streetlights illuminated cloudy circles around themselves, and every now and then, the car drove past shadows darker than the night, but Leslie noticed nothing else as she wavered between dozing and waking. At some point, a blacker darkness closed in around their lonely car. Then, before too long, the headlights lit up a driveway surrounded by trees, and they rumbled down it until they reached a small stone house.

"Yer home for the next three weeks," Tamsin announced. As if on cue, an automatic light switched on over the front door, triggered by the car.

Leslie blinked her heavy eyes. She couldn't make any judgments on the house or property this time of night, but it all looked promising. "Wonderful."

Tamsin helped her take her luggage inside, then showed her the important rooms: the kitchen–slash–dining room, the living room, the bathroom, and finally, the guest room.

"It doubles as a study." Tamsin waved at the desk and bookshelves lining one wall. Then she gestured to thick blue-and-green-plaid blackout drapes on the adjoining wall. "When it's mornin', make sure ye open those curtains. Ye can see the sunrise."

Leslie nodded, having eyes only for the full-size bed piled high with pillows and a cushy-looking dark-blue comforter.

"And perhaps one or two surprises," Tamsin added as she set down Leslie's suitcase.

"Hmm? Surprises?" Leslie dropped her backpack on the chair at the desk and glanced blearily at her hostess.

"Mm-hmm. The animals like the mornin'."

"Oh." Scottish wildlife *would* be a special thing to see. "What time is sunrise?"

"Just after eight. Then tomorra, we put the clocks back, ye know, so it'll switch to after seven. But no matter what time ye get up, open the curtains. We're in the Cairngorms, don't forget. Ye willnae regret it." Tamsin's smile crinkled the corners of her eyes.

The line through TSA stretched to an impossible length. Leslie would never make it. She tried to take a step, but she felt as if she were tied to a boulder. She tried to run, to force herself into motion, but she stayed stuck. Looking over her shoulder, she saw Blaine and realized he was holding her arms.

"Let go! I'm going to miss the plane!" she cried.

He didn't answer, just stared at her.

"Don't make me give up this dream too!" she yelled, twisting and flailing to loosen his grip. To no avail. Outside the floor-to-ceiling windows, an airplane—her airplane, she somehow knew—started taxiing.

Leslie's eyes opened, her heart pounding, cold sweat pooling under her arms. The room was too dark for her sight to adjust, that in itself reminding her she wasn't in her bedroom at her parents' house, where the streetlight always filled her window's blinds.

Scotland. She had made it to Scotland. Blaine probably didn't even know. She'd been out of his grip for six months already.

She uncurled herself and slowly straightened under the covers. Frigid air met the side of her face no longer pressed against the pillow. Didn't the heater work? Wind blustered past the house. Definitely not in southeast Texas anymore.

Leslie calmed her mind with reassurances. *Blaine has no power over you. His opinions don't matter. You are free to pursue your hopes, goals, and dreams without anyone holding you back.* An awareness of God filtered into her thoughts. She was free to know God again as she had known Him before Blaine came into her life with his skewed theology and his overpowering personality that forced his beliefs on her.

What were those hopes, goals, and dreams? Sometimes she couldn't even remember. Other times, they felt pointless, or worse—not even attractive anymore. Like coming to Scotland. Like writing novels. Like having a job she loved. Sometimes she felt as if she could never love or desire anything ever again.

After breaking up with Blaine, she had poured herself into her job as a day care teacher. It was stressful and didn't pay a living wage, but caring for her kiddos had been the balm she needed. She had explored other means of making a living so she could stand on her own two feet. She had tried to rely on herself for once instead of on other people.

But she hadn't gotten back to relying on God. Even now, her prayers felt hollow, perfunctory. She missed real, deep, heartfelt communion with God, just like she missed reading her Bible, journaling, and writing stories, but they seemed inaccessible, as if they stood on the other side of a locked gate. She'd taken such joy in them, but that joy had gone through the gate, never to return.

Her thoughts gradually rejoined the darkness, and she drifted back to sleep.

When Leslie woke again, luminous gray lines bordered the drapes on the window opposite the bed. Tamsin's words sprang to mind: *"Open the curtains ... Ye willnae regret it."*

Leslie slid out from under the covers, her stocking feet sinking into the sheepskin rug. The room felt a little warmer; her hostess must have turned on the heat with morning. She crossed to the window and pulled aside one plaid drape.

In the clear, pale light of dawn, a scene like a painting met her eyes. A small mountain, craggy and brown, highlighted by nascent sunlight, melted into the silvery sky in the far distance. It was framed by evergreens and troops of skeletal trees holding on to their last gold leaves. Birches, perhaps? Their white bark practically glowed. Bordered by the trees, a large swathe of dull green turf rolled down toward either a drop-off or a steeper slope.

While Leslie stared, mesmerized, movement caught the corner of her eye. Two large reddish hinds stepped out from the woods to her left, nosing the old grass for fresher food. They were bigger than the white-tail deer in Texas, and their exotic color and size sent a thrill zinging through Leslie's veins. It'd been so long since she'd seen anything that brought her wonder; she'd begun to believe wonder no longer existed.

As if she were real, a tall, red-haired girl in a white shift, brown stays and petticoat, and a tartan shawl stood at the edge of the woods, watching the nearby hinds, then turned to gaze at the distant mountain. The breeze rippled her auburn tresses. She was yearning for something ... or was it someone? Did she wish to journey to that mountain because she hoped for a better life on the other side? Or because she wanted adventure? Was she waiting for someone or wishing to go to him?

The deer faded from Leslie's sight as she contemplated the imaginary girl, then followed her gaze toward the mountain. *I must go there.* Was that thought Leslie's or the Scottish lass's?

A small, polite clatter sounded from the kitchen, and the Scottish lass disappeared. Leslie gave her head a slight shake, but a tiny spark of joy remained. It'd been forever since a character or a story had visited her like that. Often, they weren't from anything she'd written yet, just products of an imagination that peopled the real world around her with layers beyond reality.

She hated to leave the deer just yet, but something must have startled them, for their heads perked up and they bounded back into the woods. And so the first hunger pang of morning beckoned her out of the bedroom. Good thing her system was adjusting well to the six-hour time difference from home, though she was still tired. It'd probably be another night or two before she caught up, judging by the last time she'd been in the UK.

"Good mornin'!" Tamsin sang out when Leslie emerged into the kitchen after a restroom stop. They exchanged pleasantries about their night's rest, and then Tamsin asked, "What do ye think of the view?"

"It's breathtaking. I saw two red hinds grazing. And that mountain!" Leslie didn't have to force enthusiasm, but further words failed her.

"I couldnae live anywhere else." Tamsin's ready smile appeared before she turned back to the stove and adjusted the flame under a pot on one burner. "Can I interest ye in some breakfast? Then we can discuss yer plans."

Tamsin had a variety of food to offer, and Leslie settled on a large bowl of porridge, which was simply classic, creamy oatmeal. Milk, brown sugar, and raisins topped it off. While waiting for it, she sipped a cup of heavily sweetened coffee.

"So are ye like me, coffee before noon, tea after?" Tamsin asked.

Leslie snickered. "Yes, that's me. No caffeine after noon."

"Now that's sensible." Tamsin joined Leslie at the table with her own porridge and coffee. "I'll cook ye plenty of Scottish foods while ye're here. I'm no' the greatest cook, but I've learned enough from me mam and granny to be passable."

"You're wonderful." Leslie smiled. She was feeling much more herself as the sweet, steaming oatmeal slid warmly into her stomach. She couldn't remember the last time she had enjoyed food so much. That scene this morning—complete with a fictional character she'd never met before—probably had something to do with it. Maybe it hadn't been a mistake to come to Scotland after all.

"What kind of leaves are those?" Leslie gestured to the twigs with golden leaves poking from a vase in the center of the table. A small branch with green leaves and clusters of vermilion berries accompanied them.

"Silver birch. And the berries are rowanberries." Tamsin nodded to the vase. "I always decorate with the outdoors. Ye probably saw the birches out yer window, but the berries are away down at the bottom of the slope, a wee bit of a scramble." She grinned. "I've a jar of rowanberry preserves I've been savin' for ye. Now, the rowan tree ... That's a tree with lots of legends and mythology round it." She side-eyed Leslie, as if to gauge her interest.

Forgetting that she'd ever lost her interests or passions, Leslie sat up straight. "Tell me more, please. I love things like that."

Tamsin obliged. "The rowan tree, or *caorann* in the Gaelic, was said to protect a house from evil fairies, so lots of folk planted it in front of their houses." She sipped her coffee. "And there's a legend about a caorann, on an island in a loch, with berries that restore yer youth. It was guarded by a dragon. An ancient hero was tricked by a wicked woman to bring her the tree because she was jealous of his love for her daughter, and when he cut it down, the dragon awoke and chased him into the loch. His lass threw him a knife, and he and the dragon killed each other in the loch. The lass died of a broken heart, and her mother ate the rowanberries and was poisoned by them because her heart was impure."

Leslie's imagination slipped to the distant time when such tales were first told. Where did they come from? Were they ever believed? "That's a sad story. But I guess most legends are."

"That's what makes them most memorable." Tamsin fingered the handle of her mug. "But rowanberries are full of health benefits, too, so despite their checkered past, they're something the Lord made to be useful and enjoyed. Just dinnae eat them plain. They're very bitter." She laughed.

"Noted," Leslie said.

Tamsin ate a few more quick bites of porridge, then said, "Now, ye've all sorts of time in these three weeks to do whatever ye like, so long as ye can stand the weather. How do ye find it, by the by?"

"Cold, but it feels good. So often in Houston, even October is hot and muggy." The *good* part of Leslie's answer was slightly untrue, but she intended to make the best of the weather. This was the only time of year she could afford to come, and beggars couldn't be choosers.

"Tell me what ye most want to do while yer here. I'll make a list so I dinnae go daft tryin' to remember." After standing, Tamsin fetched a pen and pad of paper from a drawer, sat down again, and gulped more coffee.

Leslie concentrated on scraping up the last of her breakfast. She dreaded the question. She'd basically forced herself to come to Scotland and had put off any planning. Sitting on her bedroom floor, staring into a void, seeing nothing in her mind's eye besides a swirl of things she hated—that was all she'd felt capable of for the past eight months. Work had dragged her out of herself, but she couldn't make decisions about what to do on her own time, in her own life, apart from that. Two months before the split, she'd realized that she had to break up with Blaine, but she avoided it until … she couldn't any longer. And then six months after that, until now, she'd continued to live in that daze. Living, but not really. More like drifting.

"I-I wanted mainly to relax the first few days," Leslie said when she could delay no longer. "I-I don't really have an agenda for this trip. Not much of one anyway. Just wanted to experience Scotland." Her face burned; did the blush show? She couldn't admit to her hostess she hadn't wanted to come. Besides, that wouldn't have been completely true. The deepest part of her—the part she'd lost touch with so long ago—had wanted to come. But she hadn't known it was still there and still able to decide things for her. Buying that plane ticket to Scotland back in June felt like an illusion even then. Only by her family's help and insistence had she followed through.

Tamsin nodded. "I can give ye ideas, and ye'll have plenty of time to research more while ye relax."

Silence followed. Leslie had that awkward feeling one gets when they knew something should be said but didn't want to say it. Tamsin would sooner or later catch on that Leslie wasn't "all right," but would Leslie ever know Tamsin well enough to share what was wrong with her?

"Well." Tamsin drained the last of her coffee and set her mug down with a clunk. "Since ye liked the deer so much, do ye want to see me stag?"

Leslie cocked an eyebrow. Did she mean a mounted deer head? The house reminded Leslie of a cozy, feminized hunting lodge, but the mounted head of a stag might be a bit more than Leslie could appreciate.

"It's in the livin' room." Tamsin stood and beckoned for Leslie to follow her.

Leslie didn't recall a deer's head when she passed through the dim living room last night ...

Tamsin threw open the drapes and flicked the light switch. There, above the couch, in a gold frame, a magnificent red stag stood surveying the distance, surrounded by stormy blue-gray clouds, misty brown mountains, and windswept grass. He faced three-quarters to the front, a crown of twelve-point antlers adorning his head.

Leslie forgot to say anything, so Tamsin spoke first. "Splendid, isn't he? That's *The Monarch of the Glen* by Sir Edwin Landseer. It's me favorite paintin' of all time."

"I've seen it before, I know I have, but it's so different when you see it as a big painting on the wall," Leslie said.

Tamsin grinned. "I must take ye to Edinburgh so ye can see the original."

Briefly taking her eyes off the stag to meet Tamsin's gaze, Leslie nodded and smiled. "Yes, please."

"We should spend several days explorin' Edinburgh, in fact. But we'll make seein' *him* first priority. There—we're already givin' ye ideas and gettin' ye excited about things."

Leslie looked at her hostess again. Tamsin could already read her. Maybe, at least, she wouldn't go further and ask prying questions.

"Let me show ye around the house a wee bit more," Tamsin said after a pause. "Make ye feel at home. Then how 'bout we go to the village. It'll be a nice day, just windy, but the sun may come out after a bit."

The village, Rathadglas, was about half a mile from the house, just down a road winding through patches of fading broad-leaf trees, vibrant Scots pines, and undulating stretches of green-and-brown slopes. All the Scottish songs Leslie knew—and they were many—lilted through her brain as the two women walked. The stone bridge to Rathadglas made her heart throb. She leaned over one side to watch the chortling water. It was all so picturesque ... everything she dreamed this country would look like. But she couldn't say it made her happy, exactly. More like wistful. She was still missing something, though the beauty did help. If only she could forget her real life; if only this could be the sum of her reality.

Tamsin introduced her to several villagers. Just hearing their accents perked Leslie's spirits. Life couldn't be perfect, even in Scotland, but she had to enjoy herself and get the most out of being here. Perhaps it would provide that reset she so desperately needed.

They passed a small gray church surrounded by a low wall and orderly rows of headstones. *Now* Leslie truly felt as though she'd stepped back in time. It was easier to imagine Scottish Covenanters taking a stand against the king of England's religious dictates in this churchyard than it was to picture modern-day parishioners filing out of the doors.

Leslie paused at the churchyard wall. "Do you go to church here?" she asked Tamsin.

"Aye. Most all me life. It's lovely, even if it's no' everyone's cuppa tea; do ye want to go with me tomorra?"

"Yes, please!" Leslie replied. Old churches had been her favorite places to visit the other time she had been in the UK. Surely this one would similarly wrap her with a warm assurance of God's presence. Continuing beside Tamsin down the pavement, she prayed, *God, will I be able to find You again here? If I find You, maybe I can find myself again, too.* And maybe happiness as well. And maybe even her writing voice ... She could feel the stories tugging like mischievous children, though they still eluded her grasp.

The interior of the church was just as poignant as the exterior, and Leslie did find great meaning in the Presbyterian service even if it wasn't what she was accustomed to. But the connection with her spirit remained elusive. Maybe she was striving too hard for a deeply spiritual experience when all she needed was simply to talk with God like a friend, like she used to. But somehow she couldn't. It was as if her mind refused to admit Him.

Before Leslie and Tamsin filed out of the pew, Tamsin whispered, "I'm introducin' ye to the minister, so dinnae slip past him."

Leslie immediately felt self-conscious. Maybe it was because her spiritual state seemed so inadequate. *Not a good reason to be shy. Most ministers can't see any further inside you than ordinary people can.*

At the tall double doors, both wide open, stood the minister, David MacDougall. He greeted everyone, listened to their comments, and wished them a good week. When Tamsin and Leslie finally reached him, he smoothed his thin gray hair as his blue eyes brightened.

"David, this is the American friend I told ye about, Leslie Fraser."

"Ah, sounds like a misplaced Scot." David shook Leslie's hand.

Leslie smiled despite herself. "My parents are both of Scottish ancestry, and my mom, especially, loves all things Scottish, so I guess, in a way, I am."

"Is this yer first time in the country?"

"In Scotland, yes."

Tamsin had maneuvered them so that they were the last parishioners to leave, so the three of them were able to chitchat a bit longer than the others. The conversation ended in an invitation for David to come over for dinner on Tuesday.

If Leslie had been a bit bolder and a bit less heartsore about all things romantic, she'd have asked Tamsin if her cap was set for the minister. Though Tamsin was a fairly exuberant person in general, she seemed even more animated around him, and he, in turn, seemed to relax his pastoral dignity.

Leslie would figure it out soon enough; Tuesday evening would surely make it apparent either way.

On Monday, Tamsin took Leslie for their first excursion into Edinburgh. All they accomplished that day was visiting Edinburgh Castle, St Giles' Cathedral, and the branch of the national art galleries that housed the oldest paintings: masterpieces by da Vinci, Botticelli, Rembrandt, Gainsborough, and others, including Landseer's *The Monarch of the Glen*. The stag towered above Leslie in a nearly life-size painting. Time stopped as she studied it.

"I'd love to see a red stag in person." She finally turned away. "And I mean up close, not in a far-distant field from the road." To herself, she added, *I'd write a story about him. Maybe a fantasy novel retelling a legend about the red-haired lass whose lover is turned into a stag, and she must fulfill a quest to change him back.* Thrills chased each other down her spine. That was the first concrete story idea she'd had in years. It was very different from the novels she'd written and published in the past—nineteenth- and twentieth-century historical fiction—but this was Scotland. Scotland drew from a deep well ... legends, symbolism, ancient history, wildness, an especially dramatic story of Christianity's triumph over paganism, endless ages of fighting enemies without and within, a fierce loyalty to the fatherland, and an immobile dedication to freedom and tightly gripped beliefs. A story set in Scotland needed to dip far below the surface.

Leslie left the gallery feeling hopeful that her inner life would return in full force.

"I'm gonnae try haggis on ye tonight," Tamsin said Tuesday morning at breakfast. "David loves it. I dinnae make it from scratch, though. Me granny did, but the tradition stopped there. Me mam said it was too much work. So I buy it from the butcher's in the village."

"Is it really made of sheep's intestines?" Leslie asked with raised eyebrows and a slight smile.

"No, no' intestines. Just organs like the liver. And the butcher puts it in an artificial casing, no' the sheep's stomach."

"Good to know." Leslie tried not to laugh as she crunched her toast topped with rowanberry preserves.

"I'll be makin' neeps and tatties to go with it." Tamsin buttered her toast. "Mashed turnips and potatoes. Those are the most traditional foods to have with haggis."

"I'm looking forward to it—with some trepidation."

"Dinnae be frightened. Think of it as a Scottish meatball."

Leslie helped her hostess prepare the meal—or, at least, she set the table and stayed in the kitchen for company. As Tamsin mashed turnips at the stove, she said matter-of-factly, "David and I are rather good friends ... *very* good friends. Ye could say we're datin'." She glanced sideways at Leslie. "Ye probably guessed already, eh?" Her grin looked as sheepish as the intrepid Tamsin could get.

"Well ... yes, I did." Leslie turned back to the table and refolded a napkin. "That's great." She tried to make her voice cheery, but she sighed inwardly. When would other people's relationships cease to give her that twinge? The twinge wasn't jealousy; Leslie didn't want another relationship, at least not anytime soon. Perhaps it was just soreness at the reminder of how awful her own romance had turned out to be.

"But dinnae worry." Tamsin beat her masher on the edge of the turnip pot. "We're very sane about it. We are in our fifties, after all."

David MacDougall arrived in a flurry of wind and rain precisely at six. He gave Tamsin a peck on the cheek, and she smiled up at him with a glow that Leslie must have felt when she fell in love with Blaine. The way David and Tamsin behaved toward each other that evening was "sane" enough to ward off any discomfort Leslie might feel. In fact, they acted like an old married couple already, between Tamsin's banter and David's dry jokes and their mutual ease.

For being so wiry, David made sure there were no leftovers of haggis, neeps, or tatties.

"He always makes me envious because he can walk that off on one of his long jaunts and be none the worse for it." Tamsin shook her head as she took his empty plate. "Me, no' at all." She took Leslie's plate as well. "I'm glad ye liked everything, Leslie."

"It was delicious, and I'll be sure to tell my friends back home that haggis is nothing to be scared of." Leslie truly did enjoy the herby, sausage-like haggis and buttery turnips and potatoes.

With the table cleared, they retired to the living room. Tamsin and David sat on the couch beneath *The Monarch of the Glen*, while Leslie sat across from them on the armchair. Her gaze traveled to the stag almost as often as she looked at the couple when they spoke.

"It's a grand painting, isn't it?" David remarked.

"It is." Leslie brought her eyes down to the minister. "We saw the original in the National Gallery yesterday."

"She stood there gazin' at it for a good few minutes." Tamsin gave her a grin. "I could hardly draw her away to look at the da Vinci or anything else."

Leslie lifted her palms and grinned back. "What can I say? It's a magical painting. I wish it could actually suck me in for real." It had been a while since she'd felt comfortable enough with anyone to divulge her fanciful thoughts, but Tamsin and David and their down-to-earth joy together had relaxed her, even more than when Tamsin and she were alone.

"Leslie likes books," Tamsin said. She placed her hand on her boyfriend's knee—it was odd to think of a gray-haired man as a *boyfriend*, but by all definitions, that's what he was. "How is *yer* book comin', Davy? Tell Leslie about it."

A spark leaped in Leslie's mind at the realization she was facing another writer, always a thrilling recognition in her younger days. But the next instant, the spark dropped into the hollow of her stomach, swallowed by the yearning to return to what once defined her and the dread that she never would. It had gotten so bad in the years she hadn't written that it was painful to hear about other people writing.

Tamsin didn't know any of that, of course, not even that Leslie had self-published several novels. Mom had never told her.

David shrugged and fiddled with the cuffs of his sweater. "Well, ye know people in ministry—always thinking they have a book in them because they write sermons. Well, mine's a wee different. It's no' about theology. It's a novel about William Wallace." He offered a lame smile. "As if the Scots need another book about him. But this one doesn't aim to be strictly historical; it's a time-travel story where a young man from our year goes back and learns what it means to fight for what ye believe in."

Genuine intrigue made Leslie forget her jealousy pangs for the moment. "I want to read that book. Seriously."

David chuckled self-consciously and ducked his eyes, pushing his cuffs up and down his wrists. "Well, thank ye. I'm only about halfway through, and after that ... I don't know anything about publishers, but I'm sure Tamsin can keep ye informed."

"Have you thought about self-publishing?" *Oof.* Leslie wanted to bite her tongue. That was dipping too close to what she didn't want to talk about. "That is, I've heard some authors do that. Not sure how successful it can be, but at least it's a way to get your work out there." She blushed. She was bordering on deception here, but this was not where she wanted to go. How to change the subject?

"I've heard of it, and it's something I'll explore."

Leslie didn't ask any more questions, and David soon veered away from the topic of his book despite Tamsin's prompts. He seemed to be the type of sensitive person who didn't want to talk about something when his listener didn't encourage him.

After David left and Tamsin and she said goodnight, Leslie went to bed and cried.

The days took shape and started ticking by like the minutes on Tamsin's antique grandmother clock. Every day she could, Tamsin took Leslie to do something, whether it was the three-day trip around Glencoe on Scotland's west side or the day jaunt to Inverness or a few hours of trekking through the Cairngorms close to Rathadglas. Once, deep in the Cairngorms, they saw a herd of red deer at a distance, and Leslie could have sworn a stag was among them. But it was like she'd said—at a distance didn't satisfy her. And almost every morning, there were red hinds outside her window, but never a stag. What was going on with the males? They weren't supposed to be rarely seen, especially this time of year, yet they were acting like the elusive, mythical white stag hunted by kings and queens of old.

By the end of her second full week there, well into November's brisk and cloudy days, Leslie felt at home and daily set out on her own for long walks when Tamsin occasionally filled in for the owner of the village gift shop.

On Saturday morning, Leslie bundled up, complete with a tartan wool scarf she'd recently bought, and said goodbye to Tamsin, who was heading to work. The tug of stories had increased as Leslie's days in Scotland lengthened, but she'd never once taken out the blank notebook she'd packed in a desperate act of faith. Risking words when her heart was still so unwhole would be pointless.

Never mind writing fiction, she hadn't even been able to journal since her breakup with Blaine, though journaling had always helped her process and heal before. But her feelings about Blaine had become so complex in the last months of their relationship that she couldn't even do that.

And yet, today, a new thought dawned through the clouds in her mind. Maybe the words would *help* her heart become whole again, not worsen her pain and frustration. Putting imperfect words on paper had always helped her writer's block in the past. Maybe it would do so now.

She returned to her room and took the green leather journal, embossed with leaves, out of the bottom of her near-empty suitcase. *Don't forget a pen.* She dug through her backpack, then emptied it out on the bed. It'd be best to take the whole thing if she was going to carry her water, journal, and a snack, leaving the unnecessary items behind.

Leslie shut the creaky front door and stepped onto the lawn with a strong feeling of liberation and adventure. There was something about going into nature alone ... One could go anywhere they chose, ooh and ah over the smallest things without judgment, feel like a child again when the great outdoors was an infinite wonderland. Possibilities abounded, and yet it wasn't about people. It was about the wonders of creation.

Gray clouds overhead threatened drizzle, but those farther away were white and thin. Just like nearly every day, the drizzle would come, the drizzle would go, and the pale sun would emerge. Sometimes the cycle ran twice. Maybe one day while she was here, Leslie would get the brilliant autumn sunshine that poured from a blue sky, so common in Texas.

She wound her scarf around her neck one more time and pulled her beanie farther down. Also wearing a rainproof jacket, a thick sweater underneath, a T-shirt under that, jeans, and hiking boots, she felt as insulated as Tamsin's teapot in its cozy.

Leslie circled to the back of the house and descended the steep slope overlooking the moor. The craggy mountain watched her from across the vast swells of land. She'd head toward it. Not that she'd reach it, but it was a signpost to ensure she wouldn't get lost, as well as a target to aim for so she wouldn't turn back too soon. Despite all the days spent here, she'd only gone as far as the area between the bottom of the slope and the edge of the stream.

She'd cross that stream today and discover nature's hidden treasures beyond it.

Maybe, just maybe, she'd write down her thoughts—describe what she saw or let a story take shape or splash a handful of random, heartfelt words. Like *wild. Misty. Silent.* Simple words that conjured meanings far beyond their dictionary definitions.

Shouldn't she stop and jot down those words right now? Why wait? Why save them for later, when her impressions might grow weaker?

Leslie dropped her backpack and fished out her journal and pen. Disregarding the moisture that flecked the cream page, she stood there and sewed those three words to the lines. *Silent.* Why did she write *silent*? The stream babbled a stone's throw away. Ah. *Silent* because the noise of the modern world was nowhere to be heard, not even the drone of an airplane. The sounds of nature were of a far different quality, at one with silence, rising out of it and falling back into it instead of shattering it.

The small stream meandered through a rocky bed, easily crossed. Leslie's waterproof boots barely touched the water. More words came to mind. *Fresh. Cold. Silvery.* They described the stream and the day itself. *Scots pine cones. Needles scattered in the grass.* She stopped and wrote them down. It felt wonderful to savor words again simply for their looks, their sounds, and the images and sensations they evoked. Simply that. She wasn't trying to express anything more, merely remembering that words were beautiful and healing things, intimately tying her to her environment. Making her feel present and grounded.

Oh, God, thank You so much for bringing me here.

She walked on into the belt of pines bordering the stream. The wind blew a last smattering of drops into her face and then the rain seemed done for the time being. The babble of the stream receded as the mountain drew her on, never losing sight of her even through the tree branches.

God, the only thing that would make this day more perfect is for me to meet that monarch stag I've been wanting to see. Leslie quirked a grin, breaking free of the pines and facing a vast sweep of moor, dotted here and there by scrubby trees and dense piles of rocks. What were the chances of that happening so close to civilization when Tamsin and she had gone so far out and not seen him?

One can hope.

Hope ... the thing that faith substantiated. She needed to have faith that her life would get better, that there were still things to live for, even if she never got married or published another novel or made a living doing what she loved. She could always hope those things would happen and work toward them; that would pull her through each day. But *faith* came when she remembered that God loved her more than she imagined, that He had a purpose for whatever she endured, and that He had a purpose for her *now*.

"'Faith is the substance of things hoped for, the evidence of things not seen,'" she murmured.

The gray sky, so broad and all-encompassing, felt more present and tangible than the land Leslie walked on. Mountainous hills reached for it but fell far short. Hollows in the moor shrank from its majesty but could not hide, not even from its breath, the wind. Never had Leslie felt smaller. Seen from anywhere in this landscape, she'd be only a speck. It was a delicious sensation. Her life woes became their proper size—minuscule, so small they couldn't be seen, and all but forgotten.

She skirted a tall, rocky hill somewhere in the middle of the moor. Boulders that had seemed pebbles from a distance loomed over her. On the far side of the hill, she had to look twice because her peripheral vision caught an oddly square boulder that turned out not to be one at all.

She stopped and faced it. It was a stone hut with a thatched roof—a shepherd's bothy, a centuries-old structure that had been preserved or renovated in Scotland's wilds to shelter hikers and campers. Tamsin hadn't told her there was one in this very glen.

Leslie couldn't resist its clarion call. Exploring the bothy would also provide a little break from the wind. She picked her way around the rocks and longer tufts of grass partway up the hill. The hut, its wooden door a closed mouth and its two windows open eyes, seemed to stare past her to the hills beyond. She smiled at the irony. She wasn't even acknowledged by the youngest and smallest entity in this moor.

When she reached the door but before she could open it, it swung outward, nearly hitting her. With a small gasp, she jumped back just in time.

The eyes of a gray-haired man decked in hiking clothes shot upward to meet her. "Sorry, sorry!" he exclaimed in a rich burr. "Are ye all right? Oh! It's ye, Leslie!"

David McDougall stood, slightly bent, just inside the low doorway.

Leslie dropped her hand from her chest. "Why, hello!"

He smiled. "Hello. I'm very sorry again. I didn't hit ye, did I?"

Leslie smiled back. "No, no. I'm fine. Just surprised."

David stepped out of the doorway. "Going in?"

"I just wanted a peek. I've never seen a bothy before."

"This is a bonny specimen." A twinkle showed up in his blue eyes, giving Leslie the sense he'd used that Scottish word for her benefit, the American tourist.

Leslie ducked inside and surveyed the dark, rustic room—its plastered stone walls, peaked tin ceiling, and cement floor weren't the comfiest but still cozier than a rainstorm or a cold night. She could see the appeal, especially with the table topped by a portable gas stove and kettle in the corner.

When she stepped away from the structure, David had gone partway down the hill. Leslie was happy to run into him, of course, but the solitude she had expected—and desired—today didn't let go of her so easily. If he planned to continue hiking, she could easily say she was going to rest here for a while ... which was truthfully exactly what she wanted. She could sit on a rock, drink water, maybe write. This view would never weary her.

"Having a pleasant day?" David asked.

"Oh yes." Where to sit? If she did sit, he wouldn't join her, would he? "And you?" She perched on the nearest smooth rock and shrugged off her backpack.

David nodded. "Very. As Tamsin told ye, I'm an incurable hiker." He raised his eyes to the towering hills that surrounded them. "Nothing like the mountains to put ye in yer place." He turned slightly and waved his arm toward the mountain Leslie had been heading for but didn't expect to reach.

"I agree. Do you know how far that mountain is, by the way?" Leslie took a quick drink while he answered.

"I believe it's three to four miles. I've done this jaunt before, climbed it even; I camped right here in this bothy. Are ye trying to reach it?"

"Would be nice, but no, I don't have the time or proper hiking equipment. Plus, I'm reasonably sure Tamsin wouldn't appreciate me going by myself."

He smirked. "Ye're probably right. Well, I hope ye have a pleasant journey wherever ye do get to. I've been walking all morning and took a half hour in the bothy to warm up. Ye can even make tea in there, if ye'd like. Ye saw the gas stove and packets of tea on the table, aye? No cups, though."

"That's so cool. Hospitable, even in the wilderness. If you call it that." Leslie shooed away strands of hair blowing into her eyes and mouth.

"Fair enough to call it that, I think." David tightened the backpack strap across his chest, then looked back at her, his blue-eyed gaze made keener by his aquiline nose. "I hope ye find what ye're searching for, too, Leslie. Ye strike me as a seeker. A place like this draws them."

A shiver went down her spine. This Scotsman, more than twenty years her senior, spoke like a kindred spirit. "I can see that." She managed a small laugh as she pulled out her journal. "I'm a writer trying to find her voice again and a Christian trying to find her God, and this seemed like a good place to do both." Her heart thumped as she spoke. One such as herself did not simply spill her heart to an acquaintance. She had kept her mouth tightly closed over her deepest yearnings and concerns when meeting David before, and she still hadn't opened up to Tamsin despite living with her for two weeks. Yet what did Leslie have to lose? Being in Scotland had changed her; she might go back to her normal self when she returned to the States, but for now, she could be that different person who took risks.

David's eyes softened. "Now I hope even more that ye find what ye're seeking. Those are important things to recover."

"Thank you."

He stood still, but his khaki-clad knees twitched as if he was undecided whether to stay or depart. Then his nose twitched, too, and he spoke. "Leslie, if ye need prayer or have any questions, do let me know."

There went another shiver. Leslie stared at him. The words *divine appointment* whispered in her mind. "I-I ..." She gulped. "I'm sure you've heard it all. I don't have that much of a story compared to many, but it's been rough for me personally over the past—" How long? It'd been six months since Blaine, but the years with him had all been tough. "Three years or so," she croaked and took another drink of water, willing tears away from her aching eyes.

"Everyone has a story that is 'much,'" David said quietly, taking a step or two nearer. "Would ye like me to sit down?"

"Please, if you want to, that is." Leslie clutched her water bottle and looked toward the mountain. She had to get a grip on herself. Just because he was a minister didn't mean she could crumble to pieces in front of him. "I'll keep it simple." She breathed in deeply, then out slowly. "I was in an emotionally abusive relationship for two and a half years. We even got engaged. But it never felt right. I broke it off six months ago. He's left me alone ever since, thank God, but I suffered a lot of mindset issues."

Tears pricked, but Leslie soldiered on. "I feel like my real self was so suppressed that I don't know who I am anymore. I'm thirty now, and I'm afraid I'll never get married or even want to. I don't have a well-paying job, so I live with my parents. I don't know if I'll ever be able to support myself or have the confidence to." She took her blurring eyes from the mountains and looked onto her lap. "My confidence is shattered. I'm a writer, a novelist, and I've published books, but that was years ago. They don't sell anymore. So that's another dream I've given up on."

She paused, gathering the thoughts that remained to be spoken. "With all this, I don't know where to go anymore. God is there, I know He is, but I don't see Him at work in my life, and He feels so distant, like He doesn't care. But also, it's like I've failed Him because I haven't clung to Him like I should, so why should He help me? I used to talk to Him like a friend and tell Him everything." Realizing that her cheeks were wet, she swiped them with her palm. She still hadn't looked at David; he might as well not even be present.

"My ex-fiancé messed with my view of God, too; he constantly negated my personality, ideas, and interests and told me they didn't matter. But I was in love with him, and I was such a coward that I thought he was right, and ... and ..." She coughed to hide the tears in her voice, then desperately swallowed more water. This was *so* embarrassing if she allowed herself to think about it. What would David tell Tamsin? And, Lord God, did it hurt! Like a ripped-open wound.

"And I don't know what more to say, what else to do. I feel stuck, trapped, in a place with no direction, no hope. I'm just existing, and I've often thought it would be easier to just ... die." She sucked in a shaky breath. "But at the same time, I berate myself for feeling that way because I'm a Christian, I have a loving family, I have friends ... There's no reason to be so hopeless. But *I can't help it*." She finished in a rasp that became shuddering sobs.

For the first time, Leslie heard David move as he knelt next to her and put his hand on her shoulder. "It sounds to me, ye've been holding this all in, and now that ye've said it, things will automatically start to look better." His soothing voice salved her nerves, and she tried to quiet her gasps. "It also sounds to me that ye are already on the road to healing because ye're here, in a place ye've always wanted to visit. Ye didn't let *that* dream die." He paused. "Six months after breaking off an abusive relationship is no' a long time. It's understandable and normal for ye to feel this way. Don't despair that ye'll never be yerself again."

Leslie pressed her swollen, aching eyes shut.

"And with being 'not yerself' for more years than that, it'll be a little while yet before ye do. But don't give up. Even if ye don't feel like doing something, do it. Write. Explore other job opportunities. And above all, pray and read yer Bible." David chuckled ever so softly. "Reaching out to God is the single most important thing ye can do right now, all the more if ye feel yer relationship is no' top-notch. We always feel in a state of fluctuating 'proximity' to God because of our emotions. But remember that emotions are no' reality; they're just how we relate to reality. The truth is, He's as close to ye as He ever was, and perhaps even more so because ye are in such pain."

Fresh tears trickled from Leslie's eyes. Oh, did it feel good to hear someone say that with so much authority.

"One of my favorite verses is Psalm 34:18, 'The Lord is nigh unto them that are of a broken heart; and saveth such as be of a contrite spirit.' And I like it in King James's English, too." David chuckled again. "But however ye say it, the words are true." He patted her shoulder. "I'm gonnae let go for a minute and dig out a handkerchief for ye. I'm that old-fashioned."

A moment later, the soft white square was in Leslie's hands. It felt so comforting pressed into her eyes, laying against her cheek. Like the hem of Jesus's robe.

David remained silent for another minute or two. "The fact is, Leslie, God created ye for very specific reasons, and He won't let ye leave this earth until He wants ye to. So ye have an important purpose here: to glorify Him in yer life. What that looks like depends on ye, mostly. Reaching out to Him will be the quickest and surest way of getting back on yer feet, spiritually and emotionally speaking, and maybe even physically."

Leslie finally felt capable of peeling her eyes open and looking at David.

"Ye're a writer. And since I like to write, too, I know that writing brings me close to God and sorts my thoughts. Helps me feel I have a purpose. It's prayer and worship. And since ye haven't written creatively for so long, that may be a key part of yer problem."

Leslie nodded. David's mouth was open to continue when she coughed and held up her finger. "I-I brought a journal and a pen out here."

"Brilliant! What did I tell ye about being on the road to healing already?" He sat back on his heels. "Imagine how much deeper yer work will be with all that ye've suffered. Do I need to give ye some room now? I can go away as far as ye need me to so that ye can have that alone time connecting with God—praying and writing. I can also stay here and pray with ye first."

"That'd be wonderful," Leslie whispered.

And so he did. David's prayer was so heartfelt that she sensed he'd been in her same position. Maybe he had. Or maybe it was the Holy Spirit giving him the words. Regardless, when he said, "Amen," Leslie felt more understood, more whole, and more loved by God than she'd felt in ages.

David suggested they walk back toward Tamsin's ridge together before he left Leslie alone, in case she was overtired. She agreed; it was sublime out here in the open elements, but the belt of woods by the stream would be a cozier place to pray and write.

David promised to say nothing of their talk to Tamsin unless Leslie gave him permission. Leslie decided to tell Tamsin that evening, not wanting to hurt her friend's feelings by having David relate what she could have shared herself.

And so, well into the afternoon, just as the clouds were rolling back over the sky, Leslie was alone again in the woods, sitting against a pine on a bed of springy needles, listening to the stream, feeling an ache that was different than before: an ache that would promote healing, as if she'd been adjusted by a chiropractor or experienced a deep-tissue massage. She opened her journal. What to write? Maybe pray first. *Oh, God, thank You for Your comfort and healing. Please draw me close to You. Let me reach for You as never before. Make me into who You want me to be. Please give me words to write that will help restore my soul.*

She ate her trail mix, drank some water, then opened her journal again. Silent, motionless minutes went by as Leslie's spirit grew quieter. The stream babbled, and branches whispered in the wind. Trees towered above her, sheltering as if she were in a sanctuary. *What to write, what to write?* The familiar pinching panic started coming to life in her soul. *No,* she prayed. *Please give me words.*

Leaves crunched; twigs snapped. Leslie's head jerked up, and she held her breath. The sounds continued, gradually drawing closer. Chills ran up her spine and over her arms. Should she bolt? But at this point, she couldn't even turn her head, she was so tense.

Then the corner of her eye caught a dark form among the gray and brown tree trunks to her left. Her head swiveled that direction, immobility forgotten. It was so big ... Could it be ...

A magnificent red stag, powerfully alive, trod toward her, footfall by footfall, steady and slow. The monarch of the glen had stepped from his portrait and graced her with his presence at last. He moved nearer, copper flank and shaggy neck rippling over muscles, bright dark eyes calm, his rack of antlers a vast crown of thorny branches.

Leslie's whole body was a mass of tingles, her scalp feeling as if it would prickle right off her head. *Oh, God,* she prayed, hardly daring to breathe. *Oh, God, oh, God.*

The stag looked at her and paused. They stared into each other's eyes, and time ceased. Small clouds of mist puffed from his nose. Then he continued his tread toward the stream, passing in and out behind tree trunks just a few yards from her. Leslie's breath came a little easier as he got farther away, and her gaze stayed riveted as he bent his head and drank. Fearless, he didn't even glance back at her.

After satisfying his thirst, the stag followed the stream to the south. Leslie watched until the trees hid him. The last thing she saw was his swaying crown.

Every muscle taut, she gave him a few more minutes, then stood and stretched. Her pounding pulse decelerated. One did not recover quickly from an experience like that. She could do nothing now but soak in the memory.

She walked to where he had been, noting his faint hoofprints, then went to the stream and looked in the direction he had disappeared. No sign of him, of course. A thought struck her. Taking a picture with her phone had never even crossed her mind. It was as if she had been so far back in time that such technology did not exist.

But that was all right, she decided in the next breath. Such experiences lived better in one's memory than in a conglomeration of pixels.

She returned to her tree and looked down at her journal. *Thank You, God. You brought him.* She sat down, picked up and opened her journal, and began to write.

The Monarch of the Glen
A Tale of Wonder
by Leslie Fraser

She flipped the page.

Every so often, something from another realm breaks into what we thought was reality and shatters our safe, tight box of ordinary existence. Red-haired Jennie MacPherson had always lived an ordinary life ...